D0794428

THE FIRST THREE NOVELS

THE FIRST THREE NOVELS

John le Carré

B L O O M S B U R Y

NEW YORK • LONDON • NEW DELHI • SYDNEY

Call for the Dead
Copyright © 1961 by le Carré Productions
Copyright © renewed 1989 by David Cornwell
Foreword © copyright 2004 by P.D. James

A Murder of Quality
Copyright © 1962 by le Carré Productions
Copyright © renewed 1990 by David Cornwell
Foreword copyright © 2004 by Otto Penzler

The Spy Who Came In from the Cold
Copyright © 1963 by le Carré Productions
Copyright © renewed 1991 by David Cornwell
Foreword copyright © 2005 by Joseph Kanon

All rights reserved. No part of this book may be used or reproduced in any
manner whatsoever without written permission from the publisher except
in the case of brief quotations embodied in critical articles or reviews. For
information address Bloomsbury USA, 1385 Broadway, New York, NY 10018.

Published by Bloomsbury USA, New York
Bloomsbury is a trademark of Bloomsbury Publishing Plc

All papers used by Bloomsbury USA are natural, recyclable products made
from wood grown in well-managed forests. The manufacturing processes
conform to the environmental regulations of the country of origin.

LIBRARY OF CONGRESS CATALOGING-IN-PUBLICATION DATA HAS BEEN APPLIED FOR.

ISBN: 978-1-63286-196-2

First U.S. Edition 2014

1 3 5 7 9 10 8 6 4 2

Book design by Marlene Tungseth
Book composition by Coghill Composition Company
Printed and bound in the U.S.A. by Thomson-Shore Inc., Dexter, Michigan

Bloomsbury books may be purchased for business or promotional use.
For information on bulk purchases please contact Macmillan Corporate
and Premium Sales Department at specialmarkets@macmillan.com.

CONTENTS

CALL FOR THE DEAD

FOREWORD

Call for the Dead, John le Carré's first George Smiley novel, is also his shortest, but it shares with his later and longer books the virtues that have placed him high among the best of contemporary novelists. The novel is a finely wrought and compelling admixture of three types of crime writing: the novel of action and excitement that we commonly call a thriller, the spy story, which explores the seedy labyrinths of international espionage, and the detective story, which has at its heart a mystery, usually a violent death, and by the end of the novel provides a rational solution, which the reader should be able to arrive at by logical deduction from clues that, although cunningly placed, are essentially fair.

The mystery in *Call for the Dead* is straightforward. The Cold War is at its height. George Smiley of the Secret Service is asked to interview Samuel Fennan, a Foreign Office official, about whom there are some slight suspicions arising from his alleged involvement with the Communist Party while at Oxford. These are never serious, and after the interview Smiley goes as far as regulations permit in assuring Fennan that he is cleared. The man is left in no doubt that he has nothing to worry about. Why then does Fennan subsequently allege that doubt has been cast on his loyalty, his career ruined, and that he's a victim of paid informers? More dramatically, why does he kill himself? Smiley has the job of investigating what, to him, is an inexplicable act that becomes even more mysterious when he finds that Fennan, before dying, had rung the telephone exchange and asked for a wake-up call the next morning. One of the incidental pleasures of the novel is to find oneself in the 1960s world when it was first published, when mobile phones were unknown, the telephone services provided wake-up calls, and the more sophisticated appurtenances of a criminal investigation were to come.

One of the most interesting achievements of the novel is le Carré's percipient skill in creating in George Smiley a hero who develops in later novels but remains in character essentially the same man. The George Smiley in *Call for the Dead* is the George Smiley we meet in *Tinker, Tailor, Soldier, Spy* and *Smiley's People*, but younger and more physically capable of a fight. We meet, too, several familiar characters for the first time: the retired policeman Mendel, living his quiet suburban life, who is to be called in on later, more onerous occasions, and young Peter Guillam, Smiley's loyal and courageous comrade-in-arms. One of the pleasures lies in meeting Smiley's wife, Lady Ann, for the first time. In the later novels she is usually absent from home and we know her through the words of others, most of whom are concerned to use her infidelities as barbs to sting Smiley. Here, briefly, she speaks for herself. The dialogue is not extensive but, as always with le Carré, it tells us more than the words. At the end of the novel, at Ann's invitation, Smiley travels to meet her for the inevitable reconciliation and the acceptance of a treachery more painful than anything the Service or his enemies can inflict on him.

Call for the Dead has all the qualities we come to expect in John le Carré novels: the ability to create an atmosphere of tension, menace, and anxiety, the cleverly controlled thrust of the action, and the descriptive power that brings to life the hidden corners of London, the deceptive safety of suburban avenues and sitting rooms, the government offices, and the haunts of ambitious men concerned to protect their political masters and further their own careers. How vividly the characters come alive, particularly Fennan's wife Elsa, with her prison-camp worn face and cropped hair died the colour of nicotine, her fixed uncompromising intensity. What part, if any, had she played in her husband's death?

Le Carré's secret world, the rivalry, the sad bureaucracy, the tradecraft and the arcane language, may or may not be very like the real world of international espionage. But it is a world of intense reality and we enter it with a frisson of excitement in the assurance that we are in the hands of a fine writer and a consummate storyteller. Above all, in this novel and in all his others, this brilliant explorer of the murky labyrinths of treachery and betrayal is a sensitive chronicler of the byways of the human heart.

P. D. James
May 2004

INTRODUCTION

With the possible exception of the person interviewed, there is nobody more predictable than an interviewer, and in my experience they come in two sorts, you might almost say two ages. The over-forties look nervously at my grey locks, and ask, in one way or another: how much longer can I last? The under-forties, who still have some hope for themselves as future writers, ask the other question: how did I get started? *Call for the Dead* is my first novel, so I will ignore the first question, which is anyway unanswerable, and tell you how I got started.

I began writing because I was going mad with boredom. Not the apathetic, listless kind of boredom that doesn't want to get out of bed in the morning, but the screaming, frenetic sort that races around in circles looking for real work and finding none. I had tried teaching "backward" children, and most of them were suffering from exactly what I was suffering from: boredom. They had sat at the back of their classes, and been bored stiff. I had tried teaching at Eton, but at Eton I often felt younger than the boys, and quite as much in need of a good tutor as they were. And I certainly wasn't ready to see straight down the corridor to the end of my life: housemaster at forty, retirement at sixty, cottage in Devon, and oh God, let me please go gentle into that good night.

While teaching I had dabbled in commercial art during the school holidays, but not with much success. To satisfy me, everything I drew or painted should have explained the meaning of life. But you don't get many opportunities to express your soul when you are knocking out children's book jackets at eight pounds a crack.

As to writing—yes, since abandoning boyhood poetry, I had had one shot. While I was still teaching at Eton, the Bodley Head asked me to write a German reader for them, to be aimed at the Ordinary Level examination students. So I wrote them a story about a pavement artist who one afternoon produced a masterpiece in pastels on a paving stone in Trafalgar Square: a Mona Lisa. Better. And he knew. Rain was coming, so was the rush hour. He had no fixative. The paving stone belonged to the Council, not to him. My story was a nice little metaphor, now that I come to recall it, for my frustrated talent, even if I didn't know what talent it was that was lying on the ground unregarded by the hurrying passersby. Needless to say, the story was unsuited to the Bodley Head's purposes, and they turned it down. Years later, Graham Greene, who was some kind of co-opted director of the Bodley Head, who published him, wrote to me suggesting that I go to them. But that's writers for you: I had not forgiven them, and I never will.

Escaping from teaching, I re-entered the world of Whitehall's large back rooms, and was soon working in a terribly secret building in the West End, which even the taxi drivers knew was M15. Five days a week I rose at six, breakfasted, walked half-an-hour to the railway station at Great Missenden where I lived, rode the sixty-five minutes to Marylebone, then took the bus to Leconfield House in Curzon Street and showed my pass. Each evening I returned, sometimes not arriving home to my loyal wife and small son till ten or eleven at night.

The world I inhabited in London was a paper world. A security service marches on its files, and I was one of the infantry. Like Bob Cratchit in his Tank, I toiled from morning and often till late into the evening at the dossiers of people I would never meet: should we trust him? Or her? Should their employers trust them? Might he be a traitor, spy, lonely decider, a suitable case for blackmail by the unscrupulous opposition? Thus I, who seemed to have no adult understanding of myself, was being asked to sit in judgement on the lives and loves of others. I was not versed in the ways of the real world, only of my own. The only tools I possessed were the possibilities of my own nature. These were of many sorts in those days, and the imaginative bridges that I built to my paper suspects earned me a reputation for, of all things, perspicuity. Nothing could have been further from the truth. All I was doing was inventing people out of the meagre clay of telephone taps, purloined mail, and investigators' reports. What else I gave my suspects came from myself. It wasn't good intelligence work, but in that mediocre world it could easily pass for such. And it turned out to be excellent training for the career I had not yet consciously embarked upon: namely that of the novelist.

The novelist, I know now, frequently regards his characters with the veiled mystification of a child among grown-ups. He views them with the same callousness and the same suspicion, the same pain, marvel, and the same fickle love. And as he watches them, he adds them to his secret bestiary, to admire, to imitate, to reject, to punish. For its inmates, the sheltered world of intelligence can be wonderfully conducive to preserving this childish vision. From inside its walls, we young recruits were able to regard ourselves as mature to a fault. But let us loose upon the grown-ups, and most of us were lost children.

Which is precisely what Elsa Fennan tells George Smiley in *Call for the Dead* on the first occasion when they meet.

In addition to my files, of course, I had my colleagues, and I never met such an odd bunch. The secret world is exactly the same as the real world, but, as Koestler said of the Jews, more so. The egregious Peter Wright walked our corridors and perhaps, like me, he was subconsciously preparing himself for a literary career. Our senior officers hated each other for reasons we were not allowed to know. They hated our sister service even more. They hated politicians, Communists, and quite a lot of journalists. And as we now know, they hated Harold Wilson and his kitchen cabinet. The nervousness of the place was eerie. Men who were close colleagues one day disappeared from sight the next, whether sacked, or despatched on some delicate mission, again we couldn't know. Usually it turned out to be the sack. From these mysterious comings and goings, I later wove together the tale of Alec Leamas in *The Spy Who Came In from the Cold,* whose sacking turned out to be a fiendish ploy. Alas, few in reality were. Great ability rubbed shoulders with breathtaking incompetence, and when you were new you never knew which to expect.

For a while you even wondered whether the fools were pretending to be fools, as some kind of wonderful deception. Or whether there was a real, efficient secret service somewhere else. Later, in my fiction, I invented one. But alas, the reality was the mediocrity. Ex-colonial policemen mingled with failed academics; failed lawyers, failed missionaries, and failed debutantes gave our fabled canteen the amorphous quality of an Old School outing on the Orient Express. Everyone seemed to smell a little of failure. With time, I began to believe that there was a Service face after all, and that they all had it: a glance that catches yours, then looks downward, then away, eyes that reach and then refuse; a separateness to each one of us, like those strange bubbles in the paintings of Hieronymus Bosch, that never lets us kiss or touch. I later wrote about that too, in *The Secret Pilgrim.*

Perhaps it was our secrets that kept us apart, the feeling that we knew more than our neighbour, or (oh Lord) less. Our secrets were our money, and the man who knew the most was the most conceited. Only on my occasional visits to the BBC, or at luncheons with "great" British newspapers, have I sensed something of the same malign, resentful atmosphere.

But for a writer in the making who didn't even know that's what he was, this sad, secret world could scarcely have been bettered. John Bingham started me off, there is no doubt of it. John looked a bit like Smiley and wrote his thrillers in the lunch hour. Later he became, through no fault of his own, an Earl, a transition I can never quite forgive in anybody with a sense of humour. He was one of the good ones, all the same, Earl or spy: a kindly, gracious, astute man, ex-journalist, ex–Control Commission, intelligence professional to his fingertips. And he reminded me of another and deeper influence in my early life: Vivian Green, who had been Chaplain at my public school, and ended his career triumphantly as Rector of Lincoln College, Oxford. If I ever had a confessor, it was Green; and John Bingham, with his bumbly manners and shrewd eye and shrewder ear, was like an intelligence version of him. But where Vivian Green had written scholarly works on Wesley and the later Plantagenets, Bingham wrote fiction, and I watched him do it.

His example was all I needed. I was ready to try my hand. And it is no surprise to me that, when I came to invent my leading character, George Smiley, I should give him something of Vivian Green's unlikely wisdom, wrapped in academic learning, and something of Bingham's devious resourcefulness and simple patriotism also. All fictional characters are amalgams; all spring from much deeper wells than their apparent counterparts in life. All in the end, like the poor suspects in my files, are refitted and remoulded in the writer's imagination, until they are probably closer to his own nature than to anybody else's. But now that Bingham is dead—not to mention blown sky-high by self-styled historians of the Service—it seems only right that I should acknowledge my debt to him: not merely as a component of George Smiley, but as the man who first put the spark to my writing career.

I wrote in penny notebooks. On the train to and from Great Missenden, in lunch hours, in the grey morning hours before going off to work. Ann, my wife at the time, typed the stuff out; we were broke, but we risked an Olivetti portable on hire purchase at a few shillings a week. I pitched straight into the story, no messing with outlines, skeletons or flow charts. I hadn't the smallest idea where I was going. But I had Smiley, I had my trays of files of men and women I was supposed to suspect, but had never met. And I had in my memory a little crushed French-woman in the hospital at Chamonix when I had been skiing there soon after the war. She had been staying at my hotel, and when the manager told me she had broken not just one but both her legs, I went to visit her.

She was on her back, both legs in traction, a little scrap of a woman in her fifties with short peroxide hair, and a fat lipstick mouth drawn over the little thin one underneath. She had been all through the Resistance, she told me with a laugh. She had been parachuted into France, she forgot how many times. And she had never broken anything till she went skiing! More laughter. And the hair, she explained excitedly. Her hair, she now feared, would never grow properly again. She had spent the last year of the war in one of the camps, she said, as if she were talking of a few weeks on the Riviera: so of course they had shaved her head. Other people's hair had grown perfectly well, but hers for some reason, as she told me with the same self-deprecating laugh, hers just hadn't. It didn't matter what she did to it—ointments, lotions, powders, you name it, they were all a flop. I appointed her my Elsa Fennan.

When I had written the book, I feared that my troubles had just begun. I had talked to nobody about the proprieties of writing a spy story while I was still inside the spy business, and nowadays, I am told, new entrants have to sign away their literary lives before they are allowed to join. Certainly I knew enough about the subterranean connections of my service not to attempt to publish without official consent. So I sent the book to the Legal Adviser, Bernard Hill, who had always seemed to me to be the dullest old stick in the whole outfit, and he returned it a couple of days later with a note saying how much he had enjoyed it. He asked for one change and I made it. Not for security reasons: he thought it might be libellous. He also asked me to use a pseudonym. He thought it wiser and, sucking on his pipe, he wished me luck.

When Victor Gollancz accepted the book, I asked Victor what sort of pseudonym I should choose. He recommended two Anglo-Saxon monosyllables—something like Chunk Smith or Hank Brown. I chose le Carré. God alone knows why, or where I had it from, but I didn't like Victor's advice. When people press me, I say I saw the name on a shop front from the top of a London bus. I didn't. I just don't know. But never trust a novelist when he tells you the truth.

John le Carré
March 1992

1 ❈
A BRIEF HISTORY OF GEORGE SMILEY

When Lady Ann Sercomb married George Smiley towards the end of the war, she described him to her astonished Mayfair friends as breathtakingly ordinary. When she left him two years later in favour of a Cuban motor racing driver, she announced enigmatically that if she hadn't left him then, she never could have done; and Viscount Sawley made a special journey to his club to observe that the cat was out of the bag.

This remark, which enjoyed a brief season as a *mot*, can only be understood by those who knew Smiley. Short, fat, and of a quiet disposition, he appeared to spend a lot of money on really bad clothes, which hung about his squat frame like skin on a shrunken toad. Sawley, in fact, declared at the wedding that "Sercomb was mated to a bullfrog in a sou'wester." And Smiley, unaware of this description, had waddled down the aisle in search of the kiss that would turn him into a Prince.

Was he rich or poor, peasant or priest? Where had she got him from? The incongruity of the match was emphasized by Lady Ann's undoubted beauty, its mystery stimulated by the disproportion between the man and his bride. But gossip must see its characters in black and white, equip them with sins and motives easily conveyed in the shorthand of conversation. And so Smiley, without school, parents, regiment or trade, without wealth or poverty, travelled without labels in the guard's van of the social express, and soon became lost luggage, destined, when the divorce had come and gone, to remain unclaimed on the dusty shelf of yesterday's news.

When Lady Ann followed her star to Cuba, she gave some thought to Smiley. With grudging admiration she admitted to herself that if there were an only man in her life, Smiley would be he. She was gratified in retrospect that she had demonstrated this by holy matrimony.

The effect of Lady Ann's departure upon her former husband did not interest society—which indeed is unconcerned with the aftermath of sensation. Yet it would be interesting to know what Sawley and his flock might have made of Smiley's reaction; of that fleshy, bespectacled face puckered in energetic concentration as he read so deeply among the lesser German poets, the chubby wet hands clenched beneath the tumbling sleeves. But Sawley profited by the occasion with the merest of shrugs by remarking *partir c'est courir un peu,* and he appeared to be unaware that though Lady Ann just ran away, a little of George Smiley had indeed died.

That part of Smiley which survived was as incongruous to his appearance as love, or a taste for unrecognized poets: it was his profession, which was that of intelligence officer. It was a profession he enjoyed, and which mercifully provided him with colleagues equally obscure in character and origin. It also provided him with what he had once loved best in life: academic excursions into the mystery of human behaviour, disciplined by the practical application of his own deductions.

Some time in the twenties when Smiley had emerged from his unimpressive school and lumbered blinking into the murky cloisters of his unimpressive Oxford College, he had dreamed of Fellowships and a life devoted to the literary obscurities of seventeenth-century Germany. But his own tutor, who knew Smiley better, guided him wisely away from the honours that would undoubtedly have been his. On a sweet July morning in 1928, a puzzled and rather pink Smiley had sat before an interviewing board of the Overseas Committee for Academic Research, an organization of which he had unaccountably never heard. Jebedee (his tutor) had been oddly vague about the introduction: "Give these people a try, Smiley, they might have you and they pay badly enough to guarantee you decent company." But Smiley was annoyed and said so. It worried him that Jebedee, usually so precise, was so evasive. In a slight huff he agreed to postpone his reply to All Souls until he had seen Jebedee's "mysterious people."

He wasn't introduced to the Board, but he knew half of its members by sight. There was Fielding, the French medievalist from Cambridge, Sparke from the School of Oriental Languages, and Steed-Asprey, who had been dining at High Table the night Smiley had been Jebedee's guest. He had to admit he was impressed. For Fielding to leave his rooms, let alone Cambridge, was in itself a miracle. Afterwards Smiley always thought of that interview as a fan dance; a calculated progression of disclosures, each revealing different parts of a mysterious entity. Finally Steed-Asprey, who seemed to be Chairman, removed the last veil, and the truth stood before him in all its dazzling nakedness. He was being offered a post in what, for want of a better name, Steed-Asprey blushingly described as the Secret Service.

Smiley had asked for time to think. They gave him a week. No one mentioned pay.

That night he stayed in London at somewhere rather good and took himself to the theatre. He felt strangely light-headed and this worried him. He knew very well that he would accept, that he could have done so at the interview. It was only an instinctive caution, and perhaps a pardonable desire to play the coquette with Fielding, which prevented him from doing so.

Following his affirmation came training: anonymous country houses, anonymous instructors, a good deal of travel and, looming ever larger, the fantastic prospect of working completely alone.

His first operational posting was relatively pleasant: a two-year appointment as *englischer Dozent* at a provincial German University: lectures on Keats and vacations in Bavarian hunting lodges with groups of earnest and solemnly promiscuous German students. Towards the end of each long vacation he brought some of them back to England, having already earmarked the likely ones and conveyed his recommendations by clandestine means to an address in Bonn; during the entire two years he had no idea of whether his recommendations had been accepted or ignored. He had no means of knowing even whether his candidates were approached. Indeed he had no means of knowing whether his messages ever reached their destination; and he had no contact with the Department while in England.

His emotions in performing this work were mixed, and irreconcilable. It intrigued him to evaluate from a detached position what he had learnt to describe as "the agent potential" of a human being; to devise minuscule tests of character and behaviour which could inform him of the qualities of a candidate. This part of him was bloodless and inhuman—Smiley in this role was the international mercenary of his trade, amoral and without motive beyond that of personal gratification.

Conversely it saddened him to witness in himself the gradual death of natural pleasure. Always withdrawn, he now found himself shrinking from the temptations of friendship and human loyalty; he guarded himself warily from spontaneous reaction. By the strength of his intellect, he forced himself to observe humanity with clinical objectivity, and because he was neither immortal nor infallible he hated and feared the falseness of his life.

But Smiley was a sentimental man and the long exile strengthened his deep love of England. He fed hungrily on memories of Oxford; its beauty, its rational ease, and the mature slowness of its judgments. He dreamt of windswept autumn holidays at Hartland Quay, of long trudges over the Cornish cliffs, his face smooth and hot against the sea wind. This was his other secret life, and he grew to hate the bawdy intrusion of the new Germany, the stamping and shouting of uniformed students, the scarred, arrogant faces and their cheapjack answers. He resented, too, the way in which the Faculty had tampered with his subject—*his* beloved German literature. And there had been a night, a terrible night in the winter of 1937, when Smiley had stood at his window and watched a great bonfire in the university court: round it stood hundreds of students, their faces exultant and glistening in the dancing light. And into the pagan fire they threw books in their hundreds. He knew whose books they were: Thomas Mann, Heine, Lessing and a host of others. And Smiley, his damp hand cupped round the end of his cigarette, watching and hating, triumphed that he knew his enemy.

Nineteen thirty-nine saw him in Sweden, the accredited agent of a well-known Swiss small-arms manufacturer, his association with the firm conveniently backdated. Conveniently, too, his appearance had somehow altered, for Smiley had discovered in himself a talent for the part which went beyond the rudimentary change to his hair and the addition of a small moustache. For four years he had played the part, travelling back and forth between Switzerland, Germany, and Sweden. He had never guessed it was possible to be frightened for so long. He developed a nervous irritation in his left eye which remained with him fifteen years later; the strain etched lines on his fleshy cheeks and brow. He learnt what it was never to sleep, never to relax, to feel at any time of day or night the restless beating of his own heart, to know the extremes of solitude and self-pity, the sudden unreasoning desire for a woman, for drink, for exercise, for any drug to take away the tension of his life.

Against this background he conducted his authentic commerce and his work as a spy. With the progress of time the network grew, and other countries repaired their lack of foresight and preparation. In 1943 he was recalled. Within six weeks he was yearning to return, but they never let him go.

"You're finished," Steed-Asprey said. "Train new men, take time off. Get married or something. Unwind."

Smiley proposed to Steed-Asprey's secretary, the Lady Ann Sercomb.

The war was over. They paid him off, and he took his beautiful wife to Oxford to devote himself to the obscurities of seventeenth-century Germany. But two years later Lady Ann was in Cuba, and the revelations of a young Russian cypher-clerk in Ottawa had created a new demand for men of Smiley's experience.

The job was new, the threat elusive and at first he enjoyed it. But younger men were coming in, perhaps with fresher minds. Smiley was no material for promotion and it dawned on him gradually that he had entered middle age without ever being young, and that he was—in the nicest possible way—on the shelf.

Things changed. Steed-Asprey was gone; fled from the new world to India, in search of another civilization. Jebedee was dead. He had boarded a train at Lille in 1941 with his radio operator, a young Belgian, and neither had been heard of again. Fielding was wedded to a new thesis on Roland—only Maston remained, Maston the career man, the war-time recruit, the Ministers' Adviser on Intelligence; "the first man," Jebedee had said, "to play power tennis at Wimbledon." The NATO alliance, and the desperate measures contemplated by the Americans, altered the whole nature of Smiley's Service. Gone forever were the days of Steed-Asprey, when as like as not you took your orders over a glass of port in his rooms at Magdalen; the inspired amateurism of a handful of highly qualified, under-paid men had given way to the efficiency, bureaucracy, and intrigue of a large Government department— effectively at the mercy of Maston, with his expensive clothes and his knighthood, his distinguished grey hair and silver-coloured ties; Maston, who even remembered his secretary's birthday, whose manners were a by-word among the ladies of the registry; Maston, apologetically extending his empire and regretfully moving to even larger offices; Maston, holding smart house parties at Henley and feeding on the success of his subordinates.

They had brought him in during the war, the professional civil servant from an orthodox department, a man to handle paper and integrate the brilliance of his staff with the cumbersome machine of bureaucracy. It comforted the Great to deal with a man they knew, a man who could reduce any colour to grey, who knew his masters and could walk among them. And he did it so well. They liked his diffidence when he apologized for the company he kept, his insincerity when he defended the vagaries of his subordinates, his flexibility when formulating new commitments. Nor did he let go the advantages of a cloak and dagger man *malgré lui,* wearing the cloak for his masters and preserving the dagger for his servants. Ostensibly, his position was an odd one. He was not the nominal Head of Service, but the Ministers' Adviser on Intelligence, and Steed-Asprey had described him for all time as the Head Eunuch.

This was a new world for Smiley: the brilliantly lit corridors, the smart young men. He felt pedestrian and old-fashioned, homesick for the dilapidated terrace house in Knightsbridge where it had all begun. His appearance seemed to reflect this discomfort in a kind of physical recession which made him more hunched and frog-like than ever. He blinked more, and acquired the nickname of "Mole." But his debutante secretary adored him, and referred to him invariably as "My darling teddy-bear."

Smiley was now too old to go abroad. Maston had made that clear: "Anyway, my dear fellow, as like as not you're blown after all the ferreting about in the war. Better stick at home, old man, and keep the home fires burning."

Which goes some way to explaining why George Smiley sat in the back of a London taxi at two o'clock on the morning of Wednesday, 4 January, on his way to Cambridge Circus.

2 ✾

WE NEVER CLOSE

He felt safe in the taxi. Safe and warm. The
warmth was contraband, smuggled from his bed and hoarded
against the wet January night. Safe because unreal: it was his
ghost that ranged the London streets and took note of their
unhappy pleasure-seekers, scuttling under commissionaires'
umbrellas; and of the tarts, gift-wrapped in polythene. It was
his ghost, he decided, which had climbed from the well of
sleep and stopped the telephone shrieking on the bedside
table . . . Oxford Street . . . why was London the only capital
in the world that lost its personality at night? Smiley, as he
pulled his coat more closely about him, could think of
nowhere, from Los Angeles to Berne, which so readily gave
up its daily struggle for identity.

The cab turned into Cambridge Circus, and Smiley sat up
with a jolt. He remembered why the Duty Officer had rung, and
the memory woke him brutally from his dreams. The conversation came back to him word for word—a feat of recollection
long ago achieved.

"Duty Officer speaking, Smiley. I have the Adviser on the line . . ."

"Smiley; Maston speaking. You interviewed Samuel Arthur Fennan at the Foreign Office on Monday, am I right?"

"Yes . . . yes I did."

"What was the case?"

"Anonymous letter alleging Party membership at Oxford. Routine interview, authorized by the Director of Security."

(Fennan *can't* have complained, thought Smiley; he knew I'd clear him. There was nothing irregular, nothing.)

"Did you go for him at all? Was it hostile, Smiley, tell me that?" (Lord, he does sound frightened. Fennan must have put the whole Cabinet on to us.)

"No. It was a particularly friendly interview; we liked one another, I think. As a matter of fact I exceeded my brief in a way."

"How, Smiley, how?"

"Well, I more or less told him not to worry."

"You *what?*"

"I told him not to worry; he was obviously in a bit of a state, and so I told him."

"*What* did you tell him?"

"I said I had no powers and nor had the Service; but I could see no reason why we should bother him further."

"Is that all?"

Smiley paused for a second; he had never known Maston like this, never known him so dependent.

"Yes, that's all. Absolutely all." (He'll never forgive me for this. So much for the studied calm, the cream shirts and silver ties, the smart luncheons with Ministers.)

"He says you cast doubts on his loyalty, that his career in the FO is ruined, that he is the victim of paid informers."

"He said *what?* He must have gone stark mad. He knows he's cleared. What else does he want?"

"Nothing. He's dead. Killed himself at 10:30 this evening. Left a letter to the Foreign Secretary. The police rang one of his secretaries and got permission to open the letter. Then they told

24

us. There's going to be an inquiry. Smiley, you're sure, aren't you?"

"Sure of what?"

". . . never mind. Get round as soon as you can."

It had taken him hours to get a taxi. He rang three cab ranks and got no reply. At last the Sloane Square rank replied, and Smiley waited at his bedroom window wrapped in his overcoat until he saw the cab draw up at the door. It reminded him of the air raids in Germany, this unreal anxiety in the dead of night.

At Cambridge Circus he stopped the cab a hundred yards from the office, partly from habit and partly to clear his head in anticipation of Maston's febrile questioning.

He showed his pass to the constable on duty and made his way slowly to the lift.

The Duty Officer greeted him with relief as he emerged, and they walked together down the bright cream corridor.

"Maston's gone to see Sparrow at Scotland Yard. There's a squabble going on about which police department handles the case. Sparrow says Special Branch, Evelyn says CID and the Surrey police don't know what's hit them. Bad as a will. Come and have coffee in the DO's glory hole. It's out of a bottle but it does."

Smiley was grateful it was Peter Guillam's duty that night. A polished and thoughtful man who had specialized in Satellite espionage, the kind of friendly spirit who always has a timetable and a penknife.

"Special Branch rang at twelve five. Fennan's wife went to the theatre and didn't find him till she got back alone at quarter to eleven. She eventually rang the police."

"He lived down in Surrey somewhere."

"Walliston, off the Kingston by-pass. Only just outside the Metropolitan area. When the police arrived they found a letter to the Foreign Secretary on the floor beside the body. The Superintendent rang the Chief Constable, who rang the Duty Officer at the Home Office, who rang the Resident Clerk at the Foreign

Office, and eventually they got permission to open the letter. Then the fun started."

"Go on."

"The Director of Personnel at the Foreign Office rang us. He wanted the Adviser's home number. Said this was the last time Security tampered with his staff, that Fennan had been a loyal and talented officer, bla . . . bla . . . bla . . ."

"So he was. So he was."

"Said the whole affair demonstrated conclusively that Security had got out of hand—Gestapo methods which were not even mitigated by a genuine threat . . . bla . . .

"I gave him the Adviser's number and dialled it on the other phone while he went on raving. By a stroke of genius I got the FO off one line and Maston on the other and gave him the news. That was at 12:20. Maston was here by one o'clock in a state of advanced pregnancy—he'll have to report to the Minister tomorrow morning."

They were silent for a moment, while Guillam poured coffee essence into the cups and added boiling water from the electric kettle.

"What was he like?" he asked.

"Who? Fennan? Well, until tonight I could have told you. Now he doesn't make sense. To look at, obviously a Jew. Orthodox family, but dropped all that at Oxford and turned Marxist. Perceptive, cultured . . . a reasonable man. Soft spoken, good listener. Still educated; you know, facts galore. Whoever denounced him was right of course: he was in the Party."

"How old?"

"Forty-four. Looks older really." Smiley went on talking as his eyes wandered round the room. ". . . sensitive face—mop of straight dark hair undergraduate fashion, profile of a twenty-year-old, fine dry skin, rather chalky. Very lined too—lines going all ways, cutting the skin into squares. Very thin fingers . . . compact sort of chap; self-contained unit. Takes his pleasures alone. Suffered alone too, I suppose."

They got up as Maston came in.

"Ah, Smiley. Come in." He opened the door and put out his left arm to guide Smiley through first. Maston's room contained not a single piece of government property. He had once bought a collection of nineteenth-century watercolours, and some of these were hanging on the walls. The rest was off the peg, Smiley decided. Maston was off the peg, too, for that matter. His suit was just too light for respectability; the string of his monocle cut across the invariable cream shirt. He wore a light grey woollen tie. A German would call him *flott*, thought Smiley; chic, that's what he is—a barmaid's dream of a real gentleman.

"I've seen Sparrow. It's a clear case of suicide. The body has been removed and beyond the usual formalities the Chief Constable is taking no action. There'll be an inquest within a day or two. It has been agreed—I can't emphasize this too strongly, Smiley—that no word of our former interest in Fennan is to be passed to the Press."

"I see." (You're dangerous, Maston. You're weak and frightened. Anyone's neck before yours, I know. You're looking at me that way—measuring me for the rope.)

"Don't think I'm criticizing, Smiley; after all if the Director of Security authorized the interview you have nothing to worry about."

"Except Fennan."

"Quite so. Unfortunately the Director of Security omitted to sign off your minute suggesting an interview. He authorized it verbally, no doubt?"

"Yes. I'm sure he'll confirm that."

Maston looked at Smiley again, sharp, calculating; something was beginning to stick in Smiley's throat. He knew he was being uncompromising, that Maston wanted him nearer, wanted him to conspire.

"You know Fennan's office has been in touch with me?"

"Yes."

"There will have to be an inquiry. It may not even be possible to keep the Press out. I shall certainly have to see the Home

27

Secretary first thing tomorrow." (Frighten me and try again . . .
I'm getting on . . . pension to consider . . . unemployable, too,
. . . but I won't share your lie, Maston.) "I must have all the
facts, Smiley. I must do my duty. If there's anything you feel
you should tell me about that interview, anything you haven't
recorded, perhaps, tell me now and let me be the judge of its
significance."

"There's nothing to add, really, to what's already on the
file, and what I told you earlier tonight. It might help you to
know (the "you" was a trifle strong, perhaps)—it might help
you to know that I conducted the interview in an atmosphere
of exceptional informality. The allegation against Fennan was
pretty thin—university membership in the thirties and vague
talk of current sympathy. Half the Cabinet were in the Party
in the thirties." Maston frowned. "When I got to his room in
the Foreign Office it turned out to be rather public—people
trotting in and out the whole time, so I suggested we should
go out for a walk in the park."

"Go on."

"Well, we did. It was a sunny, cold day and rather pleasant.
We watched the ducks." Maston made a gesture of impatience.
"We spent about half an hour in the park—he did all the talking.
He was an intelligent man, fluent and interesting. But nervous,
too, not unnaturally. These people love talking about themselves,
and I think he was pleased to get it off his chest. He told me the
whole story—seemed quite happy to mention names—and then
we went to an espresso cafe he knew near Millbank."

"A what?"

"An espresso bar. They sell a special kind of coffee for a
shilling a cup. We had some."

"I see. It was under these . . . convivial circumstances that
you told him the Department would recommend no action."

"Yes. We often do that, but we don't normally record it."
Maston nodded. That was the kind of thing he understood,
thought Smiley; goodness me, he really is rather contemptible. It
was exciting to find Maston being as unpleasant as he expected.

28

"And I may take it therefore that his suicide—and his letter, of course—come as a complete surprise to you? You find no explanation?"

"It would be remarkable if I did."

"You have no idea who denounced him?"

"No."

"He was married, you know."

"Yes."

"I wonder . . . it seems conceivable that his wife might be able to fill in some of the gaps. I hesitate to suggest it, but perhaps someone from the Department ought to see her and, so far as good feeling allows, question her on all this."

"Now?" Smiley looked at him, expressionless.

Maston was standing at his big flat desk, toying with the businessman's cutlery—paper knife, cigarette box, lighter—the whole chemistry set of official hospitality. He's showing a full inch of cream cuff, thought Smiley, and admiring his white hands.

Maston looked up, his face composed in an expression of apathy. "Smiley, I know how you feel, but despite this tragedy you must try to understand the position. The Minister and the Home Secretary will want the fullest possible account of this affair and it is my specific task to provide one. Particularly any information which points to Fennan's state of mind immediately after his interview with . . . with us. Perhaps he spoke to his wife about it. He's not supposed to have done but we must be realistic."

"You want me to go down there?"

"Someone must. There's a question of the inquest. The Home Secretary will have to decide about that of course, but at present we just haven't the facts. Time is short and you know the case, you made the background inquiries. There's no time for anyone else to brief himself. If anyone goes it will have to be you, Smiley."

"When do you want me to go?"

"Apparently Mrs. Fennan is a somewhat unusual woman. Foreign. Jewish, too, I gather, suffered badly in the war, which

29

adds to the embarrassment. She is a strong-minded woman and relatively unmoved by her husband's death. Only superficially, no doubt. But sensible and communicative. I gather from Sparrow that she is proving cooperative and would probably see you as soon as you can get there. Surrey police can warn her you're coming and you can see her first thing in the morning. I shall telephone you there later in the day."

Smiley turned to go.

"Oh—and Smiley . . ." He felt Maston's hand on his arm and turned to look at him: Maston wore the smile normally reserved for the older ladies of the Service. "Smiley, you can count on me, you know; you can count on my support."

My God, thought Smiley; you really do work round the clock. A twenty-four-hour cabaret, you are—"We Never Close." He walked out into the street.

3 ❀

ELSA FENNAN

Merridale Lane is one of those corners of Surrey where the inhabitants wage a relentless battle against the stigma of suburbia. Trees, fertilized and cajoled into being in every front garden, half obscure the poky "Character dwellings" which crouch behind them. The rusticity of the environment is enhanced by the wooden owls that keep guard over the names of houses, and by crumbling dwarfs indefatigably poised over goldfish ponds. The inhabitants of Merridale Lane do not paint their dwarfs, suspecting this to be a suburban vice, nor, for the same reason, do they varnish the owls; but wait patiently for the years to endow these treasures with an appearance of weathered antiquity, until one day even the beams on the garage may boast of beetle and woodworm.

The lane is not exactly a cul-de-sac although estate agents insist that it is; the further end from the Kingston by-pass dwindles nervously into a gravel path, which in turn degenerates into a sad little mud track across Merries Field—leading to another lane indistinguishable from Merridale. Until about 1920 this path had

31

led to the parish church, but the church now stands on what is virtually a traffic island adjoining the London road, and the path which once led the faithful to worship provides a superfluous link between the inhabitants of Merridale Lane and Cadogan Road. The strip of open land called Merries Field has already achieved an eminence far beyond its own aspirations; it has driven a wedge deep into the District Council, between the developers and the preservers, and so effectively that on one occasion the entire machinery of local government in Walliston was brought to a standstill. A kind of natural compromise has now established itself: Merries Field is neither developed nor preserved by the three steel pylons, placed at regular intervals across it. At the centre is a cannibal but with a thatched roof called "The War Memorial Shelter," erected in 1951 in grateful memory to the fallen of two wars, as a haven for the weary and old. No one seems to have asked what business the weary and old would have in Merries Field, but the spiders have at least found a haven in the roof, and as a sitting-out place for pylon-builders the but was unusually comfortable.

Smiley arrived there on foot just after eight o'clock that morning, having parked his car at the police station, which was ten minutes' walk away.

It was raining heavily, driving cold rain, so cold it felt hard upon the face.

Surrey police had no further interest in the case, but Sparrow had sent down independently a Special Branch officer to remain at the police station and act if necessary as liaison between Security and the police. There was no doubt about the manner of Fennan's death. He had been shot through the temple at point blank range by a small French pistol manufactured in Lille in 1957. The pistol was found beneath the body. All the circumstances were consistent with suicide.

Number fifteen Merridale Lane was a low, Tudor-style house with the bedrooms built into the gables, and a half-timbered garage. It had an air of neglect, even disuse. It might have been occupied by artists, thought Smiley. Fennan didn't

32

seem to fit here. Fennan was Hampstead and au-pair foreign girls.

He unlatched the gate and walked slowly up the drive to the front door, trying vainly to discern some sign of life through the leaded windows. It was very cold. He rang the bell.

Elsa Fennan opened the door.

"They rang and asked me if I minded. I didn't know what to say. Please come in." A trace of a German accent.

She must have been older than Fennan. A slight, fierce woman in her fifties with hair cut very short and dyed to the colour of nicotine. Although frail, she conveyed an impression of endurance and courage, and the brown eyes that shone from her crooked little face were of an astonishing intensity. It was a worn face, racked and ravaged long ago, the face of a child grown old on starving and exhaustion, the eternal refugee face, the prison-camp face, thought Smiley.

She was holding out her hand to him—it was scrubbed and pink, bony to touch. He told her his name.

"You're the man who interviewed my husband," she said; "about loyalty." She led him into the low, dark drawing-room. There was no fire. Smiley felt suddenly sick and cheap. Loyalty to whom, to what? She didn't sound resentful. He was an oppressor, but she accepted oppression.

"I liked your husband very much. He would have been cleared."

"Cleared? Cleared of what?"

"There was a prima facie case for investigation—an anonymous letter—I was given the job." He paused and looked at her with real concern. "You have had a terrible loss, Mrs. Fennan . . . you must be exhausted. You can't have slept all night . . ."

She did not respond to his sympathy: "Thank you, but I can scarcely hope to sleep today. Sleep is not a luxury I enjoy." She looked down wryly at her own tiny body; "My body and I must put up with one another twenty hours a day. We have lived longer than most people already.

"As for the terrible loss. Yes, I suppose so. But you know,

33

Mr. Smiley, for so long I owned nothing but a toothbrush, so I'm not really used to possession, even after eight years of marriage. Besides, I have the experience to suffer with discretion."

She bobbed her head at him, indicating that he might sit, and with an oddly old-fashioned gesture she swept her skirt beneath her and sat opposite him. It was very cold in that room. Smiley wondered whether he ought to speak; he dared not look at her, but peered vaguely before him, trying desperately in his mind to penetrate the worn, travelled face of Elsa Fennan. It seemed a long time before she spoke again.

"You said you liked him. You didn't give him that impression, apparently."

"I haven't seen your husband's letter, but I have heard of its contents." Smiley's earnest, pouchy face was turned towards her now: "It simply doesn't make sense. I as good as told him he was . . . that we would recommend that the matter be taken no further."

She was motionless, waiting to hear. What could he say: "I'm sorry I killed your husband, Mrs. Fennan, but I was only doing my duty. (Duty to *whom* for God's sake?) He was in the Communist Party at Oxford twenty-four years ago; his recent promotion gave him access to highly secret information. Some busybody wrote us an anonymous letter and we had no option but to follow it up. The investigation induced a state of melancholia in your husband, and drove him to suicide." He said nothing.

"It was a game," she said suddenly, "a silly balancing trick of ideas; it had nothing to do with him or any real person. Why do you bother yourself with us? Go back to Whitehall and look for more spies on your drawing boards." She paused, showing no sign of emotion beyond the burning of her dark eyes. "It's an old illness you suffer from, Mr. Smiley," she continued, taking a cigarette from the box; "and I have seen many victims of it. The mind becomes separated from the body; it thinks without reality, rules a paper kingdom and devises without emotion the ruin of its paper victims. But sometimes the division between your world and ours is incomplete; the files grow heads and arms and legs, and that's a terrible moment, isn't it? The names have families as well as records, and human motives to explain the sad little dossiers and their make-believe sins. When that happens I am sorry for you." She paused for a moment, then continued:

"It's like the State and the People. The State is a dream, too, a symbol of nothing at all, an emptiness, a mind without a body, a game played with clouds in the sky. But States make war, don't they, and imprison people? To dream in doctrines— how tidy! My husband and I have both been tidied now, haven't we?" She was looking at him steadily. Her accent was more noticeable now.

"You call yourself the State, Mr. Smiley; you have no place among real people. You dropped a bomb from the sky: don't come down here and look at the blood, or hear the scream."

She had not raised her voice, she looked above him now, and beyond.

"You seem shocked. I should be weeping, I suppose, but I've no more tears, Mr. Smiley—I'm barren; the children of my grief are dead. Thank you for coming, Mr. Smiley; you can go back, now—there's nothing you can do here."

He sat forward in his chair, his podgy hands nursing one another on his knees. He looked worried and sanctimonious, like a grocer reading the lesson. The skin of his face was white and glistened at the temples and on the upper lip. Only under his eyes was there any colour: mauve half-moons bisected by the heavy frame of his spectacles.

"Look, Mrs. Fennan; that interview was almost a formality. I think your husband enjoyed it, I think it even made him happy to get it over."

"How *can* you say that, how can you, now this . . ."

"But I tell you it's true: why, we didn't even hold the thing in a Government office—when I got there I found Fennan's of-fice was a sort of right of way between two other rooms, so we walked out into the park and finished up at a cafe—scarcely an inquisition, you see. I even told him not to worry—I told him that. I just don't understand the letter—it doesn't . . ."

"It's not the letter, Mr. Smiley, that I'm thinking of. It's what he said to me."

"How do you mean?"

"He was deeply upset by the interview, he told me so. When he came back on Monday night he was desperate, almost incoherent. He collapsed in a chair and I persuaded him to go to bed. I gave him a sedative which lasted him half the night. He was still talking about it the next morning. It occupied his whole mind until his death."

The telephone was ringing upstairs. Smiley got up. "Excuse me—that will be my office. Do you mind?"

"It's in the front bedroom, directly above us."

Smiley walked slowly upstairs in a state of complete bewilderment. What on earth should he say to Maston now?

He lifted the receiver, glancing mechanically at the number on the apparatus.

"Walliston 2944."

"Exchange here. Good morning. Your eight-thirty call."

"Oh—Oh yes, thank you very much."

He rang off, grateful for the temporary respite. He glanced briefly round the bedroom. It was the Fennans' own bedroom, austere but comfortable. There were two armchairs in front of the gas fire. Smiley remembered now that Elsa Fennan had been bedridden for three years after the war. It was probably a survival from those years that they still sat in the bedroom in the evenings. The alcoves on either side of the fireplace were full of books. In the furthest corner, a typewriter on a desk. There was something intimate and touching about the arrangement, and perhaps for the first time Smiley was filled with an immediate sense of the tragedy of Fennan's death. He returned to the drawing-room.

"It was for you. Your eight-thirty call from the exchange."

He was aware of a pause and glanced incuriously towards her. But she had turned away from him and was standing looking out of the window, her slender back very straight and still, her stiff, short hair dark against the morning light.

Suddenly he stared at her. Something had occurred to him which he should have realized upstairs in the bedroom, something so improbable that for a moment his brain was unable to grasp it.

Mechanically he went on talking; he must get out of there, get away from the telephone and Maston's hysterical questions, get away from Elsa Fennan and her dark, restless house. Get away and think.

"I have intruded too much already, Mrs. Fennan, and I must now take your advice and return to Whitehall."

Again the cold, frail hand, the mumbled expressions of sympathy. He collected his coat from the hall and stepped out into the early sunlight. The winter sun had just appeared for a moment after the rain, and it repainted in pale, wet colours the trees and houses of Merridale Lane. The sky was still dark grey, and the world beneath it strangely luminous, giving back the sunlight it had stolen from nowhere.

He walked slowly down the gravel path, fearful of being called back.

He returned to the police station, full of disturbing thoughts. To begin with it was not Elsa Fennan who had asked the exchange for an eight-thirty call that morning.

37

4 ✻

COFFEE AT THE FOUNTAIN

The CID Superintendent at Walliston was a large, genial soul who measured professional competence in years of service and saw no fault in the habit. Sparrow's Inspector Mendel on the other hand was a thin, weasel-faced gentleman who spoke very rapidly out of the corner of his mouth. Smiley secretly likened him to a gamekeeper—a man who knew his territory and disliked intruders.

"I have a message from your Department, sir. You're to ring the Adviser at once." The Superintendent indicated his telephone with an enormous hand and walked out through the open door of his office. Mendel remained. Smiley looked at him owlishly for a moment, guessing his man.

"Shut the door." Mendel moved to the door and pulled it quietly to.

"I want to make an inquiry of the Walliston telephone exchange. Who's the most likely contact?"

"Assistant Supervisor normally. Supervisor's always in the clouds; Assistant Supervisor does the work."

"Someone at 15 Merridale Lane asked to be called by the exchange at eight-thirty this morning. I want to know what time the request was made and who by. I want to know whether there's a standing request for a morning call, and if so let's have the details."

"Know the number?"

"Walliston 2944. Subscriber Samuel Fennan, I should think." Mendel moved to the telephone and dialled O. While he waited for a reply he said to Smiley: "You don't want anyone to know about this, do you?"

"No one. Not even you. There's probably nothing in it. If we start bleating about murder we'll . . ."

Mendel was through to the exchange, asking for the Assistant Supervisor.

"Walliston CID here, Superintendent's office. We have an inquiry . . . yes, of course . . . ring me back then . . . CID outside line, Walliston 2421."

He replaced the receiver and waited for the exchange to ring him. "Sensible girl," he muttered, without looking at Smiley. The telephone rang and he began speaking at once.

"We're investigating a burglary in Merridale Lane. Number 18. Just possible they used No. 15 as an observation point for a job on the opposite house. Have you got any way of finding out whether calls were originated or received on Walliston 2944 in the last twenty-four hours?"

There was a pause. Mendel put his hand over the mouthpiece and turned to Smiley with a very slight grin. Smiley suddenly liked him a good deal.

"She's asking the girls," said Mendel; "and she'll look at the dockets." He turned back to the telephone and began jotting down figures on the Superintendent's pad. He stiffened abruptly and leaned forward on the desk.

"Oh yes." His voice was casual, in contrast to his attitude; "I wonder when she asked for that?" Another pause . . . "19:55 hours . . . a man, eh? The girl's sure of that, is she? . . . Oh, I see, oh, well, that fixes that. Thanks very much indeed all the same.

Well, at least we know where we stand . . . not at all, you've been very helpful . . . just a theory, that's all . . . have to think again, won't we? Well, thanks very much. Very kind, keep it under your hat . . . Cheerio." He rang off, tore the page from the pad, and put it in his pocket.

Smiley spoke quickly: "There's a beastly cafe down the road. I need some breakfast. Come and have a cup of coffee." The telephone was ringing; Smiley could almost feel Maston on the other end. Mendel looked at him for a moment and seemed to understand. They left it ringing and walked quickly out of the police station towards the High Street.

The Fountain Cafe (Proprietor Miss Gloria Adam) was all Tudor and horse brasses and local honey at sixpence more than anywhere else. Miss Adam herself dispensed the nastiest coffee south of Manchester and spoke of her customers as "My Friends." Miss Adam did not do business with friends, but simply robbed them, which somehow added to the illusion of genteel amateurism which Miss Adam was so anxious to preserve. Her origin was obscure, but she often spoke of her late father as "The Colonel." It was rumoured among those of Miss Adam's friends who had paid particularly dearly for their friendship that the colonelcy in question had been granted by the Salvation Army.

Mendel and Smiley sat at a corner table near the fire, waiting for their order. Mendel looked at Smiley oddly: "The girl remembers the call clearly; it came right at the end of her shift—five to eight last night. A request for an 8:30 call this morning. It was made by Fennan himself—the girl is positive of that."

"How?"

"Apparently this Fennan had rung the exchange on Christmas Day and the same girl was on duty. Wanted to wish them all a Happy Christmas. She was rather bucked. They had quite a chat. She's sure it was the same voice yesterday, asking for the call. 'Very cultured gentleman,' she said."

"But it doesn't make sense. He wrote a suicide letter at 10:30. What happened between 8 and 10:30?"

40

Mendel picked up a battered old briefcase. It had no lock—more like a music case, thought Smiley. He took from it a plain buff folder and handed it to Smiley. "Facsimile of the letter. Super said to give you a copy. They're sending the original to the FO and another copy straight to Marlene Dietrich."

"Who the devil's she?"

"Sorry, sir. What we call your Adviser, sir. Pretty general in the Branch, sir. Very sorry, sir."

How beautiful, thought Smiley, how absolutely beautiful. He opened the folder and looked at the facsimile. Mendel went on talking: "First suicide letter I've ever seen that was typed. First one I've seen with the time on it, for that matter. Signature looks OK, though. Checked it at the station against a receipt he once signed for lost property. Right as rain."

The letter was typed, probably a portable. Like the anonymous denunciation; that was a portable too. This one was signed with Fennan's neat, legible signature. Beneath the printed address at the head of the page was typed the date, and beneath that the time: 10:30 P.M.

Dear Sir David,

    After some hesitation I have decided to take my life. I cannot spend my remaining years under a cloud of disloyalty and suspicion. I realize that my career is ruined, that I am the victim of paid informers.

                            Yours sincerely,
                            Samuel Fennan

Smiley read it through several times, his mouth pursed in concentration, his eyebrows raised a little as if in surprise. Mendel was asking him something:

"How d'you get on to it?"

"On to what?"

"This early call business."

"Oh, I took the call. Thought it was for me. It wasn't—it was the exchange with this thing. Even then the penny didn't drop. I assumed it was for her, you see. Went down and told her."

"Down?"

"Yes. They keep the telephone in the bedroom. It's a sort of bed-sitter, really . . . she used to be an invalid, you know, and they've left the room as it was then, I suppose. It's like a study, one end; books, typewriter, desk and so forth."

"Typewriter?"

"Yes. A portable. I imagine he did this letter on it. But you see when I took that call I'd forgotten it couldn't possibly be Mrs. Fennan who'd asked for it."

"Why not?"

"She's an insomniac—she told me. Made a sort of joke of it. I told her to get some rest and she just said: 'My body and I must put up with one another twenty hours a day. We have lived longer than most people already.' There was more of it—something about not enjoying the luxury of sleep. So why should she want a call at 8:30?"

"Why should her husband—why should anyone? It's damn nearly lunch-time. God help the Civil Service."

"Exactly. That puzzles me too. The Foreign Office admittedly starts late—ten o'clock, I think. But even then Fennan would be pushed to dress, shave, breakfast, and catch the train on time if he didn't wake till 8:30. Besides, his wife could call him."

"She might have been shooting a line about not sleeping," said Mendel. "Women do, about insomnia and migraine and stuff. Makes people think they're nervous and temperamental. Cock, most of it."

Smiley shook his head: "No, she couldn't have made the call, could she? She wasn't home till 10:45. But even supposing she made a mistake about the time she got back, she couldn't have gone to the telephone without seeing her husband's body first. And you're not going to tell me that her reaction on finding her husband dead was to go upstairs and ask for an early call?"

They drank their coffee in silence for a while.

"Another thing," said Mendel.

42

"Yes?"

"His wife got back from the theatre at quarter to eleven, right?"

"That's what she says."

"Did she go alone?"

"No idea."

"Bet she didn't. I'll bet she *had* to tell the truth there, and timed the letter to give herself an alibi."

Smiley's mind went back to Elsa Fennan, her anger, her submission. It seemed ridiculous to talk about her in this way. No: not Elsa Fennan. No.

"Where was the body found?" Smiley asked.

"Bottom of the stairs."

"Bottom of the stairs?"

"True. Sprawled across the hall floor. Revolver underneath him."

"And the note. Where was that?"

"Beside him on the floor."

"Anything else?"

"Yes. A mug of cocoa in the drawing-room."

"I see. Fennan decides to commit suicide. He asks the exchange to ring him at 8:30. He makes himself some cocoa and puts it in the drawing-room. He goes upstairs and types his last letter. He comes down again to shoot himself, leaving the cocoa undrunk. It all hangs together nicely."

"Yes, doesn't it. Incidentally, hadn't you better ring your office?"

He looked at Mendel equivocally. "That's the end of a beautiful friendship," he said. As he walked towards the coin box beside a door marked "Private" he heard Mendel saying: "I bet you say that to all the boys." He was actually smiling as he asked for Maston's number.

Maston wanted to see him at once.

He went back to their table. Mendel was stirring another cup of coffee as if it required all his concentration. He was eating a very large bun.

43

Smiley stood beside him. "I've got to go back to London."

"Well, this will put the cat among the pigeons." The weasel face turned abruptly towards him; "Or will it?" He spoke with the front of his mouth while the back of it continued to deal with the bun.

"If Fennan was murdered, no power on earth can prevent the Press from getting hold of the story," and to himself added: "I don't think Maston would like that. He'd prefer suicide."

"Still, we've got to face that, haven't we?"

Smiley paused, frowning earnestly. Already he could hear Maston deriding his suspicions, laughing them impatiently away. "I don't know," he said, "I really don't know."

Back to London, he thought, back to Maston's Ideal Home, back to the rat-race of blame. And back to the unreality of containing a human tragedy in a three-page report.

It was raining again, a warm incessant rain now, and in the short distance between the Fountain Cafe and the police station he got very wet. He took off his coat and threw it into the back of the car. It was a relief to be leaving Walliston—even for London. As he turned on to the main road he saw out of the corner of his eye the figure of Mendel stoically trudging along the pavement towards the station, his grey trilby shapeless and blackened by the rain. It hadn't occurred to Smiley that he might want a lift to London, and he felt ungracious. Mendel, untroubled by the niceties of the situation, opened the passenger door and got in.

"Bit of luck," he observed. "Hate trains. Cambridge Circus you going to? You can drop me Westminster way, can't you?"

They set off and Mendel produced a shabby green tobacco tin and rolled himself a cigarette. He directed it towards his mouth, changed his mind and offered it to Smiley, lighting it for him with an extraordinary lighter that threw a two-inch blue flame. "You look worried sick," said Mendel.

"I am."

There was a pause. Mendel said: "It's the devil you don't know that gets you."

They had driven another four or five miles when Smiley drew the car onto the side of the road. He turned to Mendel.

"Would you mind awfully if we drove back to Walliston?"

"Good idea. Go and ask her."

He turned the car and drove slowly back to Walliston, back to Merridale Lane. He left Mendel in the car and walked down the familiar gravel path.

She opened the door and showed him into the drawing-room without a word. She was wearing the same dress, and Smiley wondered how she had passed the time since he had left her that morning.

Had she been walking about the house or sitting motionless in the drawing-room? Or upstairs in the bedroom with the leather chairs? How did she see herself in her new widowhood? Could she take it seriously yet, was she still in that secretly elevated state which immediately follows bereavement? Still looking at herself in mirrors, trying to discern the change, the horror in her own face, and weeping when she could not?

Neither of them sat down—both instinctively avoided a repetition of that morning's meeting.

"There was one thing I felt I must ask you, Mrs. Fennan. I'm very sorry to have to bother you again."

"About the call, I expect; the early morning call from the exchange."

"Yes."

"I thought that might puzzle you. An insomniac asks for an early morning call." She was trying to speak brightly.

"Yes. It did seem odd. Do you often go to the theatre?"

"Yes. Once a fortnight. I'm a member of the Weybridge Repertory Club, you know. I try and go to everything they do. I have a seat reserved for me automatically on the first Tuesday of each run. My husband worked late on Tuesdays. He never came; he'd only go to classical theatre."

"But he liked Brecht, didn't he? He seemed very thrilled with the Berliner Ensemble performances in London."

She looked at him for a moment, and then smiled suddenly,

45

the first time he had seen her do so. It was an enchanting smile; her whole face lit up like a child's.

Smiley had a fleeting vision of Elsa Fennan as a child—a spindly, agile tomboy like George Sand's "Petite Fadette"—half woman, half glib, lying girl. He saw her as a wheedling *Back-fisch*, fighting like a cat for herself alone, and he saw her too, starved and shrunken in prison camp, ruthless in her fight for self-preservation. It was pathetic to witness in that smile the light of her early innocence, and a steeled weapon in her fight for survival.

"I'm afraid the explanation of that call is very silly," she said. "I suffer from a terrible memory—really awful. Go shopping and forget what I've come to buy, make an appointment on the telephone and forget it the moment I replace the receiver. I ask people to stay the weekend and we are out when they arrive. Occasionally, when there is something I simply have to remember, I ring the exchange and ask for a call a few minutes before the appointed time. It's like a knot in one's handkerchief, but a knot can't ring a bell at you, can it?"

Smiley peered at her. His throat felt rather dry, and he had to swallow before he spoke.

"And what was the call for this time, Mrs. Fennan?"

Again the enchanting smile: "There you are. I completely forget."

5 ❀
MASTON AND CANDLELIGHT

As he drove slowly back towards London, Smiley
ceased to be conscious of Mendel's presence.

There had been a time when the mere business of driving a
car was a relief to him; when he had found in the unreality of a
long, solitary journey a palliative to his troubled brain, when the
fatigue of several hours' driving had allowed him to forget more
sombre cares.

It was one of the subtler landmarks of middle age, perhaps, that he could no longer thus subdue his mind. It needed
sterner measures now: he even tried on occasion to plan in his
head a walk through a European city—to record the shops
and buildings he would pass, for instance, in Berne on a walk
from the Munster to the University. But despite such energetic mental exercise, the ghosts of time present would in-
trude and drive his dreams away. It was Ann who had robbed
him of his peace, Ann who had once made the present so important and taught him the habit of reality, and when she went
there was nothing.

He could not believe that Elsa Fennan had killed her husband. Her instinct was to defend, to hoard the treasures of her life, to build about herself the symbols of normal existence. There was no aggression in her, no will but the will to preserve.

But who could tell? What did Hesse write? "Strange to wander in the mist, each is alone. No tree knows his neighbour. Each is alone." We know nothing of one another, nothing, Smiley mused. However closely we live together, at whatever time of day or night we sound the deepest thoughts in one another, we know nothing. How am I judging Elsa Fennan? I think I understand her suffering and her frightened lies, but what do I know of her? Nothing.

Mendel was pointing at a sign-post.

". . . That's where I live. Mitcham. Not a bad spot really. Got sick of bachelor quarters. Bought a decent little semi-detached down here. For my retirement."

"Retirement? That's a long way off."

"Yes. Three days. That's why I got this job. Nothing to it; no complications. Give it to old Mendel; he'll muck it up."

"Well, well. I expect we shall both be out of a job by Monday." He drove Mendel to Scotland Yard and went on to Cambridge Circus.

He realized as he walked into the building that everyone knew. It was the way they looked; some shade of difference in their glance, their attitude. He made straight for Maston's room. Maston's secretary was at her desk and she looked up quickly as he entered.

"Adviser in?"

"Yes. He's expecting you. He's alone. I should knock and go in." But Maston had opened the door and was already calling him. He was wearing a black coat and pinstripe trousers. Here goes the cabaret, thought Smiley.

"I've been trying to get in touch with you. Did you not receive my message?" said Maston.

"I did, but I couldn't possibly have spoken to you."

"I don't quite follow?"

"Well, I don't believe Fennan committed suicide—I think he was murdered. I couldn't say that on the telephone."

Maston took off his spectacles and looked at Smiley in blank astonishment.

"Murdered? Why?"

"Well, Fennan wrote his letter at 10:30 last night, if we are to accept the time on his letter as correct."

"Well?"

"Well, at 7:55 he rang up the exchange and asked to be called at 8:30 the next morning."

"How on earth do you know that?"

"I was there this morning when the exchange rang. I took the call thinking it might be from the Department."

"How can you possibly say that it was Fennan who ordered the call?"

"I had inquiries made. The girl at the exchange knew Fennan's voice well; she was sure it was he, and that he rang at five to eight last night."

"Fennan and the girl knew each other, did they?"

"Good heavens no. They just exchanged pleasantries occasionally."

"And how do you conclude from this that he was murdered?"

"Well, I asked his wife about this call . . ."

"And?"

"She lied. Said she ordered it herself. She claimed to be frightfully absentminded—she gets the exchange to ring her occasionally, like tying a knot in a handkerchief, when she has an important appointment. And another thing—just before shooting himself he made some cocoa. He never drank it."

Maston listened in silence. At last he smiled and got up.

"We seem to be at cross-purposes," he said. "I send you down to discover why Fennan shot himself. You come back and say he didn't. We're not policemen, Smiley."

"No. I sometimes wonder what we are."

"Did you hear of anything that affects our position here—anything that explains his action at all? Anything to substantiate the suicide letter?"

Smiley hesitated before replying. He had seen it coming.

"Yes. I understood from Mrs. Fennan that her husband was very upset after the interview." He might as well hear the whole story. "It obsessed him, he couldn't sleep after it. She had to give him a sedative. Her account of Fennan's reaction to my interview entirely substantiates the letter." He was silent for a minute, blinking rather stupidly before him. "What I am trying to say is that I don't believe her. I don't believe Fennan wrote that letter, or that he had any intention of dying." He turned to Maston. "We simply cannot dismiss the inconsistencies. Another thing," he plunged on, "I haven't had an expert comparison made but there's a similarity between the anonymous letter and Fennan's suicide note. The type looks identical. It's ridiculous I know but there it is. We must bring the police in—give them the facts."

"Facts?" said Maston. "What facts? Suppose she did lie—she's an odd woman by all accounts, foreign, Jewish. Heaven knows the tributaries of her mind. I'm told she suffered in the war, persecuted and so forth. She may see in you the oppressor, the inquisitor. She spots you're on to something, panics, and tells you the first lie that comes into her head. Does that make her a murderess?"

"Then why did Fennan make the call? Why make himself a nightcap?"

"Who can tell?" Maston's voice was richer now, more persuasive. "If you or I, Smiley, were ever driven to that dreadful point where we were determined to destroy ourselves, who can tell what our last thoughts on earth would be? And what of Fennan? He sees his career in ruins, his life has no meaning. Is it not conceivable that he should wish, in a moment of weakness or irresolution, to hear another human voice, feel again the warmth of human contact before he dies? Fanciful, sentimental, perhaps;

50

but not improbable in a man so overwrought, so obsessed that he takes his own life."

Smiley had to give him credit—it was a good performance and he was no match for Maston when it came to this. Abruptly he felt inside himself the rising panic of frustration beyond endurance. With panic came an uncontrollable fury with this posturing sycophant, this obscene cissy with his greying hair and his reasonable smile. Panic and fury welled up in a sudden tide, flooding his breast, suffusing his whole body. His face felt hot and red, his spectacles blurred, and tears sprang to his eyes, adding to his humiliation.

Maston went on, mercifully unaware: "You cannot expect me to suggest to the Home Secretary on this evidence that the police have reached a false conclusion; you know how tenuous our police liaison is. On the one hand we have your suspicions: that in short Fennan's behavior last night was not consistent with the intent to die. His wife has apparently lied to you. Against that we have the opinion of trained detectives, who found nothing disturbing in the circumstances of death, and we have Mrs. Fennan's statement that her husband was upset by his interview. I'm sorry, Smiley, but there it is."

There was complete silence. Smiley was slowly recovering himself, and the process left him dull and inarticulate. He peered myopically before him, his pouchy, lined face still pink, his mouth slack and stupid. Maston was waiting for him to speak, but he was tired and suddenly utterly disinterested. Without a glance at Maston he got up and walked out.

He reached his own room and sat down at the desk. Mechanically he looked through his work. His in-tray contained little—some office circulars and a personal letter addressed to G. Smiley Esq., Ministry of Defence. The handwriting was unfamiliar; he opened the envelope and read the letter.

Dear Smiley,

It is essential that I should lunch with you tomorrow at the Compleat Angler at Marlow. Please do your

51

best to meet me there at one o'clock. There is something
I have to tell you.

Yours,
Samuel Fennan

The letter was handwritten and dated the previous day, Tuesday, 3 January. It had been postmarked in Whitehall at 6:00 P.M.

He looked at it stodgily for several minutes, holding it stiffly before him and inclining his head to the left. Then he put the letter down, opened a drawer of the desk, and took out a single clean sheet of paper. He wrote a brief letter of resignation to Maston and attached Fennan's invitation with a pin. He pressed the bell for a secretary, left the letter in his out-tray, and made for the lift. As usual it was stuck in the basement with the registry's tea trolley, and after a short wait he began walking downstairs. Halfway down he remembered that he had left his mackintosh and a few bits and pieces in his room. Never mind, he thought, they'll send them on.

He sat in his car in the car park, staring through the drenched windscreen.

He didn't care, he just damn well didn't care. He was surprised certainly. Surprised that he had so nearly lost control. Interviews had played a great part in Smiley's life, and he had long ago come to consider himself proof against them all: disciplinary, scholastic, medical, and religious. His secretive nature detested the purpose of all interviews, their oppressive intimacy, their inescapable reality. He remembered one deliriously happy dinner with Ann at Quaglino's when he had described to her the Chameleon-Armadillo system for beating the interviewer.

They had dined by candlelight; white skin and pearls—they were drinking brandy—Ann's eyes wide and moist, only for him; Smiley playing the lover and doing it wonderfully well; Ann loving him and thrilled by their harmony.

". . . and so I learned first to be a chameleon."

"You mean you sat there burping, you rude toad?"

"No, it's a matter of colour. Chameleons change colour."

"Of course they change colour. They sit on green leaves and go green. Did you go green, toad?"

His fingers ran lightly over the tips of hers. "Listen, minx, while I explain the Smiley Chameleon-Armadillo technique for the impertinent interviewer." Her face was very close to his and she adored him with her eyes.

"The technique is based on the theory that the interviewer, loving no one as well as himself, will be attracted by his own image. You therefore assume the exact social, temperamental, political, and intellectual colour of your inquisitor."

"Pompous toad. But intelligent lover."

"Silence. Sometimes this method founders against the idiocy or ill-disposition of the inquisitor. If so, become an armadillo."

"And wear linear belts, toad?"

"No, place him in a position so incongruous that you are superior to him. I was prepared for confirmation by a retired bishop. I was his whole flock, and received on one half holiday sufficient guidance for a diocese. But by contemplating the bishop's face and imagining that under my gaze it became covered in thick fur, I maintained the ascendancy. From then on the skill grew. I could turn him into an ape, get him stuck in sash windows, send him naked to Masonic banquets, condemn him, like the serpent, to go about on his belly . . ."

"*Wicked* lover-toad."

And so it had been. But in his recent interviews with Maston the power of detachment had left him; he was getting too involved. When Maston made the first moves, Smiley had been too tired and disgusted to compete. He supposed Elsa Fennan had killed her husband, that she had some good reason and it just did not bother him anymore. The problem no longer existed; suspicion, experience, perception, common sense—for Maston these were not the organs of fact. Paper was fact, Ministers were fact, Home Secretaries were hard fact. The Department did not concern itself with the vague impressions of a single officer when they conflicted with policy.

Smiley was tired, deeply, heavily tired. He drove slowly

homewards. Dinner out tonight. Something rather special. It was only lunch-time now—he would spend the afternoon pursuing Olearius across the Russian continent on his Hansa voyage. Then dinner at Quaglino's, and a solitary toast to the successful murderer, to Elsa perhaps, in gratitude for ending the career of George Smiley with the life of Sam Fennan.

He remembered to collect his laundry in Sloane Street, and finally turned into Bywater Street, finding a parking space about three houses down from his own. He got out carrying the brown paper parcel of laundry, locked the car laboriously, and walked all round it from habit, testing the handles. A thin rain was still falling. It annoyed him that someone had parked outside his house again. Thank goodness Mrs. Chapel had closed his bedroom window, otherwise the rain would have . . .

He was suddenly alert. Something had moved in the drawing-room. A light, a shadow, a human form; something, he was certain. Was it sight or instinct? Was it the latent skill of his own tradecraft which informed him? Some fine sense or nerve, some remote faculty of perception warned him now and he heeded the warning.

Without a moment's thought he dropped his keys back into his overcoat pocket, walked up the steps to his own front door and rang the bell.

It echoed shrilly through the house. There was a moment's silence, then came to Smiley's ears the distinct sound of footsteps approaching the door, firm and confident. A scratch of the chain, a click of the Ingersoll latch and the door was opened, swiftly, cleanly.

Smiley had never seen him before. Tall, fair, handsome, thirty-five odd. A light grey suit, white shirt, and silver tie—*habillé en diplomate*. German or Swede. His left hand remained nonchalantly in his jacket pocket.

Smiley peered at him apologetically:

"Good afternoon. Is Mr. Smiley in, please?"

The door was opened to its fullest extent. A tiny pause. "Yes. Won't you come in?"

For a fraction of a second he hesitated. "No thanks. Would you please give him this?" He handed him the parcel of laundry, walked down the steps again, to his car. He knew he was still being watched. He started the car, turned and drove into Sloane Square without a glance in the direction of his house. He found a parking space in Sloane Street, pulled in, and rapidly wrote in his diary seven sets of numbers. They belonged to the seven cars parked along Bywater Street.

What should he do? Stop a policeman? Whoever he was, he was probably gone by now. Besides there were other considerations. He locked the car again and crossed the road to a telephone kiosk. He rang Scotland Yard, got through to Special Branch, and asked for Inspector Mendel. But it appeared that the Inspector, having reported back to the Superintendent, had discreetly anticipated the pleasures of retirement and left for Mitcham. Smiley got his address after a good deal of prevarication, and set off once more in his car, covering three sides of a square and emerging at Albert Bridge. He had a sandwich and a large whisky at a new pub overlooking the river, and a quarter of an hour later was crossing the bridge on the way to Mitcham, the rain still beating down on his inconspicuous little car. He was worried, very worried indeed.

6 ❋
TEA AND SYMPATHY

It was still raining as he arrived. Mendel was in his garden wearing the most extraordinary hat Smiley had ever seen. It had begun life as an Anzac hat but its enormous brim hung low all the way round, so that he resembled nothing so much as a very tall mushroom. He was brooding over a tree stump, a wicked looking pick-axe poised obediently in his sinewy right hand.

He looked at Smiley sharply for a moment, then a grin slowly crossed his thin face as he extended his hand.

"Trouble," said Mendel.

"Trouble."

Smiley followed him up the path and into the house. Suburban and comfortable.

"There's no fire in the living-room—only just got back. How about a cup of tea in the kitchen?"

They went into the kitchen. Smiley was amused to notice the extreme tidiness, the almost feminine neatness of everything about him. Only the police calendar on the wall spoilt the illusion. While Mendel put a kettle on and busied himself with cups and saucers, Smiley related dispassionately what had happened in Bywater Street. When he had finished, Mendel looked at him for a long time in silence.

"But why did he ask you in?"

Smiley blinked and coloured a little. "That's what I wondered. It put me off my balance for a moment. It was lucky I had the parcel."

He took a drink of tea. "Though I don't believe he was taken in by the parcel. He may have been, but I doubt it. I doubt it very much."

"Not taken in?"

"Well, I wouldn't have been. Little man in a Ford delivering parcels of linen. Who could I have been? Besides, I asked for Smiley and then didn't want to see him—he must have thought that was pretty queer."

"But what was he after? What would he have done with you? Who did he think you were?"

"That's just the point, that's just it, you see. I think it was me he was waiting for, but of course he didn't expect me to ring the bell. I put him off balance. I think he wanted to kill me. That's why he asked me in: he recognized me but only just, probably from a photograph."

Mendel looked at him in silence for a while.

"Christ," he said.

"Suppose I'm right," Smiley continued, "all the way. Suppose Fennan *was* murdered last night and I *did* nearly follow him this morning. Well, unlike your trade, mine doesn't normally run to a murder a day."

"Meaning what?"

"I don't know. I just don't know. Perhaps before we go much further you'd check on these cars for me. They were parked in Bywater Street this morning."

"Why not do it yourself?"

Smiley looked at him, puzzled, for a second. Then it dawned on him that he hadn't mentioned his resignation.

57

"Sorry. I didn't tell you, did I? I resigned this morning. Just managed to get it in before I was sacked. So I'm free as air. And about as employable."

Mendel took the list of numbers from him and went into the hall to telephone. He returned a couple of minutes later.

"They'll ring back in an hour," he said. "Come on. I'll show you round the estate. Know anything about bees, do you?"

"Well, a very little, yes. I got bitten with the natural history bug at Oxford." He was going to tell Mendel how he had wrestled with Goethe's metamorphoses of plants and animals in the hope of discovering, like Faust, "what sustains the world at its inmost point." He wanted to explain why it was impossible to understand nineteenth-century Europe without a working knowledge of the naturalistic sciences, he felt earnest and full of important thoughts, and knew secretly that this was because his brain was wrestling with the day's events, that he was in a state of nervous excitement. The palms of his hands were moist.

Mendel led him out of the back door: three neat beehives stood against the low brick wall which ran along the end of the garden. Mendel spoke as they stood in the fine rain.

"Always wanted to keep them, see what it's all about. Been reading it all up—frightens me stiff, I can tell you. Odd little beggars." He nodded a couple of times in support of this statement, and Smiley looked at him again with interest. His face was thin but muscular, its expression entirely uncommunicative; his iron grey hair was cut very short and spiky. He seemed quite indifferent to the weather, and the weather to him. Smiley knew exactly the life that lay behind Mendel, had seen in policemen all over the world the same leathern skin, the same reserves of patience, bitterness, and anger. He could guess the long, fruitless hours of surveillance in every kind of weather, waiting for someone who might never come . . . or come and go too quickly. And he knew how much Mendel and the rest of them were at the mercy of personalities—capricious and bullying, nervous and changeful, occasionally wise and sympathetic.

58

He knew how intelligent men could be broken by the stupidity of their superiors, how weeks of patient work night and day could be cast aside by such men.

Mendel led him up the precarious path laid with broken stone to the beehives and, still oblivious of the rain, began taking one to pieces, demonstrating and explaining. He spoke in jerks, with quite long pauses between phrases, indicating precisely and slowly with his slim fingers.

At last they went indoors again, and Mendel showed him the two downstairs rooms. The drawing-room was all flowers: flowered curtains and carpet, flowered covers on the furniture. In a small cabinet in one corner were some Toby jugs and a pair of very handsome pistols beside a cup for target shooting.

Smiley followed him upstairs. There was a smell of paraffin from the stove on the landing, and a surly bubbling from the cistern in the lavatory.

Mendel showed him his own bedroom.

"Bridal chamber. Bought the bed at a sale for a quid. Box spring mattress. Amazing what you can pick up. Carpets are ex–Queen Elizabeth. They change them every year. Bought them at a store in Watford."

Smiley stood in the doorway, somehow rather embarrassed. Mendel turned back and passed him to open the other bedroom door.

"And that's your room. If you want it." He turned to Smiley. "I wouldn't stay at your place tonight if I were you. You never know, do you? Besides, you'll sleep better here. Air's better."

Smiley began to protest.

"Up to you. You do what you like." Mendel grew surly and embarrassed. "Don't understand your job, to be honest, any more than you know police work. You do what you like. From what I've seen of you, you can look after yourself."

They went downstairs again. Mendel had lit the gas fire in the drawing-room.

"Well, at least you must let me give you dinner tonight," said Smiley.

The telephone rang in the hall. It was Mendel's secretary about the car numbers.

Mendel came back. He handed Smiley a list of seven names and addresses. Four of the seven could be discounted; the registered addresses were in Bywater Street. Three remained: a hired car from the firm of Adam Scarr and Sons of Battersea; a trade van belonging to the Severn Tile Company, Eastbourne; and the third was listed specially as the property of the Panamanian Ambassador.

"I've got a man on the Panamanian job now. There'll be no difficulty there—they've only got three cars on the Embassy strength."

"Battersea's not far," Mendel continued. "We could pop over there together. In your car."

"By all means, by all means," Smiley said quickly, "and we can go in to Kensington for dinner. I'll book a table at the Entrechat."

It was four o'clock. They sat for a while talking in a rather desultory way about bees and housekeeping. Mendel quite at ease and Smiley still bothered and awkward, trying to find a way of talking, trying not to be clever. He could guess what Ann would have said about Mendel. She would have loved him, made a person of him, had a special voice and face for imitating him, would have made a story of him until he fitted into their lives and wasn't a mystery anymore: "Darling, who'd have thought he could be so cosy! The last man I'd ever thought would tell me where to buy cheap fish. And what a darling little house—*no bother*—he must know Toby jugs are hell and he just doesn't care. I think he's a pet. Toad, do ask him to dinner. You must. Not to giggle at but to *like*." He wouldn't have asked him, of course, but Ann would be content—she'd found a way to like him. And having done so, forgotten him.

That was what Smiley wanted, really—a way to like Mendel. He was not as quick as Ann at finding one. But Ann was Ann— she practically murdered an Etonian nephew once for drinking

60

claret with fish, but if Mendel had lit a pipe over her *crepe Suzette,* she probably would not have noticed.

Mendel made more tea and they drank it. At about a quarter past five they set off for Battersea in Smiley's car. On the way Mendel bought an evening paper. He read it with difficulty, catching the light from the street lamps. After a few minutes he spoke with sudden venom:

"Krauts. Bloody Krauts. God, I hate them!"

"Krauts?"

"Krauts. Huns. Jetties. Bloody Germans. Wouldn't give you sixpence for the lot of them. Carnivorous ruddy sheep. Kicking Jews about again. Us all over. Knock 'em down, set 'em up. Forgive and forget. Why bloody well forget, I'd like to know? Why forget theft, murder, and rape just because millions committed it? Christ, one poor little sod of a bank clerk pinches ten bob and the whole of the Metropolitan's on to him. But Krupp and all that mob—oh no. Christ, if I was a Jew in Germany I'd . . ."

Smiley was suddenly wide awake: "What would you do? What would you do, Mendel?"

"Oh, I suppose I'd sit down under it. It's statistics now, politics. It isn't sense to give them H-bombs so it's politics. And there's the Yanks—millions of ruddy Jews in America. What do they do? Damn all: give the Krauts more bombs. All chums together—blow each other up."

Mendel was trembling with rage, and Smiley was silent for a while, thinking of Elsa Fennan.

"What's the answer?" he asked, just for something to say.

"Christ knows," said Mendel savagely.

They turned into Battersea Bridge Road and drew up beside a constable standing on the pavement. Mendel showed his police card.

"Scarr's garage? Well it isn't hardly a garage, sir, just a yard. Scrap metal he handles mostly, and secondhand cars. If they won't do for one they'll do for the other, that's what Adam says. You want to go down Prince of Wales Drive till you come to the hospital. It's tucked in there between a couple of pre-fabs. Bomb site it is really. Old Adam straightened it out with some cinders and no one's ever moved him."

"You seem to know a lot about him," said Mendel.

"I should do, I've run him in a few times. There's not much in the book that Adam hasn't been up to. He's one of our hardy perennials, Scarr is."

"Well, well. Anything on him at present?"

"Couldn't say, sir. But you can have him any time for illegal betting. And Adam's practically under the Act already."

They drove towards Battersea Hospital. The park on their right looked black and hostile behind the street lamps.

"What's 'under the Act'?" asked Smiley.

"Oh, he's only joking. It means your record's so long you're eligible for Preventive Detention—years of it. He sounds like my type," Mendel continued. "Leave him to me."

They found the yard as the constable had described, between two dilapidated pre-fabs in an uncertain row of hutments erected on the bomb site. Rubble, clinker, and refuse lay everywhere. Bits of asbestos, timber, and old iron, presumably acquired by Mr. Scarr for resale or adaptation, were piled in a corner, dimly lit by the pale glow which came from the farther pre-fab. The two men looked round them in silence for a moment. Then Mendel shrugged, put two fingers in his mouth and whistled shrilly.

"Scarr!" he called. Silence. The outside light on the far pre-fab went on, and three or four pre-war cars in various stages of dilapidation became dimly discernible.

The door opened slowly and a girl of about twelve stood on the threshold.

"Your dad in, dear?" asked Mendel.

"Nope. Gone to the Prod, I 'spect."

"Righto, dear. Thanks."

They walked back to the road.

"What on earth's the Prod, or daren't I ask?" said Smiley. "Prodigal's Calf. Pub round the corner. We can walk it—only a hundred yards. Leave the car here."

It was only just after opening time. The public bar was

empty, and as they waited for the landlord to appear the door swung open and a very fat man in a black suit came in. He walked straight to the bar and hammered on it with a half-crown.

"Wilf," he shouted. "Take your finger out, you got customers, you lucky boy." He turned to Smiley; "Good evening, friend."

From the rear of the pub a voice replied: "Tell 'em to leave their money on the counter and come back later."

The fat man looked at Mendel and Smiley blankly for a moment, then suddenly let out a peal of laughter: "Not them, Wilf—they're busies!" The joke appealed to him so much that he was finally compelled to sit on the bench that ran along the side of the room, with his hands on his knees, his huge shoulders heaving with laughter, the tears running down his cheeks. Occasionally he said "Oh dear, oh dear," as he caught his breath before another outburst.

Smiley looked at him with interest. He wore a very dirty stiff white collar with rounded edges, a flowered red tie carefully pinned outside the black waistcoat, army boots and a shiny black suit, very threadbare and without a vestige of a crease in the trousers. His shirt cuffs were black with sweat, grime, and motor oil and held in place by paper-clips twisted into a knot.

The landlord appeared and took their orders. The stranger bought a large whisky and ginger wine and took it at once to the saloon bar, where there was a coal fire. The landlord watched with disapproval.

"That's him all over, mean sod. Won't pay saloon prices, but likes the fire."

"Who is he?" asked Mendel.

"Him? Scarr, his name is. Adam Scarr. Christ knows why Adam. See him in the Garden of Eden: bloody grotesque, that's what it is. They say round here that if Eve gave him an apple he'd eat the ruddy core." The landlord sucked his teeth and shook his head. Then he shouted to Scarr. "Still, you're good for business, aren't you, Adam? They come bloody miles to see you, don't they? Teenage monster from outer space, that's what you are. Come and see. Adam Scarr: one look and you'll sign the pledge."

More hilarious laughter. Mendel leant over to Smiley. "You go and wait in the car—you're better out of this. Got a fiver?" Smiley gave him five pounds from his wallet, nodded his agreement, and walked out. He could imagine nothing more frightful than dealing with Scarr.

"You Scarr?" said Mendel.

"Friend, you are correct."

"TRX 0891. That your car?"

Mr. Scarr frowned at his whisky and ginger. The question seemed to sadden him.

"Well?" said Mendel.

"She was, squire, she was."

"What the hell do you mean?"

Scarr raised his right hand a few inches then let it gently fall. "Dark waters, squire, murky waters."

"Listen, I've got bigger fish to fry than ever you dreamed of. I'm not made of glass, see? I couldn't care bloody less about your racket. Where's that car?"

Scarr appeared to consider this speech on its merits. "I see the light, friend. You wish for information."

"Of course I bloody well do."

"These are hard times, squire. The cost of living, dear boy, is a rising star. Information is an item, a saleable item, is it not?"

"You tell me who hired that car and you won't starve."

"I don't starve now, friend. I want to eat better."

"A fiver."

Scarr finished his drink and replaced his glass noisily on the table. Mendel got up and bought him another.

"It was pinched," said Scarr. "I had it a few years for self-drive, see. For the deepo."

"The *what?*"

"The deepo—the deposit. Bloke wants a car for a day. You

64

take twenty quid deposit in notes, right? When he comes back he owes you forty bob, see? You give him a cheque for thirty-eight quid, show it on your books as a loss, and the job's worth a tenner. Got it?"

Mendel nodded.

"Well, three weeks ago a bloke come in. Tall Scotsman. Well-to-do, he was. Carried a stick. He paid the deepo, took the car, and I never see him nor the car again. Robbery."

"Why not report it to the police?"

Scarr paused and drank from his glass. He looked at Mendel sadly.

"Many factors would argue against, squire."

"Meaning you'd pinched it yourself?"

Scarr looked shocked. "I have since heard distressing rumours about the party from which I obtained the vehicle. I will say no more," he added piously.

"When you rented him the car he filled in forms, didn't he? Insurance, receipt, and so on? Where are they?"

"False, all false. He gave me an address in Ealing. I went there and it didn't exist. I have no doubt the name was also fictitious."

Mendel screwed the money into a roll in his pocket and handed it across the table to Scarr. Scarr unfolded it and, quite unselfconscious, counted it in full view of anyone who cared to look.

"I know where to find you," said Mendel; "and I know a few things about you. If that's a load of cock you've sold me, I'll break your bloody neck."

It was raining again and Smiley wished he had brought a hat. He crossed the road, entered the side street which accommodated Mr. Scarr's establishment, and walked towards the car. There was no one in the street, and it was oddly quiet. Two hundred yards down the road, Battersea General Hospital, small and neat, shed multiple beams of light from its uncurtained windows. The pavement was very wet and the echo of his own footsteps was crisp and startling.

He drew level with the first of the two pre-fabs which bordered Scarr's yard. A car was parked in the yard with its sidelights on. Curious, Smiley turned off the street and walked towards it. It was an old MG saloon, green probably, or that brown they went in for before the war. The numberplate was barely lit, and caked in mud. He stooped to read it, tracing the letters with his forefinger: TRX 0891. Of course—that was one of the numbers he had written down this morning.

He heard a footstep behind him and stood up, half turning. He had begun to raise his arm as the blow fell.

It was a terrible blow—it seemed to split his skull in two. As he fell he could feel the warm blood running freely over his left ear. Not again, oh Christ, not again, thought Smiley. But he hardly felt the rest—just a vision of his own body, far away, being slowly broken like rock; cracked and split into fragments, then nothing. Nothing but the warmth of his own blood as it ran over his face into the cinders, and far away the beating of the stonebreakers. But not here. Far away.

7 ❀
MR. SCARR'S STORY

Mendel looked at him and wondered whether he was dead. He emptied the pockets of his own overcoat and laid it gently over Smiley's shoulders, then he ran, ran like a madman, towards the hospital, crashed through the swing-doors of the out-patients' department into the bright, twenty-four-hour interior of the hospital. A young coloured doctor was on duty. Mendel showed him his card, shouted something to him, took him by the arm, tried to lead him down the road. The doctor smiled patiently, shook his head, and telephoned for an ambulance.

Mendel ran back down the road and waited. A few minutes later the ambulance arrived and skilful men gathered Smiley up and took him away.

"Bury him," thought Mendel; "I'll make the bastard pay."

He stood there for a moment, staring down at the wet patch of mud and cinders where Smiley had fallen; the red glow of the car's rear lights showed him nothing. The ground had been hopelessly churned by the feet of the ambulance men and a few inhabitants from the pre-fabs who had come and gone like shadowy vultures. Trouble was about. They didn't like trouble.

"Bastard," Mendel hissed, and walked slowly back towards the pub.

The saloon bar was filling up. Scarr was ordering another drink. Mendel took him by the arm. Scarr turned and said:

"Hello, friend, back again. Have a little of what killed Auntie."

"Shut up," said Mendel; "I want another word with you. Come outside."

Mr. Scarr shook his head and sucked his teeth sympathetically. "Can't be done, friend, can't be done. Company." He indicated with his head an eighteen-year-old blonde with off-white lipstick and an improbable bosom, who sat quite motionless at a corner table. Her painted eyes had a permanently startled look. "Listen," whispered Mendel; "in just two seconds I'll tear your bloody ears off, you lying sod."

Scarr consigned his drinks to the care of the landlord and made a slow, dignified exit. He didn't look at the girl.

Mendel led him across the street towards the pre-fabs. The sidelights of Smiley's car shone towards them eighty yards down the road. They turned into the yard. The MG was still there. Mendel had Scarr firmly by the arm, ready if necessary to force the forearm back and upwards, breaking or dislocating the shoulder joint.

"Well, well," cried Scarr with apparent delight. "She's returned to the bosom of her ancestors."

"Stolen, was it?" said Mendel. "Stolen by a tall Scotsman with a walking stick and an address in Ealing. Decent of him to bring it back, wasn't it? Friendly gesture, after all this time. You've mistaken your bloody market, Scarr." Mendel was shaking with anger. "And why are the sidelights on? Open the door."

Scarr turned to Mendel in the dark, his free hand slapping his pockets in search of keys. He extracted a bunch of three or four, felt through them, and finally unlocked the car door. Mendel got in, found the passenger light in the roof, and switched it on. He began methodically to search the inside of the car. Scarr stood outside and waited.

He searched quickly but thoroughly. Glove tray, seats, floor, rear window-ledge: nothing. He slipped his hand inside the map pocket on the passenger door and drew out a map and an envelope. The envelope was long and flat, grey-blue in colour with a linen finish. Continental, thought Mendel. There was no writing on it. He tore it open. There were ten used five-pound notes inside and a piece of plain postcard. Mendel held it to the light and read the message printed on it with a ballpoint pen:

FINISHED NOW. SELL IT.

There was no signature.

He got out of the car and seized Scarr by the elbows. Scarr stepped back quickly. "What's your problem, friend?" he asked.

Mendel spoke softly. "It's not my problem, Scarr, it's yours. The biggest bloody problem you ever had. Conspiracy to murder, attempted murder, offences under the Official Secrets Act. And you can add to that contravention of the Road Traffic Act, conspiracy to defraud the Inland Revenue, and about fifteen other charges that will occur to me while you nurse your problem on a cell bed."

"Just a minute, copper, let's not go over the moon. What's the story? Who the hell's talking about murder?"

"Listen, Scarr, you're a little man, come in on the fringe of the big spenders, aren't you? Well, now you're the big spender. I reckon it'll cost you fifteen years."

"Look, shut up, will you."

"No I won't, little man. You're caught between two big ones, see, and you're the mug. And what will I do? I'll bloody well laugh myself sick while you rot in the Scrubs and contemplate your fat belly. See that hospital, do you? There's a bloke dying there, murdered by your tall Scotsman. They found him half an hour ago bleeding like a pig in your yard. There's another one dead in Surrey, and for all I know there's one in every

69

bloody home county. So it's your problem, you poor sod, not mine. Another thing—you're the only one who knows who he is, aren't you? He might want to tidy that up a bit, mightn't he?"

Scarr walked slowly round to the other side of the car.

Mendel sat in the driving seat and unlocked the passenger door from the inside. Scarr sat himself beside him. They didn't put the light on.

"I'm in a nice way of business round here," said Scarr quietly, "and the pickings is small but regular. Or was till this bloke come along."

"What bloke?"

"Bit by bit, copper, don't rush me. That was four years ago. I didn't believe in Father Christmas till I met him. Dutch, he said he was, in the diamond business. I'm not pretending I thought he was straight, see, because you're not barmy and nor am I. I never asked what he done and he never told me, but I guessed it was smuggling. Money to burn he had, came off him like leaves in autumn. 'Scarr,' he said; 'you're a man of business. I don't like publicity, never did, and I hears we're birds of a feather. I want a car. Not to keep, but to borrow.' He didn't put it quite like that because of the lingo, but that's the sense of it. 'What's your proposition?' I says. 'Let's have a proposition.'

" 'Well,' he says; 'I'm shy. I want a car that no one can ever get on to, supposing I had an accident. Buy a car for me, Scarr, a nice old car with something under the bonnet. Buy it in your own name,' he says, 'and keep it wrapped up for me. There's five hundred quid for a start, and twenty quid a month for garaging. And there's a bonus, Scarr, for every day I take it out. But I'm shy, see, and you don't know me. That's what the money's for,' he says. 'It's for not knowing me.'

"I'll never forget that day. Raining cats and dogs it was, and me bent over an old taxi I'd got off a bloke in Wandsworth. I owed a bookie forty quid, and the coppers were sensitive about a car I'd bought on the never never and flogged in Clapham."

Mr. Scarr drew breath and let it out again with an air of comic resignation.

70

"And there he was, standing over me like my own conscience, showering old singles on me like used tote tickets."

"What did he look like?" asked Mendel.

"Quite young he was. Tall, fair chap. But cool—cool as charity. I never saw him after that day. He sent me letters posted in London and typed on plain paper. Just 'Be ready Monday night,' 'Be ready Thursday night,' and so on. We had it all arranged. I left the car out in the yard, full of petrol and teed up. He never said when he'd be back. Just ran it in about closing time or later, leaving the lights on and the doors locked. He'd put a couple of quid in the map pocket for each day he'd been away."

"What happened if anything went wrong, if you got pinched for something else?"

"We had a telephone number. He told me to ring and ask for a name."

"What name?"

"He told me to choose one. I chose Blondie. He didn't think that was very funny but we stuck to it. Primrose 0098."

"Did you ever use it?"

"Yes, a couple of years ago I took a bint to Margate for ten days. I thought I'd better let him know. A girl answered the phone—Dutch too, by the sound of her. She said Blondie was in Holland, and she'd take a message. But after that I didn't bother."

"Why not?"

"I began to notice, see. He came regular once a fortnight, the first and third Tuesdays except January and February. This was the first January he come. He brought the car back Thursday usually. Odd him coming back tonight. But this is the end of him, isn't it?" Scarr held in his enormous hand the piece of postcard he had, taken from Mendel.

"Did he miss at all? Away long periods?"

"Winters he kept away more. January he never come, nor February. Like I said."

Mendel still had the £50 in his hand. He tossed them into Scarr's lap.

"Don't think you're lucky. I wouldn't be in your shoes for ten times that lot. I'll be back."

Mr. Scarr seemed worried.

"I wouldn't have peached," he said; "but I don't want to be mixed up in nothing, see. Not if the old country's going to suffer, eh, squire?"

"Oh, shut up," said Mendel. He was tired. He took the postcard back, got out of the car, and walked away towards the hospital.

There was no news at the hospital. Smiley was still unconscious. The CID had been informed. Mendel would do better to leave his name and address and go home. The hospital would telephone as soon as they had any news. After a good deal of argument, Mendel obtained from the sister the key to Smiley's car.

Mitcham, he decided, was a lousy place to live.

8 ✻

REFLECTIONS IN A HOSPITAL WARD

He hated the bed as a drowning man hates the sea. He hated the sheets that imprisoned him so that he could move neither hand nor foot.

And he hated the room because it frightened him. There was a trolley by the door with instruments on it, scissors, bandages, and bottles, strange objects that carried the terror of the unknown, swathed in white linen for the last Communion. There were jugs, tall ones half covered with napkins, standing like white eagles waiting to tear at his entrails, little glass ones with rubber tubing coiled inside them like snakes. He hated everything, and he was afraid. He was hot and the sweat ran off him, he was cold and the sweat held him, trickling over his ribs like cold blood. Night and day alternated without recognition from Smiley. He fought a relentless battle against sleep, for when he closed his eyes they seemed to turn inwards on the chaos of his brain; and when sometimes by sheer weight his eyelids drew themselves together, he would summon all his strength to tear them apart and stare again at the pale light wavering somewhere above him.

Then came a blessed day when someone must have drawn the blinds and let in the grey winter light. He heard the sound of traffic outside and knew at last that he would live.

So the problem of dying once more became an academic one—a debt he would postpone until he was rich and could pay in his own way. It was a luxurious feeling, almost of purity. His mind was wonderfully lucid, ranging like Prometheus over his whole world; where had he heard that: "the mind becomes separated from the body, rules a paper kingdom . . ."? He was bored by the light above him, and wished there was more to look at. He was bored by the grapes, the smell of honeycomb and flowers, the chocolates. He wanted books, and literary journals; how could he keep up with his reading if they gave him no books? There was so little research done on his period as it was, so little creative criticism on the seventeenth century.

It was three weeks before Mendel was allowed to see him. He walked in holding a new hat and carrying a book about bees. He put his hat on the end of the bed and the book on the bedside table. He was grinning.

"I bought you a book," he said; "about bees. They're clever little beggars. Might interest you."

He sat on the edge of the bed. "I got a new hat. Daft really. Celebrate my retirement."

"Oh yes, I forgot. You're on the shelf, too." They both laughed, and were silent again.

Smiley blinked. "I'm afraid you're not very distinct at the moment. I'm not allowed to wear my old glasses. They're getting me some new ones." He paused. "You don't know who did this to me, do you?"

"May do. Depends. Got a lead, I think. I don't know enough, that's the trouble. About your job, I mean. Does the East German Steel Mission mean anything to you?"

"Yes, I think so. It came here four years ago to try and get a foot in the Board of Trade."

Mendel gave an account of his transactions with Mr. Scarr. "... Said he was Dutch. The only way Scarr had of getting in touch with him was by ringing a Primrose telephone number. I checked the subscriber. Listed as the East German Steel Mission, in Belsize Park. I sent a bloke to sniff round. They've cleared out. Nothing there at all, no furniture, nothing. Just the telephone, and that's been ripped out of its socket."

"When did they go?"

"The third of January. Same day as Fennan was murdered." He looked at Smiley quizzically. Smiley thought for a minute and said: "Get hold of Peter Guillam at the Ministry of Defence and bring him here tomorrow. By the scruff of the neck."

Mendel picked up his hat and walked to the door. "Goodbye," said Smiley; "thank you for the book."

"See you tomorrow," said Mendel, and left.

Smiley lay back in bed. His head was aching. Damn, he thought, I never thanked him for the honey. It had come from Fortnums, too.

Why the early morning call? That was what puzzled him more than anything. It was silly, really, Smiley supposed, but of all the unaccountables in the case, that worried him most.

Elsa Fennan's explanation had been so stupid, so noticeably unlikely. Ann, yes; she would make the exchange stand on its head if she'd felt like it, but not Elsa Fennan. There was nothing in that alert, intelligent little face, nothing in her total independence to support the ludicrous claim to absentmindedness. She could have said the exchange had made a mistake, had called the wrong day, anything. Fennan, yes; he had been absentminded. It was one of the odd inconsistencies about Fennan's character which had emerged in the inquiries before the interview. A voracious reader of Westerns and a passionate chess player, a musician and a spare-time philosopher, a deep thinking man—but absentminded. There had been a frightful row once about him taking some secret papers out of the Foreign Office, and it turned out that he had put them in his despatch case with his *Times* and the evening paper before going home to Walliston.

Had Elsa Fennan, in her panic, taken upon herself the mantle of her husband? Or the motive of her husband? Had Fennan asked for the call to remind him of something, and had Elsa borrowed the motive? Then what did Fennan need to be reminded of—and what did his wife so strenuously wish to conceal?

Samuel Fennan. The new world and the old met in him. The eternal Jew, cultured, cosmopolitan, self-determinate, industrious, and perceptive: to Smiley, immensely attractive. The child of his century; persecuted, like Elsa, and driven from his adopted Germany to University in England. By the sheer weight of his ability he had pushed aside disadvantage and prejudice, finally to enter the Foreign Office. It had been a remarkable achievement, owed to nothing but his own brilliance. And if he was a little conceited, a little disinclined to bide the decision of minds more pedestrian than his own, who could blame him? There had been some embarrassment when Fennan pronounced himself in favour of a divided Germany, but it had all blown over, he had been transferred to an Asian desk, and the affair was forgotten. For the rest, he had been generous to a fault, and popular both in Whitehall and in Surrey, where he devoted several hours each weekend to charity work. His great love was skiing. Every year he took all his leave at once and spent six weeks in Switzerland or Austria. He had visited Germany only once, Smiley remembered—with his wife about four years ago.

It had been natural enough that Fennan should join the Left at Oxford. It was the great honeymoon period of University Communism, and its causes, heaven knows, lay close enough to his heart. The rise of Fascism in Germany and Italy, the Japanese invasion of Manchuria, the Franco rebellion in Spain, the slump in America, and above all the wave of anti-Semitism that

76

was sweeping across Europe: it was inevitable that Fennan should seek an outlet for his anger and revulsion. Besides, the Party was respectable then; the failure of the Labour Party and the Coalition Government had convinced many intellectuals that the Communists alone could provide an effective alternative to Capitalism and Fascism. There was the excitement, an air of conspiracy and comradeship which must have appealed to the flamboyance in Fennan's character and given him comfort in his loneliness. There was talk of going to Spain; some *had* gone, like Cornford from Cambridge, never to return.

Smiley could imagine Fennan in those days—volatile and earnest, no doubt bringing to his companions the experience of real suffering, a veteran among cadets. His parents had died— his father had been a banker with the foresight to keep a small account in Switzerland. There had not been much, but enough to see him through Oxford, and protect him from the cold wind of poverty.

Smiley remembered so well that interview with Fennan; one among many, yet different. Different because of the language. Fennan was so articulate, so quick, so sure. "Their greatest day," he had said, "was when the miners came. They came from the Rhondda, you know, and to the comrades it seemed the spirit of Freedom had come down with them from the hills. It was a hunger march. It never seemed to occur to the Group that the marchers might actually *be* hungry, but it occurred to me. We hired a truck and the girls made stew—tons of it. We got the meat cheap from a sympathetic butcher in the market. We drove the truck out to meet them. They ate the stew and marched on. They didn't like us really, you know, didn't trust us." He laughed. "They were so small—that's what I remember best—small and dark like elves. We hoped they'd sing and they did. But not for us—for themselves. That was the first time I had met Welshmen.

"It made me understand my own race better, I think—I'm a Jew, you know."

Smiley had nodded.

"They didn't know what to do when the Welshmen had gone. What do you do when a dream has come true? They realized then why the Party didn't much care about intellectuals. I think they felt cheap, mostly, and ashamed. Ashamed of their beds and their room, their full bellies and their clever essays. Ashamed of their talents and their humour. They were always saying how Keir Hardie taught himself shorthand with a piece of chalk: on the coal face, you know. They were ashamed of having pencils and paper. But it's no good just throwing them away, is it? That's what I learnt in the end. That's why I left the Party, I suppose."

Smiley wanted to ask him how Fennan himself had felt, but Fennan was talking again. He had shared nothing with them, he had come to realize that. They were not men, but children, who dreamed of freedom-fires, gipsy music, and one world tomorrow, who rode on white horses across the Bay of Biscay or with a child's pleasure bought beer for starving elves from Wales; children who had no power to resist the Eastern sun, and obediently turned their tousled heads towards it. They loved each other and believed they loved mankind; they fought each other and believed they fought the world.

Soon he found them comic and touching. To him, they might as well have knitted socks for soldiers. The disproportion between the dream and reality drove him to a close examination of both; he put all his energy into philosophical and historical reading, and found, to his surprise, comfort and peace in the intellectual purity of Marxism. He feasted on its intellectual ruthlessness, was thrilled by its fearlessness, its academic reversal of traditional values. In the end it was this and not the Party that gave him strength in his solitude, a philosophy which exacted total sacrifice to an unassailable formula, which humiliated and inspired him; and when he finally found success, prosperity, and integration, he turned his back sadly upon it as a treasure he had outgrown and must leave at Oxford with the days of his youth.

This was how Fennan had described it, and Smiley had understood. It was scarcely the story of anger and resentment that

Smiley had come to expect in such interviews, but (perhaps because of that) it seemed more real. There was another thing about that interview: Smiley's conviction that Fennan had left something important unsaid.

Was there any *factual* connection between the incident in Bywater Street and Fennan's death? Smiley reproached himself for being carried away. Seen in perspective, there was nothing but the sequence of events to suggest that Fennan and Smiley were part of a single problem.

The sequence of events, that is, and the weight of Smiley's intuition, experience or what you will—the extra sense that had told him to ring the bell and not use his key, the sense that did not, however, warn him that a murderer stood in the night with a piece of lead piping.

The interview had been informal, that was true. The walk in the park reminded him more of Oxford than of Whitehall. The walk in the park, the café in Millbank—yes, there had been a procedural difference too, but what did it amount to? An official of the Foreign Office walking in the park, talking earnestly with an anonymous little man . . . Unless the little man was not anonymous!

Smiley took a paperback book and began to write in pencil on the flyleaf:

"Let us assume what is by no means proven: that the murder of Fennan and the attempted murder of Smiley are related. What circumstances connected Smiley with Fennan *before* Fennan's death?

1. Before the interview on Monday, 2 January, I had never met Fennan. I read his file at the Department and I had certain preliminary inquiries made.
2. On 2 January I went alone to the Foreign Office by taxi. The FO arranged the interview, but did not, repeat not, know in advance who would conduct it. Fennan therefore had no prior knowledge of my identity, nor had anyone else outside the Department.

79

3. The interview fell into two parts; the first at the FO, when people wandered through the room and took no notice of us at all, the second outside when anyone could have seen us.

What followed? Nothing, unless . . .

Yes, that was the only possible conclusion: unless whoever saw them together recognized not only Fennan but Smiley as well, and was violently opposed to their association.

Why? In what way was Smiley dangerous? His eyes suddenly opened very wide. Of course—in one way, in one way only—*as a security officer.*

He put down his pencil.

And so whoever killed Sam Fennan was anxious that he should not talk to a security officer. Someone in the Foreign Office, perhaps. But essentially someone who knew Smiley, too. Someone Fennan had known at Oxford, known as a Communist, someone who feared exposure, who thought that Fennan would talk, had talked already, perhaps? And if he had talked already, then of course Smiley would have to be killed quickly before he could put in his report.

That would explain the murder of Fennan and the assault on Smiley. It made some sense, but not much. He had built a cardhouse as high as it would go, and he still had cards in his hand. What about Elsa, her lies, her complicity, her fear? What about the car and the 8:30 call? What about the anonymous letter? If the murderer was frightened of contact between Smiley and Fennan, he would scarcely call attention to Fennan by denouncing him. Who then? Who?

He lay back and closed his eyes. His head was throbbing again. Perhaps Peter Guillam could help. He was the only hope. His head was going round. It hurt terribly.

9 ❀
TIDYING UP

Mendel showed Peter Guillam into the ward, grinning hugely.

"Got him," he said.

The conversation was awkward; strained for Guillam at least, by the recollection of Smiley's abrupt resignation and the incongruity of meeting in a hospital ward. Smiley was wearing a blue bedjacket, his hair was spiky and untidy above the bandages and he still had the trace of a heavy bruise on his left temple.

After a particularly awkward pause, Smiley said: "Look, Peter, Mendel's told you what happened to me. You're the expert—what do we know about the East German Steel Mission?"

"Pure as the driven snow, dear boy, except for their sudden departure. Only about three men and a dog in the thing. They hung out in Hampstead somewhere. No one quite knew why they were here when they first came, but they've done quite a decent job in the last four years."

"What are their terms of reference?"

"God knows. I think they thought when they arrived that they were going to persuade the Board of Trade to break the European steel rings, but they got the cold shoulder. Then they went in for consular stuff with the accent on machine tools and finished products, exchange of industrial and technical information and so on. Nothing to do with what they came for but rather more acceptable, I gather."

"Who were they?"

"Oh—couple of technicians—Professor Doktor someone and Doktor someone else—couple of girls and a general dogsbody."

"Who was the dogsbody?"

"Don't know. Some young diplomat to iron out the wrinkles. We have them recorded at the Department. I can send you details, I suppose."

"If you don't mind."

"No, of course not."

There was another awkward pause. Smiley said: "Photographs would be a help, Peter. Could you manage that?"

"Yes, yes, of course." Guillam looked away from Smiley in some embarrassment. "We don't know much about the East Germans, really, you know. We get odd bits here and there, but on the whole they're something of a mystery. If they operate at all they don't do it under Trade or Diplomatic cover—that's why, if you're right about this chap, it's so odd him coming from the Steel Mission."

"Oh," said Smiley flatly.

"How do they operate?" asked Mendel.

"It's hard to generalize from the very few isolated cases we do know of. My impression is that they run their agents direct from Germany with no contact between controller and agent in the operational zone."

"But that must limit them terribly," cried Smiley. "You may have to wait months before your agent can travel to a meeting place outside his own country. He may not have the necessary cover to make the journey at all."

"Well, obviously it does limit him, but their targets seem to be so insignificant. They prefer to run foreign nationals—Swedes, expatriate Poles and whatnot, on short-term missions, where the limitations of their technique don't matter. In exceptional cases where they have an agent resident in the target country, they work on a courier system, which corresponds to the Soviet pattern."

Smiley was listening now.

"As a matter of fact," Guillam went on, "the Americans intercepted a courier quite recently, which is where we learnt the little we do know about GDR technique."

"Such as what?"

"Oh well, never waiting at a rendezvous, never meeting at the stated time but twenty minutes before; recognition signals—all the usual conjuring tricks that give a gloss to low-grade information. They muck about with names, too. A courier may have to contact three or four agents—a controller may run as many as fifteen. They never invent cover names for themselves."

"What do you mean? Surely they must."

"They get the agent to do it for them. The agent chooses a name, any name he likes, and the controller adopts it. A gimmick really—" He stopped, looking at Mendel in surprise.

Mendel had leapt to his feet.

Guillam sat back in his chair and wondered if he were allowed to smoke. He decided reluctantly that he wasn't. He could have done with a cigarette.

"Well?" said Smiley. Mendel had described to Guillam his interview with Mr. Scarr.

"It fits," said Guillam. "Obviously it fits with what we know. But then we don't know all that much. If Blondie was a courier, it is exceptional—in my experience at least—that he should use a trade delegation as a staging post."

"You said the Mission had been here four years," said Mendel. "Blondie first came to Scarr four years ago."

No one spoke for a moment. Then Smiley said earnestly: "Peter, it is possible, isn't it? I mean they might under certain operational conditions need to have a station over here as well as couriers."

"Well, of course, if they were on to something really big they might."

"Meaning if they had a highly placed resident agent in play?"

"Yes, roughly."

"And assuming they had such an agent, a Maclean or Fuchs, it is conceivable that they would establish a station here under trade cover with no operational function except to hold the agent's hand?"

"Yes, it's conceivable. But it's a tall order, George. What you're suggesting is that the agent is run from abroad, serviced by courier, and the courier is serviced by the Mission, which is also the agent's personal guardian angel. He'd have to be some agent."

"I'm not suggesting quite that—but near enough. And I accept that the system demands a high-grade agent. Don't forget we only have Blondie's word for it that he came from abroad."

Mendel chipped in: "This agent—would he be in touch with the Mission direct?"

"Good lord, no," said Guillam. "He'd probably have an emergency procedure for getting in touch with them—a telephone code or something of the sort."

"How does that work?" asked Mendel.

"Varies. Might be on the wrong number system. You dial the number from a call box and ask to speak to George Brown. You're told George Brown doesn't live there so you apologize and ring off. The time and the rendezvous are prearranged—the emergency signal is contained in the name you ask for. Someone will be there."

"What else would the Mission do?" asked Smiley.

"Hard to say. Pay him probably. Arrange a collecting place

for reports. The controller would make all those arrangements for the agent, of course, and tell him his part of it by courier. They work on the Soviet principle a good deal, as I told you—even the smallest details are arranged by control. The people in the field are allowed very little independence."

There was another silence. Smiley looked at Guillam and then at Mendel, then blinked and said:

"Blondie didn't come to Scarr in January and February, did he?"

"No," said Mendel; "this was the first year."

"Fennan always went skiing in January and February. This was the first time in four years he'd missed."

"I wonder," said Smiley, "whether I ought to go and see Maston again."

Guillam stretched luxuriously and smiled: "You can always try. He'll be thrilled to hear you've been brained. I've a sneaking feeling he'll think Battersea's on the coast, but not to worry. Tell him you were attacked while wandering about in someone's private yard—he'll understand. Tell him about your assailant, too, George. You've never seen him, mind, and you don't know his name, but he's a courier of the East German Intelligence Service. Maston will back you up; he always does. Specially when he's got to report to the Minister."

Smiley looked at Guillam and said nothing.

"After your bang on the head, too," Guillam added; "he'll understand."

"But, Peter—"

"I know, George, I know."

"Well, let me tell you another thing. Blondie collected his car on the first Tuesday of each month."

"So?"

"Those were the nights Elsa Fennan went to the Weybridge Rep. Fennan worked late on Tuesdays, she said."

Guillam got up. "Let me dig about, George. Cheerio, Mendel, I'll probably give you a ring tonight. I don't see what we can do now, anyway, but it would be nice to know, wouldn't it?" He reached the door. "Incidentally, where are Fennan's possessions—wallet, diary, and so forth? Stuff they found on the body?"

"Probably still at the Station," said Mendel; "until after the inquest."

Guillam stood looking at Smiley for a moment, wondering what to say.

"Anything you want, George?"

"No thanks—oh, there is one thing."

"Yes?"

"Could you get the CID off my back? They've visited me three times now and of course they've got nowhere locally. Could you make this an Intelligence matter for the time being? Be mysterious and soothing?"

"Yes, I should think so."

"I know it's difficult, Peter, because I'm not—"

"Oh, another thing just to cheer you up. I had that comparison made between Fennan's suicide note and the anonymous letter. They were done by different people on the same machine. Different pressures and spacing but identical typeface. So long, old dear. Tuck into the grapes."

Guillam closed the door behind him. They heard his footsteps echoing crisply down the bare corridor.

Mendel rolled himself a cigarette.

"Lord," said Smiley; "does nothing frighten you? Haven't you seen the Sister here?"

Mendel grinned and shook his head.

"You can only die once," he said, putting the cigarette between his thin lips. Smiley watched him light it. He produced his lighter, took the hood off it and rotated the wheel with his stained thumb, swiftly cupping both hands around it and nursing the flame towards the cigarette. There might have been a hurricane blowing.

"Well, you're the crime expert," said Smiley. "How are we doing?"

"Messy," said Mendel. "Untidy."

86

"Why?"

"Loose ends everywhere. No police work. Nothing checked. Like algebra."

"What's algebra got to do with it?"

"You've got to prove what can be proved, first. Find the constants. Did she really go to the theatre? Was she alone? Did the neighbours hear her come back? If so, what time? Was Fennan really late Tuesdays? Did his Missus go to the theatre regularly *every* fortnight like she said?"

"And the 8:30 call. Can you tidy that for me?"

"You've got that call on the brain, haven't you?"

"Yes. Of all the loose ends, that's the loosest. I brood over it, you know, and there just isn't any sense in it. I've been through his train timetable. He was a punctual man—often got to the FO before anyone else, unlocked his own cupboard. He would have caught the 8:54, the 9:08, or at worst the 9:14. The 8:54 got him in at 9:38—he liked to be at his office by a quarter to ten. He couldn't possibly want to be woken at 8:30."

"Perhaps he just liked bells," said Mendel, getting up.

"And the letters," Smiley continued. "Different typists but the same machine. Discounting the murderer, two people had access to that machine: Fennan and his wife. If we accept that Fennan typed the suicide note—and he certainly signed it—we must accept that it was Elsa who typed the denunciation. Why did she do that?"

Smiley was tired out, relieved that Mendel was going.

"Off to tidy up. Find the constants."

"You'll need money," said Smiley, and offered him some from the wallet beside his bed. Mendel took it without ceremony, and left.

Smiley lay back. His head was throbbing madly, burning hot. He thought of calling the nurse and cowardice prevented him. Gradually the throbbing eased. He heard from outside the ringing of an ambulance bell as it turned off Prince of Wales Drive into the hospital yard. "Perhaps he just liked bells," he muttered, and fell asleep.

He was woken by the sound of argument in the corridor—he heard the Sister's voice raised in protest; he heard footsteps and Mendel's voice, urgent in contradiction. The door opened suddenly and someone put the light on. He blinked and sat up, glancing at his watch. It was a quarter to six. Mendel was talking to him, almost shouting. What was he trying to say? Something about Battersea Bridge . . . the river police . . . missing since yesterday . . . He was wide awake. Adam Scarr was dead.

10 ✺
THE VIRGIN'S STORY

Mendel drove very well, with a kind of school-ma'amish pedantry that Smiley would have found comic. The Weybridge road was packed with traffic as usual. Mendel hated motorists. Give a man a car of his own and he leaves humility and common sense behind him in the garage. He didn't care who it was—he'd seen bishops in purple doing seventy in a built-up area, frightening pedestrians out of their wits. He liked Smiley's car. He liked the fussy way it had been maintained, the sensible extras, wing mirrors and reversing light. It was a decent little car.

He liked people who looked after things, who finished what they began. He liked thoroughness and precision. No skimping. Like this murderer. What had Scarr said? "Young, mind, but cool. Cool as charity." He knew that look, and Scarr had known it too . . . the look of complete negation that reposes in the eyes of a young killer. Not the look of a wild beast, not the grinning savagery of a maniac, but the look born of supreme efficiency, tried and proven. It was a stage beyond the experience of war.

The witnessing of death in war brings a sophistication of its own; but beyond that, far beyond, is the conviction of supremacy in the heart of the professional killer. Yes, Mendel had seen it before: the one that stood apart from the gang, pale-eyed, expressionless, the one the girls went after, spoke of without smiling. Yes, he was a cool one all right.

Scarr's death had frightened Mendel. He made Smiley promise not to go back to Bywater Street when he was released from hospital. With any luck they'd think he was dead, anyway. Scarr's death proved one thing, of course: the murderer was still in England, still anxious to tidy up. "When I get up," Smiley had said last night, "we must get him out of his hole again. Put out bits of cheese." Mendel knew who the cheese would be: Smiley. Of course if they were right about the motive, there would be other cheese too: Fennan's wife. In fact, Mendel thought grimly, it doesn't say much for her that she hasn't been murdered. He felt ashamed of himself and turned his mind to other things. Such as Smiley again.

Odd little beggar, Smiley was. Reminded Mendel of a fat boy he'd played football with at school. Couldn't run, couldn't kick, blind as a bat but played like hell, never satisfied till he'd got himself torn to bits. Used to box, too. Came in wide open swinging his arms about: got himself half killed before the referee stopped it. Clever bloke, too.

Mendel stopped at a roadside cafe for a cup of tea and a bun, then drove into Weybridge. The Repertory Theatre was in a one-way street leading off the High Street where parking was impossible. Finally he left the car at the railway station and walked back into the town.

The front doors of the theatre were locked. Mendel walked round to the side of the building under a brick archway. A green door was propped open. It had push bars on the inside and the words "stage door" scribbled in chalk. There was no bell; a faint smell of coffee issued from the dark green corridor within. Mendel stepped through the doorway and walked down the corridor, at the end of which he found a stone staircase with a metal handrail leading upwards to another green door. The smell of coffee was stronger, and he heard the sound of voices.

"Oh rot, darling, frankly. If the culture vultures of blissful Surrey want Barrie three months running let them have it, say I. It's either Barrie or *A Cuckoo in the Nest* for the third year running and for me Barrie gets it by a short head"—this from a middle-aged female voice.

A querulous male replied: "Well, Ludo can always do Peter Pan, can't you, Ludo?"

"Bitchie, bitchie," said a third voice, also male, and Mendel opened the door.

He was standing in the wings of the stage. On his left was a piece of thick hardboard with about a dozen switches mounted on a wooden panel. An absurd rococo chair in gilt and embroidery stood beneath it for the prompter and factotum.

In the middle of the stage two men and a woman sat on barrels smoking and drinking coffee. The decor represented the deck of a ship. A mast with rigging and rope ladders occupied the centre of the stage, and a large cardboard cannon pointed disconsolately towards a backcloth of sea and sky.

The conversation stopped abruptly as Mendel appeared on the stage. Someone murmured: "My dear, the ghost at the feast," and they all looked at him and giggled.

The woman spoke first: "Are you looking for someone, dear?"

"Sorry to butt in. Wanted to talk about becoming a subscriber to the theatre. Join the club."

"Why yes, of course. How nice," she said, getting up and walking over to him. "How very nice." She took his left hand in both of her own and squeezed it, stepping back at the same time and extending her arms to their full length. It was her chatelaine gesture—Lady Macbeth receives Duncan. She put her head to one side and smiled girlishly, retained his hand and led him across the stage to the opposite wing. A door led into a tiny office littered with old programmes and posters, greasepaint, false hair, and tawdry pieces of nautical costume.

"Have you seen our panto this year? *Treasure Island.* Such a *gratifying* success. And so much more *social content,* don't you think, than those vulgar nursery tales?"

Mendel said: "Yes, wasn't it," without the least idea of what she was talking about, when his eye caught a pile of bills rather neatly assembled and held together by a bulldog clip. The top one was made out to Mrs. Ludo Oriel and was four months overdue.

She was looking at him shrewdly through her glasses. She was small and dark, with lines on her neck and a great deal of makeup. The lines under her eyes had been levelled off with greasepaint, but the effect had not lasted. She was wearing slacks and a chunky pullover liberally splashed with distemper. She smoked incessantly. Her mouth was very long, and she held her cigarette in the middle of it in a direct line beneath her nose; her lips formed an exaggerated convex curve, distorting the lower half of her face and giving her an ill-tempered and impatient look. Mendel thought she would probably be difficult and clever. It was a relief to think she couldn't pay her bills.

"You *do* want to join the club, don't you?"

"No."

She suddenly flew into a rage: "If you're another bloody tradesman you can get out. I've said I'll pay and I will, just don't pester me. If you let people think I'm finished, I *will* be and you'll be the losers, not me."

"I'm not a creditor, Mrs. Oriel. I've come to offer you money."

She was waiting.

"I'm a divorce agent. Rich client. Like to ask you a few questions. We're prepared to pay for your time."

"Christ," she said with relief. "Why didn't you say so in the first place?" They both laughed. Mendel put five pounds on top of the bills, counting them down.

"Now," said Mendel; "how do you keep your club subscription list? What are the benefits of joining?"

"Well, we have watery coffee on stage every morning at

eleven sharp. Members of the club can mix with the cast during the break between rehearsals from 11:00 to 11:45. They pay for whatever they have, of course, but entry is strictly limited to club members."

"Quite."

"That's probably the part that interests you. We seem to get nothing but pansies and nymphos in the morning."

"It may be. What else goes on?"

"We put on a different show each fortnight. Members can reserve seats for a particular day of each run—the second Wednesday of each run, and so on. We always begin a run on the first and third Mondays of the month. The show begins at 7:30 and we hold the club reservations until 7:20. The girl at the box office has the seating plan and strikes off each seat as it's sold. Club reservations are marked in red and aren't sold off till last."

"I see. So if one of your members doesn't take his usual seat, it will be marked off on the seating plan."

"Only if it's sold."

"Of course."

"We're not often full after the first week. We're trying to do a show a week, you see, but it's not easy to get the—er—facilities. There isn't the support for two-week runs really."

"No, no, quite. Do you keep old seating plans?"

"Sometimes, for the accounts."

"How about Tuesday the third of January?"

She opened a cupboard and took out a sheaf of printed seating plans. "This is the second fortnight of our pantomime, of course. Tradition."

"Quite," said Mendel.

"Now who is it you're so interested in?" asked Mrs. Oriel, picking up a ledger from the desk.

"Small blonde party, aged about forty-two or -three. Name of Fennan, Elsa Fennan."

Mrs. Oriel opened her ledger. Mendel quite shamelessly looked over her shoulder. The names of club members were entered neatly in the left-hand column. A red tick on the extreme

93

left of the page indicated that the member had paid his subscription. On the right-hand side of the page were notes of standing reservations made for the year. There were about eighty members.

"Name doesn't ring a bell. Where does she sit?"

"No idea."

"Oh, yes, here we are. Merridale Lane, Walliston. Merridale!—I *ask* you. Let's look. A rear stall at the end of a row. Very odd choice, don't you think? Seat number R2. But God knows whether she took it on the third of January. I shouldn't think we've got the plan anymore, though I've never thrown anything away in my life. Things just evaporate, don't they?" She looked at him out of the corner of her eye, wondering whether she'd earned her five pounds. "Tell you what, we'll ask the Virgin." She got up and walked to the door; "Fennan . . . Fennan . . ." she said. "Half a sec, that does ring a bell. I wonder why. Well I'm damned—of course—the music case." She opened the door. "Where's the Virgin?" she said, talking to someone on the stage.

"God knows."

"Helpful pig," said Mrs. Oriel, and closed the door again. She turned to Mendel: "The Virgin's our white hope. English rose, local solicitor's stagestruck daughter, all lisle stockings and get-me-if-you-can. We loathe her. She gets a part occasionally because her father pays tuition fees. She does seating in the evenings sometimes when there's a rush—she and Mrs. Torr, the cleaner, who does cloaks. When things are quiet, Mrs. Torr does the whole thing and the Virgin mopes about in the wings hoping the female lead will drop dead." She paused. "I'm damned sure I remember 'Fennan.' Damn sure I do. I wonder where that cow is." She disappeared for a couple of minutes and returned with a tall and rather pretty girl with fuzzy blonde hair and pink cheeks—good at tennis and swimming.

"This is Elizabeth Pidgeon. She may be able to help. Darling, we want to find out a Mrs. Fennan, a club member. Didn't you tell me something about her?"

"Oh, yes, Ludo." She must have thought she sounded sweet. She smiled vapidly at Mendel, put her head to one side and twined her fingers together. Mendel jerked his head towards her.

"Do you know her?" asked Mrs. Oriel.

"Oh *yes*, Ludo. She's madly musical; at least I think she must be because she always brings her music. She's madly thin and odd. She's foreign, isn't she, Ludo?"

"Why odd?" asked Mendel.

"Oh, well, last time she came she got in a frightful pet about the seat next to her. It was a club reservation you see and simply hours after twenty past. We'd just started the panto season and there were millions of people wanting seats so I let it go. She kept on saying she was sure the person would come because he always did."

"Did he?" asked Mendel.

"No. I let the seat go. She must have been in an awful pet because she left after the second act and forgot to collect her music case."

"This person she was sure would turn up," said Mendel, "is he friendly with Mrs. Fennan?"

Ludo Oriel gave Mendel a suggestive wink.

"Well, gosh, I should think *so*, he's her husband, isn't he?" Mendel looked at her for a minute and then smiled: "Couldn't we find a chair for Elizabeth?" he said.

"Gosh, thanks," said the Virgin, and sat on the edge of an old gilt chair like the prompter's chair in the wings. She put her red, fat hands on her knees and leaned forward, smiling all the time, thrilled to be the centre of so much interest. Mrs. Oriel looked at her venomously.

"What makes you think he was her husband, Elizabeth?" There was an edge to his voice which had not been there before.

"Well, I know they arrive separately, but I thought that as they had seats apart from the rest of the club reservations, they must be husband and wife. And of course he always brings a music case, too."

95

"I see. What else can you remember about that evening, Elizabeth?"

"Oh, well, lots really because you see I felt awful about her leaving in such a pet and then later that night she rang up. Mrs. Fennan did, I mean. She said her name and said she'd left early and forgotten her music case. She'd lost the ticket for it, too, and was in a frightful state. It sounded as if she was crying. I heard someone's voice in the background, and then she said someone would drop in and get it if that would be all right without the ticket. I said of course, and half an hour later the man came. He's rather super. Tall and fair."

"I see," said Mendel; "thank you very much, Elizabeth, you've been very helpful."

"Gosh, that's OK." She got up.

"Incidentally," said Mendel. "This man who collected her music case—he wasn't by any chance the same man who sits beside her in the theatre, was he?"

"Rather. Gosh, sorry, I should have said that."

"Did you talk to him?"

"Well, just to say here you are, sort of thing."

"What kind of voice had he?"

"Oh, foreign, like Mrs. Fennan's—she *is* foreign, isn't she? That's what I put it down to—all her fuss and state—foreign temperament."

She smiled at Mendel, waited a moment, then walked out like Alice.

"Cow," said Mrs. Oriel, looking at the closed door. Her eyes turned to Mendel. "Well, I hope you've got your five quids' worth."

"I think so," said Mendel.

11 ❧
THE UNRESPECTABLE CLUB

Mendel found Smiley sitting in an armchair fully dressed. Peter Guillam was stretched luxuriously on the bed, a pale green folder held casually in his hand. Outside, the sky was black and menacing.

"Enter the third murderer," said Guillam as Mendel walked in. Mendel sat down at the end of the bed and nodded happily to Smiley, who looked pale and depressed.

"Congratulations. Nice to see you on your feet."

"Thank you. I'm afraid if you did see me on my feet you wouldn't congratulate me. I feel as weak as a kitten."

"When are they letting you go?"

"I don't know when they expect me to go—"

"Haven't you asked?"

"No."

"Well, you'd better. I've got news for you. I don't know what it means but it means something."

"Well, well," said Guillam; "everyone's got news for everyone else. Isn't that exciting. George has been looking at my

97

family snaps"—he raised the green folder a fraction of an inch—"and recognizes all his old chums."

Mendel felt baffled and rather left out of things. Smiley intervened: "I'll tell you all about it over dinner tomorrow evening. I'm getting out of here in the morning, whatever they say. I think we've found the murderer and a lot more besides. Now let's have your news." There was no triumph in his eyes. Only anxiety.

Membership of the club to which Smiley belonged is not quoted among the respectable acquisitions of those who adorn the pages of *Who's Who*. It was formed by a young renegade of the junior Carlton named Steed-Asprey, who had been warned off by the Secretary for blaspheming within the hearing of a South African bishop. He persuaded his former Oxford landlady to leave her quiet house in Hollywell and take over two rooms and a cellar in Manchester Square which a monied relative put at his disposal. It had once had forty members who each paid fifty guineas a year. There were thirty-one left. There were no women and no rules, no secretary and no bishops. You could take sandwiches and buy a bottle of beer, you could take sandwiches and buy nothing at all. As long as you were reasonably sober and minded your own business, no one gave twopence what you wore, did, or said, or whom you brought with you. Mrs. Sturgeon no longer devilled at the bar or brought you your chop in front of the fire in the cellar but presided in genial comfort over the ministrations of two retired sergeants from a small border regiment.

Naturally enough, most of the members were approximate contemporaries of Smiley at Oxford. It had always been agreed that the club was to serve one generation only, that it would grow old and die with its members. The war had taken its toll of Jebedee and others, but no one had ever suggested they should elect new members. Besides, the premises were now their own, Mrs. Sturgeon's future had been taken care of, and the club was solvent.

It was a Saturday evening and only half a dozen people were there. Smiley had ordered their meal, and a table was set for them in the cellar, where a bright coal fire burned in a brick hearth. They were alone, there was sirloin and claret; outside the rain fell continuously. For all three of them the world seemed an untroubled and decent place that night, despite the strange business that brought them together.

"To make sense of what I have to tell you," began Smiley at last, addressing himself principally to Mendel, "I shall have to talk at length about myself. I'm an intelligence officer by trade as you know—I've been in the Service since the Flood, long before we were mixed up in power politics with Whitehall. In those days we were understaffed and underpaid. After the usual training and probation in South America and Central Europe, I took a job lecturing at a German University, talent spotting for young Germans with an agent potential." He paused, smiled at Mendel, and said: "Forgive the jargon." Mendel nodded solemnly and Smiley went on. He knew he was being pompous, and didn't know how to prevent himself.

"It was shortly before the last war, a terrible time in Germany then, intolerance run mad. I would have been a lunatic to approach anyone myself. My only chance was to be as nondescript as I could, politically and socially colourless, and to put forward candidates for recruitment by someone else. I tried to bring some back to England for short periods on students' tours. I made a point of having no contact at all with the Department when I came over because we hadn't any idea in those days of the efficiency of German Counter Intelligence. I never knew who was approached, and of course it was much better that way. In case I was blown, I mean.

"My story really begins in 1938. I was alone in my rooms one summer evening. It had been a beautiful day, warm and peaceful. Fascism might never have been heard of. I was working in my shirt sleeves at a desk by my window, not working very hard because it was such a wonderful evening."

He paused, embarrassed for some reason, and fussed a little

with the port. Two pink spots appeared high on his cheeks. He felt slightly drunk though he had had very little wine.

"To resume," he said, and felt an ass. "I'm sorry, I feel a little inarticulate. . . . Anyway, as I sat there, there was a knock on the door and a young student came in. He was nineteen, in fact, but he looked younger. His name was Dieter Frey. He was a pupil of mine, an intelligent boy and remarkable to look at." Smiley paused again, staring before him. Perhaps it was his illness, his weakness, which brought the memory so vividly before him.

"Dieter was a very handsome boy, with a high forehead and a lot of unruly black hair. The lower part of his body was deformed, I think by infantile paralysis. He carried a stick and leaned heavily upon it when he walked. Naturally he cut a rather romantic figure at a small university; they thought him Byronic and so on. In fact I could never find him romantic myself. The Germans have a passion for discovering young genius, you know, from Herder to Stefan George—somebody lionized them practically from the cradle. But you couldn't lionize Dieter. There was a fierce independence, a ruthlessness about him which scared off the most determined patron. This defensiveness in Dieter derived not only from his deformity, but his race, which was Jewish. How on earth he kept his place at University I could never understand. It was possible that they didn't know he was a Jew—his beauty might have been southern, I suppose, Italian, but I don't really see how. To me he was obviously Jewish.

"Dieter was a socialist. He made no secret of his views even in those days. I once considered him for recruitment, but it seemed futile to take on anyone who was so obviously earmarked for concentration camp. Besides he was too volatile, too swift to react, too brightly painted, too vain. He led all the societies at the University—debating, political, poetry and so on. In all the athletic guilds he held honorary positions. He had the nerve not to drink in a University where you proved your manhood by being drunk most of your first year.

"That was Dieter, then: a tall, handsome, commanding cripple, the idol of his generation; a Jew. And that was the man who came to see me that warm summer evening.

"I sat him down and offered him a drink, which he refused. I made some coffee, I think, on a gas ring. We spoke in a desultory way about my last lecture on Keats. I had complained about the application of German critical methods to English poetry, and this had led to some discussion—as usual—on the Nazi interpretation of 'decadence' in art. Dieter dragged it all up again and became more and more outspoken in his condemnation of modern Germany and finally of Nazism itself. Naturally, I was guarded—I think I was less of a fool in those days than I am now. In the end he asked me point blank what I thought of the Nazis. I replied rather pointedly that I was disinclined to criticize my hosts, and that anyway I didn't think politics were much fun. I shall never forget his reply. He was furious, struggled to his feet and shouted at me: '*Von Freude ist nicht die Rede!*'—'We're not talking about fun!'" Smiley broke off and looked across the table to Guillam: "I'm sorry, Peter, I'm being rather long-winded."

"Nonsense, old dear. You tell the story in your own way." Mendel grunted his approval; he was sitting rather stiffly with both hands on the table before him. There was no light in the room now except the bright glow of the fire, which threw tall shadows on the roughcast wall behind them. The port decanter was three parts empty; Smiley gave himself a little and passed it on.

"He raved at me. He simply did not understand how I could apply an independent standard of criticism to art and remain so insensitive to politics, how I could bleat about artistic freedom when a third of Europe was in chains. Did it mean nothing to me that contemporary civilization was being bled to death? What was so sacred about the eighteenth century that I could throw the twentieth away? He had come to me because he enjoyed my seminars and thought me an enlightened man, but he now realized that I was worse than all of them.

"I let him go. What else could I do? On paper he was suspect

101

anyway—a rebellious Jew with a University place still mysteriously free. But I watched him. The term was nearly over and the long vacation soon to begin. In the closing debate of the term three days later he was dreadfully outspoken. He really frightened people, you know, and they grew silent and apprehensive. The end of the term came and Dieter departed without a word of farewell to me. I never expected to see him again.

"It was about six months before I did. I had been visiting friends near Dresden, Dieter's home town, and I arrived half an hour early at the station. Rather than hang around on the platform I decided to go for a stroll. A couple of hundred metres from the station was a tall, rather grim seventeenth-century house. There was a small courtyard in front of it with tall iron railings and a wrought-iron gate. It had apparently been converted into a temporary prison: a group of shaven prisoners, men and women, were being exercised in the yard, walking round the perimeter. Two guards stood in the centre with tommy guns. As I watched I caught sight of a familiar figure, taller than the rest, limping, struggling to keep up with them. It was Dieter. They had taken his stick away.

"When I thought about it afterwards, of course, I realized that the Gestapo would scarcely arrest the most popular member of the University while he was still up. I forgot about my train, went back into the town and looked for his parents in the telephone book. I knew his father had been a doctor so it wasn't difficult. I went to the address and only his mother was there. The father had died already in a concentration camp. She wasn't inclined to talk about Dieter, but it appeared that he had not gone to a Jewish prison but to a general one, and ostensibly for 'a period of correction' only. She expected him back in about three months. I left him a message to say I still had some books of his and would be pleased to return them if he would call on me.

"I'm afraid the events of 1939 must have got the better of me, because I don't believe I gave Dieter another thought that year. Soon after I returned from Dresden my Department ordered me back to England. I packed and left within forty-eight

102

hours, to find London in a turmoil. I was given a new assignment which required intensive preparation, briefing, and training. I was to go back to Europe at once and activate almost untried agents in Germany who had been recruited against such an emergency. I began to memorize the dozen odd names and addresses. You can imagine my reaction when I discovered Dieter Frey among them.

"When I read his file I found he had more or less recruited himself by bursting in on the consulate in Dresden and demanding to know why no one lifted a finger to stop the persecution of the Jews." Smiley paused and laughed to himself, "Dieter was a great one for getting people to do things." He glanced quickly at Mendel and Guillam. Both had their eyes fixed on him.

"I suppose my first reaction was pique. The boy had been right under my nose and I hadn't considered him suitable—what was some ass in Dresden up to? And then I was alarmed to have this firebrand on my hands, whose impulsive temperament could cost me and others our lives. Despite the slight changes in my appearance and the new cover under which I was operating, I should obviously have to declare myself to Dieter as plain George Smiley from the University, so he could blow me sky high. It seemed a most unfortunate beginning, and I was half resolved to set up my network without Dieter. In the event I was wrong. He was a magnificent agent.

"He didn't curb his flamboyance but used it skilfully as a kind of double bluff. His deformity kept him out of the Services and he found himself a clerical job on the railways. In no time he worked his way to a position of real responsibility, and the quantity of information he obtained was fantastic. Details of troop and ammunition transports, their destination and date of transit. Later he reported on the effectiveness of our bombing, pinpointed key targets. He was a brilliant organizer and I think that was what saved him. He did a wonderful job on the railways, made himself indispensable, worked all hours of the night and day; became almost inviolate. They even gave him a civilian decoration for exceptional merit, and I suppose the Gestapo conveniently lost his file.

"Dieter had a theory that was pure Faust. Thought alone was valueless. You must act for thought to become effective. He used to say that the greatest mistake man ever made was to distinguish between the mind and the body: an order does not exist if it is not obeyed. He used to quote Kleist a great deal: 'if all eyes were made of green glass, and if all that seems white was really green, who would be the wiser?' Something like that.

"As I say, Dieter was a magnificent agent. He even went so far as to arrange for certain freights to be transported on good flying nights for the convenience of our bombers. He had tricks all his own—a natural genius for the nuts and bolts of espionage. It seemed absurd to suppose it could last, but the effect of our bombing was often so widespread that it would have been childish to attribute it to one person's betrayal—let alone a man so notoriously outspoken as Dieter.

"Where he was concerned my job was easy. Dieter put in a lot of travelling as it was—he had a special pass to get him around. Communication was child's play by comparison with some agents. Occasionally we would actually meet and talk in a cafe, or he would pick me up in a Ministry car and drive me sixty or seventy miles along a main road, as if he were giving me a lift. But more often we would take a journey in the same train and swap briefcases in the corridor or go to the theatre with parcels and exchange cloakroom tickets. He seldom gave me actual reports but just carbon copies of transit orders. He got his secretary to do a lot—he made her keep a special float which he 'destroyed' every three months by emptying it into his briefcase in the lunch hour.

"Well, in 1943 I was recalled. My trade cover was rather thin by then I think, and I was getting a bit shopsoiled." He stopped and took a cigarette from Guillam's case.

"But don't let's get Dieter out of perspective," he said. "He was my best agent, but he wasn't my only one. I had a lot of headaches of my own—running him was a picnic by comparison with some. When the war was over I tried to find out from my successor what had become of Dieter and the rest of them. Some were resettled in Australia and Canada, some just drifted away to what was left of their home towns. Dieter hesitated, I gather. The Russians were in Dresden, of course, and he may have had doubts. In the end he went—he had to really, because of his mother. He hated the Americans, anyway. And of course he was a Socialist.

"I heard later that he had made his career there. The administrative experience he had picked up during the war got him some Government job in the new republic. I suppose that his reputation as a rebel and the suffering of his family cleared the way for him. He must have done pretty well for himself."

"Why?" asked Mendel.

"He was over here until a month ago running the Steel Mission."

"That's not all," said Guillam quickly. "In case you think your cup is full, Mendel, I spared you another visit to Weybridge this morning and called on Elizabeth Pidgeon. It was George's idea." He turned to Smiley: "She's a sort of Moby Dick, isn't she—big white man-eating whale."

"Well?" said Mendel.

"I showed her a picture of that young diplomat by the name of Mundt they kept in tow there to pick up the bits. Elizabeth recognized him at once as the nice man who collected Elsa Fennan's music case. Isn't that jolly?"

"But—"

"I know what you're going to ask, you clever youth. You want to know whether George recognized him, too. Well, George did. It's the same nasty fellow who tried to lure him into his house in Bywater Street. Doesn't he get around?"

Mendel drove to Mitcham. Smiley was dead tired. It was raining again and cold. Smiley hugged his greatcoat round him and, despite his tiredness, watched with quiet pleasure the busy London night go by. He had always loved travelling. Even now, if he had the choice, he would cross France by train rather than fly. He could still respond to the magic noises of a night journey across Europe, the oddly cacophonous chimes and the French voices suddenly waking him from English dreams. Ann had loved it too, and they had twice travelled overland to share the dubious joys of that uncomfortable journey.

When they got back Smiley went straight to bed while Mendel made some tea. They drank it in Smiley's bedroom. "What do we do now?" asked Mendel.

"I thought I might go to Walliston tomorrow."

"You ought to spend the day in bed. What do you want to do there?"

"See Elsa Fennan."

"You're not safe on your own. You'd better let me come. I'll sit in the car while you do the talking. She's a Yid, isn't she?"

Smiley nodded.

"My dad was Yid. He never made such a bloody fuss about it."

12 ✻

DREAM FOR SALE

She opened the door and stood looking at him for a moment in silence.

"You could have let me know you were coming," she said.

"I thought it safer not to."

She was silent again. Finally she said: "I don't know what you mean." It seemed to cost her a good deal.

"May I come in?" said Smiley. "We haven't much time."

She looked old and tired, less resilient perhaps. She led him into the drawing-room and with something like resignation indicated a chair.

Smiley offered her a cigarette and took one himself. She was standing by the window. As he looked at her, watched her quick breathing, her feverish eyes, he realized that she had almost lost the power of self-defence.

When he spoke, his voice was gentle, concessive. To Elsa Fennan it must have seemed like a voice she had longed for, irresistible, offering all strength, comfort, compassion, and safety. She gradually moved away from the window and her right hand, which had been pressed against the sill, trailed wistfully along it, then fell to her side in a gesture of submission. She sat opposite him, her eyes upon him in complete dependence, like the eyes of a lover.

"You must have been terribly lonely," he said. "No one can stand it forever. It takes courage, too, and it's hard to be brave alone. They never understand that, do they? They never know what it costs—the sordid tricks of lying and deceiving, the isolation from ordinary people. They think you can run on their kind of fuel—the flag waving and the music. But you need a different kind of fuel, don't you, when you're alone? You've got to hate, and it needs strength to hate all the time. And what you must love is so remote, so vague when you're not part of it." He paused. Soon, he thought, soon you'll break. He prayed desperately that she would accept him, accept his comfort. He looked at her. Soon she would break.

"I said we hadn't much time. Do you know what I mean?"

She had folded her hands on her lap and was looking down at them. He saw the dark roots of her yellow hair and wondered why on earth she dyed it. She showed no sign of having heard his question.

"When I left you that morning a month ago I drove to my home in London. A man tried to kill me. That night he nearly succeeded—he hit me on the head three or four times. I've just come out of hospital. As it happens I was lucky. Then there was the garage man he hired the car from. The river police recovered his body from the Thames not long ago. There were no signs of violence—he was just full of whisky. They can't understand it—he hadn't been near the river for years. But then we're dealing with a competent man, aren't we? A trained killer. It seems he's trying to remove anyone who can connect him with Samuel Fennan. Or his wife, of course. Then there's that young blonde girl at the Repertory Theatre . . ."

"What are you saying?" she whispered. "What are you trying to tell me?"

Smiley suddenly wanted to hurt her, to break the last of her will, to remove her utterly as an enemy. For so long she had haunted him as he had lain helpless, had been a mystery and a power.

"What games did you think you were playing, you two? Do you think you can flirt with power like theirs, give a little and not give all? Do you think that you can stop the dance—control the strength you give them? What dreams did you cherish, Mrs. Fennan, that had so little of the world in them?"

She buried her face in her hands and he watched the tears run between her fingers. Her body shook with great sobs and her words came slowly, wrung from her.

"No, no dreams. I had no dream but him. He had one dream, yes . . . one great dream." She went on crying, helpless, and Smiley, half in triumph, half in shame, waited for her to speak again. Suddenly she raised her head and looked at him, the tears still running down her cheeks. "Look at me," she said. "What dream did they leave me? I dreamed of long golden hair and they shaved my head; I dreamed of a beautiful body and they broke it with hunger. I have seen what human beings are, how could I believe in a formula for human beings? I said to him, oh I said to him a thousand times, 'only make no laws, no fine theories, no judgements, and the people may love, but give them one theory, let them invent one slogan, and the game begins again.' I told him that. We talked whole nights away. But no, that little boy must have his dream, and if a new world was to be built, Samuel Fennan must build it. I said to him, 'Listen,' I said. 'They have given you all you have, a home, money, and trust. Why do you do it to them?' And he said to me: 'I do it *for* them. I am the surgeon and one day they will understand.' He was a child, Mr. Smiley, they led him like a child."

He dared not speak, dared put nothing to the test.

"Five years ago he met that Dieter. In a ski hut near Garmisch. Freitag told us later that Dieter had planned it that way—Dieter couldn't ski anyway because of his legs. Nothing seemed real then; Freitag wasn't a real name. Fennan christened him Freitag like Man Friday in *Robinson Crusoe*. Dieter found that so funny and afterwards we never talked of Dieter but always of Mr. Robinson and Freitag." She broke off now and looked at him with a very faint smile: "I'm sorry," she said; "I'm not very coherent."

"I understand," said Smiley.

"That girl—what did you say about that girl?"

"She's alive. Don't worry. Go on."

"Fennan liked you, you know. Freitag tried to kill you . . . why?"

"Because I came back, I suppose, and asked you about the 8:30 call. You told Freitag that, didn't you?"

"Oh, God," she said, her fingers at her mouth.

"You rang him up, didn't you? As soon as I'd gone?"

"Yes, yes. I was frightened. I wanted to warn him to go, him and Dieter, to go away and never come back, because I knew you'd find out. If not today then one day, but I knew you'd find out in the end. Why would they never leave me alone? They were frightened of me because they knew I had no dreams, that I only wanted Samuel, wanted him safe to love and care for. They relied on that."

Smiley felt his head throbbing erratically. "So you rang him straight away," he said. "You tried the Primrose number first and couldn't get through."

"Yes," she said vaguely. "Yes, that's right. But they're both Primrose numbers."

"So you rang the *other* number, the alternative . . ."

She drifted back to the window, suddenly exhausted and limp; she seemed happier now—the storm had left her reflective and, in a way, content.

"Yes. Freitag was a great one for alternative plans."

"What was the other number?" Smiley insisted. He watched her anxiously as she stared out of the window into the dark garden. "Why do you want to know?"

He came and stood beside her at the window, watching her profile. His voice was suddenly harsh and energetic.

"I said the girl was all right. You and I are alive, too. But don't think that's going to last."

She turned to him with fear in her eyes, looked at him for a moment, then nodded. Smiley took her by the arm and guided her to a chair. He ought to make her a hot drink or something. She sat down quite mechanically, almost with the detachment of incipient madness.

"The other number was 9747."

"Any address—did you have an address?"

"No, no address. Only the telephone. Tricks on the telephone. No address," she repeated, with unnatural emphasis, so that Smiley looked at her and wondered. A thought suddenly struck him—a memory of Dieter's skill in communication.

"Freitag didn't meet you the night Fennan died, did he? He didn't come to the theatre?"

"No."

"That was the first time he had missed, wasn't it? You panicked and left early."

"No . . . yes, yes, I panicked."

"No you didn't! You left early because you had to, it was the arrangement. *Why* did you leave early? Why?"

Her hands hid her face.

"Are you still mad?" Smiley shouted. "Do you still think you can control what you have made? Freitag will kill you, kill the girl, kill, kill, kill. Who are you trying to protect, a girl or a murderer?"

She wept and said nothing. Smiley crouched beside her, still shouting.

"I'll tell you why you left early, shall I? I'll tell you what I think. It was to catch the last post that night from Weybridge. He hadn't come, you hadn't exchanged cloakroom tickets, had you, so you obeyed the instructions, you posted your ticket to him, and you *have* got an address, not written down but re-

111

membered, remembered forever: 'if there is a crisis, if I do not come, this is the address': is that what he said? An address never to be used or spoken of, an address forgotten and remembered forever? Is that right? Tell me!"

She stood up, her head turned away, went to the desk and found a piece of paper and a pencil. The tears still ran freely over her face. With agonizing slowness she wrote the address, her hand faltering and almost stopping between the words.

He took the paper from her, folded it carefully across the middle, and put it in his wallet.

Now he would make her some tea.

She looked like a child rescued from the sea. She sat on the edge of the sofa holding the cup tightly in her frail hands, nursing it against her body. Her thin shoulders were hunched forward, her feet and ankles pressed tightly together. Smiley, looking at her, felt he had broken something he should never have touched because it was so fragile. He felt an obscene, coarse bully, his offerings of tea a futile recompense for his clumsiness.

He could think of nothing to say. After a while, she said: "He liked you, you know. He really liked you . . . he said you were a clever little man. It was quite a surprise when Samuel called anyone clever." She shook her head slowly. Perhaps it was the reaction that made her smile: "He used to say there were two forces in the world, the positive and the negative. 'What shall I do then?' he would ask me. 'Let them ruin their harvest because they give me bread? Creation, progress, power, the whole future of mankind waits at their door: shall I not let them in?' And I said to him: 'But Samuel, maybe the people are happy without these things?' But you know he didn't think of people like that.

"But I couldn't stop him. You know the strangest thing about Fennan? For all that thinking and talking, he had made up his mind long ago what he would do. All the rest was poetry. He wasn't coordinated, that's what I used to tell him . . ."

"...and yet you helped him," said Smiley.

"Yes, I helped him. He wanted help so I gave it to him. He was my life."

"I see."

"That was a mistake. He was a little boy, you know. He forgot things just like a child. And so vain. He had made up his mind to do it and he did it so badly. He didn't think of it as you do, or I do. He simply didn't think of it like that. It was his work and that was all.

"It began so simply. He brought home a draft telegram one night and showed it to me. He said: 'I think Dieter ought to see that'—that was all. I couldn't believe it to begin with—that he was a spy, I mean. Because he was, wasn't he? And gradually, I realized. They began to ask for special things. The music case I got back from Freitag began to contain orders, and sometimes money. I said to him: 'Look at what they are sending you—do you want this?' We didn't know what to do with the money. In the end we gave it away mostly, I don't know why. Dieter was very angry that winter, when I told him."

"What winter was that?" asked Smiley.

"The second winter with Dieter—1956 in Mürren. We met him first in January 1955. That was when it began. And shall I tell you something? Hungary made no difference to Samuel, not a tiny bit of difference. Dieter was frightened about him then, I know, because Freitag told me. When Fennan gave me the things to take to Weybridge that November I nearly went mad. I shouted at him: 'Can't you see it's the same? The same guns, the same children dying in the streets? Only the dream has changed, the blood is the same colour. Is that what you want?' I asked him: 'Would you do this for Germans, too? It's me who lies in the gutter, will you let them do it to me?' But he just said: 'No, Elsa, this is different.' And I went on taking the music case. Do you understand?"

"I don't know. I just don't know. I think perhaps I do."

"He was all I had. He was my life. I protected myself, I

suppose. And gradually I became a part of it, and then it was too late to stop . . . And then you know," she said, in a whisper; "there were times when I was glad, times when the world seemed to applaud what Samuel was doing. It was not a pretty sight for us, the new Germany. Old names had come back, names that had frightened us as children. The dreadful, plump pride returned, you could see it even in the photographs in the papers, they marched with the old rhythm. Fennan felt that, too, but then thank God he hadn't seen what I saw.

"We were in a camp outside Dresden, where we used to live. My father was paralysed. He missed tobacco more than anything and I used to roll cigarettes from any rubbish I could find in the camp—just to pretend with. One day a guard saw him smoking and began laughing. Some others came and they laughed too. My father was holding the cigarette in his paralysed hand and it was burning his fingers. He didn't know, you see.

"Yes, when they gave guns to the Germans again, gave them money and uniforms, then sometimes—just for a little while—I was pleased with what Samuel had done. We are Jews, you know, and so . . ."

"Yes, I know, I understand," said Smiley. "I saw it, too, a little of it."

"Dieter said you had."

"Dieter said that?"

"Yes. To Freitag. He told Freitag you were a very clever man. You once deceived Dieter before the war, and it was only long afterwards that he found out, that's what Freitag said. He said you were the best he'd ever met."

"When did Freitag tell you that?"

She looked at him for a long time. He had never seen in any face such hopeless misery. He remembered how she had said to him before: "The children of my grief are dead." He understood that now, and heard it in her voice when at last she spoke:

"Why, isn't it obvious? The night he murdered Samuel. That's the great joke, Mr. Smiley. At the very moment when Samuel could have done so much for them—not just a piece here and a piece there, but all the time—so many music cases—at that moment their own fear destroyed them, turned them into animals and made them kill what they had made.

"Samuel always said: 'They will win because they *know* and the others will perish because they do not: men who work for a dream will work forever'—that's what he said. But I knew their dream, I knew it would destroy us. What has not been destroyed? Even the dream of Christ."

"It was Dieter, then, who saw me in the park with Fennan?"

"Yes."

"And thought—"

"Yes. Thought that Samuel had betrayed him. Told Freitag to kill Samuel."

"And the anonymous letter?"

"I don't know. I don't know who wrote it. Someone who knew Samuel, I suppose, someone from the office who watched him and knew. Or from Oxford, from the Party. I don't know. Samuel didn't know either."

"But the suicide letter—"

She looked at him, and her face crumpled. She was almost weeping again. She bowed her head:

"I wrote it. Freitag brought the paper, and I wrote it. The signature was already there. Samuel's signature."

Smiley went over to her, sat beside her on the sofa, and took her hand. She turned on him in a fury and began screaming at him:

"Take your hands off me! Do you think I'm yours because I don't belong to them? Go away! Go away and kill Freitag and Dieter, keep the game alive, Mr. Smiley. But don't think I'm on *your* side, d'you hear? Because I'm the wandering Jewess, the no-man's-land, the battlefield for your toy soldiers. You can kick me and trample on me, see, but never, never touch me, never tell me you're sorry, d'you hear? Now get out! Go away and kill."

She sat there, shivering as if from cold. As he reached the door he looked back. There were no tears in her eyes.

Mendel was waiting for him in the car.

13 ❀
THE INEFFICIENCY
OF SAMUEL FENNAN

They arrived at Mitcham at lunch-time. Peter Guillam was waiting for them in his car.

"Well, children; what's the news?"

Smiley handed him the piece of paper from his wallet. "There was an emergency number, too—Primrose 9747. You'd better check it, but I'm not hopeful of that either."

Peter disappeared into the hall and began telephoning. Mendel busied himself in the kitchen and returned ten minutes later with beer, bread, and cheese on a tray. Guillam came back and sat down without saying anything. He looked worried. "Well," he said at last, "what did she say, George?"

Mendel cleared away as Smiley finished the account of his interview that morning.

"I see," said Guillam. "How very worrying. Well, that's it, George, I shall have to put this on paper today, and I'll have to go to Maston at once. Catching dead spies is a poor game really—and causes a lot of unhappiness."

"What access did he have at the FO?" asked Smiley.

"Recently a lot. That's why they felt he should be interviewed, as you know."

"What kind of stuff, mainly?"

"I don't know yet. He was on an Asian desk until a few months ago, but his new job was different."

"American, I seem to remember," said Smiley. "Peter?"

"Yes."

"Peter, have you thought at all *why* they wanted to kill Fennan so much? I mean, supposing he *had* betrayed them, as they thought, why kill him? They had nothing to gain."

"No; no, I suppose they hadn't. That does need some explaining, come to think of it . . . or does it? Suppose Fuchs or Maclean had betrayed them, I wonder what would have happened. Suppose they had reason to fear a chain reaction—not just here but in America—all over the world? Wouldn't they kill him to prevent that? There's so much we shall just never know."

"Like the 8:30 call?" said Smiley.

"Cheerio. Hang on here till I ring you, will you? Maston's bound to want to see you. They'll be running down the corridors when I tell them the glad news. I shall have to wear the special grin I reserve for bearing really disastrous tidings."

Mendel saw him out and then returned to the drawing-room. "Best thing you can do is put your feet up," he said. "You look a ruddy mess, you do."

"Either Mundt's here or he's not," thought Smiley as he lay on the bed in his waistcoat, his hands linked under his head. "If he's not, we're finished. It will be for Maston to decide what to do with Elsa Fennan, and my guess is he'll do nothing.

"If Mundt *is* here, it's for one of three reasons: A, because Dieter told him to stay and watch the dust settle; B, because he's in bad odour and afraid to go back; C, because he has unfinished business.

"A is improbable because it's not like Dieter to take needless risks. Anyway, it's a woolly idea.

"B is unlikely because, while Mundt may be afraid of Dieter he must also, presumably, be frightened of a murder charge: here. His wisest plan would be to go to another country.

"C is more likely. If I was in Dieter's shoes, I'd be worried sick about Elsa Fennan. The Pidgeon girl is immaterial—without Elsa to fill in the gaps she presents no serious danger. She was not a conspirator, and there is no reason why she should particularly remember Elsa's friend at the theatre. No, Elsa constitutes the real danger."

There was, of course, a final possibility, which Smiley was quite unable to judge: the possibility that Dieter had other agents to control here through Mundt. On the whole he was inclined to discount this, but the thought had no doubt crossed Peter's mind.

No . . . it still didn't make sense—it wasn't tidy. He decided to begin again.

What do we know? He sat up to look for pencil and paper and at once his head began throbbing. Obstinately he got off the bed and took a pencil from the inside pocket of his jacket. There was a writing pad in his suitcase. He returned to the bed, shaped the pillows to his satisfaction, took four aspirin from the bottle on the table, and propped himself against the pillows, his short legs stretched before him. He began writing. First he wrote the heading in a neat, scholarly hand, and underlined it.

What do we know?

Then he began, stage by stage, to recount as dispassionately as possible the sequence of events hitherto:

"On Monday, 2 January, Dieter Frey saw me in the park talking to his agent and concluded . . ." Yes, what *did* Dieter conclude? That Fennan had confessed, was going to confess? That Fennan was my agent? ". . . and concluded that Fennan was dangerous, for reasons still unknown. The following

119

evening, the first Tuesday in the month, Elsa Fennan took her husband's reports in a music case to the Weybridge Repertory Theatre, in the agreed way, and left the case in the cloakroom in exchange for a ticket. Mundt was to bring his own music case and do the same thing. Elsa and Mundt would then exchange tickets during the performance. Mundt did not appear. Accordingly she followed the emergency procedure and posted the ticket to a prearranged address, having left the theatre early to catch the last post from Weybridge. She then drove home to be met by Mundt, who had, by then, murdered Fennan, probably on Dieter's orders. He had shot him at point blank range as soon as he met him in the hall. Knowing Dieter, I suspect that he had long ago taken the precaution of keeping in London a few sheets of blank writing paper signed with samples, forged or authentic, of Sam Fennan's signature, in case it was ever necessary to compromise or blackmail him. Assuming this to be so, Mundt brought a sheet with him in order to type the suicide letter over the signature on Fennan's own typewriter. In the ghastly scene which must have followed Elsa's arrival, Mundt realized that Dieter had wrongly interpreted Fennan's encounter with Smiley, but relied on Elsa to preserve her dead husband's reputation—not to mention her own complicity. Mundt was therefore reasonably safe. Mundt made Elsa type the letter, perhaps because he did not trust his English. (Note: But who the devil typed the *first* letter, the denunciation?)

"Mundt then, presumably, demanded the music case he had failed to collect, and Elsa told him that she had obeyed standing instructions and posted the cloakroom ticket to the Hampstead address, leaving the music case at the theatre. Mundt reacted significantly: he forced her to telephone the theatre and to arrange for him to collect the case that night on his way back to London. Therefore, either the address to which the ticket was posted was no longer valid, or Mundt intended at that stage to return home early the next morning without having time to collect the ticket and the case.

"Smiley visits Walliston early on the morning of Wednesday,

120

4 January, and during the *first* interview takes an 8:30 call from the exchange which (beyond reasonable doubt) Fennan requested at 7:55 the previous evening. WHY?

"Later that morning S. returns to Elsa Fennan to ask about the 8:30 call—which she knew (on her own admission) would 'worry me' (no doubt Mundt's flattering description of my powers had had its effect). Having told S. a futile story about her bad memory, she panics and rings Mundt.

"Mundt, presumably equipped with a photograph or a description from Dieter, decides to liquidate S. (on Dieter's authority?) and later that day nearly succeeds. (Note: Mundt did not return the car to Scarr's garage till the night of the 4th. This does not necessarily prove that Mundt had no plans for flying earlier in the day. If he had originally meant to fly in the morning, he might well have left the car at Scarr's earlier and gone to the airport by bus.)

"It does seem pretty likely that Mundt changed his plans after Elsa's telephone call. It is not clear that he changed them *because* of her call." Would Mundt really be panicked by Elsa? Panicked into staying, panicked into murdering Adam Scarr? he wondered.

The telephone was ringing in the hall . . .

"George, it's Peter. No joy with the address or the telephone number. Dead end."

"What do you mean?"

"The telephone number and the address both led to the same place—furnished apartment in Highgate village."

"Well?"

"Rented by a pilot in Lufteuropa. He paid his two months' rent on the fifth of January and hasn't come back since."

"Damn."

"The landlady remembers Mundt quite well. The pilot's friend. A nice polite gentleman he was, for a German, very open-handed. He used to sleep on the sofa quite often."

"Oh God."

"I went through the room with a toothcomb. There was a

121

desk in the corner. All the drawers were empty except one, which contained a cloakroom ticket. I wonder where that came from. . . . Well, if you want a laugh, come round to the Circus. The whole of Olympus is seething with activity. Oh, incidentally—"

"Yes?"

"I dug around at Dieter's flat. Another lemon. He left on the fourth of January. Didn't tell the milkman."

"What about his mail?"

"He never received any, apart from bills. I also had a look at Comrade Mundt's little nest: couple of rooms over the Steel Mission. The furniture went out with the rest of the stuff. Sorry."

"I see."

"I'll tell you an odd thing though, George. You remember I thought I might get on to Fennan's personal possessions—wallet, notebook, and so on? From the police."

"Yes."

"Well, I did. His diary's got Dieter's full name entered in the address section with the Mission telephone number against it. Bloody cheek."

"It's more than that. It's lunacy. Good Lord."

"Then for the fourth of January the entry is 'Smiley C.A. Ring 8:30.' That was corroborated by an entry for the third which ran 'request call for Wed. morning.' There's your mysterious call."

"Still unexplained." A pause.

"George, I sent Felix Taverner round to the FO to do some ferreting. It's worse than we feared in one way, but better in another."

"Why?"

"Well, Taverner got his hands on the registry schedules for the last two years. He was able to work out what files have been marked to Fennan's section. Where a file was particularly requested by that section they still have a requisition form."

"I'm listening."

"Felix found that three or four files were usually marked in to Fennan on a Friday afternoon and marked out again on Monday morning; the inference is that he took the stuff home at weekends."

"Oh my Lord!"

"But the odd thing is, George, that during the last six months, since his posting in fact, he tended to take home *unclassified* stuff which wouldn't have been of interest to anyone."

"But it was during the last months that he began dealing mainly with secret files," said Smiley. "He could take home anything he wanted."

"I know, but he didn't. In fact you'd almost say it was deliberate. He took home very low-grade stuff barely related to his daily work. His colleagues can't understand it now they think about it—he even took back some files handling subjects outside the scope of his section."

"And unclassified."

"Yes—of no conceivable intelligence value."

"How about earlier, before he came into his new job? What kind of stuff went home then?"

"Much more what you'd expect—files he'd used during the day, policy and so on."

"Secret?"

"Some were, some weren't. As they came."

"But nothing unexpected—no particularly delicate stuff that didn't concern him?"

"No. Nothing. He had opportunity galore quite frankly and didn't use it. Windy, I suppose."

"So he ought to be if he puts his controller's name in his diary."

"And make what you like of this: he'd arranged at the FO to take a day off on the fourth—the day after he died. Rather an event apparently—he was a glutton for work, they say."

"What's Maston doing about all this?" asked Smiley, after a pause.

"Going through the files at the moment and rushing in to see me with bloody fool questions every two minutes. I think he gets lonely in there with hard facts."

"Oh, he'll beat them down, Peter, don't worry."

"He's already saying that the whole case against Fennan rests on the evidence of a neurotic woman."

"Thanks for ringing, Peter."

"Be seeing you, dear boy. Keep your head down."

Smiley replaced the receiver and wondered where Mendel was. There was an evening paper on the hall table, and he glanced vaguely at the headline "Lynching: World Jewry Protests" and beneath it the account of the lynching of a Jewish shopkeeper in Düsseldorf. He opened the drawing-room door—Mendel was not there. Then he caught sight of him through the window wearing his gardening hat, hacking savagely with a pick-axe at a tree stump in the front garden. Smiley watched him for a moment, then went upstairs again to rest. As he reached the top of the stairs the telephone began ringing again.

"George—sorry to bother you again. It's about Mundt."

"Yes?"

"Flew to Berlin last night by BEA. Travelled under another name but was easily identified by the air hostess. That seems to be that. Hard luck, chum."

Smiley pressed down the cradle with his hand for a moment, then dialled Walliston 2944. He heard the number ringing the other end. Suddenly the dialling tone stopped and instead he heard Elsa Fennan's voice:

"Hullo . . . Hullo . . . *Hullo?*"

Slowly he replaced the receiver. She was alive.

Why on earth *now?* Why should Mundt go home *now*, five weeks after murdering Fennan, three weeks after murdering Scarr; why had he eliminated the lesser danger—Scarr—and left Elsa Fennan unharmed, neurotic and embittered, liable at any moment to throw aside her own safety and tell the whole story? What effect might that terrible night not have had upon her? How could Dieter trust a woman now so lightly bound to him? Her husband's good name could no longer be presented; might she not, in God knows what mood of vengeance or repentance, blurt out the whole truth? Obviously, a little time must elapse between the murder of Fennan and the murder of his wife, but what event, what information, what danger, had decided Mundt to return last night? A ruthless and elaborate plan to preserve the secrecy of Fennan's treason had now apparently been thrown aside unfinished. What had happened yesterday that Mundt could know of? Or was the timing of his departure a coincidence? Smiley refused to believe it was. If Mundt had remained in England after the two murders and the assault on Smiley, he had done so unwillingly, waiting upon some opportunity or event that would release him. He would not stay a moment longer than he need. Yet what had he done since Scarr's death? Hidden in some lonely room, locked away from light and news. Then why did he now fly home so suddenly?

And Fennan—what spy was this who selected innocuous information for his masters when he had such gems at his fingertips? A change of heart, perhaps? A weakening of purpose? Then why did he not tell his wife, for whom his crime was a constant nightmare, who would have rejoiced at his conversion? It seemed now that Fennan had never shown any preference for secret papers—he had simply taken home whatever files currently might occupy him. But certainly a weakening of purpose would explain the strange summons to Marlow and Dieter's conviction that Fennan was betraying him. And who wrote the anonymous letter?

Nothing made sense, nothing. Fennan himself—brilliant, fluent, and attractive—had deceived so naturally, so expertly. Smiley had really liked him. Why then had this practised deceiver made the incredible blunder of putting Dieter's name in his diary—and shown so little judgement or interest in the selection of intelligence?

Smiley went upstairs to pack the few possessions which Mendel had collected for him from Bywater Street. It was all over.

14 ✾
THE DRESDEN GROUP

He stood on the doorstep and put down his suitcase, fumbling for his latchkey. As he opened the door he recalled how Mundt had stood there looking at him, those very
pale blue eyes calculating and steady. It was odd to think of
Mundt as Dieter's pupil. Mundt had proceeded with the inflex-
ibility of a trained mercenary—efficient, purposeful, narrow.
There had been nothing original in his technique: in everything
he had been a shadow of his master. It was as if Dieter's brilliant
and imaginative tricks had been compressed into a manual
which Mundt had learnt by heart, adding only the salt of his
own brutality.

Smiley had deliberately left no forwarding address, and a
heap of mail lay on the door mat. He picked it up, put it on the
hall table, and began opening doors and peering about him, a
puzzled, lost expression on his face. The house was strange to
him, cold and musty. As he moved slowly from one room to
another, he began for the first time to realize how empty his life
had become.

He looked for matches to light the gas fire, but there were none. He sat in an armchair in the living-room and his eyes wandered over the bookshelves and the odds and ends he had collected on his travels. When Ann had left him he had begun by rigorously excluding all trace of her. He had even got rid of her books. But gradually he had allowed the few remaining symbols that linked his life with hers to reassert themselves: wedding presents from close friends which had meant too much to be given away. There was a Watteau sketch from Peter Guillam, a Dresden group from Steed-Asprey.

He got up from his chair and went over to the corner cupboard where the group stood. He loved to admire the beauty of those figures, the tiny rococo courtesan in shepherd's costume, her hands outstretched to one adoring lover, her little face bestowing glances on another. He felt inadequate before that fragile perfection, as he had felt before Ann when he first began the conquest which had amazed society. Somehow those little figures comforted him: it was as useless to expect fidelity of Ann as of this tiny shepherdess in her glass case. Steed-Asprey had bought the group in Dresden before the war, it had been the prize of his collection and he had given it to them. Perhaps he had guessed that one day Smiley might have need of the simple philosophy it propounded.

Dresden: of all German cities, Smiley's favourite. He had loved its architecture, its odd jumble of medieval and classical buildings, sometimes reminiscent of Oxford, its cupolas, towers, and spires, its copper-green roofs shimmering under a hot sun. Its name meant "town of the forest-dwellers" and it was there that Wenceslas of Bohemia had favoured the minstrel poets with gifts and privilege. Smiley remembered the last time he had been there, visiting a University acquaintance, a Professor of Philology he had met in England. It was on that visit that he had caught sight of Dieter Frey, struggling round the prison courtyard. He could see him still, tall and angry, monstrously altered by his shaven head, somehow too big for that little prison. Dresden, he remembered, had been Elsa's birthplace.

He remembered glancing through her personal particulars at the ministry: Elsa *née* Freimann, born 1917 in Dresden, Germany, of German parents; educated Dresden: imprisoned 1938–45. He tried to place her against the background of her home, the patrician Jewish family living out its life amid insult and persecution. "I dreamed of long golden hair and they shaved my head." He realized with sickening accuracy why she dyed her hair. She might have been like this shepherdess, round-bosomed and pretty. But the body had been broken with hunger so that it was frail and ugly, like the carcass of a tiny bird.

He could picture her on the terrible night when she found her husband's murderer standing by his body; hear her breathless, sobbing explanation of why Fennan had been in the park with Smiley; and Mundt unmoved, explaining and reasoning, compelling her finally to conspire once more against her will in this most dreadful and needless of crimes, dragging her to the telephone; and forcing her to ring the theatre, leaving her finally tortured and exhausted to cope with the enquiries that were bound to follow, even to type that futile suicide letter over Fennan's signature. It was inhuman beyond belief and, he added to himself, for Mundt a fantastic risk.

She had, of course, proved herself a reliable enough accomplice in the past, cool-headed and, ironically, more skilful than Fennan in the techniques of espionage. And, heaven knows, for a woman who had been through such a night as that, her performance at their first meeting had been a marvel.

As he stood gazing at the little shepherdess, poised eternally between her two admirers, he realized dispassionately that there was another quite different solution to the case of Samuel Fennan, a solution which matched every detail of circumstance, reconciled the nagging inconsistencies apparent in Fennan's character. The realization began as an academic exercise without reference to personalities; Smiley manoeuvred the characters like pieces in a puzzle, twisting them this way and that to fit the complex framework of established facts and then, in a moment, the pattern had suddenly re-formed with such assurance that it was a game no more.

His heart beat faster, as with growing astonishment Smiley retold to himself the whole story, reconstructed scenes and incidents in the light of his discovery. Now he knew why Mundt had left England that day, why Fennan chose so little that was of value to Dieter, had asked for the 8:30 call, and why his wife had escaped the systematic savagery of Mundt. Now at last he knew who had written the anonymous letter. He saw how he had been the fool of his own sentiment, had played false with the power of his mind.

He went to the telephone and dialled Mendel's number. As soon as he had finished speaking to him he rang Peter Guillam. Then he put on his hat and coat and walked round the corner to Sloane Square. At a small newsagent's beside Peter Jones he bought a picture postcard of Westminster Abbey. He made his way to the underground station and travelled north to Highgate, where he got out. At the main post office he bought a stamp and addressed the postcard in stiff, continental capitals to Elsa Fennan. In the panel for correspondence he wrote in spiky longhand: "Wish you were here." He posted the card and noted the time, after which he returned to Sloane Square. There was nothing more he could do.

He slept soundly that night, rose early the following morning, a Saturday, and walked round the corner to buy croissants and coffee beans. He made a lot of coffee and sat in the kitchen reading *The Times* and eating his breakfast. He felt curiously calm and when the telephone rang at last he folded his paper carefully together before going upstairs to answer it.

"George, it's Peter"—the voice was urgent, almost triumphant: "George, she's bitten, I swear she has!"

"What happened?"

"The post arrived at exactly 8:35. By 9:30 she was walking briskly down the drive, booted and spurred. She made straight for the railway station and caught the 9:52 to Victoria. I put

130

Mendel on the train and hared up by car, but I was too late to meet the train this end."

"How will you make contact with Mendel again?"

"I gave him the number of the Grosvenor Hotel and I'm there now. He's going to ring me as soon as he gets a chance and I'll join him wherever he is."

"Peter, you're taking this gently, aren't you?"

"Gentle as the wind, dear boy. I think she's losing her head. Moving like a greyhound."

Smiley rang off. He picked up his *Times* and began studying the theatre column. He must be right . . . he must be.

After that the morning passed with agonizing slowness. Sometimes he would stand at the window, his hands in his pockets, watching leggy Kensington girls going shopping with beautiful young men in pale blue pullovers, or the car-cleaning brigade toiling happily in front of their houses, then drifting away to talk motoring shop and finally setting off purposefully down the road for the first pint of the weekend.

At last, after what seemed an interminable delay, the front door bell rang and Mendel and Guillam came in, grinning cheerfully, ravenously hungry.

"Hook, line, and sinker," said Guillam. "But let Mendel tell you—he did most of the dirty work. I just got in for the kill."

Mendel recounted his story precisely and accurately, looking at the ground a few feet in front of him, his thin head slightly to one side.

"She caught the 9:52 to Victoria. I kept well clear of her on the train and picked her up as she went through the barrier. Then she took a taxi to Hammersmith."

"A taxi?" Smiley interjected. "She must be out of her mind."

"She's rattled. She walks fast for a woman anyway, mind, but she damn nearly ran going down the platform. Got out at the Broadway and walked to the Sheridan Theatre. Tried the doors to the box office but they were locked. She hesitated a moment then turned back and went to a café a hundred yards down the road. Ordered coffee and paid for it at once. About forty minutes later she went back to the Sheridan. The box office was open and I ducked in behind her and joined the queue. She bought two rear stalls for next Thursday, Row T, 27 and 28. When she got outside the theatre she put one ticket in an envelope and sealed it up. Then she posted it. I couldn't see the address but there was a sixpenny stamp on the envelope."

Smiley sat very still. "I wonder," he said; "I wonder if he'll come."

"I caught up with Mendel at the Sheridan," said Guillam. "He saw her into the café and then rang me. After that he went in after her."

"Felt like a coffee myself," Mendel went on. "Mr. Guillam joined me. I left him there when I joined the ticket queue, and he drifted out of the café a bit later. It was a decent job and no worries. She's rattled, I'm sure. But not suspicious."

"What did she do after that?" asked Smiley.

"Went straight back to Victoria. We left her to it."

They were silent for a moment, then Mendel said: "What do we do now?"

Smiley blinked and gazed earnestly into Mendel's grey face. "Book tickets for Thursday's performance at the Sheridan."

They were gone and he was alone again. He still had not begun to cope with the quantity of mail which had accumulated in his absence. Circulars, catalogues from Blackwells, bills and the usual collection of soap vouchers, frozen pea coupons, football pool forms and a few private letters still lay unopened on the hall table. He took them into the drawing-room, settled in an armchair, and began opening the personal letters first. There was one from Maston, and he read it with something approaching embarrassment.

My dear George,
    I was so sorry to hear from Guillam about your accident, and I do hope that by now you have made a full recovery.

You may recall that in the heat of the moment you wrote me a letter of resignation before your misfortune, and I just wanted to let you know that I am not, of course, taking this seriously. Sometimes when events crowd in upon us our sense of perspective suffers. But old campaigners like ourselves, George, are not so easily put off the scent. I look forward to seeing you with us again as soon as you are strong enough, and in the meantime we continue to regard you as an old and loyal member of the staff.

Smiley put this to one side and turned to the next letter. Just for a moment he did not recognize the handwriting; just for a moment he looked bleakly at the Swiss stamp and the expensive hotel writing paper. Suddenly he felt slightly sick, his vision blurred, and there was scarcely strength enough in his fingers to tear open the envelope. What did she want? If money, she could have all he possessed. The money was his own, to spend as he wished; if it gave him pleasure to squander it on Ann, he would do so. There was nothing else he had to give her—she had taken it long ago. Taken his courage, his love, his compassion, carried them jauntily away in her little jewel case to fondle occasionally on odd afternoons when the time hung heavy in the Cuban sun, to dangle them perhaps before the eyes of her newest lover, to compare then even with similar trinkets which others before or since had brought her.

Darling George,
I want to make you an offer which no gentleman could accept. I want to come back to you.
I'm staying at the Baur-au-Lac at Zurich till the end of the month. Let me know.

Ann

Smiley picked up the envelope and looked at the back of it: "Madame Juan Alvida." No, no gentleman could accept that offer. No dream could survive the daylight of Ann's departure with her saccharine Latin and his orange-peel grin. Smiley had once seen a news film of Alvida winning some race in Monte Carlo. The most repellent thing about him, he remembered, had been the hair on his arms. With his goggles and the motor oil and that ludicrous laurel-wreath he had looked exactly like an anthropoid ape fallen from a tree. He was wearing a white tennis shirt with short sleeves, which had somehow remained spotlessly clean throughout the race, setting off those black monkey arms with repulsive clarity.

That was Ann: Let me know. Redeem your life, see whether it can be lived again, and let me know. I have wearied my lover, my lover has wearied me, let me shatter your world again: my own bores me. I want to come back to you ... I want, I want ...

Smiley got up, the letter still in his hand, and stood again before the porcelain group. He remained there several minutes, gazing at the little shepherdess. She was so beautiful.

15 ❀
THE LAST ACT

The Sheridan's three-act production of *Edward II* was playing to a full house. Guillam and Mendel sat in adjacent seats at the extreme end of the circle, which formed a wide U facing the stage. The left-hand end of the circle afforded a view of the rear stalls, which were otherwise concealed. An empty seat separated Guillam from a party of young students buzzing with anticipation.

They looked down thoughtfully on a restless sea of bobbing heads and fluttering programmes, stirring in sudden waves as later arrivals took their places. The scene reminded Guillam of an Oriental dance, where the tiny gestures of hand and foot animate a motionless body. Occasionally he would glance towards the rear stalls, but there was still no sign of Elsa Fennan or her guest.

Just as the recorded overture was ending, he looked again briefly towards the two empty stalls in the back row and his heart gave a sudden leap as he saw the slight figure of Elsa Fennan sitting straight and motionless, staring fixedly down the auditorium like a child learning deportment. The seat on her right, nearest the gangway, was still empty.

Outside in the street taxis were drawing up hastily at the theatre entrance and an agreeable selection of the established and the dis-established hurriedly over-tipped their cabmen and spent five minutes looking for their tickets. Smiley's taxi took him past the theatre and deposited him at the Clarendon Hotel, where he went straight downstairs to the dining room and bar.

"I'm expecting a call any moment," he said. "My name's Savage. You'll let me know, won't you?"

The barman turned to the telephone behind him and spoke to the receptionist.

"And a small whisky and soda, please; will you have one yourself?"

"Thank you sir, I never touch it."

The curtain rose on a dimly lit stage and Guillam, peering towards the back of the auditorium, tried at first without success to penetrate the sudden darkness. Gradually his eyes accustomed themselves to the faint glow cast by the emergency lamps, until he could just discern Elsa in the half light; and still the empty seat beside her.

Only a low partition separated the rear stalls from the gangway which ran along the back of the auditorium, and behind it were several doors leading to the foyer, bar, and cloakrooms. For a brief moment one of these opened and an oblique shaft of light was cast as if by design upon Elsa Fennan, illuminating with a thin line one side of her face, making its hollows black by contrast. She inclined her head slightly, as if listening to something behind her, half rose in her seat, then sat down again, deceived, and resumed her former attitude.

Guillam felt Mendel's hand on his arm, turned, and saw his lean face thrust forward, looking past him. Following Mendel's gaze, he peered down into the well of the theatre, where a tall figure was slowly making his way towards the

136

back of the stalls; he was an impressive sight, erect and handsome, a lock of black hair tumbling over his brow. It was he whom Mendel watched with such fascination, this elegant giant limping up the gangway. There was something different about him, something arresting and disturbing. Through his glasses Guillam watched his slow and deliberate progress, admired the grace and measure of his uneven walk. He was a man apart, a man you remember, a man who strikes a chord deep in your experience, a man with the gift of universal familiarity: to Guillam he was a living component of all our romantic dreams, he stood at the mast with Conrad, sought the lost Greece with Byron, and with Goethe visited the shades of classical and medieval hells.

As he walked, thrusting his good leg forward, there was a defiance, a command, that could not go unheeded. Guillam noticed how heads turned in the audience, and eyes followed him obediently.

Pushing past Mendel, Guillam stepped quickly through the emergency exit into the corridor behind. He followed the corridor down some steps and arrived at last at the foyer. The box office had closed down, but the girl was still poring hopelessly over a page of laboriously compiled figures, covered with alterations and erasures.

"Excuse me," said Guillam; "but I must use your telephone—it's urgent, do you mind?"

"Ssh!" She waved her pencil at him impatiently, without looking up. Her hair was mousy, her oily skin glistened from the fatigue of late nights and a diet of chipped potatoes. Guillam waited a moment, wondering how long it would be before she found a solution to that tangle of spidery numerals which would match the pile of notes and silver in the open cash box beside her.

"Listen," he urged; "I'm a police officer—there's a couple of heroes upstairs who are after your cash. Now will you let me use that telephone?"

"Oh Lord," she said in a tired voice, and looked at him for

137

the first time. She wore glasses and was very plain. She was neither alarmed nor impressed. "I wish they'd perishing well take the money. It sends me up the wall." Pushing her accounts to one side, she opened a door beside the little kiosk and Guillam squeezed in.

"Hardly decent, is it?" the girl said with a grin. Her voice was nearly cultured—probably a London undergraduate earning pinmoney, thought Guillam. He rang the Clarendon and asked for Mr. Savage. Almost immediately he heard Smiley's voice.

"He's here," said Guillam, "been here all the time. Must have bought an extra ticket; he was sitting in the front stalls. Mendel suddenly spotted him limping up the aisle."

"Limping?"

"Yes, it's not Mundt. It's the other one, Dieter."

Smiley did not reply and after a moment Guillam said: "George—are you there?"

"We've had it, I'm afraid, Peter. We've got nothing against Frey. Call the men off, they won't find Mundt tonight. Is the first act over yet?"

"Must be just coming up for the interval."

"I'll be round in twenty minutes. Hang on to Elsa like grim death—if they leave and separate Mendel's to stick to Dieter. You stay in the foyer for the last act in case they leave early."

Guillam replaced the receiver and turned to the girl. "Thanks," he said, and put four pennies on her desk. She hastily gathered them together and pressed them firmly into his hand.

"For God's sake," she said, "don't add to my troubles."

He went outside into the street and spoke to a plain clothes man loitering on the pavement. Then he hurried back and rejoined Mendel as the curtain fell on the first act.

Elsa and Dieter were sitting side by side. They were talking happily together, Dieter laughing, Elsa animated and articulate like a puppet brought to life by her master. Mendel watched them in

138

fascination. She laughed at something Dieter said, leant forward, and put her hand on his arm. He saw her thin fingers against his dinner jacket, saw Dieter incline his head and whisper something to her, so that she laughed again. As Mendel watched, the theatre lights dimmed and the noise of conversation subsided as the audience quickly prepared for the second act.

Smiley left the Clarendon and walked slowly along the pavement towards the theatre. Thinking about it now, he realized that it was logical enough that Dieter should come, that it would have been madness to send Mundt. He wondered how long it could be before Elsa and Dieter discovered that it was not Dieter who had summoned her, not Dieter who had sent the postcard by a trusted courier. That, he reflected, should be an interesting moment. All he prayed for now was the opportunity of one more interview with Elsa Fennan.

A few minutes later he slipped quietly into the empty seat beside Guillam. It was a long time since he had seen Dieter.

He had not changed. He was the same improbable romantic with the magic of a charlatan; the same unforgettable figure which had struggled over the ruins of Germany, implacable of purpose, satanic in fulfilment, dark and swift like the Gods of the North. Smiley had lied to them that night in his club; Dieter *was* out of proportion, his cunning, his conceit, his strength, and his dream—all were larger than life, undiminished by the moderating influence of experience. He was a man who thought and acted in absolute terms, without patience or compromise.

Memories returned to Smiley that night as he sat in the dark theatre and watched Dieter across a mass of motionless faces, memories of dangers shared, of mutual trust when each had held in his hand the life of the other. . . . Just for a second Smiley wondered whether Dieter had seen him, had the feeling that Dieter's eyes were upon him, watching him in the dim half-light.

Smiley got up as the second half drew to a close; as the

139

curtain fell he made quickly for the side exit and waited discreetly in the corridor until the bell rang for the last act. Mendel joined him shortly before the end of the interval, and Guillam slipped past them to take up his post in the foyer.

"There's trouble," Mendel said. "They're arguing. She looks frightened. She keeps on saying something and he just shakes his head. She's panicking, I think, and Dieter looks worried. He's started looking round the theatre as if he was trapped, getting the measure of the place, making plans. He glanced up to where you'd been sitting."

"He won't let her leave alone," said Smiley. "He'll wait and get out with the crowd. They won't leave before the end. He probably reckons he's surrounded: he'll bargain on flustering us by parting from her suddenly in the middle of a crowd—just losing her."

"What's our game? Why can't we go down there and get them?"

"We just wait; I don't know what for. We've no proof. No proof of murder and none of espionage until Maston decides to do something. But remember this: Dieter doesn't know that. If Elsa's jumpy and Dieter's worried, they'll do *some-thing*—that's certain. So long as *they* think the game is up, we've a chance. Let them bolt, panic, anything. So long as they do something . . ."

It was dark in the theatre again, but out of the corner of his eye Smiley saw Dieter leaning over Elsa whispering to her. His left hand held her arm, his whole attitude was one of urgent persuasion and reassurance.

The play dragged on, the shouts of soldiers and the screams of the demented king filled the theatre, until the dreadful climax of his foul death, when an audible sigh rose from the stalls beneath them. Dieter had his arm round Elsa's shoulders now, he had gathered the folds of her thin wrap about her neck and protected her as if she were a sleeping child. They remained like this until the final curtain. Neither applauded, Dieter looked about for Elsa's handbag, said something reassuring to her, and put it on her lap. She nodded very slightly. A warning roll of the drums brought the audience to its feet for the national anthem—Smiley rose instinctively and noticed to his surprise that Mendel had vanished. Dieter slowly stood up and as he did so Smiley realized that something had happened. Elsa was still sitting and though Dieter gently prevailed on her to rise, she made no answering sign. There was something oddly dislocated in the way she sat, in the way her head lolled forward on her shoulders . . .

The last line of the anthem was beginning as Smiley rushed to the door, ran down the corridor, down the stone stairs to the foyer. He was just too late—he was met by the first crowd of anxious theatre-goers hastening towards the street in search of taxis. He looked wildly among the crowd for Dieter and knew it was hopeless—that Dieter had done what he himself would have done, had chosen one of the dozen emergency exits which led to the street and safety. He pushed his bulky frame gradually through the middle of the crowd towards the entrance to the stalls. As he twisted this way and that, forcing himself between oncoming bodies, he caught sight of Guillam at the edge of the stream searching hopelessly for Dieter and Elsa. He shouted to him, and Guillam turned quickly.

Struggling on, Smiley at last found himself against the low partition, and he could see Elsa Fennan sitting motionless as all around her men stood up and women felt for their coats and handbags. Then he heard the scream. It was sudden, short, and utterly expressive of horror and disgust. A girl was standing in the gangway looking at Elsa. She was young and very pretty, the fingers of her right hand were raised to her mouth, her face was deathly white. Her father, a tall, cadaverous man, stood behind her. He grasped her shoulders quickly and drew her back as he caught sight of the dreadful thing before him.

Elsa's wrap had slipped from her shoulders and her head was lolling on to her chest.

Smiley had been right. "Let them bolt, panic, anything . . . so long as they do *something* . . ." And this was what they had done: this broken, wretched body was witness to their panic.

"You'd better get the police, Peter. I'm going home. Keep me out of it, if you can. You know where to find me." He nodded, if to himself, "I'm going home."

It was foggy, and a fine rain was falling as Mendel quickly darted across the Fulham Palace Road in pursuit of Dieter. The headlights of cars came suddenly out of the wet mist twenty yards from him; the noise of traffic was high-pitched and nervous as it groped its uncertain way.

He had no choice but to keep close on Dieter's heels, never more than a dozen paces behind him. The pubs and cinemas had closed but the coffee bars and dance halls still attracted noisy groups crowding the pavements. As Dieter limped ahead of him, Mendel staged his progression by the street lamps, watching his silhouette suddenly clarify each time it entered the next cone of light.

Dieter was walking swiftly despite his limp. As his stride lengthened, his limp became more pronounced, so that he seemed to swing his left leg forward by a sudden effort of his broad shoulders.

There was a curious expression on Mendel's face, not of hatred or iron purpose but of frank distaste. To Mendel, the frills of Dieter's profession meant nothing. He saw in his quarry only the squalor of a criminal, the cowardice of a man who paid others to do his killing. When Dieter had gently disengaged himself from the audience and moved towards the side exit, Mendel saw what he had been waiting for: the stealthy act of a common criminal. It was something he expected and understood. To Mendel there was only one criminal class, from pickpocket and sneak-thief to the big operator tampering with company law; they were outside the law and it was his distaste-

142

ful but necessary vocation to remove them to safekeeping. This one happened to be German.

The fog grew thick and yellow. Neither of them wore a coat. Mendel wondered what Mrs. Fennan would do now. Guillam would take care of her. She hadn't even looked at Dieter when he slinked off. She was an odd one that, all skin and bones and good works by the look of her. Lived on dry toast and Bovril.

Dieter turned abruptly down a side street to the right then another to the left. They had been walking for nearly an hour and he showed no sign of slowing down. The street seemed empty: certainly Mendel could hear no other footsteps but their own, crisp and short, the echo corrupted by the fog. They were in a narrow street of Victorian houses with hastily contrived Regency-style façades, heavy porches, and sash windows. Mendel guessed they were somewhere near Fulham Broadway, perhaps beyond it, nearer the King's Road. Still Dieter's pace did not flag, still the crooked shadow thrust forward into the fog, confident of its path, urgent in its purpose.

As they approached a main road, Mendel heard again the plaintive whine of traffic, brought almost to a standstill by the fog. Then from somewhere above them a yellow streetlight shed a pale glow, its outline clearly drawn like the aura of a winter sun. Dieter hesitated a moment on the kerb, then, chancing the ghostly traffic that nosed its way past them from nowhere, he crossed the road and plunged at once into one of the innumerable side streets that led, Mendel was certain, towards the river.

Mendel's clothes were soaking wet, and the thin rain ran over his face. They must be near the river now; he thought he could detect the smell of tar and coke, feel the insidious cold of the black water. Just for a moment he thought Dieter had vanished. He moved forward quickly, nearly tripped on a kerb, went forward again and saw the railings of the embankment in front of him. Steps led upwards to an iron gate in the railings and this was slightly open. He stood at the gate and peered beyond, down into the water. There was a stout wooden gangway and Mendel heard the uneven echo as Dieter, hidden by the fog, followed his strange course to the water's edge. Mendel waited, then, wary and silent, he made his way down the gangway. It was a permanent affair with heavy pine handrails on either side. Mendel reckoned it had been there some time. The low end of the gangway was joined to a long raft made of duckboard and oil-drums. Three dilapidated houseboats loomed in the fog, rocking gently on their moorings.

Noiselessly Mendel crept on to the raft, examining each of the houseboats in turn. Two were close together, connected by a plank.

The third was moored some fifteen feet away, and a light was burning in her forward cabin. Mendel returned to the embankment, closing the iron gate carefully behind him.

He walked slowly down the road, still uncertain of his bearings. After about five minutes the pavement took him suddenly to the right and the ground rose gradually. He guessed he was on a bridge. He lit his cigarette lighter, and its long flame cast a glow over the stone wall on his right. He moved the lighter back and forth, and finally came upon a wet and dirty metal plate bearing the words "Battersea Bridge." He made his way back to the iron gate and stood for a moment, orientating himself in the light of his knowledge.

Somewhere above him and to his right the four massive chimneys of Fulham Power Station stood hidden in the fog. To his left was Cheyne Walk with its row of smart little boats reaching to Battersea Bridge. The place where he now stood marked the dividing line between the smart and the squalid, where Cheyne Walk meets Lots Road, one of the ugliest streets in London. The southern side of this road consists of vast warehouses, wharves, and mills, and the northern side presents an unbroken line of dingy houses typical of the side streets of Fulham.

It was in the shadow of the four chimneys, perhaps sixty feet from the Cheyne Walk mooring, that Dieter Frey had found a sanctuary. Yes, Mendel knew the spot well. It was only a couple of hundred yards upriver from where the earthly remains of Mr. Adam Scarr had been recovered from the unyielding arms of the Thames.

16 ✺
ECHOES IN THE FOG

It was long after midnight when Smiley's telephone rang. He got up from the armchair in front of the gas fire and plodded upstairs to his bedroom, his right hand gripping the banisters tightly as he went. It was Peter, no doubt, or the police, and he would have to make a statement. Or even the Press. The murder had taken place just in time to catch today's papers and mercifully too late for last night's news broadcast. What would this be? "Maniac killer in theatre?" "Death-lock murder—woman named?" He hated the Press as he hated advertising and television, he hated mass-media, the relentless persuasion of the twentieth century. Everything he admired or loved had been the product of intense individualism. That was why he hated Dieter now, hated what he stood for more strongly than ever before: it was the fabulous impertinence of renouncing the individual in favour of the mass. When had mass philosophies ever brought benefit or wisdom? Dieter cared nothing for human life: dreamed only of armies of faceless men bound by their lowest common denominators; he wanted to shape the world as

146

if it were a tree, cutting off what did not fit the regular image; for this he fashioned blank, soulless automatons like Mundt. Mundt was faceless like Dieter's army, a trained killer born of the finest killer breed.

He picked up the telephone and gave his number. It was Mendel.

"Where are you?"

"Near Chelsea Embankment. Pub called the Balloon, in Lots Road. Landlord's a chum of mine. I knocked him up . . . Listen, Elsa's boyfriend is lying up in a houseboat by Chelsea flour mill. Bloody miracle in the fog, he is. Must have found his way by Braille."

"*Who?*"

"Her boyfriend, her escort at the theatre. Wake up, Mr. Smiley; what's eating you?"

"You followed Dieter?"

"Of course I did. That was what you told Mr. Guillam, wasn't it? He was to stick to the woman and me the man . . . How did Mr. Guillam get on, by the way? Where did Elsa get to?"

"She didn't get anywhere. She was dead when Dieter left. Mendel, are you there? Look, for God's sake, how do I find you? Where is this place, will the police know it?"

"They'll know. Tell them he's in a converted landing craft called *Sunset Haven*. She's lying against the eastern side of Sennen Wharf, between the flour mills and Fulham Power Station. They'll know . . . but the fog's thick, mind, very thick."

"Where can I meet you?"

"Cut straight down to the river. I'll meet you where Battersea Bridge joins the north bank."

"I'll come at once, as soon as I've rung Guillam."

He had a gun somewhere, and for a moment he thought of looking for it. Then, somehow, it seemed pointless. Besides, he reflected grimly, there'd be the most frightful row if he used it. He rang Guillam at his flat and gave him Mendel's message: "And Peter, they must cover all ports and airfields;

147

order a special watch on river traffic and seabound craft. They'll know the form."

He put on an old mackintosh and a pair of thick leather gloves and slipped quickly out into the fog.

Mendel was waiting for him by the bridge. They nodded to one another and Mendel led him quickly along the embankment, keeping close to the river wall to avoid the trees that grew along the road. Suddenly Mendel stopped, seizing Smiley by the arm in warning. They stood motionless, listening. Then Smiley heard it too, the hollow ring of footsteps on a wooden floor, irregular like the footsteps of a limping man. They heard the creak of an iron gate, the clang as it was closed, then the footsteps again, firm now upon the pavement, growing louder, coming towards them. Neither moved. Louder, nearer, then they faltered, stopped. Smiley held his breath, trying desperately at the same time to see an extra yard into the fog, to glimpse at the waiting figure he knew was there.

Then suddenly he came, rushing like a massive wild beast, bursting through them, knocking them apart like children and running on, lost again, the uneven echo fading in the distance. They turned and chased after him, Mendel in front and Smiley following as best he could, the image vivid in his mind of Dieter, gun in hand, bursting on them out of the night fog. Ahead, the shadow of Mendel turned abruptly to the right, and Smiley followed blindly. Then suddenly the rhythm had changed to the scuffle of fighting. Smiley ran forward, heard the unmistakable sound of a heavy weapon striking a human skull, and then he was upon them: saw Mendel on the ground, and Dieter stooping over him, raising his arm to hit him again with the heavy butt of an automatic pistol.

Smiley was out of breath. His chest was burning from the bitter, rank fog, his mouth hot and dry, filled with a taste like blood. Somehow he summoned breath, and he shouted desperately: "Dieter!"

Frey looked at him, nodded, and said:

"*Servus*, George," and hit Mendel a hard, brutal blow with

the pistol. He got up slowly, holding the pistol downwards and using both hands to cock it.

Smiley ran at him blindly, forgetting what little skill he had ever possessed, swinging with his short arms, striking with his open hands. His head was against Dieter's chest and he pushed forward, punching Dieter's back and sides. He was mad and, discovering in himself the energy of madness, pressed Dieter back still further towards the railing of the bridge while Dieter, off balance and hindered by his weak leg, gave way. Smiley knew Dieter was hitting him, but the decisive blow never came. He was shouting at Dieter; "Swine, swine!" and as Dieter receded still further Smiley found his arms free and once more struck at his face with clumsy, childish blows. Dieter was leaning back and Smiley saw the clean curve of his throat and chin, as with all his strength he thrust his open hand upwards. His fingers closed over Dieter's jaw and mouth and he pushed further and further. Dieter's hands were at Smiley's throat, then suddenly they were clutching at his collar to save himself as he sank slowly backwards. Smiley beat frantically at his arms, and then he was held no more and Dieter was falling, falling into the swirling fog beneath the bridge, and there was silence. No shout, no splash. He was gone; offered like a human sacrifice to the London fog and the foul black river lying beneath it.

Smiley leant over the bridge, his head throbbing wildly, blood pouring from his nose, the fingers of his right hand feeling broken and useless. His gloves were gone. He looked down into the fog and could see nothing.

"Dieter!" he cried in anguish. "Dieter!"

He shouted again, but his voice choked and tears sprang to his eyes. "Oh dear God what have I done, Oh Christ, Dieter, why didn't you stop me, why didn't you hit me with the gun, why didn't you shoot?" He pressed his clenched hands to his face, tasting the salt blood in the palms mixed with the salt of his tears. He leant against the parapet and cried like a child. Somewhere beneath him a cripple dragged himself through the

149

filthy water, lost and exhausted, yielding at last to the stenching blackness till it held him and drew him down.

He woke to find Peter Guillam sitting on the end of his bed pouring out tea.

"Ah, George. Welcome home. It's two in the afternoon."

"And this morning—?"

"This morning, dear boy, you were carolling on Battersea Bridge with Comrade Mendel."

"How is he . . . Mendel, I mean?"

"Suitably ashamed of himself. Recovering fast."

"And Dieter—?"

"Dead."

Guillam handed him a cup of tea and some ratafia biscuits from Fortnum's.

"How long have you been here, Peter?"

"Well, we came here in a series of tactical bounds, as it were. The first was to Chelsea Hospital where they licked your wounds and gave you a fairly substantial tranquillizer. Then we came back here and I put you to bed. That was disgusting. Then I did a spot of telephoning and, so to speak, went round with a pointed stick tidying up the mess. I looked in on you now and again. Cupid and Psyche. You were either snoring like a saddleback or reciting Webster."

"God."

"*Duchess of Malfi*, I think it was. 'I bade thee, when I was distracted of my wits, go kill my dearest friend, and thou hast done it!' Dreadful nonsense, George, I'm afraid."

"How did the police find us—Mendel and me?"

"George, you may not know it but you were bellowing pejoratives at Dieter as if—"

"Yes, of course. You heard."

"We heard."

"What about Maston? What does Maston say about all this?"

"I think he wants to see you. I have a message from him asking you to drop in as soon as you feel well enough. I don't know what he thinks about it. Nothing at all, I should imagine."

150

"What do you mean?"

Guillam poured out more tea.

"Use your loaf, George. All three principals in this little fairy tale have now been eaten by bears. No secret information has been compromised for the last six months. Do you really think Maston wants to dwell on the details? Do you really think he is bursting to tell the Foreign Office the good tidings—and admit that we only catch spies when we trip over their dead bodies?"

The front doorbell rang and Guillam went downstairs to answer it. In some alarm Smiley heard him admit the visitor to the hall, then the subdued sound of voices, footsteps coming up the stairs. There was a knock on the door and Maston came in. He was carrying an absurdly large bunch of flowers and looked as though he had just been to a garden party. Smiley remembered it was Friday: no doubt he was going to Henley this weekend. He was grinning. He must have been grinning all the way up the stairs.

"Well, George, in the wars again!"

"Yes, I'm afraid so. Another accident."

He sat on the edge of the bed, leaning across it, one arm supporting him the other side of Smiley's legs.

There was a pause and then he said:

"You got my note, George?"

"Yes."

Another pause.

"There has been talk of a new section in the Department, George. We (your Department, that is) feel we should devote more energy to technique research, with particular application to satellite espionage. That is also the Home Office view, I'm pleased to say. Guillam has agreed to advise on terms of reference. I wondered if you'd take it on for us. Running it. I mean, with the necessary promotion of course and the option of extending your service after the statutory retirement age. Our personnel people are right behind me on this."

"Thank you . . . perhaps I could think about it, may I?"

151

"Of course . . . of course," Maston looked slightly put out. "When will you let me know? It may be necessary to take on some new men and the question of space arises. . . . Have the weekend to think about it, will you, and let me know on Monday. The Secretary was quite willing for you to—"

"Yes, I'll let you know. It's very good of you."

"Not at all. Besides I am only the Adviser, you know, George. This is really an internal decision. I'm just the bringer of good news, George; my usual function of errand boy."

Maston looked at Smiley hard for a moment, hesitated, and then said: "I've put the Ministers in the picture . . . as far as is necessary. We discussed what action should be taken. The Home Secretary was also present."

"When was this?"

"This morning. Some very grave issues were raised. We considered a protest to the East Germans and an extradition order for this man Mundt."

"But we don't recognize East Germany."

"Precisely. That was the difficulty. It is however possible to lodge a protest with an intermediary."

"Such as Russia?"

"Such as Russia. In the event, however, certain factors militated against this. It was felt that publicity, whatever form it took, would ultimately rebound against the nation's interests. There is already considerable popular hostility in this country to the rearmament of Western Germany. It was felt that any evidence of German intrigue in Britain—whether inspired by the Russians or not—might encourage this hostility. There is, you see, no positive evidence that Frey was operating for the Russians. It might well be represented to the public that he was operating on his own account or on behalf of a united Germany."

"I see."

"So far very few people indeed are aware of the facts at all. That is most fortunate. On behalf of the police the Home Secretary has tentatively agreed that they will do their part in playing the affair down as far as possible. . . . Now this man Mendel, what's he like? Is he trustworthy?"

Smiley hated Maston for that.

"Yes," he said.

Maston got up. "Good," he said, "good. Well, I must get along. Anything you want at all, anything I can do?"

"No, thank you. Guillam is looking after me admirably." Maston reached the door. "Well, good luck, George. Take the job if you can." He said this quickly in a subdued voice with a pretty, sidelong smile as if it meant rather a lot to him.

"Thank you for the flowers," said Smiley.

Dieter was dead, and he had killed him. The broken fingers of his right hand, the stiffness of his body, and the sickening headache, the nausea of guilt, all testified to this. And Dieter had let him do it, had not fired the gun, had remembered their friendship when Smiley had not. They had fought in a cloud, in the rising stream of the river, in a clearing in a timeless forest: they had met, two friends rejoined, and fought like beasts. Dieter had remembered and Smiley had not. They had come from different hemispheres of the night, from different worlds of thought and conduct. Dieter, mercurial, absolute, had fought to build a civilization. Smiley, rationalistic, protective, had fought to prevent him. "Oh God," said Smiley aloud, "who was then the gentleman . . . ?"

Laboriously he got out of bed and began to dress. He felt better standing up.

17 ❦
DEAR ADVISER

Dear Adviser,

I am at last able to reply to Personnel's offer of a higher appointment in the Department. I am sorry that I have taken so long to do this, but as you know, I have not been well recently, and have also had to contend with a number of personal problems outside the scope of the Department.

As I am not entirely free of my indisposition, I feel it would be unwise for me to accept their offer. Kindly convey this decision to Personnel.

I am sure you will understand.

Yours,
George Smiley

Dear Peter,

I enclose a note on the Fennan case. This is the only copy. Please pass it to Maston when you have read it. I

154

thought it would be valuable to record the events—even if they did not take place.

Ever,
George

The Fennan Case

On Monday, 2 January, I interviewed Samuel Arthur Fennan, a senior member of the Foreign Office, in order to clarify certain allegations made against him in an anonymous letter. The interview was arranged in accordance with the customary procedure, that is to say with the consent of the FO. We knew of nothing adverse to Fennan beyond communist sympathy while at Oxford in the thirties, to which little significance was attached. The interview was therefore in a sense a strictly routine affair.

Fennan's room at the Foreign Office was found to be unsuitable, and we agreed to continue our discussion in St. James's Park, availing ourselves of the good weather.

It has subsequently transpired that we were recognized and observed in this by an agent of the East German Intelligence Service, who had cooperated with me during the war. It is not certain whether he had placed Fennan under some kind of surveillance, or whether his presence in the park was coincidental.

On the night of 3 January it was reported by Surrey police that Fennan had committed suicide. A typewritten suicide note signed by Fennan claimed that he had been victimized by the security authorities.

The following facts, however, emerged during investigation, and suggested foul play:

1. At 7:55 P.M. on the night of his death, Fennan had asked the Walliston exchange to call him at 8:30 the following morning.

2. Fennan had made himself a cup of cocoa shortly before his death, and had not drunk it.

3. He had supposedly shot himself in the hall, at the bottom of the stairs. The note was beside the body.

4. It seemed inconsistent that he should type his last letter, as he seldom used a typewriter, and even more remarkable that he should come downstairs to the hall to shoot himself.

5. On the day of his death he posted a letter inviting me in urgent terms to lunch with him at Marlow the following day.

6. Later it also transpired that Fennan had requested a day's leave for Wednesday, 4 January. He did not apparently mention this to his wife.

7. It was also noted that the suicide letter had been typed on Fennan's own machine—and that it contained certain peculiarities in the typescript similar to those in the anonymous letter. The laboratory report concluded, however, that the two letters had not been typed by the same hand, though originating from the same machine.

Mrs. Fennan, who had been to the theatre on the night her husband died, was invited to explain the 8:30 call from the exchange and falsely claimed to have requested it herself. The exchange was positive that this was not the case. Mrs. Fennan claimed that her husband had been nervous and depressed since his security interview, which corroborated the evidence of his final letter.

On the afternoon of 4 January, having left Mrs. Fennan earlier in the day, I returned to my house in Kensington. Briefly observing somebody at the window, I rang the front doorbell. A man opened the door who has since been identified as a member of the East German Intelligence Service. He invited me into the house, but I declined his offer and returned to my car, noting at the same time the numbers of cars parked nearby.

That evening I visited a small garage in Battersea to inquire into the origin of one of these cars which was registered in the name of the proprietor of the garage. I was attacked by an unknown assailant and beaten senseless. Three weeks later the proprietor himself, Adam Scarr, was found dead in the Thames near Battersea Bridge. He had been drunk at the time of drowning. There were no signs of violence, and he was known as a heavy drinker.

It is relevant that Scarr had for the last four years provided an anonymous foreigner with the use of a car, and had received generous rewards for doing so. Their arrangements were designed to conceal the identity of the borrower even from Scarr himself, who only knew his client by the nickname "Blondie" and could only reach him through a telephone number. The telephone number is of importance—it was that of the East German Steel Mission.

Meanwhile, Mrs. Fennan's alibi for the evening of the murder had been investigated and significant information came to light:

1. Mrs. Fennan attended the Weybridge Repertory Theatre twice a month, on the first and third Tuesdays. (N.B. Adam Scarr's client had collected his car on the first and third Tuesdays of each month.)

2. She always brought a music case and left it in the cloakroom.

3. When visiting the theatre she was always joined by a man whose description corresponded with that of my assailant and Scarr's client. It was even mistakenly assumed by a member of the theatre staff that this man was Mrs. Fennan's husband. He too brought a music case and left it in the cloakroom.

4. On the evening of the murder, Mrs. Fennan had left the theatre early after her friend had failed to arrive and had forgotten to reclaim her music case. Late that night she telephoned the theatre to ask if the case could be called for at once. She had lost her cloakroom ticket. The case was collected—by Mrs. Fennan's usual friend.

157

At this point the stranger was identified as an employee of the East German Steel Mission named Mundt. The principal of the Mission was Herr Dieter Frey, a war-time collaborator of our Service, with extensive operational experience. After the war he had entered Government service in the Soviet zone of Germany. I should mention that Frey had operated with me during the war in enemy territory and had shown himself to be a brilliant and resourceful agent.

I now decided to conduct a third interview with Mrs. Fennan. She broke down and confessed to having acted as an intelligence courier for her husband, who had been recruited by Frey on a skiing holiday five years ago. She herself had cooperated unwillingly, partly in loyalty to her husband and partly to protect him from his own carelessness in performing his espionage role. Frey had seen Fennan talking to me in the park. Assuming I was still operationally employed, he had concluded that Fennan was either under suspicion or a double agent. He instructed Mundt to liquidate Fennan, and his wife had been compelled into silence by her own complicity. She had even typed the text of the suicide letter on Fennan's typewriter over a specimen of her husband's signature.

The means whereby she passed to Mundt the intelligence procured by her husband is relevant. She placed notes and copied documents in a music case, which she took to the theatre. Mundt brought a similar case containing money and instructions and, like Mrs. Fennan, left it in the cloakroom. They had only to exchange cloakroom tickets. When Mundt failed to appear at the theatre on the night in question, Mrs. Fennan obeyed standing instructions and posted the ticket to an address in Highgate. She left the theatre in order to catch the last post from Weybridge. When later that night Mundt demanded the music case she told him what she had done. Mundt insisted on collecting the case that night, for he did not wish to make another journey to Weybridge.

When I interviewed Mrs. Fennan the following morning, one of my questions (about the 8:30 call) alarmed her so much that she telephoned Mundt. This accounts for the assault upon me later that day.

Mrs. Fennan provided me with the address and telephone number she used when contacting Mundt—whom she knew by the cover name of Freitag. Both led to the apartment of a "Lufteuropa" pilot who often entertained Mundt and provided accommodation for him when he required it. The pilot (presumably a courier of the East German Intelligence Service) has not returned to this country since 5 January.

This, then, was the sum of Mrs. Fennan's revelations, and in a sense they led nowhere. The spy was dead, his murderers had vanished. It only remained to assess the extent of the damage. An official approach was now made to the Foreign Office, and Mr. Felix Taverner was instructed to calculate from Foreign Office schedules what information had been compromised. This involved listing all files to which Fennan had had access since his recruitment by Frey. Remarkably, this revealed no systematic acquisition of secret files. Fennan had drawn no secret files except those which directly concerned him in his duties. During the last six months, when his access to sensitive papers was substantially increased, he had actually taken home *no* files of secret classification. The files he took home over this period were of universally low grade, and some treated subjects actually outside the scope of his section. This was not consistent with Fennan's role as a spy. It was, however, possible that he had lost heart for his work, and that his luncheon invitation to me was a first step to confession. With this in mind he might also have written the anonymous letter which could have been designed to put him in touch with the Department.

Two further facts should be mentioned at this point. Under an assumed name and with a fake passport, Mundt left the country by air on the day after Mrs. Fennan made her confession. He evaded the notice of the airport authorities, but was retrospectively identified by the air hostess. Secondly, Fennan's diary contained the full name and official telephone number of

Dieter Frey—a flagrant breach of the most elementary rule of espionage.

It was hard to understand why Mundt had waited three weeks in England after murdering Scarr, and even harder to reconcile Fennan's activities as described by his wife with the obviously unplanned and unproductive selection of files. Re-examination of the facts led repeatedly to this conclusion: the only evidence that Fennan was a spy came from his wife. If the facts were as she described them, why had she been allowed to survive the determination of Mundt and Frey to eliminate those in possession of dangerous knowledge?

On the other hand, might she not herself be the spy?

This would explain the date of Mundt's departure: he left as soon as he had been reassured by Mrs. Fennan that I had accepted her ingenious confession. It would explain the entry in Fennan's diary: Frey was a chance skiing acquaintance and an occasional visitor to Williston. It would make sense of Fennan's choice of files—if Fennan deliberately chose unclassified papers at a time when his work was mainly secret there could be only one explanation: he had come to suspect his wife. Hence the invitation to Marlow, following naturally upon our encounter the previous day. Fennan had decided to tell me of his apprehensions and had taken a day's leave to do so—a fact of which his wife was not apparently aware. This would also explain why Fennan denounced himself in an anonymous letter: he wished to put himself in touch with us *as a preliminary to denouncing his wife.*

Continuing the supposition it was remarkable that in matters of tradecraft Mrs. Fennan alone was efficient and conscientious. The technique used by herself and Mundt recalled that of Frey during the war. The secondary arrangement to post the cloakroom ticket if no meeting took place was typical of his scrupulous planning. Mrs. Fennan, it seemed, had acted with a precision scarcely compatible with her claim to be an unwilling party to her husband's treachery.

While logically Mrs. Fennan now came under suspicion as

160

a spy, there was no reason to believe that her account of what happened on the night of Fennan's murder was necessarily untrue. Had she known of Mundt's intention to murder her husband she would not have taken the music case to the theatre, and would not have posted the cloakroom ticket.

There seemed no way of proving the case against her unless it was possible to reactivate the relationship between Mrs. Fennan and her controller. During the war Frey had devised an ingenious code for emergency communication by the use of snapshots and picture postcards. The actual subject of the photograph contained the message. A religious subject such as a painting of a Madonna or a church conveyed a request for an early meeting. The recipient would send in reply an entirely unrelated letter, making sure to date it. A meeting would take place at a prearranged time and place exactly five days after the date on the letter.

It was just possible that Frey, whose tradecraft had evidently altered so little since the war, might have clung to this system which, after all, would only seldom be needed. Relying on this I therefore posted to Elsa Fennan a picture postcard depicting a church. The card was posted from Highgate. I hoped somewhat forlornly that she would assume it had come to her through the agency of Frey. She reacted at once by sending to an unknown address abroad a ticket for a London theatre performance five days ahead. Mrs. Fennan's communication reached Frey, who accepted it as an *urgent summons.* Knowing that Mundt had been compromised by Mrs. Fennan's "confession," he decided to come himself.

They therefore met at the Sheridan Theatre, Hammersmith, on Tuesday, 15 February.

At first each assumed that the other had initiated the meeting, but when Frey realized they had been brought together by a deception, he took drastic action. It may be that he suspected Mrs. Fennan of luring him into a trap, that he realized he was under surveillance. We shall never know. In any event, he murdered her. His method of doing this is best described in the coroner's report at the inquest: "a single degree of pressure had been applied on the larynx, in particular to the horns of the thyroid cartilage, causing almost immediate death. It would appear that Mrs. Fennan's assailant was no layman in these matters."

Frey was pursued to a houseboat moored near Cheyne Walk, and while violently resisting arrest he fell into the river, from which his body has now been recovered.

18 �֍
BETWEEN TWO WORLDS

Smiley's unrespectable club was usually empty on Sundays, but Mrs. Sturgeon left the door unlocked in case any of her gentlemen chose to call in. She adopted the same stern, possessive attitude towards her gentlemen as she had done in her landlady days at Oxford, when she had commanded from her fortunate boarders more respect than the entire assembly of dons and proctors. She forgave everything, but somehow managed to suggest on each occasion that her forgiveness was unique, and would never, never happen again. She had once made Steed-Asprey put ten shillings in the poor box for bringing seven guests without warning, and afterwards provided the dinner of a lifetime.

They sat at the same table as before. Mendel looked a shade sallower, a shade older. He scarcely spoke during the meal, handling his knife and fork with the same careful precision which he applied to any task. Guillam supplied most of the conversation, for Smiley, too, was less talkative than usual. They were at ease in their companionship and no one felt unduly the need to speak.

163

"Why did she do it?" Mendel asked suddenly.

Smiley shook his head slowly: "I think I know, but we can only guess. I think she dreamed of a world without conflict, ordered and preserved by the new doctrine. I once angered her, you see, and she shouted at me: 'I'm the wandering Jewess,' she said; 'the no-man's-land, the battlefield for your toy soldiers.' As she saw the new Germany rebuilt in the image of the old, saw the plump pride return, as she put it, I think it was just too much for her; I think she looked at the futility of her suffering and the prosperity of her persecutors and rebelled. Five years ago, she told me, they met Dieter on a skiing holiday in Germany. By that time the reestablishment of Germany as a prominent Western power was well under way."

"Was she a Communist?"

"I don't think she liked labels. I think she wanted to help build one society which could live without conflict. Peace is a dirty word now, isn't it? I think she wanted peace."

"And Dieter?" asked Guillam.

"God knows what Dieter wanted. Honour, I think, and a Socialist world." Smiley shrugged. "They dreamed of peace and freedom. Now they're murderers and spies."

"Christ Almighty," said Mendel.

Smiley was silent again, looking into his glass. At last he said: "I can't expect you to understand. You only saw the end of Dieter. I saw the beginning. He went the full circle. I don't think he ever got over being a traitor in the war. He had to put it right. He was one of those world-builders who seem to do nothing but destroy: that's all."

Guillam gracefully intervened: "What about the 8:30 call?"

"I think it's pretty obvious. Fennan wanted to see me at Marlow and he'd taken a day's leave. He can't have told Elsa he was having a day off or she'd have tried to explain it away to me. He staged a phone call to give himself an excuse for going to Marlow. That's my guess, anyway."

The fire crackled in the wide hearth.

. . .

He caught the midnight plane to Zurich. It was a beautiful night, and through the small window beside him he watched the grey wing, motionless against the starlit sky, a glimpse of eternity between two worlds. The vision soothed him, calmed his fears and his doubts, made him fatalistic towards the inscrutable purpose of the universe. It all seemed to matter so little—the pathetic quest for love, or the return to solitude.

Soon the lights of the French coast came in sight. As he watched, he began to sense vicariously the static life beneath him; the rank smell of Gauloises Bleues, garlic and good food, the raised voices in the bistro. Maston was a million miles off, locked away with his arid paper and his shiny politicians.

Smiley presented an odd figure to his fellow passengers—a little fat man, rather gloomy, suddenly smiling, ordering a drink. The young, fair-haired man beside him examined him closely out of the corner of his eye. He knew the type well—the tired executive out for a bit of fun. He found it rather disgusting.

A MURDER OF QUALITY

FOREWORD

Just as *The Naive and Sentimental Lover* is generally separated from John le Carré's canon as being *sui generis*, so is *A Murder of Quality*. The former is dismissed as his only romance novel, while the latter is described as his only detective novel. Nothing could be less true.

Although he is generally regarded as the author of the greatest series of espionage novels ever written, le Carré is, in fact, primarily a writer of novels of manners and social commentary. All the novels depend for their critical esteem on the author's dissection of the British class system, of which he is virulently satirical, just as Jane Austen and Charles Dickens were in novels that often gave the appearance of being about something else. It is the exquisite veneer of espionage fiction that sets le Carré apart from modern writers who are far more pretentious and obvious, even if it is they who win Booker Prizes. Unlike so many of those literary lions, le Carré is actually read, and not merely by critics and academics.

In George Smiley, le Carré has created a superb detective. That was Smiley's role in le Carré's first book, *Call for the Dead*, just as it was in later espionage novels, notably the iconic *Tinker, Tailor, Soldier, Spy*. What distinguishes the present book from the spy stories is that Smiley operates in a smaller arena, with his success being nothing more than bringing a killer to an ambivalent justice, whereas the results in the others seem to have global implications.

Smiley's methodology owes more to Sherlock Holmes, Father Brown, and Hercule Poirot, giants in the world of detective fiction, than to Joseph Conrad, Graham Greene, or Eric Ambler, the redwoods of espionage fiction.

In *Call for the Dead,* everything that transpires springs from the sort of simple paradox that sets in motion so many Holmes

169

adventures. An apparent suicide had arranged a wake-up call for the morning after he died. As in so many mystery stories, the detective (and the author) requires a fortuitous coincidence. In this case, Smiley just happens to be in the victim's house when the wake-up call comes through, and the newly widowed lady of the house just happens to let him pick up the telephone.

Although the death was politically motivated, there is very little ideological delineation of the characters, and there is nothing to suggest any significance in the struggle between East and West. It is essentially a story of observation and deduction, and finally tracking the perpetrator. The identical set of skills are required of Smiley in *A Murder of Quality* when he is asked to explore the situation of a woman at an elite boarding school who is certain that she is about to be murdered by her husband.

Before he even arrives at the school, Smiley is shocked to learn that, in fact, she had been killed the night before. It is the opening of the classic English detective novel, ultimately solved by using the techniques identical to that of an Agatha Christie or Arthur Conan Doyle character—or any of scores of other traditional heroes of cozy crime fiction. Only the elegance of le Carré's prose elevates *A Murder of Quality* above the shelves of volumes constructed in a similar fashion.

That, and the extraordinary qualities of Smiley, who would undoubtedly have gone on to be one of the memorable detectives of fiction had le Carré worked for a police department instead of MI5, the Secret Service.

Much of the Smiley character was based on le Carré's colleague John Bingham, who also wrote spy novels. Like Smiley, Bingham was short and overweight, infused with simple patriotism, and described by le Carré as being gracious, kindly, and astute—an intelligence professional to his fingertips. There can be no argument that many of le Carré's own qualities are to be found in Smiley as well, though there is no physical resemblance between the fictional spy, who looks so ordinary that he vanishes from memory instantly, and his creator, who is the very picture of the craggily handsome British diplomat.

Le Carré's personality was heavily influenced by his father, a charming rogue who moved back and forth from aristocratic circles to jail cells. Le Carré's duplicity found its manifestation on the printed page, however, rather than as a way of life. He was able to imbue his protagonists, particularly Smiley, with a moral clarity that his father lacked. This was no small accomplishment, considering the fact that being a spy discourages, even punishes, moral behavior.

It is this moral struggle, mainly between the inherent decency of the individual as opposed to the corruption of any organization, be it the Circus, or a nation, or the school in *A Murder of Quality*, that places John le Carré at the very pinnacle of contemporary world literature.

—Otto Penzler
New York, May 2004

PREFACE

There are probably a dozen great schools of whom it will be confidently asserted that Carne is their deliberate image. But he who looks among their common rooms for the D'Arcys, Fieldings, and Hechts will search in vain.

INTRODUCTION

The origins of most of my books are by now a mystery to me, even if they were not at the time, but *A Murder of Quality* is clearly set in my memory. It was my second book and I wrote it in the flush of the modest success enjoyed by my first, *Call for the Dead.* I began it in 1961 when I arrived in Bonn ahead of my family to take up a junior post at the British Embassy, and by the time it appeared I had *The Spy Who Came In from the Cold* in my sights.

I still had a notion in those days of writing a thriller a year and adding a much-needed few hundred pounds to my Foreign Service salary. Or so I told myself, even if my ambitions were secretly larger. I wrote *A Murder of Quality* first in the gloomy *pension* in Bad Godesberg where junior British diplomats were stabled while they awaited accommodation, then in the tiny house in the Gringstrasse where we lived with our two children and our au pair. In consequence, I wrote the book lying down, on beds, in notebooks, in the few snatched hours that were left to me by family and diplomatic life.

My sources were extremely present to me, as they will be to the reader. I hated English boarding schools. I found them monstrous and still do, probably because I began my boarding school career at the age of five, at a place called St. Martin's, Northwood, and did not end it till I was sixteen, when I flatly refused to return to Westcott House, Sherborne, on the solid grounds that I would take no more of such institutions.

Yet as life would have it, eight years later I was banged up once again, this time at Eton as a junior Modern Languages master.

Eton was not Sherborne at all. Sherborne in my day had been rustic, colonialist, chauvinist, militarist, religious, patriotic, and repressive. Boys beat other boys, housemasters beat boys, and

175

even the headmaster turned his hand to beating boys when the crime was held to be sufficiently heinous or school discipline was thought to be slipping. I don't know whether masters beat masters but, in any case, I loathed them, and I loathed their grotesque allegiances most of all. To this day, I can find no forgiveness for their terrible abuse of the charges entrusted to them.

Only adults had nervous breakdowns in those days, so the methods of survival for boys who refused to join the system were animal cunning, "internal immigration" as the Germans call it, or simply getting the hell out. I practised the first two, then opted for the third and took myself to Switzerland.

But Eton was an English social class of its own. A graduate of Eton is an Etonian first and a citizen second. He enjoys, during his schooling, more personal access to the staff than in any other school I am aware of, and an extremely high standard of teaching. Certainly the system had its barbarisms, but it awarded more privacy, more sovereignty to its pupils, more self-esteem— some would say arrogance—than I had imagined possible. As a young schoolmaster, I had the sensation of embarking on a second, vicarious education of my own, reacting sometimes against it, sometimes for it, but never calmly, never with any sense of integration or acceptance. Probably, since I had not yet begun to write, I had not realised quite how much of an outsider I was anyway, constantly repelled by the institutions that drew me.

So the components are there for you to dissect as you will: an outrage at my Sherborne schooling, a fascination with the mores of the Etonian class, an attraction to it all, a revulsion from it, a bestiary of frightening adults drawn from the timid chambers of my institutional and largely parentless childhood; and a spiritual brutality towards young minds that in this far-from-perfect story takes the form of bloody violence.

As to poor Stella Rode and her nonconformism, they came from even further back, from the days when my brother and I spent our Sundays in the chapels and tabernacles of coastal Dorset, listening to the counsel of a far humbler God than He who guided the untroubled conscience of the British ruling classes.

Rereading the book now, I find a flawed thriller redeemed by ferocious and quite funny social comment. Most of all I recognise the dankness of those old stone walls that formed the limits of my childhood and left me for the rest of my life with an urge to fight off whatever threatened to enclose me.

John le Carré
December 1989

1 ❀

BLACK CANDLES

The greatness of Carne School has been ascribed by common consent to Edward VI, whose educational zeal is ascribed by history to the Duke of Somerset. But Carne prefers the respectability of the monarch to the questionable politics of his adviser, drawing strength from the conviction that Great Schools, like Tudor Kings, were ordained in Heaven.

And indeed its greatness is little short of miraculous. Founded by obscure monks, endowed by a sickly boy king, and dragged from oblivion by a Victorian bully, Carne had straightened its collar, scrubbed its rustic hands and face and presented itself shining to the courts of the twentieth century. And in the twinkling of an eye, the Dorset bumpkin was London's darling: Dick Whittington had arrived. Carne had parchments in Latin, seals in wax, and Lammas Land behind the Abbey. Carne had property, cloisters, and woodworm, a whipping block and a line in the Doomsday Book—then what more did it need to instruct the sons of the rich?

And they came; each Half they came (for terms are not elegant things), so that throughout a whole afternoon the trains would unload sad groups of black-coated boys on to the station platform. They came in great cars that shone with mournful purity. They came to bury poor King Edward, trundling handcarts over the cobbled streets or carrying tuck boxes like little coffins. Some wore gowns, and when they walked they looked like crows, or black angels come for the burying. Some followed singly like undertakers' mutes, and you could hear the clip of their boots as they went. They were always in mourning at Carne; the small boys because they must stay and the big boys because they must leave, the masters because respectability was underpaid; and now, as the Lent Half (as the Easter term was called) drew to its end, the cloud of gloom was as firmly settled as ever over the grey towers of Carne.

Gloom and the cold. The cold was crisp and sharp as flint. It cut the faces of the boys as they moved slowly from the deserted playing fields after the school match. It pierced their black topcoats and turned their stiff, pointed collars into icy rings round their necks. Frozen, they plodded from the field to the long walled road which led to the main tuck shop and the town, the line gradually dwindling into groups, and the groups into pairs. Two boys who looked even colder than the rest crossed the road and made their way along a narrow path which led towards a distant but less populated tuck shop.

"I think I shall die if ever I have to watch one of those beastly rugger games again. The noise is fantastic," said one. He was tall with fair hair, and his name was Caley.

"People only shout because the dons are watching from the pavilion," the other rejoined; "that's why each house has to stand together. So that the house dons can swank about how loud their houses shout."

"What about Rode?" asked Caley. "Why does he stand with us and make us shout, then? He's not a house don, just a bloody usher."

"He's sucking up to house dons all the time. You can see him

180

in the quad between lessons buzzing round the big men. All the junior masters do." Caley's companion was a cynical red-haired boy called Perkins, Captain of Fielding's house.

"I've been to tea with Rode," said Caley.

"Rode's hell. He wears brown boots. What was tea like?"

"Bleak. Funny how tea gives them away. Mrs. Rode's quite decent, though—homely in a plebby sort of way: doyleys and china birds. Food's good: Women's Institute, but good."

"Rode's doing Corps next Half. That'll put the lid on it. He's so *keen*, bouncing about all the time. You can tell he's not a gentleman. You know where he went to school?"

"No."

"Branxome Grammar. Fielding told my mama, when she came over from Singapore last Half."

"God. Where's Branxome?"

"On the coast. Near Bournemouth. I haven't been to tea with anyone except Fielding." Perkins added after a slight pause, "You get roast chestnuts and crumpets. You're never allowed to thank him, you know. He says emotionalism is only for the lower classes. That's typical of Fielding. He's not like a don at all. I think boys bore him. The whole house goes to tea with him once a Half, he has us in turn, four at a time, and that's about the only time he talks to most men."

They walked on in silence for a while until Perkins said: "Fielding's giving another dinner party tonight."

"He's pushing the boat out these days," Caley replied, with disapproval. "Suppose the food in your house is worse than ever?"

"It's his last Half before he retires. He's entertaining every don and all the wives separately by the end of the Half. Black candles every evening. For mourning. Hells extravagant."

"Yes. I suppose it's a sort of gesture."

"My pater says he's a queer."

They crossed the road and disappeared into the tuck shop, where they continued to discuss the weighty affairs of Mr. Terence Fielding, until Perkins drew their meeting reluctantly to a close. Being a poor hand at science, he was unfortunately obliged to take extra tuition in the subject.

The dinner party to which Perkins had alluded that afternoon was now drawing to a close. Mr. Terence Fielding, senior housemaster of Carne, gave himself some more port and pushed the decanter wearily to his left. It was his port, the best he had. There was enough of the best to last the Half—and after that, be damned. He felt a little tired after watching the match, and a little drunk, and a little bored with Shane Hecht and her husband. Shane was so hideous. Massive and enveloping, like a faded Valkyrie. All that black hair. He should have asked someone else. The Snows for instance, but he was too clever. Or Felix D'Arcy, but D'Arcy interrupted. Ah well, a little later he would annoy Charles Hecht, and Hecht would get in a pet and leave early.

Hecht was fidgeting, wanting to light his pipe, but Fielding damn well wouldn't have it. Hecht could have a cigar if he wanted to smoke. But his pipe could stay in his dinner-jacket pocket, where it belonged, or didn't belong, and his athletic profile could remain unadorned.

"Cigar, Hecht?"

"No thanks, Fielding. I say, do you mind if I . . ."

"I can recommend the cigars. Young Havelake sent them from Havana. His father's ambassador there, you know."

"Yes, dear," said Shane tolerantly; "Vivian Havelake was in Charles's troop when Charles was commandant of the Cadets."

"Good boy, Havelake," Hecht observed, and pressed his lips together to show he was a strict judge.

"It's amusing how things have changed." Shane Hecht said this rapidly with a rather wooden smile, as if it weren't really amusing. "Such a grey world we live in, now.

"I remember before the war when Charles inspected the Corps on a white horse. We don't do that kind of thing now do we? I've got nothing against Mr. Iredale as commandant, nothing at all. What was his regiment, Terence, do you know? I'm sure he does it very nicely, whatever they do now in the Corps—he gets on so well with the boys, doesn't he? His wife's such a nice person . . . I wonder why they can never keep their servants. I hear Mr. Rode will be helping out with the Corps next Half."

"Poor little Rode," said Fielding slowly; "running about like a puppy, trying to earn his biscuits. He tries so hard; have you seen him cheering at school matches? He'd never seen a game of rugger before he came here, you know. They don't play rugger at grammar schools—it's all soccer. Do you remember when he first came, Charles? It was fascinating. He lay very low at first, drinking us in: the games, the vocabulary, the manners. Then, one day it was as if he had been given the power of speech, and he spoke in our language. It was amazing, like plastic surgery. It was Felix D'Arcy's work of course—I've never seen anything quite like it before."

"Dear Mrs. Rode," said Shane Hecht in that voice of abstract vagueness which she reserved for her most venomous pronouncements: "So sweet . . . and such simple taste, don't you think? I mean, whoever would have dreamed of putting those china ducks on the wall? Big ones at the front and little ones at the back. Charming, don't you think? Like one of those teashops. I wonder where she bought them. I must ask her. I'm told her father lives near Bournemouth. It must be so lonely for him, don't you think? Such a vulgar place; no one to talk to."

Fielding sat back and surveyed his own table. The silver was good. The best in Carne, he had heard it said, and he was inclined to agree. This Half he had nothing but black candles. It was the sort of thing people remembered when you'd gone: "Dear old Terence—marvellous host. He dined every member of the staff during his last Half, you know, wives too. Black candles, rather touching. It broke his heart giving up his house." But he must annoy Charles Hecht. Shane would like that. Shane would egg him on because she hated Charles, because within her great ugly body she was as cunning as a snake.

Fielding looked at Hecht and then at Hecht's wife, and she smiled back at him, the slow rotten smile of a whore. For a moment Fielding thought of Hecht pasturing in that thick body: it

183

was a scene redolent of Lautrec . . . yes, that was it! Charles pompous and top-hatted, seated stiffly upon the plush coverlet; she massive, pendulous, and bored. The image pleased him: so perverse to consign that fool Hecht from the Spartan cleanliness of Carne to the brothels of nineteenth-century Paris. . . .

Fielding began talking, pontificating rather, with an air of friendly objectivity which he knew Hecht would resent.

"When I look back on my thirty years at Carne, I realise I have achieved rather less than a road sweeper." They were watching him now—"I used to regard a road sweeper as a person inferior to myself. Now, I rather doubt it. Something is dirty, he makes it clean, and the state of the world is advanced. But I—what have I done? Entrenched a ruling class which is distinguished by neither talent, culture, nor wit; kept alive for one more generation the distinctions of a dead age."

Charles Hecht, who had never perfected the art of not listening to Fielding, grew red and fussed at the other end of the table.

"Don't we teach them, Fielding? What about our successes, our scholarships?"

"I have never taught a boy in my life, Charles. Usually the boy wasn't clever enough; occasionally, I wasn't. In most boys, you see, perception dies with puberty. In a few it persists, though where we find it we take good care at Carne to kill it. If it survives our efforts the boy wins a scholarship. . . . Bear with me, Shane; it's my last Half."

"Last Half or not, you're talking through your hat, Fielding," said Hecht, angrily.

"That is traditional at Carne. These successes, as you call them, are the failures, the rare boys who have not learned the lessons of Carne. They have ignored the cult of mediocrity. We can do nothing for them. But for the rest, for the puzzled little clerics and the blind little soldiers, for them the truth of Carne is written on the wall, and they hate us."

Hecht laughed rather heavily.

"Why do so many come back, then, if they hate us so much? Why do they remember us and come and see us?"

184

"Because we, dear Charles, are the writing on the wall! The one lesson of Carne they never forget. They come back to read us, don't you see? It was from us they learnt the secret of life: that we grow old without growing wise. They realised that nothing happened when we grew up: no blinding light on the road to Damascus, no sudden feeling of maturity." Fielding put his head back and gazed at the clumsy Victorian moulding on the ceiling and the halo of dirt round the light rose.

"We just got a little older. We made the same jokes, thought the same thoughts, wanted the same things. Year in, year out, Hecht, we were the same people, not wiser, not better; we haven't had an original thought between us for the last fifty years of our lives. They saw what a trick it all was, Carne and us: our academic dress, our schoolroom jokes, our wise little offerings of guidance. And that's why they come back year after year of their puzzled, barren lives to gaze fascinated at you and me, Hecht, like children at a grave, searching for the secret of life and death. Oh, yes, they have learnt *that* from us."

Hecht looked at Fielding in silence for a moment.

"Decanter, Hecht?" said Fielding, in a slightly conciliatory way, but Hecht's eyes were still upon him.

"If that's a joke . . ." he began, and his wife observed with satisfaction that he was very angry indeed.

"I wish I knew, Charles," Fielding replied with apparent earnestness. "I really wish I knew. I used to think it was clever to confuse comedy with tragedy. Now I wish I could distinguish them." He rather liked that.

They had coffee in the drawing room, where Fielding resorted to gossip, but Hecht was not to be drawn. Fielding rather wished he had let him light his pipe. Then he recalled his vision of the Hechts in Paris, and it restored him. He had been rather good this evening. There were moments when he convinced himself.

While Shane fetched her coat, the two men stood together in the hall, but neither spoke. Shane returned, an ermine stole, yellow with age, draped over her great white shoulders. She inclined her head to the right, smiled and held out her hand to Fielding, the fingers down.

"Terence, darling," she said, as Fielding kissed her fat knuckles; "so kind. And in your last Half. You must dine with us before you go. So sad. So few of us left." She smiled again, half closing her eyes to indicate emotional disturbance, then followed her husband into the street. It was still bitterly cold and snow was in the air.

Fielding closed and carefully bolted the door behind them—perhaps a fraction earlier than courtesy required—and returned to the dining room. Hecht's port glass was still about half full. Fielding picked it up and carefully poured the contents back into the decanter. He hoped Hecht wasn't too upset; he hated people to dislike him. He snuffed the black candles and damped their wicks between his forefinger and thumb. Switching on the light, he took from the sideboard a sixpenny notebook, and opened it. It contained his list of dining guests for the remainder of the Half. With his fountain pen he placed a neat tick against the name Hecht. They were done. On Wednesday he would have the Rodes. The husband was quite good value, but she, of course, was hell. . . . It was not always the way with married couples. The wives as a rule were so much more sympathetic.

He opened the sideboard and took from it a bottle of brandy and a tumbler. Holding them both in the same hand, he shuffled wearily back to the drawing room, resting his other hand on the wall as he went. God! He felt old, suddenly; that thin line of pain across the chest, that heaviness in the legs and feet. Such an effort being with people—on stage all the time. He hated to be alone, but people bored him. Being alone was like being tired but unable to sleep. Some German poet had said that; he'd quoted it once, "You may sleep but I must dance." Something like that.

"That's how I am," thought Fielding. "That's how Carne is, too; an old satyr dancing to the music." The music grew faster and their bodies older, but they must dance on—there were young men waiting in the wings. It had been funny once dancing

186

the old dances in a new world. He poured himself some more brandy. He'd be pleased to leave in a way, even though he'd have to go on teaching somewhere else.

But it had its beauty, Carne . . . the Abbey Close in spring . . . the flamingo figures of boys waiting for the ritual of worship . . . the ebb and flow of children, like the seasons of the year, and the old men dying among them. He wished he could paint; he would paint the pageant of Carne in the fallow browns of autumn. . . . What a shame, thought Fielding, that a mind so perceptive of beauty had no talent for creation.

He looked at his watch. Quarter to twelve. Nearly time to go out . . . to dance, and not to sleep.

2 ❧

THE THURSDAY FEELING

It was Thursday evening and the *Christian Voice* had just been put to bed. This was scarcely a historic event in Fleet Street. The pimply boy from Dispatch who took away the ragged pile of pageproofs showed no more ceremony than was strictly demanded by the eventual prospect of his Christmas bonus. And even in this respect he had learnt that the secular journals of Unipress were more provident of material charity than the *Christian Voice*; charity being in strict relationship to circulation.

Miss Brimley, the journal's editor, adjusted the air cushion beneath her and lit a cigarette. Her secretary and sub-editor—the appointment carried both responsibilities—yawned, dropped the aspirin bottle into her handbag, combed out her ginger hair, and bade Miss Brimley good night, leaving behind her as usual the smell of strongly scented powder and an empty paper-tissue box. Miss Brimley listened contentedly to the clipping echo of her footsteps as it faded down the corridor. It pleased her to be alone at last, tasting the anticlimax. She never failed to wonder at

188

herself; how every Thursday morning brought the same slight uneasiness as she entered the vast Unipress building and stood a little absurdly on one escalator after the other, like a drab parcel on a luxury liner. Heaven knows, she had run the *Voice* for fourteen years, and there were those who said its layout was the best thing Unipress did. Yet the Thursday feeling never left her, the wakeful anxiety that one day, perhaps today, they wouldn't be ready when the dispatch boy came. She often wondered what would happen then. She had heard of failures elsewhere in that vast combine, of features disapproved and staff rebuked. It was a mystery to her why they kept the *Voice* at all, with its expensive room on the seventh floor and a circulation which, if Miss Brimley knew anything, hardly paid for the paper clips.

The *Voice* had been founded at the turn of the century by old Lord Landsbury, together with a Nonconformist daily newspaper and the *Temperance Gazette.* But the *Gazette* and the daily were long since dead, and Landsbury's son had woken one morning not long ago to find his whole business and every man and woman of it, every stick of furniture, ink, paper clips, and galley-pins, bought by the hidden gold of Unipress.

That was three years ago and every day she had waited for her dismissal. But it never came; no directive, no question, no word. And so, being a sensible woman, she continued exactly as before and ceased to wonder.

And she was glad. It was easy to sneer at the *Voice.* Every week it offered humbly and without fanfares evidence of the Lord's intervention in the world's affairs, retold in simple and somewhat unscientific terms the early history of the Jews, and provided over a fictitious signature motherly advice to whomever should write and ask for it. The *Voice* scarcely concerned itself with the fifty-odd millions of the population who had never heard of it. It was a family affair, and rather than abuse those who were not members, it did its best for those who were. For them it was kind, optimistic, and informative. If a million children were dying of the plague in India, you may be sure that the weekly editorial described the miraculous es-

189

cape from fire of a Methodist family in Kent. The *Voice* did not advise you how to disguise the encroaching wrinkles round your eyes or control your spreading figure; did not dismay you, if you were old, by its own eternal youth. It was itself middle-aged and middle class, counselled caution to girls and charity to all. Nonconformity is the most conservative of habits and families which took the *Voice* in 1903 continued to take it in 1960.

Miss Brimley was not quite the image of her journal. The fortunes of war and the caprice of Intelligence work had thrown her into partnership with the younger Lord Landsbury, and for the six years of war they had worked together efficiently and inconspicuously in an unnamed building in Knightsbridge. The fortunes of peace rendered both unemployed, but Landsbury had the good sense, as well as the generosity, to offer Miss Brimley a job. The *Voice* had ceased publication during the war, and no one seemed anxious to renew it. At first Miss Brimley had felt a little ashamed at reviving and editing a journal which in no way expressed her own vague deism, but quite soon, as the touching letters came in and the circulation recovered, she developed an affection for her job—and for her readers—which outweighed her earlier misgivings. The *Voice* was her life and its readers her preoccupation. She struggled to answer their odd, troubled questions, sought advice of others where she could not provide it herself, and, in time, under a handful of pseudonyms, became, if not their philosopher, their guide, friend, and universal aunt.

Miss Brimley put out her cigarette, absently tidied the pins, paper clips, scissors, and paste into the top right-hand drawer of her desk, and gathered together the afternoon mail from her intray which, because it was Thursday, she had left untouched. There were several letters addressed to Barbara Fellowship, under which name the *Voice* had, since its foundation, answered both privately and through its published columns the many problems of its correspondents. They could wait until tomorrow. She rather enjoyed the "problem post," but Friday morning was when she read it. She opened the little filing cabinet at her elbow and dropped the letters into a box file at the front of the compartment. As she did so, one of them fell on its back and she noticed with surprise that the sealed flap was embossed with an elegant blue dolphin. She picked the envelope out of the cabinet and looked at it curiously, turning it over several times. It was of pale grey paper, very faintly lined. Expensive—perhaps handmade. Beneath the dolphin was a tiny scroll on which she could just discern the legend *Regem defendere diem videre.* The postmark was Carne, Dorset. That must be the school crest. But why was Carne familiar to her? Miss Brimley was proud of her memory, which was excellent, and she was vexed when it failed her. As a last resort she opened the envelope with her faded ivory paper knife and read the letter.

Dear Miss Fellowship,

I don't know if you are a real person but it doesn't matter, because you always give such good, kind answers. It was me who wrote last June about the pastry mix. I am not mad and I know my husband is trying to kill me. Could I please come and see you as soon as it's convenient? I'm sure you'll believe me and understand that I am normal. Could it be *as soon as possible* please, I am so afraid of the long nights. I don't know who else to turn to. I could try Mr. Cardew at the Tabernacle but he wouldn't believe me and Dad's too sensible. I might as well be dead. There's something not quite right about him. At night sometimes when he thinks I'm asleep he just lies watching the darkness. I know it's wrong to think such wicked things and have fear in our hearts, but I can't help it.

I hope you don't get many letters like this.

Yours faithfully,
Stella Rode (Mrs.)
née Glaston

191

She sat quite still at her desk for a moment, looking at the address in handsome blue engraving at the top of the page: "North Fields, Carne School, Dorset." In that moment of shock and astonishment one phrase forced itself upon her mind. "The value of intelligence depends on its breeding." That was John Landsbury's favourite dictum. Until you know the pedigree of the information you cannot evaluate a report. Yes, that was what he used to say: "We are not democratic. We close the door on intelligence without parentage."

And she used to reply: "Yes, John, but even the best families had to begin somewhere."

But Stella Rode *had* parentage. It all came back to her now. She was the Glaston girl. The girl whose marriage was reported in the editorial, the girl who won the summer competition; Samuel Glaston's daughter from Branxome. She had a card in Miss Brimley's index.

Abruptly she stood up, the letter still in her hand, and walked to the uncurtained window. Just in front of her was a contemporary window box of woven white metal. It was odd, she reflected, how she could never get anything to grow in that window box. She looked down into the street, a slight, sensible figure leaning forward a little and framed by the incandescent fog outside; fog made yellow from the stolen light of London's streets. She could just distinguish the street lamps far below, pale and sullen. She suddenly felt the need for fresh air, and on an impulse quite alien to her usual calm, she opened the window wide. The quick cold and the angry surge of noise burst in on her, and the insidious fog followed. The sound of traffic was constant, so that for a moment she thought it was the turning of some great machine. Then above its steady growl she heard the newsboys. Their cries were like the cries of gulls against a gathering storm. She could see them now, sentinels among the hastening shadows.

It might be true. That had always been the difficulty. Right through the war it was the same restless search. It might be true. It was no use relating reports to probability when there was no

192

quantum of knowledge from which to start. She remembered the first intelligence from France on flying bombs, wild talk of concrete runways in the depths of a forest. You had to resist the dramatic, you had to hold out against it. Yet it might be true. Tomorrow, the day after, those newsboys down there might be shouting it, and Stella Rode *née* Glaston might be dead. And if that was so, if there was the remotest chance that this man was plotting to kill this woman, then she, Ailsa Brimley, must do what she could to prevent it. Besides, Stella Glaston had a claim on her assistance if anyone did: both her father and her grandfather had taken the *Voice,* and when Stella married five years ago, Miss Brimley had put a couple of lines about it in the editorial. The Glastons sent her a Christmas card every year. They were one of the original families to subscribe. . . .

It was cold at the window, but she remained there, still fascinated by the half hidden shadows joining and parting beneath her, and the useless streetlights burning painfully among them. She began to imagine him as one of those shadows, pressing and jostling, his murderer's eyes turned to sockets of dark. And suddenly she was frightened and needed help.

But not the police, not yet. If Stella Rode had wanted that she would have gone herself. Why hadn't she? For love? For fear of looking a fool? Because instinct was not evidence? They wanted fact. But the fact of murder was death. Must they wait for that?

Who would help? She thought at once of Landsbury, but he was farming in Rhodesia. Who else had been with them in the war? Fielding and Jebedee were dead, Steed-Asprey vanished. Smiley—where was he? George Smiley, the cleverest and perhaps the oddest of them all. Of course, Miss Brimley remembered now. He made that improbable marriage and went back to research at Oxford. But he hadn't stayed there. . . . The marriage had broken up. . . . What *had* he done after that?

She returned to her desk and picked up the S-Z directory. Ten minutes later she was sitting in a taxi, heading for Sloane Square. In her neatly gloved hand she held a cardboard folder containing Stella Rode's card from the index and the correspondence which had passed between them at the time of the summer competition. She was nearly at Piccadilly when she remembered she'd left the office window open. It didn't seem to matter much.

"With other people it's Persian cats or golf. With me it's the *Voice* and my readers. I'm a ridiculous spinster, I know, but there it is. I won't go to the police until I've tried *something*, George."

"And you thought you'd try me?"

"Yes."

She was sitting in the study of George Smiley's house in Bywater Street; the only light came from the complicated lamp on his desk, a black spider of a thing shining brightly on to the manuscript notes which covered the desk.

"So you've left the Service?" she said.

"Yes, yes, I have." He nodded his round head vigorously, as if reassuring himself that a distasteful experience was really over, and mixed Miss Brimley a whisky and soda. "I had another spell there after . . . Oxford. It's all very different in peacetime, you know," he continued.

Miss Brimley nodded.

"I can imagine it. More time to be bitchy." Smiley said nothing, just lit a cigarette and sat down opposite her.

"And the people have changed. Fielding, Steed, Jebedee. All gone." She said this in a matter-of-fact way as she took from her large sensible handbag Stella Rode's letter. "This is the letter, George."

When he had read it, he held it briefly towards the lamp, his round face caught by the light in a moment of almost comic earnestness. Watching him, Miss Brimley wondered what impression he made on those who did not know him well. She used to think of him as the most forgettable man she had ever met; short and plump, with heavy spectacles and thinning hair, he was at first sight the very prototype of an unsuccessful middle-aged bachelor in a sedentary occupation. His natural diffidence in most practical matters was reflected in his clothes, which were

194

costly and unsuitable, for he was clay in the hands of his tailor, who robbed him.

He had put down the letter on the small marquetry table beside him and was looking at her owlishly.

"This other letter she sent you, Brim. Where is it?"

She handed him the folder. He opened it and after a moment read aloud Rode's other letter:

Dear Miss Fellowship,

I would like to submit the following suggestion for your "Kitchen Hints" competition.

Make your basic batch of cake mixture once a month. Cream equal quantities of fat and sugar and add one egg for every six ounces of the mixture. For puddings and cakes, add flour to the required quantity of basic mixture.

This will keep well for a month.

I enclose stamped addressed envelope.

Yours sincerely,
Stella Rode (*née* Glaston)

PS—Incidentally, you can prevent wire wool from rusting by keeping it in a jar of soapy water. Are we allowed two suggestions? If so, please can this be my second?

"She won the competition," Miss Brimley observed, "but that's not the point. This is what I want to tell you, George. She's a Glaston, and the Glastons have been reading the *Voice* since it started. Stella's grandfather was old Rufus Glaston, a Lancashire pottery king; he and John Landsbury's father built chapels and tabernacles in practically every village in the Midlands. When Rufus died the *Voice* put out a memorial edition and old Landsbury himself wrote the obituary. Samuel Glaston took on his father's business, but had to move south because of his health. He ended up near Bournemouth, a widower with one daughter, Stella. She's the last of all that family. The whole lot are as down to earth as you could wish, Stella included, I should think. I don't think any of them is likely to be suffering from delusions of persecution."

Smiley was looking at her in astonishment.

"My dear Brim, I can't possibly take that in. How on earth do you know all this?"

Miss Brimley smiled apologetically.

"The Glastons are easy—they're almost part of the magazine. They send us Christmas cards, and boxes of chocolates on the anniversary of our foundation. We've got about five hundred families who form what I call our Establishment. They were in on the *Voice* from the start and they've kept up ever since. They write to us, George; if they're worried they write and say so; if they're getting married, moving house, retiring from work, if they're ill, depressed, or angry, they write. Not often, Heaven knows; but enough."

"How do you remember it all?"

"I don't. I keep a card index. I always write back you see . . . only . . ."

"Yes?"

Miss Brimley looked at him earnestly.

"This is the first time anyone has written because she's frightened."

"What do you want me to do?"

"I've only had one bright idea so far. I seem to remember Adrian Fielding had a brother who taught at Carne . . ."

"He's a housemaster there, if he hasn't retired."

"No, he retires this Half—it was in *The Times* some weeks ago, in that little bit on the Court page where Carne always announces itself. It said: 'Carne School reassembles today for the Lent Half. Mr. T. R. Fielding will retire at the end of the Half, having completed his statutory fifteen years as a housemaster.'"

Smiley laughed.

"Really, Brim, your memory is absurd!"

"It was the mention of Fielding. . . . Anyway, I thought you could ring him up. You must know him."

"Yes, yes. I know him. At least, I met him once at Magdalen High Table. But—" Smiley coloured a little.

"But what, George?"

"Well, he's not quite the man his brother was, you know."

"How could he be?" Miss Brimley rejoined a little sharply. "But he can tell you something about Stella Rode. And her husband."

"I don't think I could do that on the telephone. I think I'd rather go and see him. But what's to stop you ringing up Stella Rode?"

"Well, I can't tonight, can I? Her husband will be in. I thought I'd put a letter in the post to her tonight telling her she can come to see me anytime. But," she continued, making a slight, impatient movement with her foot, "I want to do something now, George."

Smiley nodded and went to the telephone. He rang directory inquiries and asked for Terence Fielding's number. After a long delay he was told to ring Carne School central exchange, who would connect him with whomever he required. Miss Brimley, watching him, wished she knew a little more about George Smiley, how much of that diffidence was assumed, how vulnerable he was.

"The best," Adrian had said. "The strongest and the best."

But so many men learnt strength during the war, learnt terrible things, and put aside their knowledge with a shudder when it ended. The number was ringing now. She heard the dialling tone and for a moment was filled with apprehension. For the first time she was afraid of making a fool of herself, afraid of becoming involved in unlikely explanations with angular, suspicious people.

"Mr. Terence Fielding, please. . . ." A pause.

"Fielding, good evening. My name is George Smiley; I knew your brother well in the war. We have in fact met. . . . Yes, yes, quite right—Magdalen, was it not, the summer before last? Look, I wonder if I might come and see you on a personal matter . . . it's a little difficult to discuss on the telephone. A friend of mine has received a rather disturbing letter from the wife of a Carne master. . . . Well, I—Rode, Stella Rode; her husband . . ."

He suddenly stiffened, and Miss Brimley, her eyes fixed upon him, saw with alarm how his chubby face broke into an expression of pain and disgust. She no longer heard what he was saying. She could only watch the dreadful transformation of his face, the whitening knuckles of his hand clutching the receiver. He was looking at her now, saying something . . . it was too late. Stella Rode was dead. She had been murdered late on Wednesday night. They'd actually been dining with Fielding the night it happened.

3 ✿

THE NIGHT OF THE MURDER

The seven-five from Waterloo to Yeovil is not a popular train, though it provides an excellent breakfast. Smiley had no difficulty in finding a first-class compartment to himself. It was a bitterly cold day, dark and the sky heavy with snow. He sat huddled in a voluminous travelling coat of Continental origin, holding in his gloved hands a bundle of the day's papers. Because he was a precise man and did not care to be hurried, he had arrived thirty minutes before the train was due to depart. Still tired after the stresses of the previous night, when he had sat up talking with Ailsa Brimley until Heaven knew what hour, he was disinclined to read. Looking out of the window on to an almost empty station, he caught sight, to his great surprise, of Miss Brimley making her way along the platform, peering in at the windows, a carrier bag in her hand. He lowered the window and called to her.

"My dear Brim, what are you doing here at this dreadful hour? You should be in bed."

She sat down opposite him and began unpacking her bag

and handing him its contents: thermos, sandwiches, and chocolate.

"I didn't know whether there was a breakfast car," she explained; "and besides, I wanted to come and see you off. You're such a dear, George, and I wish I could come with you, but Unipress would go mad if I did. The only time they notice you is when you're not there."

"Haven't you seen the papers?" he asked.

"Just briefly, on the way here. They seem to think it wasn't him, but some madman. . . ."

"I know, Brim. That's what Fielding said, wasn't it?" There was a moment's awkward silence.

"George, am I being an awful ass, letting you go off like this? I was sure last night, but now I wonder . . ."

"After you left I rang Ben Sparrow of Special Branch. You remember him, don't you? He was with us in the war. I told him the whole story."

"George! At three in the morning?"

"Yes. He's ringing the Divisional Superintendent at Carne. He'll tell him about the letter, and that I'm coming down. Ben had an idea that a man named Rigby would be handling the case. Rigby and Ben were at police college together." He looked at her kindly for a moment. "Besides, I'm a man of leisure, Brim. I shall enjoy the change."

"Bless you, George," said Miss Brimley, woman enough to believe him. She got up to go, and Smiley said to her:

"Brim, if you should need any more help or anything, and can't get hold of me, there's a man called Mendel who lives in Mitcham, a retired police inspector. He's in the book. If you get hold of him and mention me, he'll do what he can for you. I've booked a room at the Sawley Arms."

Alone again, Smiley surveyed uneasily the assortment of food and drink which Miss Brimley had provided. He had promised himself the luxury of breakfast in the restaurant car. He would keep the sandwiches and coffee for later, that would be the best thing; for lunch, perhaps. And he would breakfast properly.

In the restaurant car Smiley read first the less sensational reports on the death of Stella Rode. It appeared that on Wednesday evening Mr. and Mrs. Rode had been guests at dinner of Mr. Terence Fielding, the senior housemaster at Carne and brother of the late Adrian Fielding, the celebrated French scholar who had vanished during the war while specially employed by the War Office. They had left Mr. Fielding's house together at about ten to eleven and walked the half mile from the centre of Carne to their house, which stood alone at the edge of the famous Carne playing fields. As they reached their house, Mr. Rode remembered that he had left at Mr. Fielding's house some examination papers which urgently required correction that night. (At this point Smiley remembered that he had failed to pack his dinner jacket, and that Fielding would almost certainly ask him to dine.) Rode determined to walk back to Fielding's house and collect the papers, therefore, starting back at about five past eleven. It appears that Mrs. Rode made herself a cup of tea and sat down in the drawing room to await his return.

Adjoining the back of the house is a conservatory, the inner door of which leads to the drawing room. It was there that Rode eventually found his wife when he returned. There were signs of a struggle, and certain inexpensive articles of jewellery were missing from the body. The confusion in the conservatory was terrible. Fortunately there had been a fresh fall of snow on Wednesday afternoon, and detectives from Dorchester were examining the footprints and other traces early on Thursday morning. Mr. Rode had been treated for shock at Dorchester Central Hospital. The police wished to interview a woman from the adjacent village of Pylle who was locally known as "Mad Janie" on account of her eccentric and solitary habits. Mrs. Rode, who was well known in Carne for her energetic work on behalf of the International Refugee Year, had apparently shown a charitable interest in her welfare, and she had vanished without trace since the night of the murder. The police were currently of the opinion that the murderer had caught sight of Mrs. Rode through the drawing-room window (she had not drawn the curtains) and that Mrs. Rode had admitted the murderer at the front door in the belief that it was her husband returning from Mr. Fielding's house. The Home Office pathologist had been asked to conduct a post-mortem examination.

The other reports were not so restrained: "Murder most foul has desecrated the hallowed playing fields of Carne" one article began, and another, "Science teacher discovers murdered wife in blood-spattered conservatory." A third screamed, "Mad woman sought in Carne murder." With an expression of distaste, Smiley screwed up all the newspapers except the *Guardian* and *The Times* and tossed them on to the luggage rack.

He changed at Yeovil for a local line to Sturminster, Okeford, and Carne. It was something after eleven o'clock when he finally arrived at Carne station.

He telephoned the hotel from the station and sent his luggage ahead by taxi. The Sawley Arms was only full at Commemoration and on St. Andrew's Day. Most of the year it was empty; sitting like a prim Victorian lady, its slate roof in the mauve of half-mourning on ill-tended lawns midway between the station and Carne Abbey.

Snow still lay on the ground, but the day was fine and dry, and Smiley decided to walk into the town and arrange to meet the police officer conducting the investigation of the murder. He left the station, with its foretaste of Victorian austerity, and walked along the avenue of bare trees which led towards the great Abbey tower, flat and black against the colourless winter sky. He crossed the Abbey Close, a serene and beautiful square of medieval houses, the roofs snow-covered, the white lawns shaded with pin strokes of grass. As he passed the west door of the Abbey, the soft snow creaking where he trod, the clock high above him struck the half hour, and two knights on horseback rode out from their little castle over the door and slowly raised their lances to each other in salute. Then, as if it were all part of the same clockwork mechanism, other doors all round the Close opened, too, releasing swarms of black-coated boys who stampeded across the snow towards the Abbey. One boy passed so close that his gown brushed against Smiley's sleeve. Smiley called to him as he ran past:

"What's going on?"

"Sext," shouted the boy in reply, and was gone.

He passed the main entrance to the school and came at once upon the municipal part of the town, a lugubrious nineteenth-century fairyland in local stone, stitched together by a complexity of Gothic chimneys and crenel windows. Here was the town hall, and beside it, with the flag of St. George floating at its masthead, the Carne Constabulary Headquarters, built ninety years ago to withstand the onslaughts of archery and battering rams.

He gave his name to the Duty Sergeant, and asked to see the officer investigating the death of Mrs. Rode. The Sergeant, an elderly, inscrutable man, addressed himself to the telephone with a certain formality, as if he were about to perform a difficult conjuring trick. To Smiley's surprise, he was told that Inspector Rigby would be pleased to see him at once, and a police cadet was summoned to show him the way. He was led at a spanking pace up the wide staircase in the centre of the hall, and in a matter of moments found himself before the Inspector.

He was a very short man, and very broad. He could have been a Celt from the tin mines of Cornwall or the collieries of Wales. His dark grey hair was cut very close; it came to a point in the centre of his brow like a devil's cap. His hands were large and powerful, he had the trunk and stance of a wrestler, but he spoke slowly, with a Dorset burr to his soft voice. Smiley quickly noticed that he had one quality rare among small men: the quality of openness. Though his eyes were dark and bright and the movements of his body swift, he imparted a feeling of honesty and straight dealing.

"Ben Sparrow rang me this morning, sir. I'm very pleased you've come. I believe you've got a letter for me."

Rigby looked at Smiley thoughtfully over his desk, and decided that he liked what he saw. He had got around in the war and had heard a little, just a very little, of the work of George

203

Smiley's Service. If Ben said Smiley was all right, that was good enough for him—or almost. But Ben had said more than that.

"Looks like a frog, dresses like a bookie, and has a brain I'd give my eyes for. Had a very nasty war. Very nasty indeed."

Well, he looked like a frog, right enough. Short and stubby, round spectacles with thick lenses that made his eyes big. And his clothes *were* odd. Expensive, mind, you could see that. But his jacket seemed to drape where there wasn't any room for drape. What did surprise Rigby was his shyness. Rigby had expected someone a little brash, a little too smooth for Carne, whereas Smiley had an earnest formality of manner which appealed to Rigby's conservative taste.

Smiley took the letter from his wallet and put it on the desk, while Rigby extracted an old pair of gold-rimmed spectacles from a battered metal case and adjusted the ends carefully over his ears.

"I don't know if Ben explained," said Smiley, "but this letter was sent to the correspondence section of a small Nonconformist journal to which Mrs. Rode subscribed."

"And Miss Fellowship is the lady who brought you the letter?"

"No; her name is Brimley. She is the editor of the magazine. Fellowship is just a pen-name for the correspondence column."

The brown eyes rested on him for a moment.

"When did she receive this letter?"

"Yesterday, the seventeenth. Thursday's the day they go to press, their busy day. The afternoon mail doesn't get opened till the evening, usually. This was opened about six o'clock, I suppose."

"And she brought it straight to you?"

"Yes."

"Why?"

"She worked for me during the war, in my department. She was reluctant to go straight to the police—I was the only person she could think of who wasn't a policeman," he added stupidly. "Who could help, I mean."

"May I ask what you yourself, sir, do for a living?"

"Nothing much. A little private research on seventeenth-century Germany." It seemed a very silly answer.

Rigby didn't seem bothered.

"What's this earlier letter she talks about?"

Smiley offered him the second envelope, and again the big, square hand received it.

"It appears she won this competition," Smiley explained. "That was her winning entry. I gather she comes from a family which has subscribed to the magazine since its foundation. That's why Miss Brimley was less inclined to regard the letter as nonsense. Not that it follows."

"Not that what follows?"

"I meant that the fact that her family had subscribed to a journal for fifty years does not logically affect the possibility that she was unbalanced."

Rigby nodded, as if he saw the point, but Smiley had an uncomfortable feeling that he did not.

"Ah," said Rigby, with a slow smile. "Women, eh?"

Smiley, completely bewildered, gave a little laugh. Rigby was looking at him thoughtfully.

"Know any of the staff, do you, sir?"

"Only Mr. Terence Fielding. We met at an Oxford dinner some time ago. I thought I'd call round and see him. I knew his brother pretty well."

Rigby appeared to stiffen slightly at the mention of Fielding, but he said nothing, and Smiley went on:

"It was Fielding I rang when Miss Brimley brought me the letter. He told me the news. That was last night."

"I see."

They looked at one another again in silence. Smiley discomfited and slightly comic, Rigby appraising him, wondering how much to say.

"How long are you staying?" he said at last.

"I don't know," Smiley replied. "Miss Brimley wanted to come herself, but she has her paper to run. She attached great importance, you see, to doing all she could for Mrs. Rode, even though she was dead. Because she was a subscriber, I mean. I promised to see that the letter arrived quickly in the right hands. I don't imagine there's much else I can do. I shall probably stay on for a day or two just to have a word with Fielding . . . go to the funeral, I suppose. I've booked in at the Sawley Arms."

"Fine hotel, that."

Rigby put his spectacles carefully back into their case and dropped the case into a drawer.

"Funny place, Carne. There's a big gap between the Town and Gown, as we say; neither side knows nor likes the other. It's fear that does it, fear and ignorance. It makes it hard in a case like this. Oh, I can call on Mr. Fielding and Mr. D'Arcy and they say, 'Good day, Sergeant,' and give me a cup of tea in the kitchen, but I can't get among them. They've got their own community, see, and no one outside it can get in. No gossip in the pubs, no contacts, nothing . . . just cups of tea and bits of seed cake, and being called Sergeant." Rigby laughed suddenly, and Smiley laughed with him in relief. "There's a lot I'd like to ask them, a lot of things; who liked the Rodes and who didn't, whether Mr. Rode's a good teacher and whether his wife fitted in with the others. I've got all the facts I want, but I've got no clothes to hang on them." He looked at Smiley expectantly. There was a very long silence.

"If you want me to help, I'd be delighted," said Smiley at last. "But give me the facts first."

"Stella Rode was murdered between about ten past eleven and quarter to twelve on the night of Wednesday the sixteenth. She must have been struck fifteen to twenty times with a cosh or bit of piping or something. It was a terrible murder . . . terrible. There are marks all over her body. At a guess I would say she came from the drawing room to the front door to answer the bell or something, when she opened the door she was struck down and dragged to the conservatory. The conservatory door was unlocked, see?"

"I see. . . . It's odd that he should have known that, isn't it?"

"The murderer may have been hiding there already: we can't

206

tell from the prints just there. He was wearing boots—Welling-ton boots, size 10½. We would guess from the spacing of the footprints in the garden that he was about six foot tall. When he had got her to the conservatory he must have hit her again and again—mainly on the head. There's a lot of what we call trav-elled blood in the conservatory, that's to say, blood spurted from an open artery. There's no sign of that anywhere else."

"And no sign of it on her husband?"

"I'll come to that later, but the short answer is, no." He paused a moment and continued:

"Now, I said there were footprints, and so there were. The murderer came through the back garden. Where he came from and went to, Heaven alone knows. You see, there are no tracks leading away—not Wellingtons. None at all. Of course, it's pos-sible the outgoing tracks followed the path to the front gate and got lost in all the to-ing and fro-ing later that night. But I don't think we'd have lost them even then." He glanced at Smiley, then went on:

"He left one thing behind him in the conservatory—an old cloth belt, navy blue, from a cheap overcoat by the look of it. We're working on that now."

"Was she . . . robbed or anything?"

"No sign of interference. She was wearing a string of green beads round her neck, and they've gone, and it looks as though he tried to get the rings off her finger, but they were too tight." He paused.

"I need hardly tell you that we've had reports from every corner of the country about tall men in blue overcoats and gum-boots. But none of them had wings as far as I know. Or seven-league boots for jumping from the conservatory to the road."

They paused, while a police cadet brought in tea on a tray. He put it on the desk, looked at Smiley out of the corner of his eye, and decided to let the Inspector pour out. He guided the teapot round so that the handle was towards Rigby and withdrew. Smi-ley was amused by the immaculate condition of the tray cloth; by the matching china and tea-strainer, laid before them by the enormous hands of the cadet. Rigby poured out the tea and they drank for a moment in silence. There was, Smiley reflected, something devastatingly competent about Rigby. The very ordinariness of the man and his room identified him with the society he protected. The nondescript furniture, the wooden filing cupboards, the bare walls, the archaic telephone with its separate earpiece, the brown frieze round the wall and the brown paint on the door, the glistening linoleum and the faint smell of carbolic, the burbling gas-fire, and the calendar from the Prudential— these were the evidence of rectitude and moderation; their austerity gave comfort and reassurance. Rigby continued:

"Rode went back to Fielding's house for the examination papers. Fielding confirms that, of course. He arrived at Fielding's house at about 11:35, near as Fielding can say. He hardly spent any time there at all—just collected his papers at the door—they were in a small writing-case he uses for carrying exercise books. He doesn't remember whether he saw anyone on the road. He thinks a bicycle overtook him, but he can't be sure. If we take Rode's word for it, he walked straight home. When he got there he rang the bell. He was wearing a dinner jacket and so he hadn't got his key with him. His wife was expecting him to ring the bell, you see. That's the devil of it. It was a moonlit night, mind, and snow on the ground, so you could see a mighty long way. He called her, but she didn't answer. Then he saw footprints going round to the side of the house. Not just footprints, but blood marks and the snow all churned up where the body had been dragged to the conservatory. But he didn't know it was blood in the moonlight, it just showed up dark, and Rode said afterwards he thought it was the dirty water from the gutters running over on to the path.

"He followed the prints round until he came to the conservatory. It was darker in there and he fumbled for the light switch, but it didn't work."

"Did he light a match?"

"No, he didn't have any. He's a nonsmoker. His wife didn't approve of smoking. He moved forward from the door. The conservatory walls are mainly glass except for the bottom three feet, but the roof is tiled. The moon was high that night, and not much light got in at all, except through the partition window between the drawing room and the conservatory—but she'd only had the little table light on in the drawing room. So he groped his way forward, talking all the time, calling Stella, his wife. As he went, he tripped over something and nearly fell. He knelt down and felt with his hands, up and down her body. He realised that his hands were covered in blood. He doesn't remember much after that, but there's a senior master living a hundred yards up the road—Mr. D'Arcy his name is, lives with his sister, and he heard him screaming on the road. D'Arcy went out to him. Rode had blood all over his hands and face and seemed to be out of his mind. D'Arcy rang the police and I got there at about one o'clock that morning. I've seen some nasty things in my time, but this is the worst. Blood everywhere. Whoever killed her must have been covered in it. There's an outside tap against the conservatory wall. The tap had been turned on, probably by the murderer to rinse his hands. The boffins have found traces of blood in the snow underneath it. The tap was lagged recently by Rode I gather. . . ."

"And fingerprints?" Smiley asked. "What about them?"

"Mr. Rode's were everywhere. On the floor, the walls and windows, on the body itself. But there were other prints; smudges of blood, little more, made with a gloved hand probably."

"And they were the murderer's?"

"They had been made *before* Rode made his. In some cases Rode's prints were partly superimposed on the glove prints." Smiley was silent for a moment.

"These examination papers he went back for. Were they as important as all that?"

"Yes. I gather they were. Up to a point anyway. The marks had to be handed in to Mr. D'Arcy by midday on Friday."

"But why did he take them to Fielding's in the first place?"

"He didn't. He'd been invigilating exams all afternoon and

the papers were handed in to him at six o'clock. He put them in his little case and had them taken to Fielding's by a boy—head boy in Mr. Fielding's house, name of Perkins. Rode was on Chapel duty last week, so he didn't have time to return home before dinner."

"Where did he change, then?"

"In the Tutors' Robing Room, next to the Common Room. There are facilities there, mainly for games tutors who live some distance from Carne."

"The boy who brought this case to Fielding's house—who was he?"

"I can't tell you much more than I've said. His name is Perkins; he's head of Mr. Fielding's house. Fielding has spoken to him and confirmed Rode's statement. . . . House tutors are very possessive about their boys, you know . . . don't like them to be spoken to by rough policemen." Rigby seemed to be slightly upset.

"I see," Smiley said at last, helplessly, and then: "But how do you explain the letter?"

"It isn't only the letter we've got to explain."

Smiley looked at him sharply.

"What do you mean?"

"I mean," said Rigby slowly, "that Mrs. Rode did several pretty queer things in the last few weeks."

4 ❋
TOWN AND GOWN

"Mrs. Rode was Chapel, of course," Rigby continued, "and we've quite a community in Carne. Truth to tell," he added with a slow smile, "my wife belongs to it.

"A couple of weeks ago our Minister called round to see me. It was in the evening, about half past six, I suppose. I was just thinking of going home, see. He walked in here and sat himself down where you're sitting now. He's a big fellow, the Minister, a fine man; comes from up North, where Mrs. Rode came from. Cardew, his name is."

"The Mr. Cardew in the letter?"

"That's him. He knew all about Mrs. Rode's family before the Rodes ever came here. Glaston's quite a name up North, and Mr. Cardew was very pleased when he heard that Stella Rode was Mr. Glaston's daughter; very pleased indeed. Mrs. Rode came to the Tabernacle regular as clockwork, you can imagine, and they like to see that round here. My wife was pleased as Punch, I can tell you. It was the first time, I suppose, that anyone from the School had done that. Most of the Chapel people

211

here are tradespeople—what we call the locals." Rigby smiled again. "It isn't often that Town and Gown come together, so to speak. Not here."

"How about her husband? Was he Chapel, too?"

"Well, he had been, so she told Mr. Cardew. Mr. Rode was born and bred in Branxome, and all his family were Chapel people. That's how Mr. and Mrs. Rode first met, I gather—at Branxome Tabernacle. Ever been there, have you? A fine church, Branxome, right up on the hill there, overlooking the sea."

Smiley shook his head and Rigby's wide brown eyes rested on him thoughtfully for a moment.

"You should," he said, "you should go and see that. It seems," he continued, "that Mr. Rode turned Church of England when he came to Carne. Even tried to persuade his wife to do the same. They're very strong at the School. I heard that from my wife, as a matter of fact. I never let her gossip as a rule, being a policeman's wife and that, but Mr. Cardew told her that himself."

"I see," said Smiley.

"Well now, Cardew came and saw me. He was all worried and bothered with himself. He didn't know what he should make of it, but he wanted to talk to me as a friend and not as a policeman." Rigby looked sour, "When people say that to me, I always know that they want to talk to me as a policeman. Then he told me his story. Mrs. Rode had called to see him that afternoon. He'd been out visiting a farmer's wife over in Okeford and didn't come home until half past five or thereabouts, so Mrs. Cardew had had to talk to her and hold the fort until the Minister came home. Mrs. Rode was white as a sheet, sitting very still by the fire. As soon as the Minister arrived, Mrs. Cardew left them alone and Stella Rode started talking about her husband."

He paused. "She said Mr. Rode was going to kill her. In the long nights. She seemed to have a kind of fixation about being murdered in the long nights. Cardew didn't take it too seriously at first, but thinking about it afterwards, he decided to let me know."

Smiley looked at him sharply.

"He couldn't make out what she meant. He thought she was out of her mind. He's a down-to-earth man, see, although he's a Minister. I think he was probably a bit too firm with her. He asked her what put this dreadful thought into her head, and she began to weep. Not hysterical, apparently, but just crying quietly to herself. He tried to calm her down, promised to help her any way he could, and asked her again what had given her this idea. She just shook her head, then got up, walked over to the door, still shaking her head in despair. She turned to him, and he thought she was going to say something, but she didn't. She just left."

"How very curious," said Smiley, "that she lied about that in her letter. She went out of her way to say she *hadn't* told Cardew."

Rigby shrugged his great shoulders.

"If you'll pardon me," he said, "I'm in a darned awkward position. The Chief Constable would sooner cut his throat than call in Scotland Yard. He wants an arrest and he wants one quick. We've got enough clues to cover a Christmas tree; footprints, time of the murder, indication of murderer's clothing, and even the weapon itself."

Smiley looked at him in surprise. "You've *found* the weapon, then?"

Rigby hesitated. "Yes, we've found it. There's hardly a soul knows this, sir, and I'll trouble you to remember that. We found it the morning after the murder, four miles north of Carne on the Okeford road, tossed into a ditch. Eighteen inches of what they call coaxial cable. Know what that is, do you? It comes in all sizes, but this piece is about two inches in diameter. It has a copper rod running down the middle and plastic insulation between the rod and the outer cover. There was blood on it: Stella Rode's blood group, and hairs from her head, stuck to the blood. We're keeping that very dark indeed. By the Grace of God, it was found by one of our own men. It pinpoints the line of the murderer's departure."

"There's no doubt, I suppose, that it is the weapon?" Smiley asked lamely.

"We found particles of copper in the wounds on the body."

"It's odd, isn't it," Smiley suggested reflectively, "that the murderer should have carried the weapon so far before getting rid of it? Specially if he was walking. You'd think he'd want to get rid of it as soon as he could."

"It is odd. Very odd. The Okeford road runs beside the canal for half of those four miles; he could have pitched the cable into the canal anywhere along there. We'd never have been the wiser."

"Was the cable old?"

"Not particularly. Just standard type. It could have come from almost anywhere." Rigby hesitated a minute, then burst out:

"Look, sir, this is what I am trying to say. The circumstances of this case demand a certain type of investigation: wide-scale search, detailed laboratory work, mass inquiry. That's what the Chief wants, and he's right. We've no case against the husband at all, and to be frank he's precious little use to us. He seems a bit lost, a bit vague, contradicting himself on little things that don't matter, like the date of his marriage or the name of his doctor. It's shock, of course, I've seen it before. I know all about your letter, sir, and it's damned odd, but if you can tell me how he could have produced Wellington boots out of a hat and got rid of them afterwards, battered his wife to death without leaving more than a few smudges of blood on himself, and got the weapon four miles from the scene of the crime, all within ten minutes of being at Fielding's house, I'll be grateful to you. We're looking for a stranger, six foot tall, wearing newish Dunlop Wellington boots size 10½, leather gloves and an old blue overcoat stained with blood. A man who travels on foot, who was in the area of North Fields between 11:10 and 11:45 on the night of the murder, who left in the direction of Okeford, taking with him one and a half feet of coaxial cable, a string of green beads with an imitation diamond clip, valued at twenty-three and six. We're looking for a maniac, a man who kills for pleasure or the price of a meal." Rigby paused, smiled wistfully, and added, "Who can fly fifty feet through the air? But with information like this how else should we spend our time? What else can we look for? I can't put men on to chasing shadows when there's work like that to be done."

"I understand that."

"But I'm an old policeman, Mr. Smiley, and I like to know what I'm about. I don't like looking for people I can't believe in, and I don't like being cut off from witnesses. I like to meet people and talk to them, nose about here and there, get to know the country. But I can't do that, not at the school. Do you follow me? So we've got to rely on laboratories, tracker dogs, and nationwide searches, but somehow in my bones I don't think it's altogether one of those cases."

"I read in the paper about a woman, a Mad Janic . . ."

"I'm coming to that. Mrs. Rode was a kindly woman, easy to talk to. I always found her so, anyway. Some of the women at Chapel took against her, but you know what women are. It seems she got friendly with this Janie creature. Janie came begging, selling herbs and charms at the back door; you know the kind of thing. She's queer, talks to birds and all that. She lives in a disused Norman chapel over to Pylle. Stella Rode used to give her food and clothes—the poor soul was often as not half-starved. Now Janie's disappeared. She was seen early Wednesday night on the lane towards North Fields and hasn't been seen since. That don't mean a thing. These people come and go in their own way. They'll be all over the neighbourhood for years, then one day they're gone like snow in the fire. They've died in a ditch, maybe, or they've took ill and crept away like a cat. Janie's not the only queer one round here. There's a lot of excitement because we found a spare set of footprints running along the fringe of trees at the far end of the garden. They were a woman's prints by the look of them, and at one point they come quite close to the conservatory. Could be a gypsy or a beggar woman. Could be anything, but I expect it's Janie right enough. I hope to Heaven it was, sir; we could do with an eye-witness, even a mad one."

Smiley stood up. As they shook hands, Rigby said, "Good-bye, sir. Ring me anytime, anytime at all." He scribbled a telephone number on the pad in front of him, tore off the sheet, and gave it to Smiley. "That's my home number." He showed Smiley to the door, seemed to hesitate, then he said, "You're not a Carnian yourself by any chance, are you, sir?"

"Good heavens, no."

Again Rigby hesitated. "Our Chief's a Carnian. Ex-Indian Army. Brigadier Havelock. This is his last year. He's very interested in this case. Doesn't like me messing around the school. Won't have it."

"I see."

"He wants an arrest quickly."

"And outside Carne, I suppose?"

"Good-bye, Mr. Smiley. Don't forget to ring me. Oh, another thing I should have mentioned. That bit of cable . . ."

"Yes?"

"Mr. Rode used a length of the same stuff in a demonstration lecture on elementary electronics. Mislaid it about three weeks ago." Smiley walked slowly back to his hotel.

My dear Brim,

As soon as I arrived I handed your letter over to the CID man in charge of the case—it was Rigby, as Ben had supposed: he looks like a mixture of Humpty-Dumpty and a Cornish elf—very short and broad—and I don't think he's anyone's fool.

To begin at the middle—our letter didn't have quite the effect we expected; Stella Rode evidently told Cardew, the local Baptist Minister, two weeks ago, that her husband was trying to kill her in the long nights, whatever they are. As for the circumstances of the murder—the account in the *Guardian* is substantially correct.

216

In fact, the more Rigby told me, the less likely it became that she was killed by her husband. Almost everything pointed away from him. Quite apart from motive, there is the location of the weapon, the footprints in the snow (which indicate a tall man in Wellingtons), the presence of unidentified glove-prints in the conservatory. Add to that the strongest argument of all: whoever killed her must have been covered in blood—the conservatory was a dreadful sight, Rigby tells me. Of course, there was blood on Rode when he was picked up by his colleague in the lane, but only smears which could have resulted from stumbling over the body in the dark. Incidentally, the footprints only go into the garden and not out.

As things stand at the moment, there is, as Rigby points out, only one interpretation—the murderer was a stranger, a tramp, a madman perhaps, who killed her for pleasure or for her jewellery (which was worthless) and made off along the Okeford road, throwing the weapon into a ditch. (But why carry it four miles—and why not throw it into the canal the other side of the ditch? The Okeford road crosses Okemoor, which is all cross-dyked to prevent flooding.) If this interpretation is correct, then I suppose we attribute Stella's letter and her interview with Cardew to a persecuted mind, or the premonition of death, depending on whether we're superstitious. If that is so, it is the most monstrous coincidence I have ever heard of. Which brings me to my final point.

I rather gathered from what Rigby *didn't* say that his Chief Constable was treading on his tail, urging him to scour the country for tramps in bloodstained blue overcoats (you remember the belt). Rigby, of course, has no alternative but to follow the signs and do as his Chief expects—but he is clearly uneasy about something—either something he hasn't told me, or something he just feels in his bones. I think he was sincere when he asked me to tell him anything I found out about the *School* end—the

Rodes themselves, the way they fitted in, and so on. Carne's monastery walls are still pretty high, he feels . . .

So I'll just sniff around a bit, I think, and see what goes on. I rang Fielding when I got back from the police station and he's asked me to supper tonight. I'll write again as soon as I have anything to tell you.

George.

Having carefully sealed the envelope, pressing down the corners with his thumbs, Smiley locked his door and made his way down the wide marble staircase, treading carefully on the meagre coconut matting that ran down the centre. There was a red wooden letter box in the hall for the use of residents, but Smiley, being a cautious man, avoided it. He walked to the pillar box at the corner of the road, posted his letter, and wondered what to do about lunch. There were, of course, the sandwiches and coffee provided by Miss Brimley. Reluctantly he returned to the hotel. It was full of journalists, and Smiley hated journalists. It was also cold, and he hated the cold. And there was something very familiar about sandwiches in a hotel bedroom.

5 ✺
CAT AND DOG

It was just after seven o'clock that evening when George Smiley climbed the steps which led up to the front door of Mr. Terence Fielding's house. He rang, and was admitted to the hall by a little plump woman in her middle fifties. To his right a log fire burned warmly on a pile of wood ash and above him he was vaguely aware of a minstrel gallery and a mahogany staircase, which rose in a spiral to the top of the house. Most of the light seemed to come from the fire, and Smiley could see that the walls around him were hung with a great number of paintings of various styles and periods, and the chimney-piece was laden with all manner of *objets d'art*. With an involuntary shudder, he noticed that neither the fire nor the pictures quite succeeded in banishing the faint smell of school—of polish bought wholesale, of cocoa and community cooking. Corridors led from the hall, and Smiley observed that the lower part of each wall was painted a dark brown or green according to the inflexible rule of school decorators. From one of these corridors the enormous figure of Mr. Terence Fielding emerged.

He advanced on Smiley, massive and genial, with his splendid mane of grey hair falling anyhow across his forehead and his gown billowing behind him.

"Smiley? Ah! You've met True, have you—Miss Truebody, my housekeeper? Marvellous this snow, isn't it? Pure Bruegel! Seen the boys skating by the Eyot? Marvellous sight! Black suits, coloured scarves, pale sun; all there, isn't it, all there! Bruegel to the life. Marvellous!" He took Smiley's coat and flung it on to a decrepit deal chair with a rush seat which stood in the corner of the hall.

"You like that chair—you recognise it?"

"I don't think I do," Smiley replied in some confusion.

"Ah, you should, you know, you should! Had it made in Provence before the war. Little carpenter I knew. Place it now? Facsimile of Van Gogh's yellow chair; some people recognise it." He led the way down a corridor and into a large comfortable study adorned with Dutch tiles, small pieces of Renaissance sculpture, mysterious bronzes, china dogs, and unglazed vases; and Fielding himself towering magnificent among them.

As senior housemaster of Carne, Fielding wore, in place of the customary academic dress, a wonderful confection of heavy black skirts and legal bib, like a monk in evening dress. All this imparted a suggestion of clerical austerity in noted contrast to the studied flamboyance of his personality. Evidently conscious of this, he sought to punctuate the solemnity of his uniform and give to it a little of his own temperament, by adorning it with flowers carefully chosen from his garden. He had scandalised the tailors of Carne, whose frosted windows carried the insignia of royal households, by having buttonholes let into his gown. These he would fill according to his mood with anything from hibernia to bluebells. This evening he wore a rose, and from its freshness Smiley deduced that he had this minute put it into place, having ordered it specially.

"Sherry wine or Madeira?"

"Thank you; a glass of sherry."

"Tart's drink, Madeira," Fielding called, as he poured from

220

a decanter, "but boys like it. Perhaps that's why. They're frightful flirts." He handed Smiley a glass and added, with a dramatic modification of his voice:

"We're all rather subdued at the moment by this dreadful business. We've never had anything quite like it, you know. Have you seen the evening papers?"

"No, I'm afraid I haven't. But the Sawley Arms is packed with journalists, of course."

"They've really gone to town. They've got the Army out in Hampshire, playing about with mine-detectors. God knows what they expect to find."

"How have the boys taken it?"

"They adore it! My own house has been particularly fortunate, of course, because the Rodes were dining here that night. Some oaf from the police even wanted to question one of my boys."

"Indeed," said Smiley innocently. "What on earth about?"

"Oh, God knows," Fielding replied abruptly, and then, changing the subject, he asked, "You knew my brother well, didn't you? He talked about you, you know."

"Yes, I knew Adrian very well. We were close friends."

"In the war, too?"

"Yes."

"Were you in his crowd, then?"

"What crowd?"

"Steed-Asprey, Jebedee. All those people."

"Yes."

"I never really heard how he died. Did you?"

"No."

"We didn't see much of one another in later years, Adrian and I. Being a fraud, I can't afford to be seen beside the genuine article," Fielding declared, with something of his earlier panache. Smiley was spared the embarrassment of a reply by a quiet knock at the door, and a tall red-haired boy came timidly into the room.

"I've called the Adsum, sir, if you're ready, sir."

221

"Damn," said Fielding, emptying his glass. "Prayers." He turned to Smiley.

"Meet Perkins, my head prefect. Musical genius, but a problem in the schoolroom. That right, Tim? Stay here or come as you like. It only lasts ten minutes."

"Rather less tonight, sir," said Perkins. "It's the Nunc Dimittis."

"Thank God for small mercies," Fielding declared, tugging briefly at his bib, as he led Smiley at a spanking pace out into the corridor and across the hall, with Perkins stalking along behind them. Fielding was speaking all the time without bothering to turn his head:

"I'm glad you've chosen this evening to come. I never entertain on Fridays as a rule because everyone else does, though none of us quite knows what to do about entertaining at the moment. Felix D'Arcy will be coming tonight, but that's hardly entertaining. D'Arcy's a professional. Incidentally, we normally dress in the evening, but it doesn't matter."

Smiley's heart sank. They turned a corner and entered another corridor.

"We have prayers at all hours here. The Master's revived the seven Day Hours for the Offices: Prime, Terce, Sext, and so on. A surfeit during the Half, abstinence during the holidays, that's the system, like games. Useful in the house for roll calls, too." He led the way down yet another corridor, flung open a double door at the end of it, and marched straight into the dining room, his gown filling gracefully behind him. The boys were waiting for him.

"More sherry? What did you think of prayers? They sing quite nicely, don't they? One or two good tenors. We tried some plainsong last Half, quite good, really quite good. D'Arcy will be here soon. He's a frightful toad. Looks like a Sickert model fifty years after—all trousers and collar. However, you're lucky his sister isn't accompanying him. She's worse!"

"What's his subject?" They were back in Fielding's study.

"Subject! I'm afraid we don't have subjects here. None of us has read a word on any subject since we left University." He lowered his voice and added darkly, "That's if we *went* to University. D'Arcy teaches French. D'Arcy is Senior Tutor by election, bachelor by profession, sublimated pansy by inclination . . ." he was standing quite still now, his head thrown back and his right hand stretched out towards Smiley, ". . . and his subject is other people's shortcomings. He is principally, however, self-appointed majordomo of Carne protocol. If you wear a gown on a bicycle, reply incorrectly to an invitation, make a fault in the *placement* of your dinner guests, or speak of a colleague as 'Mister,' D'Arcy will find you out and admonish you."

"What are the duties of Senior Tutor, then?" Smiley asked, just for something to say.

"He's the referee between the classics and the scientists; arranges the timetable and vets the exam results. But principally, poor man, he must reconcile the Arts with the Sciences." He shook his head sagely. "And it takes a better man than D'Arcy to do that. Not, mind you," he added wearily, "that it makes the least difference who wins the extra hour on Friday evenings. Who cares? Not the boys, poor dears, that's certain."

Fielding talked on, at random and always in superlatives, sometimes groping in the air with his hand as if to catch the more elusive metaphors; now of his colleagues with caustic derision, now of boys with compassion if not with understanding; now of the Arts with fervour—and the studied bewilderment of a lonely disciple.

"Carne isn't a school. It's a sanatorium for intellectual lepers. The symptoms began when we came down from University; a gradual putrefaction of our intellectual extremities. From day to day our minds die, our spirits atrophy and rot. We watch the process in one another, hoping to forget it in ourselves." He paused, and looked reflectively at his hands.

"In me the process is complete. You see before you a dead soul, and Carne is the body I live in." Much pleased by this confession, Fielding held out his great arms so that the sleeves of his

223

gown resembled the wings of a giant bat; "the Vampire of Carne," he declared, bowing deeply. *"Alcoholique et poète!"* A bellow of laughter followed this display.

Smiley was fascinated by Fielding, by his size, his voice, the wanton inconstancy of his temperament, by his whole big-screen style; he found himself attracted and repelled by this succession of contradictory poses; he wondered whether he was supposed to take part in the performance, but Fielding seemed so dazzled by the footlights that he was indifferent to the audience behind them. The more Smiley watched, the more elusive seemed the character he was trying to comprehend: changeful but sterile, daring but fugitive; colourful, un-bounded, ingenuous, yet deceitful and perverse. Smiley began to wish he could acquire the material facts of Fielding—his means, his ambitions and disappointments.

His reverie was interrupted by Miss Truebody. Felix D'Arcy had arrived.

No candles, and a cold supper admirably done by Miss True-body. Not claret, but hock, passed round like port. And at last, at long last, Fielding mentioned Stella Rode.

They had been talking rather dutifully of the Arts and the Sciences. This would have been dull (for it was uninformed) had not D'Arcy constantly been goaded by Fielding, who seemed anxious to exhibit D'Arcy in his worst light. D'Arcy's judgements of people and problems were largely coloured by what he considered "seemly" (a favourite word) and by an ef-feminate malice towards his colleagues. After a while Fielding asked who was replacing Rode during his absence, to which D'Arcy said, "No one," and added unctuously:

"It was a terrible shock to the community, this affair."

"Nonsense," Fielding retorted. "Boys love disaster. The further we are from death the more attractive it seems. They find the whole affair most exhilarating."

"The publicity has been most unseemly," said D'Arcy,

"most. I think that has been prominent in the minds of many of us in the Common Room." He turned to Smiley:

"The press, you know, is a constant worry here. In the past it could never have happened. Formerly our great families and institutions were not subjected to this intrusion. No, indeed not. But today all that is changed. Many of us are compelled to subscribe to the cheaper newspapers for this very reason. One Sunday newspaper mentioned no fewer than four of Hecht's old boys in one edition. All of them in an unseemly context, I may say. And of course such papers never fail to mention that the boy is a Carnian. You know, I suppose, that we have the young Prince here. (I myself have the honour to supervise his French studies.) The young Sawley is also at Carne. The activity of the press during his parents' divorce suit was deplorable. Quite deplorable. The Master wrote to the Press Council, you know. I drafted the letter myself. But on this tragic occasion they have excelled themselves. We even had the press at Compline last night, you know, waiting for the Special Prayer. They occupied the whole of the two rear pews on the west side. Hecht was doing Chapel Duty and tried to have them removed." He paused, raised his eyebrows in gentle reproach and smiled. "He had no business to, of course, but that never stopped the good Hecht." He turned to Smiley, "One of our *athletic* brethren," he explained.

"Stella was too common for you, Felix, wasn't she?"

"Not at all," said D'Arcy quickly. "I would not have you say that of me, Terence. I am by no means discriminatory in the matter of class; merely of manners. I grant you, in that particular field, I found her wanting."

"In many ways she was just what we needed," Fielding continued, addressing Smiley and ignoring D'Arcy. "She was everything we're forced to ignore—she was red-brick, council estates, new towns, the very antithesis of Carne!" He turned suddenly to D'Arcy and said, "But to you, Felix, she was just bad form."

"Not at all; merely unsuitable."

Fielding turned to Smiley in despair.

"Look," he said. "We talk academic here, you know, wear academic dress and hold high table dinners in the Common Room; we have long graces in Latin that none of us can translate. We go to the Abbey and the wives sit in the hencoop in their awful hats. But it's a charade. It means nothing."

D'Arcy smiled wanly.

"I cannot believe, my dear Terence, that anyone who keeps such an excellent table as yourself can have so low an opinion of the refinements of social conduct." He looked to Smiley for support and Smiley dutifully echoed the compliment. "Besides, we know Terence of old at Carne. I am afraid we are accustomed to his roar."

"I know why you disliked that woman, Felix. She was honest, and Carne has no defence against that kind of honesty."

D'Arcy suddenly became very angry indeed.

"Terence, I will not have you say this. I simply will not have it. I feel I have a certain duty at Carne, as indeed we all have, to restore and maintain those standards of behaviour which suffered so sadly in the war. I am sensible that this determination has made me on more than one occasion unpopular. But such comment or advice as I offer is never—I beg you to notice this—is *never* directed against personalities, only against behaviour, against unseemly lapses in conduct. I will acknowledge that more than once I was compelled to address Rode on the subject of his wife's conduct. That is a matter quite divorced from personalities, Terence. I will not have it said that I disliked Mrs. Rode. Such a suggestion would be disagreeable at all times, but under the present tragic circumstances it is deplorable. Mrs. Rode's own . . . background and education did not naturally prepare her for our ways; that is quite a different matter. It does, however, illustrate the point that I wish to emphasise, Terence: it was a question of enlightenment, not of criticism. Do I make myself clear?"

"Abundantly," Fielding answered dryly.

"Did the other wives like her?" Smiley ventured.

226

"Not entirely," D'Arcy replied crisply.

"The wives! My God!" Fielding groaned, putting his hand to his brow. There was a pause.

"Her clothes, I believe, were a source of distress to some of them. She also frequented the public laundry. This, too, would not make a favourable impression. I should add that she did not attend our church. . . ."

"Did she have any close friends among the wives?" Smiley persisted.

"I believe young Mrs. Snow took to her."

"And you say she was dining here the night she was murdered?"

"Yes," said Fielding quietly, "Wednesday. And it was Felix and his sister who took in poor Rode afterwards. . . ." He glanced at D'Arcy.

"Yes, indeed," said D'Arcy abruptly. His eyes were on Fielding, and it seemed to Smiley that something had passed between them. "We shall never forget, never. . . . Terence, if I may talk shop for just one moment, Perkins's construe is abysmal; I declare I have never seen work like it. Is he unwell? His mother is a most cultured woman, a cousin of the Samfords, I am told."

Smiley looked at him and wondered. His dinner-jacket was faded, green with age. Smiley could almost hear him saying it had belonged to his grandfather. The skin of his face was so un-lined that he somehow suggested fatness without being fat. His voice was pitched on one insinuating note, and he smiled all the time, whether he was speaking or not. The smile never left his smooth face, it was worked into the malleable fabric of his flesh, stretching his lips across his perfect teeth and opening the corners of his red mouth, so that it seemed to be held in place by the invisible fingers of his dentist. Yet D'Arcy's face was far from unexpressive; every mark showed. The smallest movement of his mouth or nose, the quickest glance or frown, were there to read and interpret. And he wanted to change the subject. Not away from Stella Rode (for he returned to discussing her himself a moment later), but away from the particular evening on which

227

she died, away from the precise narration of events. And what was more, there was not a doubt in Smiley's mind that Fielding had seen it too, that in that look which passed between them was a pact of fear, a warning perhaps, so that from that moment Fielding's manner changed, he grew sullen and preoccupied, in a way that puzzled Smiley long afterwards.

D'Arcy turned to Smiley and addressed him with cloying intimacy.

"*Do* forgive my deplorable descent into Carne gossip. You find us a little cut off, here, do you not? We are often held to be cut off, I know. Carne is a 'Snob School,' that is the cry. You may read it every day in the gutter press. And yet, despite the claims of the *avant-garde*," he said, glancing slyly at Fielding, "I may say that *no one* could be less of a snob than Felix D'Arcy." Smiley noticed his hair. It was very fine and ginger, growing from the top and leaving his pink neck bare.

"Take poor Rode, for instance. I certainly don't hold Rode's background against him in any way, poor fellow. The grammar schools do a splendid job, I am sure. Besides, he settled down here very well. I told the Master so. I said to him that Rode had settled down well; he does Chapel duty quite admirably—that was the very point I made. I hope I have played my part, what is more, in helping him to fit in. With careful instruction, such people can, as I said to the Master, learn our customs and even our manners; and the Master agreed."

Smiley's glass was empty and D'Arcy, without consulting Fielding, filled it for him from the decanter. His hands were polished and hairless, like the hands of a girl.

"But," he continued, "I must be honest. Mrs. Rode did not adapt herself so willingly to our ways." Still smiling, he sipped delicately from his glass. He wants to put the record straight, thought Smiley.

"She would never really have fitted in at Carne; that is my opinion—though I am sure I never voiced it while she was alive. Her background was against her. The fault was not hers—it was

228

her background, which, as I say, was unfortunate. Indeed, if we may speak frankly and in confidence, I have reason to believe it was her past that brought about her death."

"Why do you say that?" asked Smiley quickly, and D'Arcy replied with a glance at Fielding, "It appears she was expecting to be attacked."

"My sister is devoted to dogs," D'Arcy continued. "You may know that already perhaps. King Charles spaniels are her forte. She took a first at the North Dorset last year and was commended at Cruft's shortly afterwards for her 'Queen of Carne.' She sells to America, you know. I dare say there are few people in the country with Dorothy's knowledge of the breed. The Master's wife found occasion to say the very same thing a week ago. Well, the Rodes were our neighbours, as you know, and Dorothy is not a person to neglect her neighbourly duties. Where duty is concerned, you will not find her discriminatory, I assure you. The Rodes also had a dog, a large mongrel, quite an intelligent animal, which they brought with them. (I have little idea where they came from, but that is another matter.) They appeared quite devoted to the dog, and I have no doubt they were. Rode took it with him to watch the football until I had occasion to advise him against it. The practice was giving rise to unseemly humour among the boys. I have found the same thing myself when exercising Dorothy's spaniels.

"I shall come to the point presently. Dorothy uses a vet called Harriman, a superior type of person who lives over toward Sturminster. A fortnight ago she sent for him. 'Queen of Carne' was coughing badly and Dorothy asked Harriman to come over. A bitch of her quality is not to be taken lightly, I assure you."

Fielding groaned, and D'Arcy continued, oblivious:

"I happened to be at home, and Harriman stayed for a cup of coffee. He is, as I say, a superior type of person. Harriman made some reference to the Rodes' dog and then the truth came out:

Mrs. Rode had had the dog destroyed the previous day. She said it had bitten the postman. Some long and confused story; the Post Office would sue, the police had been round, and I don't know what else. And, anyway, she said, the dog couldn't really protect, it could only warn. She had said so to Harriman, 'It wouldn't do any good.'"

"Wasn't she upset about losing the dog?" asked Smiley.

"Oh, indeed, yes. Harriman said she was in tears when she arrived. Mrs. Harriman had to give her a cup of tea. They suggested she should give the dog another chance, put it in kennels for a while, but she was adamant, quite adamant. Harriman was most perplexed. So was his wife. When they discussed it afterwards they agreed that Mrs. Rode's behaviour had not been quite normal. Not normal at all, in fact. Another curious fact was the condition of the dog: it had been maltreated, seriously so. Its back was marked as if from beatings."

"Did Harriman follow up this remark she made? About not doing any good? What did Harriman make of it?" Smiley was watching D'Arcy intently.

"She repeated it to Mrs. Harriman, but she wouldn't explain it. However, I think the explanation is obvious enough."

"Oh?" said Fielding.

D'Arcy put his head to one side and plucked coyly at the lobe of his ear.

"We all have a little of the detective in us," he said. "Dorothy and I talked it over after the—death. We decided that Stella Rode had formed some unsavoury association before coming to Carne, which had recently been revived . . . possibly against her will. Some violent ruffian—an old admirer—who would resent the improvement in her station."

"How badly was the postman bitten by the dog?" Smiley asked. D'Arcy turned to him again.

"That is the extraordinary thing. That is the very crux of the story, my dear fellow: the postman hadn't been bitten at all. Dorothy inquired. Her whole story was an absolute string of lies from beginning to end."

. . .

They rose from the table and made their way to Fielding's study, where Miss Truebody had put the coffee. The conversation continued to wander back and forth over Wednesday's tragedy. D'Arcy was obsessed with the indelicacy of it all—the persistence of journalists, the insensitivity of the police, the uncertainty of Mrs. Rode's origin, the misfortune of her husband. Fielding was still oddly silent, sunk in his own thoughts, from which he occasionally emerged to glance at D'Arcy with a look of hostility. At exactly a quarter to eleven D'Arcy pronounced himself tired, and the three of them went into the great hall, where Miss Truebody produced a coat for Smiley and a coat and muffler and cap for D'Arcy. Fielding accepted D'Arcy's thanks with a sullen nod. He turned to Smiley:

"That business you rang me about. What was it exactly?"

"Oh—a letter from Mrs. Rode just before she was murdered," said Smiley vaguely, "the police are handling it now, but they do not regard it as . . . significant. Not significant at all. She seems to have had a sort of"—he gave an embarrassed grin—"persecution complex. Is that the expression? However, we might discuss it some time. You must dine with me at the Sawley before I go back. Do you come to London at all? We might meet in London, perhaps, at the end of the Half."

D'Arcy was standing in the doorway, looking at the new fall of snow which lay white and perfect on the pavement before him. "Ah," he said, with a little knowing laugh, "the long nights, eh, Terence, the long nights."

6 ❋

HOLLY FOR THE DEVIL

"**W**hat are the long nights?" Smiley asked, as he and D'Arcy walked briskly away from Fielding's house through the new snow towards the Abbey Close.

"We have a proverb that it always snows at Carne in the long nights. That is the traditional term here for the nights of Lent," D'Arcy replied. "Before the Reformation the monks of the Abbey kept a vigil during Lent between the Offices of Compline and Lauds. You may know that already perhaps. As there is no longer a religious order attached to the Abbey, the custom has fallen into disuse. We continue to observe it, however, by the saying of Compline during Lent. Compline was the last of the Canonical Day Hours and was said before retiring for the night. The Master, who has a great respect for traditions of this kind, has reintroduced the old words for our devotions. Prime was the dawn Office, as you are no doubt aware. Terce was at the third hour of daylight—that is to say at 9:00 A.M. Thus we no longer refer to Morning Prayer, but to Terce. I find it delightful. Similarly, during Advent and Lent we say Sext at midday in the Abbey."

"Are all these services compulsory?"

"Of course. Otherwise it would be necessary to make arrangements for those boys who did not attend. That is not desirable. Besides, you forget that Carne is a religious foundation."

It was a beautiful night. As they crossed the Close, Smiley looked up at the tower. It seemed smaller and more peaceful in the moonlight. The whiteness of the new snow lit the very sky itself; the whole Abbey was so sharply visible against it that even the mutilated images of saints were clear in every sad detail of their defacement, wretched figures, their purpose lost, with no eyes to see the changing world.

They reached the crossroads to the south of the Abbey.

"The parting of the ways, I fear," said D'Arcy, extending his hand.

"It's a beautiful night," Smiley replied quickly, "let me come with you as far as your house."

"Gladly," said D'Arcy dryly.

They turned down North Fields Lane. A high stone wall ran along one side; and on the other the great expanse of playing fields, twenty or more rugby pitches, bordered the road for over half a mile. They walked this distance in silence, until D'Arcy stopped and pointed with his stick past Smiley towards a small house on the edge of the playing fields.

"That's North Fields, the Rodes' house. It used to belong to the head groundsman, but the school added a wing a few years ago, and now it's a staff house. My own house is rather larger, and lies farther up the road. Happily, I am fond of walking."

"Was it along here that you found Stanley Rode that night?"

There was a pause, then D'Arcy said: "It was nearer to my house, about a quarter of a mile farther on. He was in a terrible condition, poor fellow, terrible. I am myself unable to bear the sight of blood. If I had known how he would look when I brought him into the house, I do not think I could have done it. Mercifully, my sister Dorothy is a most competent woman."

They walked on in silence, until Smiley said: "From what

233

you were saying at dinner, the Rodes were a very ill-assorted couple."

"Precisely. If her death had happened any other way, I would describe it as providential: a blessed release for Rode. She was a thoroughly mischievous woman, Smiley, who made it her business to hold her husband up to ridicule. I believe it was intentional. Others do not. I do, and I have my reasons. She took pleasure in deriding her husband."

"And Carne too, no doubt."

"Just so. This is a critical moment in Carne's development. Many public schools have conceded to the vulgar clamour for change—change at any price. Carne, I am pleased to say, has not joined these Gadarene swine. That makes it more important than ever that we protect ourselves from within as well as from without." He spoke with surprising vehemence.

"But was she really such a problem? Surely her husband could have spoken to her?"

"I never encouraged him to do so, I assure you. It is not my practice to interfere between man and wife."

They reached D'Arcy's house. A high laurel hedge entirely concealed the house from the road, except for two multiple chimneystacks which were visible over the top of it, confirming Smiley's impression that the house was large and Victorian.

"I am not ashamed of the Victorian taste," said D'Arcy as he slowly opened the gate; "but then, I am afraid we are not close to the modern idiom at Carne. This house used to be the rectory for North Fields Church, but the church is now served by a priest-in-charge from the Abbey. The vicarage is still within the school's gift, and I was fortunate enough to receive it. Good night. You must come for sherry before you go. Do you stay long?"

"I doubt it," Smiley replied, "but I am sure you have enough worries at the moment."

"What do you mean?" D'Arcy said sharply.

"The press, the police, and all the attendant fuss."

"Ah yes, just so. Quite so. Nevertheless, our community life must continue. We always have a small party in the middle of the

234

Half, and I feel it is particularly important that we should do so on this occasion. I will send a note to the Sawley tomorrow. My sister would be charmed. Good night." He clanged the gate to, and the sound was greeted by the frantic barking of dogs from somewhere behind the house. A window opened and a harsh female voice called:

"Is that you, Felix?"

"Yes, Dorothy."

"Why do you have to make such a bloody noise? You've woken those dogs again." The window closed with a significant thud, and D'Arcy, without so much as a glance in Smiley's direction, disappeared quickly into the shadow of the house.

Smiley set off along the road again, back towards the town. After walking for about ten minutes he stopped and looked again towards the Rodes' house a hundred yards across the playing fields. It lay in the shadow of a small coppice of fir trees, dark and secret against the white fields. A narrow lane led towards the house; there was a brick pillar-box on one corner and a small oak signpost, quite new, pointed along the lane, which must, he decided, lead to the village of Pylle. The legend upon the sign was obscured by a film of snow, and Smiley brushed it away with his hand, so that he could read the words "North Fields," done in a contrived suburban Gothic script which must have caused D'Arcy considerable discomfort. The snow in the lane was untrodden; obviously more had fallen recently. There could not be much traffic between Pylle and Carne. Glancing quickly up and down the main road he began making his way along the lane. The hedge rose high on either side, and soon Smiley could see nothing but the pale sky above him and the straggling willow wands reaching towards it. Once he thought he heard the sound of a footstep, close behind him, but when he stopped he heard nothing but the furtive rustle of the laden hedges. He grew more conscious of the cold: it seemed to hang in the still damp of the sunken road, to clutch and hold him like the chill air of an empty house. Soon the hedge on his

235

left gave way to a sparse line of trees, which Smiley judged to belong to the coppice he had seen from the road. The snow beneath the trees was patchy, and the bare ground looked suddenly ugly and torn. The lane took him in a gradual curve to the left and quite suddenly the house stood before him, gaunt and craggy in the moonlight. The walls were brick and flint, half obscured by the mass of ivy which grew in profusion across them, tumbling over the porch in a tangled mane.

He glanced towards the garden. The coppice which bordered the lane encroached almost as far as the corner of the house, and extended to the far end of the lawn, screening the house from the playing fields. The murderer had reached the house by a path which led across the lawn and through the trees to the lane at the farthest end of the garden. Looking carefully at the snow on the lawn, he was able to discern the course of the path. The white glazed door to the left of the house must lead to the conservatory . . . And suddenly he knew he was afraid—afraid of the house, afraid of the sprawling dark garden. The knowledge came to him like an awareness of pain. The ivy walls seemed to reach forward and hold him, like an old woman cosseting an unwilling child. The house was large, yet dingy, holding to itself unearthly shapes, black and oily in the sudden contrasts of moonlight. Fascinated despite his fear, he moved towards it. The shadows broke and reformed, darting swiftly and becoming still, hiding in the abundant ivy, or merging with the black windows.

He observed in alarm the first involuntary movement of panic. He was afraid, then suddenly the senses joined in one concerted cry of terror, where sight and sound and touch could no longer be distinguished in the frenzy of his brain. He turned round and ran back to the gate. As he did so, he looked over his shoulder towards the house.

A woman was standing in the path, looking at him, and behind her the conservatory door swung slowly on its hinges.

For a second she stood quite still, then turned and ran back towards the conservatory. Forgetting his fear, Smiley followed.

236

As he reached the corner of the house he saw to his astonishment that she was standing at the door, rocking it gently back and forth in a thoughtful, leisurely way, like a child. She had her back to Smiley, until suddenly she turned to him and spoke, with a soft Dorset drawl, and the childish lilt of a simpleton:

"I thought you was the Devil, Mister, but you'm got no wings."

Smiley hesitated. If he moved forward, she might take fright again and run. He looked at her across the snow, trying to make her out. She seemed to be wearing a bonnet or shawl over her head, and a dark cape over her shoulders. In her hand she held a sprig of leaves, and these she gently waved back and forth as she spoke to him.

"But you'm carn't do nothin', Mister, 'cos I got the holly fer to hold yer. So you do bide there, Mister, for little Jane can hold yer." She shook the leaves vehemently towards him and began laughing softly. She still had one hand upon the door, and as she spoke her head lolled to one side.

"You bide away from little Jane, Mister, however pretty she'm do be."

"Yes, Jane," said Smiley softly, "you're a very pretty girl, I can see that; and that's a pretty cape you're wearing, Jane."

Evidently pleased with this, she clutched the lapels of her cape and turned slowly round, in a child's parody of a fine lady.

As she turned, Smiley saw the two empty sleeves of an overcoat swinging at her sides.

"There's some do laugh at Janie," she said, a note of petulance in her voice, "but there's not many seen the Devil fly, Mister. But Janie seed 'im, Janie seed 'im. Silver wings like fishes 'e done 'ad, Janie saw."

"Where did you find that coat, Janie?"

She put her hands together and shook her head slowly from side to side.

"He'm a bad one. Ooh, he'm a bad one, Mister," and she laughed softly. "I seed 'im flying, riding on the wind," she

237

laughed again, "and the moon be'ind 'im, lightin' up the way! They'm close as sisters, moon and Devil."

On an impulse Smiley seized a handful of ivy from the side of the house and held it out to her, moving slowly forward as he did so.

"Do you like flowers, Janie? Here are flowers for Janie; pretty flowers for pretty Janie." He had nearly reached her when with remarkable speed she ran across the lawn, disappeared into the trees, and ran off down the lane. Smiley let her go. He was drenched in sweat.

As soon as he reached the hotel, he telephoned Detective Inspector Rigby.

7 ✤
KING ARTHUR'S CHURCH

The coffee lounge of the Sawley Arms resembles nothing so much as the Tropical Plants Pavilion at Kew Gardens. Built in an age when cactus was the most fashionable of plants and bamboo its indispensable companion, the lounge was conceived as the architectural image of a jungle clearing. Steel pillars, fashioned in segments like the trunk of a palm tree, supported a high glass roof whose regal dome replaced the African sky. Enormous urns of bronze or green-glazed earthenware contained all that was elegant and prolific in the cactus world, and between them very old residents could relax on sofas of spindly bamboo, sipping warm coffee and reliving the discomforts of safari.

Smiley's efforts to obtain a bottle of whisky and a syphon of soda at half past eleven at night were not immediately rewarded. It seemed that, like carrion from the carcass, the journalists had gone. The only sign of life in the hotel was the night porter, who treated his request with remote disapproval and advised him to go to bed. Smiley, by no means naturally persistent, discovered a half-crown in his overcoat pocket and thrust it a little irritably into the old man's hand. The result, though not magical, was effective, and by the time Rigby had made his way to the hotel, Smiley was seated in front of a bright gas fire in the coffee lounge with glasses and a whisky bottle before him.

Smiley retold his experiences of the evening with careful accuracy.

"It was the coat that caught my eye. It was a heavy overcoat like a man's," he concluded. "I remembered the blue belt and . . ." He left the sentence unfinished. Rigby nodded, got up, and walked briskly across the lounge and through the swing doors to the porter's desk. Ten minutes later, he returned.

"I think we'd better go and pull her in," he said simply. "I've sent for a car."

"We?" asked Smiley.

"Yes, if you wouldn't mind. What's the matter? Are you frightened?"

"Yes," he replied. "Yes, I am."

The village of Pylle lies to the south of North Fields, upon a high spur which rises steeply from the flat, damp pastures of the Carne valley. It consists of a handful of stone cottages and a small inn where you may drink beer in the landlord's parlour. Seen from Carne playing fields, the village could easily be mistaken for an outcrop of rock upon a tor, for the hill on which it stands appears conical from the northern side. Local historians claim that Pylle is the oldest settlement in Dorset, that its name is Anglo-Saxon for harbour, and that it served the Romans as a port when all the lowlands around were covered by the sea. They will tell you, too, that King Arthur rested there after seven months at sea, and paid homage to Saint Andrew, the patron saint of sailors, on the site of Pylle Church, where he burned a candle for each month he had spent afloat; and that in the church, built to commemorate his visit and standing to this day lonely and untended on the hillside, there is a bronze coin as

240

witness to his visit—the very one King Arthur gave to the verger before he set sail again for the Isle of Avalon.

Inspector William Rigby, himself a keen local historian, gave Smiley a somewhat terse précis of Pylle's legendary past as he drove cautiously along the snow-covered lanes.

"These small, out-of-the-way villages are pretty strange places," he concluded. "Often only three or four families, all so inbred you can no more sort them out than a barnful of cats. That's where your village idiots come from. They call it the Devil's Mark; I call it incest. They hate to have them in the village, you know—they'll drive them away at any price, like trying to wash away their shame, if you follow me."

"I follow you."

"This Jane's the religious sort. There's one or two of them turn that way. The villagers at Pylle are all Chapel now, see, so there's been no use for King Arthur's Church since Wesley. It's empty, falling to bits. There's a few from the valley go up to see it, for its history, like, but no one cares for it, or didn't, not till Janie moved in."

"Moved in?"

"Yes. She's taken to cleaning the church out night and day, bringing in wildflowers and such. That's why they say she's a witch."

They passed Rode's house in silence and after turning a sharp bend began climbing the long steep hill that led to Pylle village. The snow in the lane was untouched, and apart from occasional skidding they progressed without difficulty. The lower slopes of the hill were wooded, and the lane dark, until suddenly they emerged to find themselves on a smooth plateau, where a savage wind blew the fine snow like smoke across the fields, whipping it against the car. The snow had risen in drifts to one side of the lane, and the going became increasingly difficult.

Finally Rigby stopped the car and said:

"We'll walk from here, sir, if you don't mind."

"How far is it?"

"Short and sour, I'd say. That's the village straight ahead."

Through the windscreen, Smiley could discern behind the drifting veils of blown snow two low buildings about a quarter of a mile away. As he looked, a tall, muffled figure advanced towards them along the lane.

"That's Ted Mundy," said Rigby with satisfaction, "I told him to be here. He's the sergeant from Okeford." He leaned out of the car window and called merrily:

"Hullo, Ted there, you old buzzard, how be?" Rigby opened the back door of the car and the sergeant climbed in. Smiley and Mundy were briefly introduced.

"There's a light in the church," said Mundy, "but I don't know whether Janie's there. I can't ask no one in the village, see, or I'd have the whole lot round me. They thought she'd gone for good."

"Does she sleep there then, Ted? She got a bed there or something?" Rigby asked, and Smiley noticed with pleasure that his Dorset accent was more pronounced when he spoke to Mundy.

"So they say, Bill. I couldn't find no bed when I looked in there Saturday. But I tell you an odd thing, Bill. It seems Mrs. Rode used to come up here sometimes, to the chapel, to see Janie."

"I heard about that," said Rigby shortly. "Now which way's the church, Ted?"

"Over the hill," said Mundy. "Outside the village, in a paddock." He turned to Smiley. "That's quite common round here, sir, as I expect you know." Mundy spoke very slowly, choosing his words. "You see, when they had the plague they left their dead in the villages and moved away; not far though, on account of their land and the church. Terrible it was, terrible." Somehow Mundy managed to imply that the Black Death was a fairly recent disaster in those parts, if not actually within living memory.

They got out of the car, forcing the doors against the strong wind, and made their way towards the village, Mundy leading and Smiley in third place. The driven snow, fine and hard, stung

242

their faces. It was an unearthly walk, high on that white hill on such a night. The curve of the bleak hill's crest and the moaning of the wind, the snow cloud which sped across the moon, the dismal, unlit cottages so cautiously passed, belonged to another corner of the world.

Mundy led them sharply to the left, and Smiley guessed that by avoiding the centre of the village he hoped to escape the notice of its inhabitants. After about twenty minutes' walking, often through deep snow, they found themselves following a low hedge between two fields. In the furthest corner of the right-hand field they saw a pale light glimmering across the snow, so pale that at first Smiley had to look away from it, then run his eyes back along the line of that distant hedge to make sure he was not deceived. Rigby stopped, beckoning to the others.

"I'll take over now," he said. He turned to Smiley. "I'd be obliged, sir, if you'd stand off a little. If there's any trouble we don't want you mixed up in it, do we?"

"Of course."

"Ted Mundy, you come up by me."

They followed the hedge until they came to a stile. Through the gap in the hedge they saw the church clearly now, a low building more like a tithe barn than a church. At one end a pale glow, like the uncertain light of a candle, shone dimly through the leaded windows.

"She's there," said Mundy, under his breath, as he and Rigby moved forward, Smiley following some distance behind.

They were crossing the field now, Rigby leading, and the church drawing ever closer. New sounds disturbed the moaning of the storm: the parched creak of a door, the mutter of a crumbling roof, the incessant sigh of wind upon a dying house. The two men in front of Smiley had stopped, almost in the shadow of the church wall, and were whispering together. Then Mundy walked quietly away, disappearing round the corner of the church. Rigby waited a moment, then approached the narrow entrance in the rear wall and pushed the door.

It opened slowly, creaking painfully on its hinges. Then he

disappeared into the church. Smiley was waiting outside when suddenly above all the sounds of night he heard a scream, so taut and shrill and clear that it seemed to have no source, but to ride everywhere upon the wind, to mount the ravaged sky on wings; and Smiley had a vision of Mad Janie as he had seen her earlier that night, and he heard again in her demented cry the dreadful note of madness. For a moment he waited. The echo died. Then slowly, terrified, he walked through the snow to the open doorway.

Two candles and an oil lamp on the bare altar shed a dim light over the tiny chapel. In front of the altar, on the sanctuary step, sat Jane, looking vaguely towards them. Her vacuous face was daubed with stains of green and blue, her filthy clothes were threaded with sprigs of evergreen, and all about her on the floor were the bodies of small animals and birds.

The pews were similarly decorated with dead creatures of all kinds; and on the altar, broken twigs and little heaps of holly leaves. Between the candles stood a crudely fashioned cross. Stepping forward past Rigby, Smiley walked quickly down the aisle, past the lolling figure of Jane, until he stood before the altar. For a moment he hesitated, then turned and called softly to Rigby.

On the cross, draped over its three ends like a crude diadem, was a string of green beads.

8 ❋

FLOWERS FOR STELLA

He woke with the echo of her scream in his ears. He had meant to sleep late, but his watch said half past seven. He put on his bedside lamp, for it was still half-dark, and peered owlishly round the room. There were his trousers, flung over the chair, the legs still sodden from the snow. There were his shoes; he'd have to buy another pair. And there beside him were the notes he had made early that morning before going to sleep, transcriptions from memory of some of Mad Jane's monologue on the journey back to Carne, a journey he would never forget. Mundy had sat with her in the back. She spoke to herself as a child does, asking questions and then in the patient tones of an adult for whom the reply is self-evident, providing the answer.

One obsession seemed to fill her mind: she had seen the devil. She had seen him flying on the wind, his silver wings stretched out behind him. Sometimes the recollection amused her, sometimes inflated her with a sense of her own importance or beauty, and sometimes it terrified her, so that she moaned and

245

wept and begged him to go away. Then Mundy would speak kindly to her, and try to calm her. Smiley wondered whether policemen grew accustomed to the squalor of such things, to clothes that were no more than stinking rags wound round wretched limbs, to puling imbeciles who clutched and screamed and wept. She must have been living on the run for nights on end, finding her food in the fields and dustbins since the night of the murder. . . . What had she done that night? What had she seen? Had she killed Stella Rode? Had she seen the murderer, and fancied him to be the devil flying on the wind? Why should she think that? If Janie did not kill Stella Rode, what had she seen that so frightened her that for three long winter nights she prowled in terror like an animal in the forest? Had the devil within taken hold of Janie and given power to her arm as she struck down Stella? Was that the devil who rode upon the wind?

But the beads and the coat and the footprints which were not hers—what of them? He lay there thinking, and achieving nothing. At last it was time to get up: it was the morning of the funeral.

As he was getting out of bed, the telephone rang. It was Rigby. His voice sounded strained and urgent. "I want to see you," he said. "Can you call round?"

"Before or after the funeral?"

"Before, if possible. What about now?"

"I'll be there in ten minutes."

Rigby looked, for the first time since Smiley had met him, tired and worried.

"It's Mad Janie," he said. "The Chief thinks we should charge her."

"What for?"

"Murder," Rigby replied crisply, pushing a thin file across the table. "The old fool's made a statement . . . a sort of confession."

They sat in silence while Smiley read the extraordinary statement. It was signed with Mad Janie's mark—J.L.—drawn in a childish hand in letters an inch high. The constable who had taken it down had begun by trying to condense and simplify her account, but by the end of the first page he had obviously despaired. At last Smiley came to the description of the murder:

"So I tells my darling, I tells her: 'You are a naughty creature to go with the devil,' but her did not hearken, see, and I took angry with her, but she paid no call. I can't abide them as go with devils in the night, and I told her. She ought to have had holly, mister, there's the truth. I told her, mister, but she never would hearken, and that's all Janie's saying, but she drove the devil off, Janie did, and there's one will thank me, that's my darling and I took her jewels for the saints I did, to pretty out the church, and a coat for to keep me warm."

Rigby watched him as he slowly replaced the statement on the desk.

"Well, what do you think of it?"

Smiley hesitated. "It's pretty good nonsense as it stands," he replied at last.

"Of course it is," said Rigby, with something like contempt. "She saw something, Lord knows what, when she was out on the prowl; stealing, I shouldn't wonder. She may have robbed the body, or else she picked up the beads where the murderer dropped them. We've traced the coat. Belonged to a Mr. Jardine, a baker in Carne East. Mrs. Jardine gave it to Stella Rode last Wednesday morning for the refugees. Janie must have pinched it from the conservatory. That's what she meant by 'a coat for to keep me warm.' But she no more killed Stella Rode than you or I did. What about the footprints, the glove-marks in the conservatory? Besides, she's not strong enough, Janie isn't, to heave that poor woman forty feet through the snow. This is a man's work, as anyone can see."

"Then what exactly . . . ?"

"We've called off the search, and I'm to prepare a case against

247

one Jane Lyn of the village of Pylle for the wilful murder of Stella Rode. I wanted to tell you myself before you read it all over the papers. So that you'd know how it was."

"Thanks."

"In the meantime, if there's any help I can give you, we're still willing." He hesitated, seemed about to say something, then to change his mind.

As he made his way down the wide staircase, Smiley felt useless and very angry, which was scarcely the right frame of mind in which to attend a funeral.

It was an admirably conducted affair. Neither the flowers nor the congregation exceeded what was fitting to the occasion. She was not buried at the Abbey, out of deference perhaps to her simplicity of taste, but in the parish churchyard not far from North Fields. The Master was detained that day, as he was on most days, and had sent instead his wife, a small, very vague woman who had spent a long time in India. D'Arcy was much in evidence, fluttering here and there before the ceremony like an anxious beadle; and Mr. Cardew had come to guide poor Stella through the unfamiliarities of High Anglican procedure. The Hechts were there, Charles all in black, scrubbed and shining, and Shane in dramatic weeds and a hat with a very broad brim.

Smiley, who, like the others, had arrived early in anticipation of the unwholesome public interest which the ceremony might arouse, found himself a seat near the entrance of the church. He watched each new arrival with interest, waiting for his first sight of Stanley Rode.

Several tradesmen arrived, pressed into bulging serge and black ties, and formed a small group south of the aisle, away from the staff and their wives. Soon they were joined by other members of the town community, women who had known Mrs. Rode at the Tabernacle; and then by Rigby, who looked straight at Smiley and gave no sign. Then on the stroke of three a tall old

248

man walked slowly through the doorway, looking straight before him, neither knowing nor seeing anyone. Beside him was Stanley Rode.

It was a face which at first sight meant nothing to Smiley, seeming to have neither the imprint of temperament nor the components of character; it was a shallow, ordinary face, inclining to plumpness, and lacking quality. It matched his short, ordinary body and his black, ordinary hair; it was suitably compressed into an expression of sorrow. As Smiley watched him turn into the centre aisle and take his place among the principal mourners, it occurred to him that Rode's very walk and bearing successfully conveyed something entirely alien to Carne. If it is vulgar to wear a pen in the breast pocket of your jacket, to favour Fair Isle pullovers and brown ties, to bob a little and turn your feet out as you walk, then Rode beyond a shadow of doubt was vulgar, for though he did not now commit these sins, his manner implied them all.

They followed the coffin into the churchyard and gathered round the open grave. D'Arcy and Fielding were standing together, seemingly intent upon the service. The tall, elderly figure who had entered the churchyard with Rode was now visibly moved, and Smiley guessed that he was Stella's father, Samuel Glaston. As the service ended, the old man walked quickly away from the crowd, nodding briefly to Rode, and disappeared into the church. He seemed to struggle as he went, like a man walking against a strong wind.

The little group moved slowly away from the graveside, until only Rode remained, an oddly stiff figure, taut and constrained, his eyes wide but somehow sightless, his mouth set in a strict, pedagogic line. Then, as Smiley watched, Rode seemed to wake from a dream; his body suddenly relaxed and he too walked slowly but quite confidently away from the grave towards the small group which by now had reassembled at the churchyard gate. As he did so, Fielding, at the edge of the group, caught sight of him approaching and, to Smiley's aston-

249

ishment, walked deliberately and quite quickly away with an expression of strong distaste. It was not the calculated act of a man wishing to insult another, for it attracted the notice neither of Rode nor of anyone else standing by. Terence Fielding, for once, appeared to be in the grip of a genuine emotion, and indifferent to the impression he created.

Reluctantly Smiley approached the group. Rode was rather to one side, the D'Arcys were there, and three or four members of the staff. No one was talking much.

"Mr. Rode?" he inquired.

"That's right, yes." He spoke slowly, a trace of an accent carefully avoided.

"I'm representing Miss Brimley of the *Christian Voice*."

"Oh, yes."

"She was most anxious that the journal should be represented. I thought you would like to know that."

"I saw your wreath; very kind, I am sure."

"Your wife was one of our most loyal supporters," Smiley continued. "We regarded her almost as one of the family."

"Yes, she was very keen on the *Voice*."

Smiley wondered whether Rode was always as impassive as this, or whether bereavement had made him listless.

"When did you come?" Rode asked suddenly.

"Yesterday."

"Making a weekend of it, eh?"

Smiley was so astonished that for a moment he could think of nothing to say. Rode was still looking at him, waiting for an answer.

"I have one or two friends here . . . Mr. Fielding . . ."

"Oh, Terence."

Smiley was convinced that Rode was not on Christian-name terms with Fielding.

"I would like, if I may," Smiley ventured, "to write a small obituary for Miss Brimley. Would you have any objection?"

"Stella would have liked that."

"If you are not too upset, perhaps I could call round tomorrow for one or two details?"

"Certainly."

"Eleven o'clock?"

"It will be a pleasure," Rode replied, almost pertly, and they walked together to the churchyard gate.

9 �֍
THE MOURNERS

It was a cheap trick to play on a man who had suddenly lost his wife. Smiley knew that. As he gently unlatched the gate and entered the drive, where two nights ago he had conducted his strange conversation with Jane Lyn, he acknowledged that in calling on Rode under any pretext at such a time he was committing a thoroughly unprincipled act. It was a peculiarity of Smiley's character that throughout the whole of his clandestine work he had never managed to reconcile the means to the end. A stringent critic of his own motives, he had discovered after long observation that he tended to be less a creature of intellect than his tastes and habits might suggest; once in the war he had been described by his superiors as possessing the cunning of Satan and the conscience of a virgin, which seemed to him not wholly unjust.

He pressed the bell and waited.

Stanley Rode opened the door. He was very neatly dressed, very scrubbed.

"Oh hullo," he said, as if they were old friends. "I say, you haven't got a car, have you?"

"I'm afraid I left it in London."

"Never mind." Rode sounded disappointed. "Thought we might have gone out for a drive, had a chat as we went. I get a bit fed-up, kicking around here on my own. Miss D'Arcy asked me to stay over at their place. Very good people they are, very good indeed; but somehow I didn't wish it, not yet."

"I understand."

"Do you?" They were in the hall now, Smiley was getting out of his overcoat, Rode waiting to receive it. "I don't think many do—the loneliness I mean. Do you know what they've done, the Master and Mr. D'Arcy? They meant it well, I know. They've farmed out all my correcting—my exam correcting, you understand. What am I supposed to do here, all on my own? I've no teaching, nothing; they've all taken a hand. You'd think they wanted to get rid of me."

Smiley nodded vaguely. They moved towards the drawing room, Rode leading the way.

"I know they did it for the best, as I said. But after all, I've got to spend the time somehow. Simon Snow got some of my division to correct. Have you met him by any chance? Sixty-one percent he gave one boy—sixty-one. The boy's an absolute fool; I told Fielding at the beginning of the Half that he wouldn't possibly get his remove. Perkins his name is, a nice enough boy; head of Fielding's house. He'd have been lucky to get thirty percent . . . sixty-one, Snow gave him. I haven't seen the papers yet, of course, but it's impossible, quite impossible."

They sat down.

"Not that I don't want the boy to get on. He's a nice enough boy, nothing special, but well-mannered. Mrs. Rode and I meant to have him here to tea this Half. We would have done, in fact, if it hadn't been for . . ." There was a moment's silence. Smiley was going to speak when Rode stood up and said:

"I've a kettle on the stove, Mr. . . ."

"Smiley."

"I've a kettle on the stove, Mr. Smiley. May I make you a cup of coffee?" That little stiff voice with the corners carefully defined, like a hired morning suit, thought Smiley.

Rode returned a few minutes later with a tray and measured their coffee in precise quantities, according to their taste.

Smiley found himself continually irritated by Rode's social assumptions, and his constant struggle to conceal his origin. You could tell at the time, from every word and gesture, what he was; from the angle of his elbow as he drank his coffee, from the swift, expert pluck at the knee of his trouser leg as he sat down.

"I wonder," Smiley began, "whether perhaps I might now . . ."

"Go ahead, Mr. Smiley."

"We are, of course, largely interested in Mrs. Rode's association with . . . our Church."

"Quite."

"You were married at Branxome, I believe."

"Branxome Hill Tabernacle; fine church." D'Arcy wouldn't have liked the way he said that; cocksure lad on a motor-bike. Pencils in the outside pocket.

"When was that?"

"September, fifty-one."

"Did Mrs. Rode engage in charitable work in Branxome? I know she was very active here."

"No, not at Branxome, but a lot here. She had to look after her father at Branxome, you see. It was refugee relief she was keen on here. That didn't get going much until late 1956—the Hungarians began it, and then this last year . . ."

Smiley peered thoughtfully at Rode from behind his spectacles, forgot himself, blinked, and looked away.

"Did she take a large part in the social activities of Carne? Does the staff have its own Women's Institute and so on?" he asked innocently.

"She did a bit, yes. But, being Chapel, she kept mainly with the Chapel people from the town . . . you should ask Mr. Cardew about that; he's the Minister."

"But may I say, Mr. Rode, that she took an active part in school affairs as well?"

Rode hesitated.

"Yes, of course," he said.

"Thank you."

There was a moment's silence, then Smiley continued: "Our readers will, of course, remember Mrs. Rode as the winner of our Kitchen Hints competition. Was she a good cook, Mr. Rode?"

"Very good, for plain things, not fancy."

"Is there any little fact that you would specially like us to include, anything she herself would like to be remembered by?" Rode looked at him with expressionless eyes. Then he shrugged. "No, not really. I can't think of anything. Oh, you could say her father was a magistrate up North. She was proud of that." Smiley finished his coffee and stood up.

"You've been very patient with me, Mr. Rode. We're most grateful, I assure you. I'll take care to send you an advance copy of our notice. . . ."

"Thanks. I did it for her, you see. She liked the *Voice*; always did. Grew up with it."

They shook hands.

"By the way, do you know where I can find old Mr. Glaston? Is he staying in Carne or has he returned to Branxome?"

"He was up here yesterday. He's going back to Branxome this afternoon. The police wanted to see him before he left."

"I see."

"He's staying at the Sawley."

"Thank you. I might try and see him before I go."

"When do you leave, then?"

"Quite soon, I expect. Good-bye, then, Mr. Rode. Incidentally—" Smiley began.

"Yes?"

"If ever you're in London and at a loose end, if ever you

want a chat . . . and a cup of tea, we're always pleased to see you at the *Voice*, you know. Always."

"Thanks. Thanks very much, Mr.—"

"Smiley."

"Thanks, that's very decent. No one's said that to me for a long time. I'll take you up on that one day. Very good of you."

"Good-bye." Again they shook hands; Rode's was dry and cool. Smooth.

He returned to the Sawley Arms, sat himself at a desk in the empty residents' lounge, and wrote a note to Mr. Glaston:

> Dear Mr. Glaston,
>   I am here on behalf of Miss Brimley of the *Christian Voice*. I have some letters from Stella which I think you would like to see. Forgive me for bothering you at this sad moment: I understand you are leaving Carne this afternoon and wondered if I might see you before you left.

He carefully sealed the envelope and took it to the reception desk. There was no one there, so he rang the bell and waited. At last a porter came, an old turnkey with a grey, bristly face, and after examining the envelope critically for a long time, he agreed, against an excessive fee, to convey it to Mr. Glaston's room. Smiley stayed at the desk, waiting for his answer.

Smiley himself was one of those solitaries who seems to have come into the world fully educated at the age of eighteen. Obscurity was his nature, as well as his profession. The byways of espionage are not populated by the brash and colourful adventurers of fiction. A man who, like Smiley, has lived and worked for years among his country's enemies learns only one prayer: that he may never, never be noticed. Assimilation is his highest aim, he learns to love the crowds who pass him in the street without a glance; he clings to them for his anonymity and his safety. His fear makes him servile—he could embrace the shop-

256

pers who jostle him in their impatience and force him from the pavement. He could adore the officials, the police, the bus conductors, for the terse indifference of their attitudes.

But this fear, this servility, this dependence, had developed in Smiley a perception for the colour of human beings: a swift, feminine sensitivity to their characters and motives. He knew mankind as a huntsman knows his cover, as a fox the wood. For a spy must hunt while he is hunted, and the crowd is his estate. He could collect their gestures and their words, record the interplay of glance and movement, as a huntsman can record the twisted bracken and the broken twig, or as a fox detects the signs of danger.

Thus, while he waited patiently for Glaston's reply and recalled the crowded events of the last forty-eight hours, he was able to order and assess them with detachment. What was the cause of D'Arcy's attitude to Fielding, as if they were unwilling partners to a shabby secret? Staring across the neglected hotel gardens towards Carne Abbey, he was able to glimpse behind the lead roof of the Abbey the familiar battlements of the school: keeping the new world out and the old world secure. In his mind's eye he saw the Great Court now, as the boys came out of Chapel: the black-coated groups in the leisured attitudes of eighteenth-century England. And he remembered the other school beside the police station: Carne High School; a little tawdry place like a porter's lodge in an empty graveyard, as detached from the tones of Carne as its brick and flint from the saffron battlements of School Hall.

Yes, he reflected, Stanley Rode had made a long, long journey from the Grammar School at Branxome. And if he killed his wife, then the motive, Smiley was sure, and even the means, were to be found in that hard road to Carne.

"It was kind of you to come," said Glaston; "kind of Miss Brimley to send you. They're good people at the *Voice*, always were." He said this as if "good" were an absolute quality with which he was familiar.

"You'd better read the letters, Mr. Glaston. The second one will shock you, I'm afraid, but I'm sure you'll agree that it would be wrong of me not to show it to you." They were sitting in the lounge, the mammoth plants like sentinels beside them.

He handed Glaston the two letters, and the old man took them firmly and read them. He held them a good way from him to read, thrusting his strong head back, his eyes half closed, the crisp line of his mouth turned down at the corners. At last he said:

"You were with Miss Brimley in the war, were you?"

"I worked with John Landsbury, yes."

"I see. That's why she came to you?"

"Yes."

"Are you Chapel?"

"No."

He was silent for a while, his hands folded on his lap, the letters before him on the table.

"Stanley was Chapel when they married. Then he went over. Did you know that?"

"Yes."

"Where I come from in the North, we don't do that. Chapel was something we'd stood up for and won. Almost like the Vote."

"I know."

His back was as straight as a soldier's. He looked stern rather than sad. Quite suddenly, his eyes turned towards Smiley, and he looked at him long and carefully.

"Are you a schoolmaster?" he asked, and it occurred to Smiley that in his day Samuel Glaston had been a very shrewd man of business.

"No . . . I'm more or less retired."

"Married?"

"I was."

Again the old man fell silent, and Smiley wished he had left him alone.

"She was a great one for chatter," he said at last. Smiley said nothing.

"Have you told the police?"

"Yes, but they knew already. That is, they knew that Stella thought her husband was going to murder her. She'd tried to tell Mr. Cardew . . ."

"The Minister?"

"Yes. He thought she was overwrought and . . . deluded."

"Do you think she wasn't?"

"I don't know. I just don't know. But from what I have heard of your daughter I don't believe she was unbalanced. *Something* roused her suspicions, something frightened her very much. I don't believe we can just disregard that. I don't believe it was a coincidence that she was frightened before she died. And therefore I don't believe that the beggar-woman murdered her."

Samuel Glaston nodded slowly. It seemed to Smiley that the old man was trying to show interest, partly to be polite, and partly because if he did not it would be a confession that he had lost interest in life itself.

Then, after a long silence, he carefully folded up the letters and gave them back. Smiley waited for him to speak, but he said nothing.

After a few moments Smiley got up and walked quietly from the room.

10 ❧
LITTLE WOMEN

Shane Hecht smiled, and drank some more sherry. "You must be dreadfully important," she said to Smiley, "for D'Arcy to serve decent sherry. What are you, *Almanach de Gotha?*"

"I'm afraid not. D'Arcy and I were both dining at Terence Fielding's on Friday night and D'Arcy asked me for sherry."

"Terence is *wicked,* isn't he? Charles loathes him. I'm afraid they see Sparta in *quite* different ways. . . . Poor Terence. It's his last Half, you know."

"I know."

"So sweet of you to come to the funeral yesterday. I hate funerals, don't you? Black is so insanitary. I always remember King George V's funeral. Lord Sawley was at Court in those days, and gave Charles two tickets. So kind. I always think it's *spoilt* us for ordinary funerals in a way. Although I'm never quite sure about funerals, are you? I have a suspicion that they are largely a lowerclass recreation; cherry brandy and seed cake in the parlour. I think the tendency of people like ourselves is for a *quiet* funeral these days; no flowers, just a short obituary and a memorial service later." Her small eyes were bright with pleasure. She finished her sherry and held out her empty glass to Smiley.

"Would you mind, dear? I hate sherry, but Felix is so mean."

Smiley filled her glass from the decanter on the table.

"Dreadful about the murder, wasn't it? That beggar-woman must be mad. Stella Rode was such a nice person, I always thought . . . and so *unusual.* She did such clever things with the same dress. . . . But she had such curious friends. All for Hans the woodcutter and Pedro the fisherman, if you know what I mean."

"Was she popular at Carne?"

Shane Hecht laughed gently: "No one is popular at Carne . . . but she wasn't easy to like. . . . She would wear black crepe on Sundays. . . . Forgive me, but do the lower classes always do that? The townspeople liked her, I believe. They adore anyone who betrays Carne. But then she was a Christian Scientist or something."

"Baptist, I understand," said Smiley unthinkingly.

She looked at him for a moment with unfeigned curiosity. "How sweet," she murmured. "Tell me, what *are* you?"

Smiley made some facetious reply about being unemployed, and realised that it was only by a hair's-breadth that he had avoided explaining himself to Shane Hecht like a small boy. Her very ugliness, her size and voice, coupled with the sophisticated malice of her conversation, gave her the dangerous quality of command. Smiley was tempted to compare her with Fielding, but for Fielding other people scarcely existed. For Shane Hecht they did exist: they were there to be found wanting in the minute tests of social behaviour, to be ridiculed, cut off, and destroyed.

"I read in the paper that her father was quite well off. From the North. Second generation. Remarkable really how *unspoilt* she was . . . so natural. . . . You wouldn't think she *needed* to go to the launderette or to make friends with beggars. . . . Though,

261

of course, the Midlands are different, aren't they? Only about three good families between Ipswich and Newcastle. Where did you say you came from, dear?"

"London."

"How nice. I went to tea with Stella once. Milk in first and Indian. So different," and she looked at Smiley suddenly and said, "I'll tell you something. She almost aroused an admiration in me, I found her so insufferable. She was one of those tiresome little snobs who think that only the humble are virtuous." Then she smiled and added, "I even agreed with Charles about Stella Rode, and that's saying something. If you're a student of mankind, do go and have a look at him, the contrast is riveting." But at that moment they were joined by D'Arcy's sister, a bony, virile woman with untidy grey hair and an arrogant, hunting mouth.

"Dorothy darling," Shane murmured; "such a lovely party. So *kind.* And so *exciting* to meet somebody from London, don't you think? We were talking about poor Mrs. Rode's funeral."

"Stella Rode may have been damn' bad form, Shane, but she did a lot for my refugees."

"Refugees?" asked Smiley innocently.

"Hungarians. Collecting for them. Clothes, furniture, money. One of the few wives who *did* anything." She looked sharply at Shane Hecht, who was smiling benignly past her towards her husband: "Busy little creature, she was; didn't mind rolling her sleeves up, going from door to door. Got her little women on to it too at the Baptist chapel and brought in a mass of stuff. You've got to hand it to them, you know. They've got *spirit.* Felix, more sherry!"

There were about twenty in the two rooms, but Smiley, who had arrived a little late, found himself attached to a group of about eight who stood nearest the door: D'Arcy and his sister; Charles and Shane Hecht; a young mathematician called Snow and his wife; a curate from the Abbey, and Smiley himself, bewildered and mole-like behind his spectacles. Smiley looked quickly round the room but could see no sign of Fielding.

". . . Yes," Dorothy D'Arcy continued, "she was a good little worker, very . . . right to the end. I went over there on Friday with that parson man from the tin tabernacle—Cardew—to see if there was any refugee stuff to tidy up. There wasn't a thing out of place—every bit of clothing she had was all packed up and addressed; we just had to send it off. She was a damn' good little worker, I will say. Did a splendid job at the bazaar, you know."

"Yes, darling," said Shane Hecht sweetly. "I remember it well. It was the day I presented her to Lady Sawley. She wore such a *nice* little hat—the one she wore on Sundays, you know. And *so* respectful. She called her 'my lady.'" She turned to Smiley and breathed: "Rather feudal, don't you think, dear? I always like that: so few of us left."

The mathematician and his wife were talking to Charles Hecht in a corner and a few minutes later Smiley managed to extricate himself from the group and join them.

Ann Snow was a pretty girl with a rather square face and a turned-up nose. Her husband was tall and thin, with an agreeable stoop. He held his sherry glass between straight, slender fingers as if it were a chemical retort and when he spoke he seemed to address the sherry rather than his listener; Smiley remembered them from the funeral. Hecht was looking pink and rather cross, sucking at his pipe. They talked in a desultory way, their conversation dwarfed by the exchanges of the adjoining group. Hecht eventually drifted away from them, still frowning and withdrawn, and stood ostentatiously alone near the door.

"Poor Stella," said Ann Snow after a moment's silence. "Sorry," she added. "I can't get her out of my mind yet. It seems mad, just mad. I mean why should she *do* it, that Janie woman?"

"Did you like Stella?" Smiley asked.

"Of course we did. She was sweet. We've been here four Halves now, but she was the only person here who's ever been *kind* to us." Her husband said nothing, just nodded at his sherry. "Simon wasn't a boy at Carne, you see—most of the staff were—

263

so we didn't know anyone and no one was really interested. They all pretended to be terribly pleased with us, of course, but it was Stella who really . . ."

Dorothy D'Arcy was descending on them. "Mrs. Snow," she said crisply, "I've been meaning to talk to you. I want you to take over Stella Rode's job on the refugees." She cast an appraising look in Simon's direction: "The Master's very keen on refugees."

"Oh, my goodness!" Ann Snow replied, aghast. "I couldn't possibly, Miss D'Arcy, I . . ."

"Couldn't? Why couldn't you? You helped Mrs. Rode with her stall at the bazaar, didn't you?"

"So that's where she got her clothes from," breathed Shane Hecht behind them. Ann was fumbling on:

"But . . . well I haven't quite got Stella's nerve, if you understand what I mean; and besides, she was a Baptist: all the locals helped her and gave her things, and they all liked her. With me it would be different."

"Lot of damn' nonsense," declared Miss D'Arcy, who spoke to all her juniors as if they were grooms or erring children; and Shane Hecht beside her said: "Baptists are the people who don't like private pews, aren't they? I do so agree—one feels that if one's paid one simply has to go."

The curate, who had been talking cricket in a corner, was startled into mild protest: "Oh, come, Mrs. Hecht, the private pew had many advantages . . ." and embarked on a diffuse apologia for ancient custom, to which Shane listened with every sign of the most assiduous interest. When at last he finished she said: "Thank you, William dear, so sweet," turned her back on him, and added to Smiley in a stage whisper: "William Trumper—one of Charles's old pupils—such a triumph when he passed his Certificate."

Smiley, anxious to dissociate himself from Shane Hecht's vengeance on the curate, turned to Ann Snow, but she was still at the mercy of Miss D'Arcy's charitable intentions, and Shane was still talking to him:

"The only Smiley I ever heard of married Lady Ann Sercombe at the end of the war. She left him soon afterwards, of course. A very curious match. I understand he was quite unsuitable. She was Lord Sawley's cousin, you know. The Sawleys have been connected with Carne for four hundred years. The present heir is a pupil of Charles; we often dine at the Castle. I never did hear what became of Ann Sercombe . . . she went to Africa, you know . . . or was it India? No, it was America. So tragic. One doesn't talk about it at the Castle." For a moment the noise in the room stopped. For a moment, no more, he could discern nothing but the steady gaze of Shane Hecht upon him, and knew she was waiting for an answer. And then she released him as if to say: "I could crush you, you see. But I won't, I'll let you live," and she turned and walked away.

He contrived to take his leave at the same time as Ann and Simon Snow. They had an old car and insisted on running Smiley back to his hotel. On the way there, he said:

"If you have nothing better to do, I would be happy to give you both dinner at my hotel. I imagine the food is dreadful."

The Snows protested and accepted, and a quarter of an hour later they were all three seated in a corner of the enormous dining room of the Sawley Arms, to the great despondency of three waiters and a dozen generations of Lord Sawley's forebears, puffy men in crumbling pigment.

"We really got to know her our second Half," Ann Snow ran on. "Stella didn't do much mixing with the other wives—she'd learnt her lesson by then. She didn't go to coffee parties and things, so it was really luck that we did meet. When we first came there wasn't a staff house available for us: we had to spend the first Half in a hotel. We moved in to a little house in Bread Street at the end of our second Half. Moving was chaos—Simon was examining for the scholarships and we were terribly broke, so we had to do everything we possibly could for ourselves. It was a wet Thursday morning when we moved. The rain was simply teeming down; but none of our good pieces

265

would get in through the front door, and in the end Mulligan's just dumped me on the doorstep and let me sort it out." She laughed, and Smiley thought what an agreeable child she was. "They were absolutely foul. They would have just driven off, I think, but they wanted a cheque as soon as they'd done the delivery, and the bill was pounds more than the estimate. I hadn't got the cheque-book, of course. Simon had gone off with it. Mulligan's even threatened to take all the stuff away again. It was monstrous. I think I was nearly in tears."

She nearly is now, thought Smiley.

"Then out of the blue Stella turned up. I can't think how she even knew we were moving—I'm sure no one else did. She'd brought an overall and an old pair of shoes and she'd come to help. When she saw what was going on she didn't bother with the men at all, just went to a phone and rang Mr. Mulligan himself. I don't know what she said to him, but she made the foreman talk to him afterwards and there was no more trouble after that. She was terribly happy—happy to help. She was that sort of person. They took the door right out and managed to get everything in. She was marvellous at helping without managing. The rest of the wives," she added bitterly, "are awfully good at managing, but don't help at all."

Smiley nodded, and discreetly filled their glasses.

"Simon's leaving," Ann said, suddenly confidential. "He's got a grant and we're going back to Oxford. He's going to do a D.Phil. and get a University job."

They drank to his success, and the conversation turned to other things until Smiley asked: "What's Rode himself like to work with?"

"He's a good schoolmaster," said Simon, slowly, "but tiring as a colleague."

"Oh, he was quite different from Stella," said Ann; "terribly Carne-minded. D'Arcy adopted him and he got the bug. Simon says all the grammar school people go that way—it's the fury of the convert. It's sickening. He even changed his religion when he got to Carne. Stella didn't, though; she wouldn't dream of it."

"The Established Church has much to offer Carne," Simon observed, and Smiley enjoyed the dry precision of his delivery.

"Stella can't exactly have hit it off with Shane Hecht," Smiley probed gently.

"Of course she didn't!" Ann declared angrily. "Shane was horrid to her, always sneering at her because she was honest and simple about the things she liked. Shane hated Stella—I think it was because Stella didn't want to be a lady of quality. She was quite happy to be herself. That's what really worried Shane. Shane likes people to compete so that she can make fools of them."

"So does Carne," said Simon, quietly.

"She was awfully good at helping out with the refugees. That was how she got into real trouble." Ann Snow's slim hands gently rocked her brandy glass.

"Trouble?"

"Just before she died. Hasn't anyone told you? About her frightful row with D'Arcy's sister?"

"Of course, they wouldn't have done. Stella never gossiped."

"Let me tell you," said Simon. "It's a good story. When the Refugee Year business started, Dorothy D'Arcy was fired with charitable enthusiasm. So was the Master. Dorothy's enthusiasms always seem to correspond with his. She started collecting clothes and money and packing them off to London. All very laudable, but there was a perfectly good town appeal going, launched by the Mayor. That wasn't good enough for Dorothy, though: the school must have its own appeal; you can't mix your charity. I think Felix was largely behind it. Anyway, after the thing had been going for a few months the refugee centre in London apparently wrote to Dorothy and asked whether anyone would be prepared to accommodate a refugee couple. Instead of publicising the letter, Dorothy wrote straight back and said she would put them up herself. So far so good. The couple turned up, Dorothy and Felix pointed a proud finger at them, and the local press wrote it all up as an example of British humanity.

"About six weeks later, one afternoon, these two turned up on Stella's doorstep. The Rodes and the D'Arcys are neighbours, you see, and anyway Stella had tried to take an interest in Dorothy's refugees. The woman was in floods of tears and the husband was shouting blue murder, but that didn't worry Stella. She had them straight into the drawing room and gave them a cup of tea. Finally, they managed to explain in basic English that they had run away from the D'Arcys because of the treatment they received. The girl was expected to work from morning till night in the kitchen, and the husband was acting as unpaid kennel-boy for those beastly spaniels that Dorothy breeds. The ones without noses."

"King Charles," Ann prompted.

"It was about as awful as it could be. The girl was pregnant and he was a fully qualified engineer, so neither of them were exactly suited to domestic service. They told Stella that Dorothy was away till the evening—she'd gone to a dog show. Stella advised them to stay with her for the time being, and that evening she went round and told Dorothy what had happened. She had quite a nerve, you see. Although it wasn't nerve really. She just did the simple thing. Dorothy was furious, and demanded that Stella should return 'her refugees' immediately. Stella replied that she was sure that they wouldn't come, and went home. When Stella got home she rang up the refugee people in London and asked their advice. They sent a woman down to see Dorothy and the couple, and the result was that they returned to London the following day. . . . You can imagine what Shane Hecht would have made of that story."

"Didn't she ever find out?"

"Stella never told anyone except us, and we didn't pass it on. Dorothy just let it be known that the refugees had gone to some job in London, and that was that."

"How long ago did this happen?"

"They left exactly three weeks ago," said Ann to her husband. "Stella told me about it when she came to supper the night you were in Oxford for your interview. That was three weeks ago tonight." She turned to Smiley:

"Poor Simon's been having an awful time. Felix D'Arcy unloaded all Rode's exam correcting on to him. It's bad enough doing one person's correction—two is frantic."

"Yes," replied Simon reflectively. "It's been a bad week. And rather humiliating in a way. Several of the boys who were up to me for science last Half are now in Rode's forms. I'd regarded one or two of them as practically unreachable, but Rode seems to have brought them on marvellously. I corrected one boy's paper—Perkins—sixty-one percent for elementary science. Last Half he got fifteen percent in a much easier paper. He only got his remove because Fielding raised hell. He was in Fielding's house."

"Oh I know—a red-haired boy, a prefect."

"Good Lord," cried Simon. "Don't say you know him?"

"Oh, Fielding introduced us," said Smiley vaguely. "Incidentally—no one else ever mentioned that incident to you about Miss D'Arcy's refugees, did they? Confirmed it, as it were?"

Ann Snow looked at him oddly. "No. Stella told us about it, but of course Dorothy D'Arcy never referred to it at all. She must have hated Stella, though."

He saw them to their car, and waited despite their protests while Simon cranked it. At last they drove off, the car bellowing down the silent street. Smiley stood for a moment on the pavement, an odd, lonely figure peering down the empty road.

269

11 ❀

A COAT TO KEEP HER WARM

A dog that had not bitten the postman; a devil that rode upon the wind; a woman who knew that she would die; a little, worried man in an overcoat standing in the snow outside his hotel, and the laborious chime of the Abbey clock telling him to go to bed.

Smiley hesitated, then with a shrug crossed the road to the hotel entrance, mounted the step, and entered the cheap, yellow light of the residents' hall. He walked slowly up the stairs.

He detested the Sawley Arms. That muted light in the hall was typical: inefficient, antiquated, and smug. Like the waiters in the dining room and the lowered voices in the residents' lounge, like his own hateful bedroom with its blue and gilt urns, and the framed tapestry of a Buckinghamshire garden.

His room was bitterly cold; the maid must have opened the window. He put a shilling in the meter and lit the gas. The fire bubbled grumpily and went out. Muttering, Smiley looked around for some paper to write on, and discovered some, much to his surprise, in the drawer of the writing desk. He changed into his pyjamas and dressing-gown and crawled miserably into bed. After sitting there uncomfortably for some minutes he got up, fetched his overcoat, and spread it over the eider-down. A coat for to keep her warm. . . .

How did her statement read? "There's one will thank me, that's my darling and I took her jewels for the saints I did, and a coat for to keep me warm. . . ." The coat had been given to Stella last Wednesday for the refugees. It seemed reasonable to assume from the way the statement read that Janie had taken the coat from the outhouse at the same time as she took the beads from Stella's body. But Dorothy D'Arcy had been round there on Friday morning—of course she had, with Mr. Cardew—she was talking about it at her party that very evening: "There wasn't a thing out of place—every bit of clothing she had was all packed up and addressed—a damn' good little worker, I will say. . . ." Then why hadn't Stella packed the overcoat? If she packed everything else, why not the overcoat, too?

Or had Janie stolen the coat earlier in the day, before Stella made her parcel? If that was so, it went some way to weakening the case against her. But it was not so. It was not so because it was utterly improbable that Janie should steal a coat in the af-ternoon and return to the house the same evening.

"Start at the beginning," Smiley muttered, a little senten-tiously, to the crested paper on his lap. "Janie stole the coat at the same time as she stole the beads—that is, after Stella was dead. Therefore, either the coat was not packed with the other clothes, or . . ."

Or what? *Or somebody else, somebody who was not Stella Rode, packed up the clothes after Stella had died and before Dorothy D'Arcy and Mr. Cardew went round to North Fields on Friday morning. And why the devil, thought Smiley, should any-one do that?*

It had been one of Smiley's cardinal principles in research, whether among the incunabula of an obscure poet or the labo-riously gathered fragments of intelligence, not to proceed be-

271

yond the evidence. A fact, once logically arrived at, should not be extended beyond its natural significance. Accordingly he did not speculate with the remarkable discovery he had made, but turned his mind to the most obscure problem of all: motive for murder.

He began writing:

"Dorothy D'Arcy—resentment after refugee fiasco. As a motive for murder—definitely thin." Yet why did she seem to go out of her way to sing Stella's praises?

"Felix D'Arcy—resented Stella Rode for not observing Carne's standards. As a motive for murder—ludicrous.

"Shane Hecht—hatred.

"Terence Fielding—in a sane world, no conceivable motive." Yet was it a sane world? Year in year out they must share the same life, say the same things to the same people, sing the same hymns. They had no money, no hope. The world changed, fashion changed; the women saw it second-hand in the glossy papers, took in their dresses and pinned up their hair, and hated their husbands a little more. Shane Hecht—did she kill Stella Rode? Did she conceal in the sterile omniscience of her huge body not only hatred and jealousy, but the courage to kill? Was she frightened for her stupid husband, frightened of Rode's promotion, of his cleverness? Was she really so angry when Stella refused to take part in the rat race of gentility?

Rigby was right—it was impossible to know. You had to be ill, you had to be sick to understand, you had to be there in the sanatorium, not for weeks, but for years, had to be one in the line of white beds, to know the smell of their food and the greed in their eyes. You had to hear it and see it, to be part of it, to know their rules and recognise their transgressions. This world was compressed into a mould of anomalous conventions: blind, pharisaical but real.

Yet some things were written plain enough: the curious bond which tied Felix D'Arcy and Terence Fielding despite their mutual dislike; D'Arcy's reluctance to discuss the night of the murder; Fielding's evident preference for Stella Rode rather than her husband; Shane Hecht's contempt for everyone.

He could not get Shane out of his mind. If Carne were a rational place, and somebody had to die, then Shane Hecht should clearly be the one. She was a depository of other people's secrets; she had an infallible sense of weakness. Had she not found even Smiley out? She had taunted him with his wretched marriage, she had played with him for her own pleasure. Yes, she was an admirable candidate for murder.

But why on earth should Stella die? Why and how? Who tied up the parcel after her death? And why?

He tried to sleep, but could not. Finally, as the Abbey clock chimed three, he put the light on again and sat up. The room was much warmer and at first Smiley wondered if someone had switched on the central heating in the middle of the night, after it had been off all day. Then he became aware of the sound of rain outside; he went to the window and parted the curtains. A steady rain was falling; by tomorrow the snow would be washed away. Two policemen walked slowly down the road; he could hear the squelch of their boots as they trod in the melting snow. Their wet capes glistened in the arc of the street lamp.

And suddenly he seemed to hear Rigby's voice: "Blood everywhere. Whoever killed her must have been covered in it." And then Mad Janie calling to him across the moonlit snow: "Janie seed 'im . . . silver wings like fishes . . . flying on the wind . . . there's not many seen the devil fly . . ." Of course: the parcel! He remained a long time at the window, watching the rain. Finally, content at last, he climbed back into bed and fell asleep.

He tried to telephone Miss Brimley throughout the morning. Each time she was out and he left no message. Eventually, at about midday, he spoke to her:

"George, I'm terribly sorry—some missionary is in London—I had to go for an interview and I've got a Baptist Conference this afternoon. They've both got to be in this week. Will first thing tomorrow do?"

"Yes," said Smiley. "I'm sure it will." There was no particular hurry. There were one or two ends he wanted to tie up that afternoon, anyway.

12 ❀
UNCOMFORTABLE WORDS

He enjoyed the bus. The conductor was a very surly man with a great deal to say about the bus company, and why it lost money. Gently encouraged by Smiley, he expanded wonderfully so that by the time they arrived at Sturminster he had transformed the Directors of the Dorset and General Traction Company into a herd of Gadarene swine charging into the abyss of voluntary bankruptcy. The conductor directed Smiley to the Sturminster kennels, and when he alighted in the tiny village, he set out confidently towards a group of cottages which stood about a quarter of a mile beyond the church, on the Okeford road.

He had a nasty feeling he wasn't going to like Mr. Harriman. The very fact that D'Arcy had described him as a superior type of person inclined Smiley against him. Smiley was not opposed to social distinctions but he liked to make his own.

A notice stood at the gate: "*Sturminster Kennels, proprietor, C. J. Reid-Harriman, Veterinary Surgeon. Breeder of Alsatian and Labrador Dogs. Boarding.*"

A narrow path led to what seemed to be a backyard. There was washing everywhere, shirts, underclothes, and sheets, most of it khaki. There was a rich smell of dog. There was a rusted handpump with a dozen or so dog leads draped over it, and there was a small girl. She watched him sadly as he picked his way through the thick mud towards the door. He pulled on the bell-rope and waited. He tried again, and the child said:

"It doesn't work. It's bust. It's been bust for years."

"Is anyone at home?" Smiley asked.

"I'll see," she replied coolly, and after another long look at him she walked round the side of the house and disappeared from view. Then Smiley heard from inside the house the sound of someone approaching, and a moment later the door opened.

"Good day to you." He had sandy hair and a moustache. He wore a khaki shirt and a khaki tie of a lighter shade; old Service dress trousers and a tweed jacket with leather buttons.

"Mr. Harriman?"

"Major," he replied lightly. "Not that it matters, old boy. What can we do for you?"

"I'm thinking of buying an Alsatian," Smiley replied, "as a guard dog."

"Surely. Come in, won't you. Lady wife's out. Ignore the child: she's from next door. Just hangs around; likes the dogs." He followed Harriman into the living room and they sat down. There was no fire.

"Where are you from?" Harriman asked.

"I'm staying at Carne at the moment; my father lives over at Dorchester. He's getting on and he's nervous, and he wants me to find him a good dog. There's a gardener to look after it in the daytime, feed it and exercise it and so on. The gardener doesn't live in at night, of course, and it's at night that the old man gets so worried. I've been meaning to get him a dog for some time— this recent business at Carne rather brought it home to me." Harriman ignored the hint.

"Gardener good chap?"

"Yes, very."

"You don't want anything brilliant," said Harriman. "You want a good, steady type. I'd take a bitch if I were you." His hands were dark brown, his wrists too. His handkerchief was tucked into his cuff. Smiley noticed that his wristwatch faced inwards, conforming with the obscure rites of the military *demi-monde* from which he seemed to come.

"What will it do, a dog like that? Will it attack, or what?"

"Depends how she's trained, old boy; depends how she's trained. She'll warn, though; that's the main thing. Frighten the fellers away. Shove a notice up, 'Fierce Dog,' let her sniff at the tradesmen a bit and the word will get around. You won't get a burglar within a mile of the place."

They walked out into the garden again, and Harriman led the way to an enclosure with half a dozen Alsatian puppies yapping furiously at them through the wire.

"They're good little beasts, all of them," he shouted. "Game as hell." He unlocked the door and finally emerged with a plump bitch puppy chewing fiercely at his jacket.

"This little lady might do you," he said. "We can't show her—she's too dark."

Smiley pretended to hesitate, allowed Harriman to persuade him, and finally agreed. They went back into the house.

"I'd like to pay a deposit," said Smiley, "and collect her in about ten days. Would that be all right?" He gave Harriman a cheque for five pounds and again they sat down, Harriman foraging in his desk for inoculation certificates and pedigrees. Then Smiley said:

"It's a pity Mrs. Rode didn't have a dog, isn't it? I mean, it might have saved her life."

"Oh, she *had* a dog, but she had it put down just before she was killed," said Harriman. "Damned odd story between ourselves. She was devoted to the beast. Odd little mongrel, bit of everything, but she loved it. Brought it here one day with some tale about it biting the postman, got me to put it down—said it was dangerous. It wasn't anything of the sort. Some friends of mine in Carne made inquiries. No complaints anywhere. Postman liked the brute. Damned silly sort of lie to tell in a small community. Bound to be found out."

"Why on earth did she tell it then?"

Harriman made a gesture which particularly irritated Smiley. He ran his forefinger down the length of his nose, then flicked either side of his absurd moustache very quickly. There was something shamefaced about the whole movement, as if he were assuming the ways of senior officers, and fearful of rebuke.

"She was trouble," he said crisply. "I can spot 'em. I've had a few in the regiment, wives who are trouble. Little simpering types. Butter-wouldn't-melt, holier-than-thou. Arrange the flowers in the church and all that—pious as you please. I'd say she was the hysterical kind, self-dramatising, weeping all over the house for days on end. Anything for a bit of drama."

"Was she popular?" Smiley offered him a cigarette.

"Shouldn't think so. Thanks. She wore black on Sundays, I gather. Typical. We used to call them 'crows' out East, the ones who wore black—Sunday virgins. They were OD mostly—other denominations. Not C of E—some were Romans, mind. . . . I hope I'm not . . ."

"Not at all."

"You never know, do you? Can't stand 'em myself; no prejudice, but I don't like Romans—that's what my old father used to say."

"Did you know her husband?"

"Not so well, poor devil, not so well."

Harriman, Smiley reflected, seemed to have a great deal more sympathy for the living than the dead. Perhaps soldiers were like that. He wouldn't know.

"He's terribly cut up, I hear. Dreadful shock—fortunes of war, eh?" he added and Smiley nodded. "He's the other type. Humble origin, good officer qualities, credit to the mess. Those are the ones that cut up most, the ones women get at."

They walked along the path to the gate. Smiley said goodbye and promised to return in a week or so to collect the puppy.

277

As he walked away Harriman called to him: "Oh—incidentally . . ." Smiley stopped and turned round.

"I'll pay that cheque in, shall I, and credit you with the amount?"

"Of course," said Smiley. "That will do very well," and he made his way to the bus stop pondering on the strange byways of the military mind.

The same bus took him back to Carne, the same conductor railed against his employers, the same driver drove the entire distance in second gear. He got out at the station and made his way to the red-brick Tabernacle. Gently opening the Gothic door, made of thickly-varnished ochre pine, he stepped inside. An elderly woman in an apron was polishing the heavy brass chandelier which hung over the centre aisle. He waited a moment, then tiptoed up to her and asked for the Minister. She pointed towards the vestry door. Obeying her mimed directions, he crossed to it, knocked, and waited. A tall man in a clerical collar opened the door.

"I'm from the *Christian Voice*," said Smiley quietly. "Can I have a word with you?"

Mr. Cardew led him through the side entrance and into a small vegetable garden, carefully tilled, with bright yellow paths running between the empty beds. The sun shone through the crisp air. It was a cold, beautiful day. They crossed the garden and entered a paddock. The ground was hard despite last night's rain, and the grass short. They strolled side by side, talking as they went.

"This is Lammas Land, belonging to the School. We hold our fetes here in the summer. It's very practical."

Cardew seemed a little out of character. Smiley, who had a rather childish distrust of clergymen, had expected a Wesleyan hammer, a wordy, forbidding man with a taste for imagery.

"Miss Brimley, our editor, sent me," Smiley began. "Mrs. Rode subscribed to our journal; her family has taken it since it began. She was almost a part of the family. We wanted to write an obituary about her work for the Church."

"I see."

"I managed to have a word with her husband; we wanted to be sure to strike the right note."

"What did he say?"

"He said I should speak to you about her work—her refugee work particularly."

They walked on in silence for a while, then Cardew said, "She came from up North, near Derby. Her father used to be a man of substance in the North—though money never altered him."

"I know."

"I've known the family for years, off and on. I saw her old father before the funeral."

"What may I say about her work for the Church, her influence on the Chapel community here? May I say she was universally loved?"

"I'm afraid," said Cardew, after a slight pause, "that I don't hold much with that kind of writing, Mr. Smiley. People are never universally loved, even when they're dead." His North Country accent was strong.

"Then what may I say?" Smiley persisted.

"I don't know," Cardew replied evenly. "And when I don't know, I usually keep quiet. But since you're good enough to ask me, I've never met an angel, and Stella Rode was no exception."

"But was she not a leading figure in refugee work?"

"Yes. Yes, she was."

"And did she not encourage others to make similar efforts?"

"Of course. She was a good worker."

They walked on together in silence. The path across the field led downwards, then turned and followed a stream which was almost hidden by the tangled gorse and hawthorn on either side. Beyond the stream was a row of stark elm trees, and behind them the familiar outline of Carne.

"Is that all you wanted to ask me?" said Cardew suddenly.

"No," replied Smiley. "Our editor was very worried by a letter she received from Mrs. Rode just before her death. It was a kind of . . . accusation. We put the matter before the police. Miss Brimley reproaches herself in some way for not having been able to help her. It's illogical, perhaps, but there it is. I would like to be able to assure her that there was no connexion between Stella Rode's death and this letter. That is another reason for my visit. . . ."

"Whom did the letter accuse?"

"Her husband."

"I should tell your Miss Brimley," said Cardew slowly, and with some emphasis, "that she has nothing whatever for which to reproach herself."

13 ❧

THE JOURNEY HOME

It was Monday evening. At about the time that Smiley returned to his hotel after his interview with Mr. Cardew, Tim Perkins, the Head of Fielding's house, was taking his leave of Mrs. Harlowe, who taught him the 'cello. She was a kindly woman, if neurotic, and it distressed her to see him so worried. He was quite the best pupil that Carne had sent her, and she liked him.

"You played foully today, Tim," she said as she wished him good-bye at the door, "quite foully. You needn't tell me—you've only got one more Half and you still haven't got three passes in A Level and you've got to get your remove, and you're in a fizz. We won't practise next Monday if you don't want—just come and have buns and we'll play some records."

"Yes, Mrs. Harlowe." He strapped his music-case on to the carrier of his bicycle.

"Lights working, Tim?"

"Yes, Mrs. Harlowe."

"Well, don't try and beat the record tonight, Tim. You've

plenty of time till Boys' Tea. Remember the lane's still quite slippery from the snow."

Perkins said nothing. He pushed the bicycle on to the gravel path and started towards the gate.

"Haven't you forgotten something, Tim?"

"Sorry, Mrs. Harlowe."

He turned back and shook hands with her in the doorway. She always insisted on that.

"Look, Tim, what *is* the matter? Have you done something silly? You can tell me, can't you? I'm not Staff, you know." Perkins hesitated, then said:

"It's just exams, Mrs. Harlowe."

"Are your parents all right? No trouble at home?"

"No, Mrs. Harlowe; they're fine." Again he hesitated, then: "Good night, Mrs. Harlowe."

"Good night."

She watched him close the gate behind him and cycle off down the narrow lane. He would be in Carne in a quarter of an hour; it was downhill practically all the way.

Usually he loved the ride home. It was the best moment of the week. But tonight he hardly noticed it. He rode fast, as he always did; the hedge raced against the dark sky and the rabbits scuttled from the beam of his lamp, but tonight he hardly noticed them.

He would have to tell somebody. He should have told Mrs. Harlowe; he wished he had. She'd know what to do. Mr. Snow would have been all right, but he wasn't up to him for science any longer, he was up to Rode. That was half the trouble. That and Fielding.

He could tell True—yes, that's who he'd tell, he'd tell True. He'd go to Miss Truebody tonight after evening surgery and he'd tell her the truth. His father would never get over it, of course, because it meant failure and perhaps disgrace. It meant not getting to Sandhurst at the end of next Half, it meant more money they couldn't afford. . . .

282

He was coming to the steepest part of the hill. The hedge stopped on one side and instead there was a marvellous view of Sawley Castle against the night sky, like a backcloth for *Macbeth*. He loved acting—he wished the Master let them act at Carne.

He leant forward over the handlebars and allowed himself to gather speed to go through the shallow ford at the bottom of the hill. The cold air bit into his face, and for a moment he almost forgot . . . Suddenly he braked; felt the bike skid wildly beneath him.

Something was wrong; there was a light ahead, a flashing light, and a familiar voice calling to him urgently across the darkness.

14 ❀
THE QUALITY OF MERCY

The Public Schools Committee for Refugee Relief (Patroness: Sarah, Countess of Sawley) has an office in Belgrave Square. It is not at all clear whether this luxurious situation is designed to entice the wealthy or encourage the dispossessed—or, as some irreverent voices in Society whispered, to provide the Countess of Sawley with an inexpensive *pied-à-terre* in the West End of London. The business of assisting refugees has been suitably relegated to the south of the river, to one of those untended squares in Kennington which are part of London's architectural schizophrenia. York Gardens, as the square is called, will one day be discovered by the world, and its charm lost, but go there now, and you may see real children playing hopscotch in the road, and their mothers, shod in bedroom slippers, abusing them from doorways.

Miss Brimley, dispatched on her way by Smiley's telephone call the previous morning, had the rare gift of speaking to children as if they were human beings, and thus discovered without difficulty the dilapidated, unnamed house which served the

284

Committee as a collecting centre. With the assistance of seven small boys, she pulled on the bell and waited patiently. At last she heard the clatter of feet descending an uncarpeted staircase, and the door was opened by a very beautiful girl. They looked at one another with approval for a moment.

"I'm sorry to be a nuisance," Miss Brimley began, "but a friend of mine in the country has asked me to make some inquiries about a parcel of clothes that was sent up a day or two ago. She's made rather a stupid mistake."

"Oh, goodness, how awful," said the girl pleasantly. "Would you like to come in? Everything's frightfully chaotic, I'm afraid, and there's nothing to sit on, but we can give you powdered coffee in a mug."

Miss Brimley followed her in, closing the door firmly on the seven children, who were edging gently forward in her wake. She was in the hall, and everywhere she looked there were parcels of every kind, some wrapped in jute with smart labels, some in brown paper, torn and clumsy, some in crates and laundry baskets, old suitcases, and even an antiquated cabin trunk with a faded yellow label on it which read: "Not wanted on voyage."

The girl led the way upstairs to what was evidently the office, a large room containing a deal table littered with correspondence, and a kitchen chair. An oil stove sputtered in one corner, and an electric kettle was steaming in a melancholy way beside it. "I'm sorry," said the girl as they entered the room, "but there just isn't anywhere to talk downstairs. I mean, one can't talk on one leg like the Incas. Or isn't it Incas? Perhaps it's Afghans. However did you find us?"

"I went to your West End office first," Miss Brimley replied, "and they told me I should come and see you. I think they were rather cross. After that I relied on children. They always know the way. You are Miss Dawney, aren't you?"

"Lord, no. I'm the sort of daily help. Jill Dawney's gone to see the Customs people at Rotherhithe—she'll be back at tea time if you want to see her."

"Gracious, my dear, I'm sure I shan't keep you two minutes. A friend of mine who lives in Carne—("Goodness! How grand," said the girl) she's a sort of cousin really, but it's simpler to call her a friend, isn't it?—gave an old grey dress to the refugee people last Thursday and now she's convinced she left her brooch pinned to the bodice. I'm sure she hasn't done anything of the sort, mind you—she's a scatter-brain creature—but she rang me yesterday morning in a dreadful state and made me promise to come round at once and ask. I couldn't come yesterday, unfortunately—tied to my little paper from dawn till dusk. But I gather you're a bit behind, so it won't be too late?"

"Gosh, no! We're miles behind. That's all the stuff downstairs, waiting to be unpacked and sorted. It comes from the voluntary reps at each school—sometimes boys and sometimes Staff—and they put all the clothes together and send them up in big parcels, either by train or ordinary mail, usually by train. We sort them here before sending abroad."

"That's what I gathered from Jane. As soon as she realised she'd made this mistake she got hold of the woman doing the collecting and sending, but of course it was too late. The parcel had gone."

"How frantic. . . . Do you know when the parcel was sent off?"

"Yes. On Friday morning."

"From Carne? Train or post?"

Miss Brimley had been dreading this question, but she made a guess:

"Post, I believe."

Darting past Miss Brimley, the girl foraged among the pile of papers on her desk and finally produced a stiff-backed exercise book with a label on it marked "Ledger." Opening it at random, she whisked quickly back and forth through the pages, licking the tip of one finger now and then in a harassed sort of way.

"Wouldn't have arrived till yesterday at the earliest," she said. "We certainly won't have opened it yet. Honestly, I don't know how we shall *ever* cope, and with Easter coming up we shall just get worse and worse. On top of that, half our stuff is rotting in the Customs sheds—hullo, here we are!" She pushed the ledger over to Miss Brimley, her slim finger pointing to a pencilled entry in the central column: "Carne, parcel post, 27 lb."

"I wonder," said Miss Brimley, "whether you would mind awfully if we had a quick look inside?"

They went downstairs to the hall.

"It's not quite as hideous as it looks," the girl called over her shoulder. "All the Monday lot will be nearest the door."

"How do you know where they come from if you can't read the postmark?" asked Miss Brimley as the girl began to forage among the parcels.

"We issue volunteer reps with our printed labels. The labels have an originator's number on. In other cases we just ask them to write the name of the school in capitals on the outside. You see, we simply can't allow covering letters; it would be too desperate. When we get a parcel all we have to do is send off a printed card acknowledging with thanks receipt of a parcel of such and such a date weighing so and so much. People who aren't reps won't send parcels to this address, you see—they'll send to the advertised address in Belgrave Square."

"Does the system work?"

"No," replied the girl, "it doesn't. The reps either forget to use our labels or they run out and can't be bothered to tell us. Ten days later they ring up in a rage because they haven't had an acknowledgement. Reps change, too, without letting us know, and the packing and labelling instructions don't get passed on. Sometimes the boys will suddenly decide to do it themselves, and no one tells them the way to go about it. Lady Sarah gets as mad as a snake if parcels turn up at Head Office—they all have to be carted over here for repacking and inventories."

"I see." Miss Brimley watched anxiously as the girl foraged among the parcels, still talking.

"Did you say your friend actually *taught* at Carne? She must be terribly grand. I wonder what the Prince is like: he looks rather soft in his photographs. My cousin went to Carne—he's an utter wet. Do you know what he told me? During Ascot week they all . . . Hello! Here we are!" The girl stood up, a large square parcel in her arms, and carried it to a table which stood in the shadow of the staircase. Miss Brimley, standing beside her as she began carefully to untie the stout twine, looked curiously at the printed label. In its top left-hand corner was stamped the symbol which the Committee had evidently allocated to Carne: C4. After the four the letter B had been written in with ballpoint pen.

"What does the B mean?" asked Miss Brimley.

"Oh, that's a local arrangement at Carne. Miss D'Arcy's the rep there, but they've done so well recently that she coopted a friend to help with dispatch. When we acknowledge we always mention whether it was A or B. B must be terribly keen, whoever she is."

Miss Brimley forbore from inquiring what proportion of the parcels from Carne had originated from Miss D'Arcy, and what proportion from her anonymous assistant.

The girl removed the string and turned the parcel upside down in order to liberate the overlap of wrapping paper. As she did so Miss Brimley caught sight of a faint brown smudge, no more, about the size of a shilling, near the join. It was consistent with her essential rationalism that she should search for any explanation other than that which so loudly presented itself. The girl continued the work of unwrapping, saying suddenly: "I say, Carne was where they had that dreadful murder, wasn't it—that master's wife who got killed by the gipsy? It really is awful, isn't it, how much of that kind of thing goes on? Hm! Thought as much," she remarked, suddenly interrupting herself. She had removed the outer paper, and was about to unwrap the bundle inside when her attention was evidently arrested by the appearance of the inner parcel.

"What?" Miss Brimley said quickly.

The girl laughed. "Oh, only the packing," she said. "The C4Bs are usually so neat—quite the best we get. This is quite different. Not the same person at all. Must be a stand-in. I thought so from the outside."

"How can you be so sure?"

"Oh, it's like handwriting. We can tell." She laughed again, and without more ado removed the last wrapping. "Grey dress, you said, didn't you? Let's see." With both hands she began picking clothes from the top of the pile and laying them to either side. She was nearly halfway through when she exclaimed, "Well, honestly! They must be having a brainstorm," and drew from the bundle of partworn clothes a transparent plastic mackintosh, a very old pair of leather gloves, and a pair of rubber overshoes.

Miss Brimley was holding the edge of the table very tightly. The palms of her hands were throbbing.

"Here's a cape. Damp, too," the girl added in disgust, and tossed the offending articles on to the floor beside the table. Miss Brimley could only think of Smiley's letter: "Whoever killed her must have been covered in blood." Yes, and whoever killed her wore a plastic cape and a hood, rubber overshoes, and those old leather gloves with the terra-cotta stains. Whoever killed Stella Rode had not chanced upon her in the night, but had plotted long ahead, had waited. "Yes," thought Miss Brimley, "had waited for the long nights."

The girl was talking to her again: "I'm afraid it really isn't here."

"No, my dear," Miss Brimley replied, "I see that. Thank you. You've been very sweet." Her voice faltered for a moment, then she managed to say: "I think, my dear, you should leave the parcel exactly as it is now, the wrapping and everything in it. Something very dreadful has happened, and the police will want to . . . know about it and see the parcel. . . . You must trust me, my dear—things aren't quite what they seem. . . ." And somehow she escaped to the comforting freedom of York Gardens and the large-eyed wonder of its waiting children.

289

• • •

She went to a telephone box. She got through to the Sawley Arms and asked a very bored receptionist for Mr. Smiley. Total silence descended on the line until the Trunks operator asked her to put in another three and sixpence. Miss Brimley replied sharply that all she had so far had for her money was a three-minute vacuum; this was followed by the unmistakable sound of the operator sucking her teeth, and then, quite suddenly, by George Smiley's voice:

"George, it's Brim. A plastic mackintosh, a cape, rubber overshoes, and some leather gloves that look as though they're stained with blood. Smudges on some of the wrapping paper, too, by the look of it."

A pause.

"Handwriting on the outside of the parcel?"

"None. The Charity organisers issue printed labels."

"Where is the stuff now? Have you got it?"

"No. I've told the girl to leave everything exactly as it is. It'll be all right for an hour or two. . . . George, are you there?"

"Yes."

"Who did it? Was it the husband?"

"I don't know. I just don't know."

"Do you want me to do anything—about the clothes, I mean? Phone Sparrow or anything?"

"No. I'll see Rigby at once. Good-bye, Brim. Thanks for ringing."

She put back the receiver. He sounded strange, she thought. He seemed to lose touch sometimes. As if he'd switched off.

She walked northwest towards the Embankment. It was long after ten o'clock—the first time she'd been late for Heaven knows how long. She had better take a taxi. Being a frugal woman, however, she took a bus.

Ailsa Brimley did not believe in emergencies, for she enjoyed a discipline of mind uncommon in men and even rarer in women.

290

The greater the emergency, the greater her calm. John Landsbury had remarked upon it: "You have sales resistance to the dramatic, Brim; the rare gift of contempt for what is urgent. I know of a dozen people who would pay you five thousand a year for telling them every day that what is important is seldom urgent. Urgent equals ephemeral, and ephemeral equals unimportant."

She got out of the bus, carefully putting the ticket in the rubbish compartment. As she stood in the warm sunlight of the street, she caught sight of the hoardings advertising the first edition of the evening papers. If it hadn't been for the sun, she might never have looked; but the sun dazzled her and made her glance downwards. And so she did see; she read it in the plump black of the wet newsprint, in the prepacked hysteria of Fleet Street: "All-night search for missing Carne boy."

15 ✻
THE ROAD TO FIELDING

Smiley put down the receiver and walked quickly past the reception desk towards the front door. He must see Rigby at once. Just as he was leaving the hotel he heard his name called. Turning, he saw his old enemy, the night porter, braving the light of day, beckoning to him like Charon with his grey hand.

"They've been on to you from the police station," he observed with undisguised pleasure. "Mr. Rigby wants you, the Inspector. You're to go there at once. At once, see?"

"I'm on my way there now," Smiley replied irritably, and as he pushed his way through the swing doors he heard the old man repeat; "At once, mind; they're waiting for you."

Making his way through the Carne streets, he reflected for the hundredth time on the obscurity of motive in human action: there is no true thing on earth. There is no constant, no dependable point, not even in the purest logic or the most obscure mysticism; least of all in the motives of men when they are moved to act violently.

Had the murderer, now so near discovery, found contentment in the meticulous administration of his plans? For now it was clear beyond a doubt; this was a murder devised to the last detail, even to the weapon inexplicably far from the place of its use; a murder with clues cast to mislead, a murder planned to look unplanned, a murder for a string of beads. Now the mystery of the footprints was solved: having put the overshoes into the parcel, the murderer had walked down the path to the gate, and his own prints had been obscured by the subsequent traffic of feet.

Rigby looked tired.

"You've heard the news, sir, I suppose?"

"What news?"

"About the boy, the boy in Fielding's house, missing all night?"

"No." Smiley felt suddenly sick. "No, I've heard nothing."

"Good Lord, I thought you knew! Half past eight last night Fielding rang us here. Perkins, his head boy, hadn't come back from a music lesson with Mrs. Harlowe, who lives over to Longemede. We put out an alert and started looking for him. They sent a patrol car along the road he should have come back on—he was cycling, you see. The first time they didn't see anything, but on the way back the driver stopped the car at the bottom of Longemede Hill, just where the water-splash is. It occurred to him the lad might have taken a long run at the water-splash from the top of the hill, and come to grief in the dip. They found him half in the ditch, his bike beside him. Dead."

"Oh, my dear God."

"We didn't let on to the press at first. The boy's parents are in Singapore. The father's an Army officer. Fielding sent them a telegram. We've got on to the War Office, too."

They were silent for a moment, then Smiley asked, "How did it happen?"

"We've closed the road and we've been trying to reconstruct the accident. I've got a detective over there now, just having a look. Trouble is, we couldn't do much till the morning. Besides, the men trampled everywhere; you can't blame them. It looks as though he must have fallen near the bottom of the hill and hit his head on a stone: his right temple."

"How did Fielding take it?"

"He was very shaken. Very shaken indeed. I wouldn't have believed it, to be quite honest. He just seemed to . . . give up. There was a lot that had to be done—telegraph the parents, get in touch with the boy's uncle at Windsor, and so on. But he just left all that to Miss Truebody, his housekeeper. If it hadn't been for her, I don't know how he'd have managed. I was with him for about half an hour, then he just broke down, completely, and asked to be left alone."

"How do you mean, broke down?" Smiley asked quickly.

"He cried. Wept like a child," said Rigby evenly. "I'd never have thought it."

Smiley offered Rigby a cigarette and took one himself. "I suppose," he ventured, "it was an accident?"

"I suppose so," Rigby replied woodenly.

"Perhaps," said Smiley, "before we go any farther, I'd better give you my news. I was on my way to see you when you rang. I've just heard from Miss Brimley." And in his precise, rather formal way he related all that Ailsa Brimley had told him, and how he had become curious about the contents of the parcel.

Smiley waited while Rigby telephoned to London. Almost mechanically, Rigby described what he wanted done: the parcel and its contents were to be collected and arrangements made to subject them immediately to forensic examination; the surfaces should be tested for fingerprints. He would be coming up to London himself with some samples of a boy's handwriting and an examination paper; he would want the opinion of a handwriting expert. No, he would be coming by train on the 4:25 from Carne, arriving at Waterloo at 8:05. Could a car be sent to the station to collect him? There was silence, then Rigby said testily, "All right, I'll take a ruddy taxi," and rang off rather abruptly. He looked at Smiley angrily for a moment, then grinned, plucked at his ear and said:

"Sorry, sir; getting a bit edgy." He indicated the far wall with his head and added, "Fighting on too many fronts, I suppose. I shall have to tell the Chief about that parcel, but he's out shooting at the moment—only pigeon, with a couple of friends, he won't be long—but I haven't mentioned your presence here in Carne, as a matter of fact, and if you don't mind I'll . . ."

"Of course," Smiley cut in quickly. "It's much simpler if you keep me out of it."

"I shall tell him it was just a routine inquiry. We shall have to mention Miss Brimley later . . . but there's no point in making things worse, is there?"

"No."

"I shall have to let Janie go, I suppose. . . . She was right, wasn't she? Silver wings in the moonlight."

"I wouldn't—no, I wouldn't let her go, Rigby," said Smiley with unaccustomed vehemence. "Keep her with you as long as you can possibly manage. No more accidents, for heaven's sake. We've had enough."

"Then you don't believe Perkins's death was an accident?"

"Good Lord, no," cried Smiley suddenly, "and nor do you, do you?"

"I've put a detective on to it," Rigby replied coolly. "I can't take the case myself. I shall be needed on the Rode murder. The Chief will have to call the Yard in now; there'll be hell to pay, I can tell you. He thought it was all over bar the shouting."

"And in the meantime?"

"In the meantime, sir, I'm going to do my damnedest to find out who killed Stella Rode."

"If," said Smiley slowly, "if you find fingerprints on that mackintosh, which I doubt, will you have anything . . . local . . . to compare them with?"

"We've got Rode's, of course, and Janie's."

295

"But not Fielding's?"

Rigby hesitated.

"As a matter of fact, we have," he said at last. "From long ago. But nothing to do with this kind of thing."

"It was during the war," said Smiley. "His brother told me. Up in the North. It was hushed up, wasn't it?"

Rigby nodded. "So far as I heard, only the D'Arcys knew; and the Master, of course. It happened in the holidays—some Air Force boy. The Chief was very helpful . . ."

Smiley shook hands with Rigby and made his way down the familiar pine staircase. He noticed again the vaguely institutional smell of floor polish and carbolic soap, like the smell at Fielding's house.

He walked slowly back towards the Sawley Arms. At the point where he should have turned left to his hotel, however, he hesitated, then seemed to change his mind. Slowly, almost reluctantly, he crossed the road to the Abbey Close, and walked along the southern edge towards Fielding's house. He looked worried, almost frightened.

16 ✻
A TASTE FOR MUSIC

Miss Truebody opened the door. The rims of her eyes were pink, as though she had been weeping.

"I wonder if I might see Mr. Fielding? To say good-bye."

She hesitated: "Mr. Fielding's very upset. I doubt whether he'll want to see anyone." He followed her into the hall and watched her go to the study door. She knocked, inclined her head, then gently turned the handle and let herself in. It was a long time before she returned. "He'll be out shortly," she said, without looking at him. "Will you take off your coat?" She waited while he struggled out of his overcoat, then took it from him and hung it beside the Van Gogh chair. They stood together in silence, both looking towards the study door.

Then, quite suddenly, Fielding was standing in the half-open doorway, unshaven and in his shirt-sleeves. "For Christ's sake," he said thickly. "What do you want?"

"I just wanted to say good-bye, Fielding, and to offer you my condolences."

Fielding looked at him hard for a moment; he was leaning

heavily against the doorway. "Well, good-bye. Thank you for calling." He waved one hand vaguely in the air. "You needn't have bothered really, need you?" he added rudely. "You could have sent me a card, couldn't you?"

"I could have done, yes; it just seemed so very tragic, when he was so near success."

"What do you mean? What the devil do you mean?"

"I mean in his work . . . the improvement. Simon Snow was telling me all about it. Amazing really, the way Rode brought him on."

A long silence, then Fielding spoke: "Good-bye, Smiley. Thanks for coming." He was turning back into the study as Smiley called:

"Not at all . . . not at all. I suppose poor Rode must have been bucked with those exam results, too. I mean it was more or less a matter of life and death for Perkins, passing that exam, wasn't it? He wouldn't have got his remove next Half if he'd failed in science. They might have superannuated him, I suppose, even though he was head of the house; then he couldn't have sat for the Army. Poor Perkins, he had a lot to thank Rode for, didn't he? And you, too, Fielding, I'm sure. You must have helped him wonderfully . . . both of you did, you and Rode; Rode and Fielding. His parents ought to know that. They're rather hard up, I gather; the father's in the Army, isn't he, in Singapore? It must have been a great effort keeping the boy at Carne. It will comfort them to know how much was done for him, won't it, Fielding?"

Smiley was very pale. "You've heard the latest, I suppose," he continued. "About that wretched gipsy woman who killed Stella Rode? They've decided she's fit to plead. I suppose they'll hang her. That'll be the third death, won't it? You know, I'll tell you an odd thing—just between ourselves, Fielding. I don't believe she did it. Do you? I don't believe she did it at all."

He was not looking at Fielding. He had clasped his little hands tightly behind his back, and he stood with his shoulders bowed and his head inclined to one side, as though listening for an answer.

Fielding seemed to feel Smiley's words like a physical pain. Slowly he shook his head:

"No," he said; "no. Carne killed them; it was Carne. It could only happen here. It's the game we play: the exclusion game. Divide and rule!" He looked Smiley full in the face, and shouted: "Now for God's sake go! You've got what you want, haven't you? You can pin me on your little board, can't you?" And then, to Smiley's distress, he began sobbing in great uncontrollable gulps, holding his hand across his brow. He appeared suddenly grotesque, stemming the childish tears with his chalky hand, his cumbersome feet turned inwards. Gently, Smiley coaxed him back into the study, gently sat him before the dead fire. Then he began talking to him softly and with compassion.

"If what I think is true, there isn't much time," he began. "I want you to tell me about Tim Perkins—about the exam." Fielding, his face buried in his hands, nodded.

"He would have failed, wouldn't he? He would have failed and not got his remove; he'd have had to leave." Fielding was silent. "After the exam that day, Rode gave him the writing-case to bring here, the case that contained the papers; Rode was doing chapel duty that week and wouldn't be going home before dinner, but he wanted to correct the papers that night, after his dinner with you."

Fielding took his hands from his face and leant back in his chair, his great head tilted back, his eyes closed. Smiley continued:

"Perkins came home, and that evening he brought the case to you, as Rode told him to, for safe keeping. Perkins, after all, was head of your house, a responsible boy. . . . He gave you the case and you asked him how he'd done in the exam."

"He wept," said Fielding suddenly. "He wept as only a child can."

"And after breaking down he told you he had cheated? That he had looked up the answers and copied them on to his paper. Is that right? And after the murder of Stella Rode he remembered what else he had seen in the suitcase?"

Fielding was standing up. "No! Don't you see? Tim wouldn't have cheated to save his life! That's the whole point, the whole bloody irony of it," he shouted. "He never cheated at all. I cheated for him."

"But you couldn't! You couldn't copy his handwriting!"

"He wrote with a ball-pen. It was only formulae and diagrams. When he'd gone, and left me alone with the case, I looked at his paper. It was hopeless—he'd only done two out of seven questions. So I cheated for him. I just cribbed them from the science book, and wrote them with blue ballpoint, the kind we all use. Abbots' sell them. I copied his hand as best I could. It only needed about three lines of figures. The rest was diagrams."

"Then it was you who opened the case? You who saw . . ."

"Yes. It was me, I tell you, not Tim! He couldn't cheat to save his life! But Tim paid for it, don't you see? When the marks were published. Tim must have known something was wrong with them. After all, he'd only attempted two questions out of seven and yet he'd got sixty-one percent. But he knew nothing else, nothing!"

For a long time neither spoke. Fielding was standing over Smiley, exultant with the relief of sharing his secret, and Smiley was looking vaguely past him, his face drawn in deep concentration.

"And of course," he said finally, "when Stella was murdered, you knew who had done it."

"Yes," replied Fielding. "I knew that Rode had killed her."

Fielding poured himself a brandy and gave one to Smiley. He seemed to have recovered his self-control. He sat down and looked at Smiley thoughtfully for a time.

"I've got no money," he said at last. "None. Nobody knows that except the Master. Oh, they know I'm more or less broke, but they don't know how broke. Long ago I made an ass of myself. I got into trouble. It was in the war, when staff was impossible. I had a boys' house and was practically running the school— D'Arcy and I. We were running it together, and the Master running us. Then I made an ass of myself. It was during the holidays. I was up North at the time, giving a course of talks at an RAF educational place. And I stepped out of line. Badly. They pulled me in. And along came D'Arcy wearing his country overcoat and bringing the Master's terms: Come back to Carne, my dear fellow, and we'll say no more about it; go on running your house, my dear fellow, and giving of your wisdom. There's been no publicity. We know it will never happen again, my dear fellow, and we're dreadfully hard up for staff. Come back as a temporary. So I did, and I've been one ever since, going cap in hand to darling D'Arcy every December asking for my contract to be renewed. And, of course—no pension. I shall have to teach at a crammer's. There's a place in Somerset where they'll take me. I'm seeing their Headmaster in London on Thursday. It's a sort of breaker's yard for old dons. The Master had to know, because he gave me a reference."

"That was why you couldn't tell anyone? Because of Perkins?"

"In a way, yes. I mean they'd want to know all sorts of things. I did it for Tim, you see. The Governors wouldn't have liked that much . . . inordinate affection. . . . It looks bad, doesn't it? But it wasn't that kind of affection, Smiley, not anymore. You never heard him play the 'cello. He wasn't marvellous, but just sometimes he would play so beautifully, with a kind of studious simplicity, that was indescribably good. He was an awkward boy, and when he played well it was such a surprise. You should have heard him play."

"You didn't want to drag him into it. If you told the police what you had seen it would ruin Tim, too?"

Fielding nodded. "In the whole of Carne, he was the one thing I loved."

"Loved?" asked Smiley.

"For God's sake," said Fielding in an exhausted voice, "why not?"

"His parents wanted him to go to Sandhurst; I didn't, I'm afraid. I thought that if I could keep him here another Half or two I might be able to get him a music scholarship. That's why I made him Head of House: I wanted his parents to keep him on because he was doing so well." Fielding paused. "He was a rotten Head of House," he added.

"And what exactly was in the writing-case," Smiley asked, "when you opened it that evening to look at Tim's exam paper?"

"A sheet of transparent plastic . . . it may have been one of those pack-away cape things—an old pair of gloves, and a pair of homemade galoshes."

"Homemade?"

"Yes. Hacked from a pair of Wellington boots, I should think."

"That's all?"

"No. There was a length of heavy cable, I presumed for demonstrating something in his science lessons. It seemed natural enough in winter to carry waterproofs about. Then, after the murder, I realised how he had done it."

"Did you know," Smiley asked him, "why he had done it?"

Fielding seemed to hesitate: "Rode's a guinea pig," he began, "the first man we've had from a grammar school. Most of us are old Carnians ourselves, in fact. Focused when we start. Rode wasn't, and Carne thrilled him. The very name Carne means quality, and Rode loved quality. His wife wasn't like that. She had her standards and they were different, but just as good. I used to watch Rode in the Abbey sometimes on Sunday mornings. Tutors sit at the end of pews, right by the aisle, you know. I used to watch his face as the choir processed past him in white and scarlet, and the Master in his doctor's robes and the Governors and Guardians behind him. Rode was drunk—drunk with the pride of Carne. We're heady wine for the grammar school men, you know. It must have hurt him terribly that Stella wouldn't share any of that. You could see it did. The night they came to dinner with me, the night she died, they argued. I never told anyone, but they did. The Master had preached a sermon at Compline that evening: 'Hold fast to that which is good.' Rode talked about it at dinner; he couldn't take much drink, you know, he wasn't used to it. He was full of this sermon and of the eloquence of the Master. She never came to the Abbey—she went to that drab tabernacle by the station. He went on and on about the beauty of the Abbey service, the dignity, the reverence. She kept quiet till he'd finished, then laughed, and said: 'Poor old Stan. You'll always be Stan to me.' I've never seen anyone so angry as he was then. He went quite pale."

Fielding swept his white hair from his eyes and went on, with something like the old panache: "I've watched her, too, at meals. Not just here, but at dinner parties elsewhere, when we've both been invited. I've watched her do the simplest things—like eating an apple. She'd peel it in one piece, round and round till the whole peel fell off. Then she'd cut the apple and dice the quarters, getting it all ready before she ate it. She might have been a miner's wife preparing it for her husband. She must have seen how people do things here, but it never occurred to her that she ought to copy them. I admire that. So do you, I expect. But Carne doesn't—and Rode didn't; above all, Rode didn't. He'd watch her, and I think he grew to hate her for not conforming. He came to see her as the bar to his success, the one factor which would deprive him of a great career. Once he'd reached that conclusion, what could he do? He couldn't divorce her—that would do him more harm than remaining married to her. Rode knew what Carne would think of divorce; we're a Church foundation, remember. So he killed her. He plotted a squalid murder, and with his little scientist's mind he gave them all the clues they wanted. Fabricated clues. Clues that would point to a murderer who didn't exist. But something went wrong; Tim Perkins got sixty-one percent. He'd got an impossible mark—he must have cheated. He'd had the opportunity—he'd had the papers in the case. Rode put his little mind to it and decided what had happened: Tim

303

had opened the case and he'd seen the cape and the boots and the gloves. And the cable. So Rode killed him, too."

With surprising energy, Fielding got up and gave himself more brandy. His face was flushed, almost exultant.

Smiley stood up. "When did you say you'll be coming to London? Thursday, wasn't it?"

"Yes. I had arranged to lunch with my crammer man at one of those dreadful clubs in Pall Mall. I always go into the wrong one, don't you? But I'm afraid there's not much point in my seeing him now, is there, if all this is going to come out? Not even a crammer's will take me then."

Smiley hesitated.

"Come and dine with me that evening. Spend the night if you want. I'll ask one or two other people. We'll have a party. You'll feel better by then. We can talk a bit. I might be able to help you . . . for Adrian's sake."

"Thank you. I should like to. Interview apart, I've got some odds and ends to clear up in London, anyway."

"Good. Quarter to eight. Bywater Street, Chelsea, number 9A." Fielding wrote it down in his diary. His hand was quite steady.

"Black tie?" asked Fielding, his pen poised, and some imp made Smiley reply:

"I usually do, but it doesn't matter." There was a moment's silence.

"I suppose," Fielding began tentatively, "that all this *will* come out in the trial, about Tim and me? I'll be ruined if it does, you know, ruined."

"I don't see how they can prevent it."

"I feel much better now, anyway," said Fielding, "much."

With a cursory good-bye, Smiley left him alone. He walked quickly back to the police station, reasonably confident that Terence Fielding was the most accomplished liar he had met for a long time.

17 ✺
RABBIT RUN

He knocked on Rigby's door and walked straight in.

"I'm awfully afraid you'll have to arrest Stanley Rode," he began, and recounted his interview with Fielding.

"I shall have to tell the Chief," said Rigby doubtfully. "Would you like to repeat all that in front of him? If we're going to pull in a Carne master, I think the Chief had better know first. He's just come back. Hang on a minute." He picked up the telephone on his desk and asked for the Chief Constable. A few minutes later they were walking in silence down a carpeted corridor. On either wall hung photographs of rugby and cricket teams, some yellow and faded from the Indian sun, others done in a sepia tint much favoured by Carne photographers in the early part of the century. At intervals along the corridor stood empty buckets of brilliant red, with FIRE printed carefully in white on the outside. At the far end of the corridor was a dark oak door. Rigby knocked and waited. There was silence. He knocked again and was answered with a cry of "Come!"

Two very large spaniels watched them come in. Behind the spaniels, at an enormous desk, Brigadier Havelock, O.B.E., Chief Constable of Carne, sat like a water rat on a raft.

The few strands of white hair which ran laterally across his otherwise bald head were painstakingly adjusted to cover the maximum area. This gave him an oddly wet look, as if he had just emerged from the river. His moustache, which lavishly compensated for the scarcity of other hair, was yellow and appeared quite solid. He was a very small man, and he wore a brown suit and a stiff white collar with rounded corners.

"Sir," Rigby began, "may I introduce Mr. Smiley from London?" He came out from behind his desk as if he were giving himself up, unconvinced but resigned. Then he pushed out a little, knobbly hand and said, "From London, eh? How d'you do, sir," all at once, as if he'd learnt it by heart.

"Mr. Smiley's here on a private visit, sir," Rigby continued. "He is an acquaintance of Mr. Fielding."

"Quite a card, Fielding, quite a card," the Chief Constable snapped.

"Yes, indeed, sir," said Rigby, and went on:

"Mr. Smiley called on Mr. Fielding just now, sir, to take his leave before returning to London." Havelock shot a beady glance at Smiley, as if wondering whether he were fit to make the journey.

"Mr. Fielding made a kind of statement, which he substantiated with new evidence of his own. About the murder, sir."

"Well, Rigby?" he said challengingly. Smiley intervened:

"He said that the husband had done it; Stanley Rode. Fielding said that when his head boy brought him Rode's writing-case containing the examination papers . . ."

"What examination papers?"

"Rode was invigilating that afternoon, you remember. He was also doing chapel duty before going on to dinner at Fielding's house. As an expediency, he gave the papers to Perkins to take. . . ."

"The boy who had the accident?" Havelock asked.

"Yes."

"You know a lot about it," said Havelock darkly.

"Fielding said that when Perkins brought him the case, Fielding opened it. He wanted to see how Perkins had done in the science paper. It was vital to the boy's future that he should get his remove," Smiley went on.

"Oh, work's the only thing now," said Havelock bitterly. "Wasn't the way when I was a boy here, I assure you."

"When Fielding opened the case, the papers were inside. So was a plastic cape, an old pair of leather gloves, and a pair of rubber overshoes, cut from Wellingtons."

A pause.

"Good God! Good God! Hear that, Rigby? That's what they found in the parcel in London. Good God!"

"Finally, there was a length of cable, heavy cable, in the case as well. It was this writing-case that Rode went back for, you remember, on the night of the murder," Smiley concluded. It was like feeding a child—you couldn't overload the spoon.

There was a very long silence indeed. Then Rigby, who seemed to know his man, said:

"Motive was self-advancement in the profession, sir. Mrs. Rode showed no desire to improve her station, dressed in a slovenly manner, and took no part in the religious life of the school."

"Just a minute," said Havelock. "Rode planned the murder from the start, correct?"

"Yes, sir."

"He wanted to make it look like robbery with violence."

"Yes, sir."

"Having collected the writing-case, he walked back to North Fields. Then what does he do?"

"He puts on the plastic cape and hood, overshoes and gloves. He arms himself with the weapon, sir. He lets himself in by the garden gate, crosses the back garden, goes to the front door, and rings the bell, sir. His wife comes to the door. He knocks her down, drags her to the conservatory, and murders her. He rinses the clothes under the tap and puts them in the parcel. Having sealed the parcel, he walks down the drive this time to the front gate, following the path, sir, knowing that his own footprints will soon be obscured by other people's. Having got to the road, where the snow was hard and showed no prints, he turned round and reentered the house, playing the part of the distressed husband, taking care, when he discovers the body, sir, to put his own fingerprints over the glove-marks. There was one article that was too dangerous to send, sir. The weapon."

"All right, Rigby. Pull him in. Mr. Borrow will give you a warrant if you want one; otherwise I'll ring Lord Sawley."

"Yes, sir. And I'll send Sergeant Low to take a full statement from Mr. Fielding, sir?"

"Why the devil didn't he speak up earlier, Rigby?"

"Have to ask him that, sir," said Rigby woodenly, and left the room.

"You a Carnian?" Havelock asked, pushing a silver cigarette-box across the desk.

"No. No, I'm afraid not," Smiley replied.

"How d'you know Fielding?"

"We met at Oxford after the war."

"Queer card, Fielding, very queer. Say your name was Smiley?"

"Yes."

"There was a fellow called Smiley married Ann Sercombe, Lord Sawley's cousin. Damned pretty girl, Ann was, and went and married this fellow. Some funny little beggar in the Civil Service with an OBE and a gold watch. Sawley was damned annoyed." Smiley said nothing. "Sawley's got a son at Carne. Know that?"

"I read it in the press, I think."

"Tell me—this fellow Rode. He's a grammar school chap, isn't he?"

"I believe so, yes."

"Damned odd business. Experiments never pay, do they? You can't experiment with tradition."

"No. No, indeed."

"That's the trouble today. Like Africa. Nobody seems to understand you can't build society overnight. It takes centuries to make a gentleman." Havelock frowned to himself and fiddled with the paper-knife on his desk.

"Wonder how he got his cable into that ditch, the thing he killed her with. He wasn't out of our sight for forty-eight hours after the murder."

"That," said Smiley, "is what puzzles me. So does Jane Lyn."

"What d'you mean?"

"I don't believe Rode would have had the nerve to walk back to the house after killing his wife knowing that Jane Lyn had seen him do it. Assuming, of course, that he *did* know, which seems likely. It's too cool . . . too cool altogether."

"Odd, damned odd," muttered Havelock. He looked at his watch, pushing his left elbow outwards to do so, in a swift equestrian movement which Smiley found comic, and a little sad. The minutes ticked by. Smiley wondered if he should leave, but he had a vague feeling that Havelock wanted his company.

"There'll be a hell of a fuss," said Havelock. "It isn't every day you arrest a Carne tutor for murder." He put down the paper-knife sharply on the desk.

"These bloody journalists ought to be horsewhipped!" he declared. "Look at the stuff they print about the Royal Family. Wicked, wicked!" He got up, crossed the room and sat himself in a leather armchair by the fire. One of the spaniels went and sat at his feet.

"What made him do it, I wonder. What the devil made him do it? His own wife, I mean; a fellow like that." Havelock said this simply, appealing for enlightenment.

"I don't believe," said Smiley slowly, "that we can ever entirely know what makes anyone do anything."

"My God, you're dead right. . . . What do you do for a living, Smiley?"

"After the war I was at Oxford for a bit. Teaching and research. I'm in London now."

"One of those clever coves, eh?"

Smiley wondered when Rigby would return.

"Know anything about this fellow's family? Has he got people, or anything?"

"I think they're both dead," Smiley answered, and the telephone on Havelock's desk rang sharply. It was Rigby. Stanley Rode had disappeared.

18 ✾
AFTER THE BALL

He caught the 1:30 train to London. He just made it after an argument at his hotel about the bill. He left a note for Rigby giving his address and telephone number in London and asking him to telephone that night when the laboratory tests were completed. There was nothing else for him to do in Carne.

As the train pulled slowly out of Carne and one by one the familiar landmarks disappeared into the cold February mist, George Smiley was filled with a feeling of relief. He hadn't wanted to come, he knew that. He'd been afraid of the place where his wife had spent her childhood, afraid to see the fields where she had lived. But he had found nothing, not the faintest memory, neither in the lifeless outlines of Sawley Castle, nor in the surrounding countryside, to remind him of her. Only the gossip remained, as it would while the Hechts and the Havelocks survived to parade their acquaintance with the first family in Carne.

He took a taxi to Chelsea, carried his suitcase upstairs and unpacked with the care of a man accustomed to living alone. He

311

thought of having a bath, but decided to ring Ailsa Brimley first. The telephone was by his bed. He sat on the edge of the bed and dialled the number. A tinny model-voice sang: "Unipress, good afternoon," and he asked for Miss Brimley. There was a long silence, then, "Ah'm afraid Miss Brimley is in conference. Can someone else answer your query?"

Query, thought Smiley. Good God! Why on earth "query"— why not "question" or "inquiry"?

"No," he replied. "Just tell her Mr. Smiley rang." He put back the receiver and went into the bathroom and turned on the hot tap. He was fiddling with his cuff links when the telephone rang. It was Ailsa Brimley:

"George? I think you'd better come round at once. We've got a visitor. Mr. Rode from Carne. He wants to talk to us." Pulling on his jacket, he ran out into the street and hailed a taxi.

19 ❋
DISPOSAL OF A LEGEND

The descending escalator was packed with the staff of Unipress, homebound and heavy-eyed. To them, the sight of a fat, middle-aged gentleman bounding up the adjoining staircase provided unexpected entertainment, so that Smiley was hastened on his way by the jeers of office boys and the laughter of typists. On the first floor he paused to study an enormous board carrying the titles of a quarter of the national dailies. Finally, under the heading of "Technical and Miscellaneous," he spotted the *Christian Voice,* Room 619. The lift seemed to go up very slowly. Formless music issued from behind its plush, while a boy in a monkey jacket flicked his hips on the heavier beats. The golden doors parted with a sigh, the boy said "Six," and Smiley stepped quickly into the corridor. A moment or two later, he was knocking on the door of Room 619. It was opened by Ailsa Brimley.

"George, how nice," she said brightly. "Mr. Rode will be dreadfully pleased to see you." And without any further introduction

313

she led him into her office. In an armchair near the window sat Stanley Rode, tutor of Carne, in a neat black overcoat. As Smiley entered he stood up and held out his hand. "Good of you to come, sir," he said woodenly. "Very." The same flat manner, the same cautious voice.

"How can I help you?" asked Smiley.

They all sat down. Smiley offered Miss Brimley a cigarette and lit it for her.

"It's about this article you're writing about Stella," he began. "I feel awful about it really, because you've been so good to her, and her memory, if you see what I mean. I know you wish well, but I don't want you to write it."

Smiley said nothing, and Ailsa was wise enough to keep quiet. From now on it was Smiley's interview. The silence didn't worry him, but it seemed to worry Rode.

"It wouldn't be right; it wouldn't do at all. Mr. Glaston agreed; I spoke to him yesterday before he left and he agreed. I just couldn't let you write that stuff."

"Why not?"

"Too many people know, you see. Poor Mr. Cardew, I asked him. He knows a lot; and a lot about Stella, so I asked him. He understands why I gave up Chapel, too; I couldn't bear to see her going there every Sunday and going down on her knees." He shook his head. "It was all wrong. It just made a fool of your faith."

"What did Mr. Cardew say?"

"He said we should not be the judges. We should let God judge. But I said to him it wouldn't be right, those people knowing her and knowing what she'd done, and then reading all that stuff in the *Voice*. They'd think it was crazy. He didn't seem to see that, he just said to leave it to God. But I can't, Mr. Smiley."

Again no one spoke for a time. Rode sat quite still, save for a very slight rocking movement of his head. Then he began to talk again:

"I didn't believe old Mr. Glaston at first. He said she was bad, but I didn't believe it. They lived up on the hill then, Gorse Hill, only a step from the Tabernacle; Stella and her father. They never seemed to keep servants for long, so she did most of the work. I used to call in Sunday mornings sometimes after church. Stella looked after her father, cooked for him and everything, and I always wondered how I'd ever have the nerve to ask Mr. Glaston for her. The Glastons were big people in Branxome. I was teaching at Grammar School in those days. They let me teach part-time while I read for my degree, and I made up my mind that if I passed the exam I'd ask her to marry me.

"The Sunday after the results came out, I went round to the house after morning service. Mr. Glaston opened the door himself. He took me straight into the study. You could see half the potteries in Poole from the window, and the sea beyond. He sat me down and he said: 'I know what you're here for, Stanley. You want to marry Stella. But you don't know her,' he said, 'you don't know her.' 'I've been visiting two years, Mr. Glaston,' I said, 'and I think I know my mind.' Then he started talking about her. I never thought to hear a human being talk like that of his own child. He said she was bad—bad in her heart. That she was full of malice. That was why no servants would stay at the Hill. He told me how she'd lead people on, all kind and warm, till they'd told her everything, then she'd hurt them, saying wicked, wicked things, half true, half lies. He told me a lot more besides, and I didn't believe it, not a word. I think I lost my head; I called him a jealous old man who didn't want to lose his housekeeper, a lying, jealous old man who wanted his child to wait on him till he died. I said it was him who was bad, not Stella, and I shouted at him liar, liar. He didn't seem to hear, just shook his head, and I ran out into the hall and called Stella. She'd been in the kitchen, I think, and she came to me and put her arms round me and kissed me.

"We were married a month later, and the old man gave her away. He shook my hand at the wedding and called me a fine man, and I thought what an old hypocrite he was. He gave us money—to me, not her—two thousand pounds. I thought

315

perhaps he was trying to make up for the dreadful things he'd said, and later I wrote to him and said I forgave him. He never answered and I didn't see him often after that.

"For a year or more we were happy enough at Branxome. She was just what I thought she'd be, neat and simple. She liked to go for walks and kiss at the stiles; she liked to be a bit grand sometimes, going to the Dolphin for dinner all dressed up. It meant a lot to me then, I don't mind admitting, going to the right places with Mr. Glaston's daughter. He was Rotary and on the Council and quite a figure in Branxome. She used to tease me about it—in front of other people, too, which got me a bit. I remember one time we went to the Dolphin, one of the waiters there was a bloke called Johnnie Raglan. We'd been to school together. Johnnie was a bit of a tear-about and hadn't done anything much since he'd left school except run after girls and get into trouble. Stella knew him, I don't know how, and she waved to him as soon as we'd sat down. Johnnie came over and Stella made him bring another chair and sit with us. The Manager looked daggers, but he didn't dare to do anything because she was Samuel Glaston's daughter. Johnnie stayed there all the meal and Stella talked to him about school and what I was like. Johnnie was pleased as punch and got cheeky, saying I'd been a swat and a good boy and all the rest, and how Johnnie had knocked me about—lies most of it, and she egged him on. I went for her afterwards and said I didn't pay good money at the Dolphin to hear Johnnie Raglan tell a lot of tall stories, and she turned on me fast like a cat. It was her money, she said, and Johnnie was as good as me any day. Then she was sorry and kissed me and I pretended to forgive her."

Sweat was forming on his face; he was talking fast, the words tripping over each other. It was like a man recalling a nightmare, as if the memory were still there, the fear only half gone. He paused and looked sharply at Smiley as if expecting him to speak, but Smiley seemed to be looking past him, his face impassive, its soft contours grown hard.

"Then we went to Carne. I'd just started reading *The Times* and I saw the advert. They wanted a science tutor and I applied. Mr. D'Arcy interviewed me and I got the job. It wasn't till we got to Carne that I knew that what her father had said was true. She hadn't been very keen on Chapel before, but as soon as she got here she went in for it in a big way. She knew it would look wrong, that it would hurt me. Branxome's a fine big church, you see; there was nothing funny about going to Branxome Tabernacle. But at Carne it was different; Carne Tabernacle's a little out-of-the-way place with a tin roof. She wanted to be different, to spite the school and me, by playing the humble one. I wouldn't have minded if she'd been sincere, but she wasn't, Mr. Cardew knew that. He got to know Stella, Mr. Cardew did. I think her father told him; anyway, Mr. Cardew was up North before, and he knew the family well. For all I know he wrote to Mr. Glaston, or went and saw him or something.

"She began there well enough. The townspeople were all pleased enough to see her—a wife from the School coming to the Tabernacle, that had never happened before. Then she took to running the appeal for the refugees—to collecting clothes and all that. Miss D'Arcy was running it for the school, Mr. D'Arcy's sister, and Stella wanted to beat her at her own game—to get more from the Chapel people than Miss D'Arcy got from the School. But I knew what she was doing, and so did Mr. Cardew, and so did the townspeople in the end. She listened. Every drop of gossip and dirt, she hoarded it away. She'd come home of an evening sometimes—Wednesdays and Fridays she did her Chapel work—and she'd throw off her coat and laugh till I thought she'd gone mad.

" 'I've got them! I've got them all,' she'd say, 'I know all their little secrets and I've got them in the hollow of my hand, Stan.' That's what she'd say. And those that realised grew to be frightened of her. They all gossiped, Heaven knows, but not to profit from it, not like Stella. Stella was cunning; anything decent, anything good, she'd drag it down and spoil it. There were a dozen she'd got the measure of. There was Mulligan the furniture man; he's got a daughter with a kid near Leamington. Somehow she found out the girl wasn't married—they'd sent her to an aunt to have her baby and begin again up there. She rang up Mulligan once, something to do with a bill for moving Simon Snow's furniture, and she said 'Greetings from Leamington Spa, Mr. Mulligan. We need a little cooperation.' She told me that—she came home laughing her head off and told me. But they got her in the end, didn't they? They got their own back!"

Smiley nodded slowly, his eyes now turned fully upon Rode. "Yes," he said at last, "they got their own back."

"They thought Mad Janie did it, but I didn't. Janie'd as soon have killed her own sister as Stella. They were as close as moon and stars, that's what Stella said. They'd talk together for hours in the evenings when I was out late on Societies or Extra Tuition. Stella cooked food for her, gave her clothes and money. It gave her a feeling of power to help a creature like Janie, and have her fawning round. Not because she was kind, but because she was cruel.

"She'd brought a little dog with her from Branxome, a mongrel. One day a few months ago I came home and found it lying in the garage whimpering, terrified. It was limping and had blood on its back. She'd beaten it. She must have gone mad. I knew she'd beaten it before, but never like that; never. Then something happened—I shouted at her and she laughed and then I hit her. Not hard, but hard enough. In the face. I gave her twenty-four hours to have the dog destroyed or I'd tell the police. She screamed at me—it was her dog and she'd damn' well do what she liked with it—but next day she put on her little black hat and took the dog to the vet. I suppose she told him some tale. She could spin a good tale about anything, Stella could. She kind of stepped into a part and played it right through. Like the tale she told the Hungarians. Miss D'Arcy had some refugees to stay from London once and Stella told them such a tale they ran away and had to be taken back to London. Miss D'Arcy paid for their fares and everything, even had the welfare officer down to see them and try and put things right. I don't think Miss D'Arcy ever knew who'd got at them,

318

but I did—Stella told me. She laughed, always that same laugh: 'There's your fine lady, Stan. Look at her charity now.'

"After the dog, she took to pretending I was violent, cringing away whenever I came near, holding her arm up as though I was going to hit her again. She even made out I was plotting to murder her: she went and told Mr. Cardew I was. She didn't believe it herself; she'd laugh about it sometimes. She said to me: 'It's no good killing me now, Stan; they'll all know who's done it.' But other times she'd whine and stroke me, begging me not to kill her. 'You'll kill me in the long nights!' She'd scream it out—it was the words that got her, the long nights, she liked the sound of them the way an actor does, and she'd build a whole story round them. 'Oh, Stan,' she'd say, 'keep me safe in the long nights.' You know how it is when you never meant to do anything anyway, and someone goes on begging you not to do it? You think you might do it after all, you begin to consider the possibility."

Miss Brimley drew in her breath rather quickly. Smiley stood up and walked over to Rode.

"Why don't we go back to my house for some food?" he said. "We can talk this over quietly. Among friends."

They took a taxi to Bywater Street. Rode sat beside Ailsa Brimley, more relaxed now, and Smiley, opposite him on a dropseat, watched him and wondered. And it occurred to him that the most important thing about Rode was that he had no friends. Smiley was reminded of Büchner's fairy tale of the child left alone in an empty world who, finding no one to talk to, went to the moon because it smiled at him, but the moon was made of rotten wood. And when the sun and moon and stars had all turned to nothing, he tried to go back to the earth, but it had gone.

Perhaps because Smiley was tired, or perhaps because he was getting a little old, he felt a movement of sudden compassion towards Rode, such as children feel for the poor and parents for their children. Rode had tried so hard—he had used

319

Carne's language, bought the right clothes, and thought as best he could the right thoughts, yet remained hopelessly apart, hopelessly alone.

He lit the gas-fire in the drawing room while Ailsa Brimley went to the delicatessen in the King's Road for soup and eggs. He poured out whisky and soda and gave one to Rode, who drank it in short sips, without speaking.

"I had to tell somebody," he said at last. "I thought you'd be a good person. I didn't want you to print that article, though. Too many knew, you see."

"How many really knew?"

"Only those she'd gone for, I think. I suppose about a dozen townspeople. And Mr. Cardew, of course. She was terribly cunning, you see. She didn't often pass on gossip. She knew to a hair how far she could go. Those who knew were the ones she'd got on the hook. Oh, and D'Arcy, Felix D'Arcy, he knew. She had something special there, something she never told me about. There were nights when she'd put on her shawl and slip out, all excited as if she was going to a party. Quite late sometimes, eleven or twelve. I'd never ask her where she was going because it only bucked her, but sometimes she'd nod at me all cunning and say, 'You don't know, Stan, but D'Arcy does. D'Arcy knows and he can't tell,' and then she'd laugh again and try and look mysterious, and off she'd go."

Smiley was silent for a long time, watching Rode and thinking. Then he asked suddenly: "What was Stella's blood group, do you know?"

"Mine's B. I know that. I was a donor at Branxome. Hers was different."

"How do you know that?"

"She had a test before we were married. She used to suffer from anaemia. I remember hers being different, that's all. Probably A. I can't remember for sure. Why?"

"Where were you registered as a donor?"

"North Poole Transfusion Centre."

"Will they know you there still? Are you still recorded there?"

"I suppose so."

The front doorbell rang. It was Ailsa Brimley, back from her shopping.

Ailsa installed herself in the kitchen, while Rode and Smiley sat in the warm comfort of the drawing room.

"Tell me something else," said Smiley, "about the night of the murder. Why did you leave the writing-case behind? Was it absentmindedness?"

"No, not really. I was on Chapel duty that night, so Stella and I arrived separately at Fielding's house. She got there before I did and I think Fielding gave the case to her—right at the start of the evening so that it wouldn't get forgotten. He said something about it later that evening. She'd put the case beside her coat in the hall. It was only a little thing about eighteen inches by twelve. I could have sworn she was carrying it as we stood in the hall saying good-bye, but I must have been mistaken. It wasn't till we got to the house that she asked me what I'd done with it."

"*She* asked *you* what you'd done with it?"

"Yes. Then she threw a temper and said I expected her to remember everything. I didn't particularly want to go back, I could have rung Fielding and arranged to collect it first thing next morning, but Stella wouldn't hear of it. She made me go. I didn't like to tell the police all this stuff about us quarrelling, it didn't seem right."

Smiley nodded. "When you got back to Fielding's, you rang the bell?"

"Yes. There's the front door, then a glass door inside, a sort of french window to keep out draughts. The front door was still open, and the light was on in the hall. I rang the bell and collected the case from Fielding."

321

. . .

They had finished supper when the telephone rang.

"Rigby here, Mr. Smiley. I've got the laboratory results. They're rather puzzling."

"The exam paper first: it doesn't tally?"

"No, it doesn't. The boffins here say all the figures and writing were done with the same ballpoint pen. They can't be sure about the diagrams but they say the legend on all the diagrams corresponds to the rest of the script on the sheet."

"All done by the boy after all in fact?"

"Yes. I brought up some other samples of his handwriting for comparison. They match the exam paper right the way through. Fielding couldn't have tinkered with it."

"Good. And the clothing? Nothing there either?"

"Traces of blood, that's all. No prints on the plastic."

"What was her blood group, by the way?"

"Group A."

Smiley sat down on the edge of the bed. Pressing the receiver to his ear, he began talking quietly. Ten minutes later he was walking slowly downstairs. He had come to the end of the chase, and was already sickened by the kill.

It was nearly an hour before Rigby arrived.

20 ❧

THE DROSS OF THE RIVER

Albert Bridge was as preposterous as ever; bony steel, rising to Wagnerian pinnacles, against the patient London sky; the Thames crawling beneath it with resignation, edging its filth into the wharves of Battersea, then sliding towards the mist down river.

The mist was thick. Smiley watched the driftwood, as it touched it, turning first to white dust, then seeming to lift, dissolve, and vanish.

This was how it would end, on a foul morning like this when they dragged the murderer whimpering from his cell and put the hempen rope round his neck. Would Smiley have the courage to recall this two months from now, as the dawn broke outside his window and the clock rang out the time? When they broke a man's neck on the scaffold and put him away like the dross of the river?

He made his way along Beaumont Street towards the King's Road. The milkman chugged past him in his electric van. He would breakfast out this morning, then take a cab to Curzon

Street and order the wine for dinner. He would choose something good. Fielding would like that.

Fielding closed his eyes and drank, his left hand held lightly across his chest.

"Divine," he said, "divine!" And Ailsa Brimley, opposite him, smiled gently.

"How are you going to spend your retirement, Mr. Fielding?" she asked. "Drinking Frankenwein?"

His glass still held before his lips, he looked into the candles. The silver was good, better than his own. He wondered why they were only dining three. "In peace," he replied at last. "I have recently made a discovery."

"What's that?"

"That I have been playing to an empty house. But now I'm comforted to think that no one remembers how I forgot my words or missed an entry. So many of us wait patiently for our audience to die. At Carne no one will remember for more than a Half or two what a mess I've made of life. I was too vain to realise that until recently." He put the glass down in front of him and smiled suddenly at Ailsa Brimley. "That is the peace I mean. Not to exist in anyone's mind but my own; to be a secular monk, safe and forgotten."

Smiley gave him more wine: "Miss Brimley knew your brother Adrian well in the war. We were all in the same department," he said. "She was Adrian's secretary for a while. Weren't you, Brim?"

"It's depressing how the bad live on," Fielding declared. "Rather embarrassing. For the bad, I mean." He gave a little gastronomic sigh. "The moment of truth in a good meal! *Übergangsperiode* between *entremets* and dessert," and they all laughed, and then were silent. Smiley put down his glass, and said:

"The story you told me on Thursday, when I came and saw you . . ."

"Well?" Fielding was irritated.

324

"About cheating for Tim Perkins . . . how you took the paper from the case and altered it . . ."

"Yes?"

"It isn't true." He might have been talking about the weather. "They've examined it and it isn't true. The writing was all one person's . . . the boy's. If anyone cheated, it must have been the boy."

There was a long silence. Fielding shrugged.

"My dear fellow, you can't expect me to believe that. These people are practically moronic."

"Of course, it doesn't necessarily signify anything. I mean you could be protecting the boy, couldn't you? By lying for him, for his honour so to speak. Is that the explanation?"

"I've told you the truth," he replied shortly. "Make what you want of it."

"I mean, I can see a situation where there might have been collusion, where you were moved by the boy's distress when he brought you the papers; and on the spur of the moment you opened the case and took out his paper and told him what to write."

"Look here," said Fielding hotly, "why don't you keep off this? What's it got to do with you?" And Smiley replied with sudden fervour:

"I'm trying to help, Fielding. I beg you to believe me, I'm trying to help. For Adrian's sake. I don't want there to be . . . more trouble than there need, more pain. I want to get it straight before Rigby comes. They've dropped the charge against Janie. You know that, don't you? They seem to think it's Rode, but they haven't pulled him in. They could have done, but they haven't. They just took more statements from him. So you see, it matters terribly about the writing-case. Everything hangs by whether you really saw inside it; and whether Perkins did. Don't you see that? If it was Perkins who cheated after all, if it was only the boy who opened the case and not you, then they'll want to know the answer to a very important question: *they'll want to know how you knew what was inside it.*"

325

"What are you trying to say?"

"They're not really moronic, you know. Let's start from the other end for a moment. Suppose it was you who killed Stella Rode, suppose you had a reason, a terribly good reason, and they knew what that reason might be; suppose you went ahead of Rode after giving him the case that night—by bicycle, for instance, like Janie said, riding on the wind. If that were really so, none of those things you saw would have been in the case at all. You could have made it up. And when later the exam results came out and you realised that Perkins had cheated, then you guessed he had seen inside the case, had seen that it contained nothing, *nothing but exam papers*. I mean that would explain why you had to kill the boy." He stopped and glanced towards Fielding. "And in a way," he added almost reluctantly, "it makes better sense, doesn't it?"

"And what, may I ask, was the reason you speak of?"

"Perhaps she blackmailed you. She certainly knew about your conviction in the war from when she was up North. Her father was a magistrate, wasn't he? I understand they've looked up the files. The police, I mean. It was her father who heard the case. She knew you're broke and need another job and she kept you on a hook. It seems D'Arcy knew too. She told him. She'd nothing to lose; he was in on the story from the start, he'd never allow the papers to get hold of it; she knew that, she knew her man. Did you tell D'Arcy as well, Fielding? I think you may have done. When she came to you and told you she knew, jeered and laughed at you, you went to D'Arcy and told him. You asked him what to do. And he said—what would he say?—perhaps he said find out what she wants. But she wanted nothing; not money at least, but something more pleasing, more gratifying to her twisted little mind: she wanted to command and own you. She loved to conspire, she summoned you to meetings at absurd times and places; in woods, in disused churches, and above all at night. And she wanted nothing from you but your will, she made you listen to her boasts and her mad intrigues, made you fawn and cringe, then let you run away till the next time." He looked up again. "They might think along those lines, you see. That's why we need to know who saw inside the case. And who cheated in the exam." They were both looking at him, Ailsa in horror, Fielding motionless, impassive.

"If they think that," asked Fielding at last, "how do they suppose I knew Rode would come back for the case that night?"

"Oh, they knew she was expecting you to meet her that night, after the dinner at your house." Smiley threw this off as if it were a tedious detail, "It was part of the game she liked to play."

"How do they know that?"

"From what Rode says," Smiley continued, "Stella was carrying the case in the hall, actually had it in her hand. When they arrived at North Fields she was without it; she flew into a rage and accused him of forgetting it. She made him go back for it. You see the inference?"

"Oh, clearly," said Fielding, and Smiley heard Ailsa Brimley whisper his name in horror.

"In other words, when Stella devised this trick to gratify her twisted will, you saw it as an opportunity to kill her, putting the blame on a nonexistent tramp, or, failing that, on Rode, as a second line of defence. Let us suppose you had been meaning to kill her. You had meant, I expect, to ride out there one night when Rode was teaching late. You had your boots and your cape, even the cable stolen from Rode's room, and you meant to lay a false trail. But what a golden opportunity when Perkins turned up with the hand-case! Stella wanted her meeting—the forgotten hand-case was agreed upon as the means of achieving it. That, I fear, is the way their minds may work. And you see, they *know* it wasn't Rode."

"How do they know? How *can* they know; he's got no alibi." Smiley didn't seem to hear. He was looking towards the window and the heavy velvet curtains stirring uneasily.

"What's that? What are you looking at?" Fielding asked with sudden urgency, but Smiley did not answer.

"You know, Fielding," he said at last, "we just don't know

what people are like, we can never tell; there isn't any truth about human beings, no formula that meets each one of us. And there are some of us—aren't there?—who are nothing, who are so labile that we astound ourselves; we're the chameleons. I read a story once about a poet who bathed himself in cold fountains so that he could recognise his own existence in the contrast. He had to reassure himself, you see, like a child being hateful to its parents. You might say he had to make the sun shine on him so that he could see his shadow and feel alive."

Fielding made an impatient movement with his hand. "How do you know it wasn't Rode?"

"The people who are like that—there really are some, Fielding—do you know their secret? They can't feel anything inside them, no pleasure or pain, no love or hate; they're ashamed and frightened that they can't feel. And their shame, this shame, Fielding, drives them to extravagance and colour; they must make themselves feel that cold water, and without that they're nothing. The world sees them as showmen, fantasists, liars, as sensualists perhaps, not for what they are: the living dead."

"How do you know? How do you know it wasn't Rode?" Fielding cried with anger in his voice, and Smiley replied: "I'll tell you."

"If Rode murdered his wife, he had planned to do so long ago. The plastic cape, the boots, the weapon, the intricate timing, the use of Perkins to carry the case to your house—these are evidence of long premeditation. Of course one could ask: if that's so, why did he bother with Perkins at all—why didn't he keep the case with him all the time? But never mind. Let's see how he does it. He walks home with his wife after dinner, having deliberately forgotten the writing-case. Having left Stella at home, he returns to your house to collect it. It was a risky business, incidentally, leaving that case behind. Quite apart from the fact that one would expect him to have locked it, his wife might have noticed he hadn't got it as they left—or you might have noticed, or Miss Truebody—but luckily no one did. He collects

328

the case, hurries back, kills her, fabricating the clues which mislead the police. He thrusts the cape, boots, and gloves into the refugees' parcel, ties it up, and prepares to make good his escape. He is alarmed by Mad Janie, perhaps, but reaches the lane and reenters the house as Stanley Rode. Five minutes later he is with the D'Arcys. From then on for the next forty-eight hours he is under constant supervision. Perhaps you didn't know this, Fielding, but the police found the murder weapon four miles down the road in a ditch. They found it within ten hours of the murder being discovered, long before Rode had a chance to throw it there.

"This is the point, though, Fielding. This is what they can't get over. I suppose it would be possible to make a phoney murder weapon. Rode could have taken hairs from Stella's comb, stuck them with human blood to a length of coaxial cable, and planted the thing in a ditch *before* he committed the murder. But the only blood he could use was his own—which belongs to a different blood group. The blood on the weapon they found belonged to Stella's blood group. He didn't do it. There's a rather more concrete piece of evidence, to do with the parcel. Rigby had a word with Miss Truebody yesterday. It seems she telephoned Stella Rode on the morning of the day she was murdered. Telephoned at your request, Fielding, to say a boy would be bringing some old clothes up to North Fields on Thursday morning—would she be sure to keep the parcel open till then? . . . What did Stella threaten to do, Fielding? Write an anonymous letter to your next school?"

Then Smiley put his hand on Fielding's arm and said: "Go now, in God's name go now. There's very little time, for Adrian's sake go now," and Ailsa Brimley whispered something he could not hear.

Fielding seemed not to hear. His great head was thrown back, his eyes half closed, his wine glass still held between his thick fingers.

And the front doorbell rang out, like the scream of a woman in an empty house.

329

. . .

Smiley never knew what made the noise, whether it was Fielding's hands on the table as he stood up, or his chair, falling backwards. Perhaps it was not a noise at all, but simply the shock of violent movement when it was least expected; the sight of Fielding, who a moment before had sat lethargic in his chair, springing forward across the room. Then Rigby was holding him, had taken Fielding's right arm and done something to it so that Fielding cried out in pain and fear, swinging round to face them under the compulsion of Rigby's grip. Then Rigby was saying the words, and Fielding's terrified gaze fell upon Smiley.

"Stop him, stop him, Smiley, for God's sake! They'll hang me." And he shouted the last two words again and again: "Hang me, hang me," until the detectives came in from the street and shoved him without ceremony into a waiting car.

Smiley watched the car go. It didn't hurry, just picked its way down the wet street and disappeared. He remained there long after it had gone, looking towards the end of the road, so that passersby stared oddly at him, or tried to follow his gaze. But there was nothing to see. Only the half-lit street, and the shadows moving along it.

330

THE SPY WHO CAME IN
FROM THE COLD

FOREWORD

In the early morning hours of August 13, 1961, East German troops sealed off the western sectors of Berlin with barbed wire and began building a wall. The Wall (the capital letter came almost at once) would stay up for 28 years and inspire loud ideological saber rattling, numerous, usually futile, acts of heroism, a shorthand symbol for the movies, and one great work of popular literature. John le Carré has said that he conceived the idea for *The Spy Who Came In from the Cold* after seeing the Wall on a visit from Bonn, and certainly no other book is so closely associated with it—its story line begins and ends there, Leamas's outstretched hands an iconic Cold War image. To think of one now is to see the other. Only a few books have had this effect, so much a part of their time that they become emblematic of it, a way of looking in. Is Kipling's the real Raj or Fitzgerald's the real twenties? No matter. Most of us see them now as Kipling and Fitzgerald did, worlds on a page. If you want to know about the Cold War in the early sixties, how it felt to people, then you must read *The Spy Who Came In from the Cold*.

Spy came out in Britain in 1963 and was noticed immediately as something special. Graham Greene, in a now famous blurb, called it "the best spy story I have ever read." But it was the American publication a few months later, in 1964, that made it an international phenomenon. It held the best-seller list for over a year (a feat as extraordinary then as it is now), was translated everywhere, and a year later was made into a successful, remarkably faithful film. Even at the time, it was recognized as marking a cultural shift, something new in spy fiction. But what, exactly?

It is usually suggested that *Spy* transformed the genre by infusing it with a gritty cynicism (le Carré himself has said that part of its popular success was as a "counter market" to the glitzy Bond series), but espionage fiction had been gritty and cynical at least as far back as Ambler and Greene. Le Carré's influence was subtler and more subversive. He took a genre pumped up with fantasy and atmospherics and brought it down to earth. There is no glamour in *Spy*, no mysterious seductress (just a drab librarian), and no adventure (only the first and last chapters, the Wall chapters, have what could be called "action" scenes). No chases, no footsteps in the fog. Le Carré took the trench coats off the rain-slicked streets and put them in offices, just like yours and mine. His books, in fact, are filled with office life—the routing slips, the indifferent clerks, the petty rivalries. In *A Small Town in Germany* the office is virtually a character in its own right. Agents became organization men, not seedy romantics. Even when Alec Leamas *plays* seedy, his cover story a kind of ironic tip of the hat to the conventions of the genre, what supposedly prompts his disillusion is an inadequate pension payment. In 1963 this was fresh, even a little startling. Spies, once thought to be risk-taking loners, were just the men down the hall—disappointed about promotion, covering their backs, maybe simply marking time until retirement. And—who could not identify?—being let down by their bosses.

But of course there is much more here than bureaucratic realism. What made *Spy* different from its predecessors, and so timely, was its unblinking recognition of a political stalemate that had nowhere to go. Even in Ambler and Greene, there is still a larger war to win. But all le Carré's soldiers can do is pick each other off—the battle itself doesn't change and, worse, a death makes no difference. There is remarkably little violence in le Carré's world, and not even many real secrets. Agents are rarely looking for the 39 Steps, just the other side's agents. Real war has become not only unwinnable but unthinkable. After years of stockpiling warheads that only the mad or suicidal would launch, the Cold War had finally reached its endgame, at once absurd (*Dr. Strangelove* was released the same year as *Spy*) and morally bankrupt.

What *Spy* captures so neatly is this sense of a great power struggle reduced to sniping on the margins, the human cost of empty rhetoric. What's left now is posturing, and an ethical blurring that makes one side little better than the other. Everyone, in a sense, is beating his head against the Wall. The only thing left worth fighting for is the individual, and that's the one thing neither side any longer cares about. In this climate, the sacrifice of one's own men (and women—the disposable Liz) is worse than a betrayal—it's a pointless sacrifice, just another move in a game where we have all been reduced to manipulated pieces.

All this might suggest a certain sociopolitical time capsule quality, but *Spy*, as entertainment as well as commentary, has by now outlived its period and has held up better than the wall that inspired it. Over forty years later, with the Wall long gone, the book is still as vivid as a headline. The plot, even when we know it, still has the ability to surprise, by its pacing as well as its twists. The characters are still recognizable people, contemporaries. Best of all, we see the first confident staging of that shadow world le Carré was to make his own—Smiley and Guillam and Control, the files at the Circus, the house in Bywater Street, the squalid bedsits, the tradecraft, all the elements that make up the great, even richer Smiley novels that were to come.

Some of these elements (even Smiley) had been introduced earlier, but it is in *Spy* that they begin to acquire the substance of a real, alternative world. To reread *Spy* so many years later is to be reminded (if we need to be reminded) what a good *writer* le Carré is: how he can bring minor characters to life with a few brushstrokes; how his antennae pick up the fine nuances of the social pecking order (he has a Henry Higgins–like ear for placing people the minute they open their mouths); how rhythmic and evocative the prose is. It may be, finally, that le Carré's most profound contribution to the spy novel was not realism or even his sense of the zeitgeist, but simply the quality of his writing. The genre had always been entertaining, but now it could offer something more—intelligence, a knowledge of the world, style, the virtues of literature. And, most important, it could offer character, right at the center, not hiding behind the mechanics of plot. *Tinker, Tailor, Soldier, Spy*, for instance, is driven by the hunt for

335

a traitor, but it's *about* Smiley and Ann and Bill Haydon. This kind of exploration of character lies at the heart of all serious writing—including, since le Carré, all serious spy fiction. He raised the bar for everyone who followed. He may have raised it to its fullest expression with Smiley, but it begins here, with weary Alex Leamas and trusting Liz and a wall that was finally too high for both of them. Few writers have had a more enduring, or more enjoyable, beginning.

—Joseph Kanon
June 2005

INTRODUCTION

The Spy Who Came In from the Cold, my third book, changed
my life and put me on bare-knuckle terms with my abilities.
Until its publication I had written literally in secret, from inside
the walls of the secret world, under another name, and free of
serious critical attention. Once this book hit the stands, my
time of quiet and gradual development was over for good, however much I tried to re-create it by, for example, fleeing with my
family to a remote Greek island. Therefore, *The Spy Who Came
In from the Cold* is the last book of my period of innocence, and
after it, for better or worse, my experimentations would have to
take place in public. For years to come there would be no such
thing, for the publishing industry, as a "small" le Carré book—
a distortion both longed for and abhorred by any artist worth
his salt.

I wrote the book in a great rush over a period of about five
weeks. I wrote it in the small hours of the morning, in my British
Embassy hiring in Königswinter, in odd moments at my desk in
the Embassy, and even at the wheel of my car as I crossed the
Rhine back and forth by ferry, sometimes parked alongside
Chancellor Adenauer's huge armoured Mercedes (or was it a
BMW?) as he made his own stately way to work. There was excitement in Chancery when I was able to report what newspaper
he was reading, and the Embassy Press Section was always quick
to deduce which leader-writers might have influenced the great
man's mind, but I suspect none did: he was long past being influenced. Sometimes I caught his eye, and occasionally it seemed to
me he even smiled at me in my little Hillman Huskie with diplomatic plates. But he resembled by then an ancient Red Indian
chief, and his expressions did not follow the patterns of other
mortals.

It was the Berlin Wall that had got me going, of course: I had flown from Bonn to take a look at it as soon as it started going up. I went with a colleague from the Embassy and as we stared back at the weasel faces of the brainwashed little thugs who guarded the Kremlin's latest battlement, he told me to wipe the grin off my face. I was not aware I had been grinning, so it must have been one of those soupy grins that comes over me at dreadfully serious moments. There was certainly nothing to grin at in what I saw, and inside myself I felt nothing but disgust and terror, which was exactly what I was supposed to feel: the Wall was perfect theatre as well as a perfect symbol of the monstrosity of ideology gone mad.

We forget the terror too easily. In my house at Königswinter, workmen had been painting the dining-room walls when the news of the first barricades came through. As good Germans they quietly washed their brushes and, as good family men, went home. In secret conclave, the Embassy discussed its evacuation plans. But where do you evacuate to, when the world is about to end? At Checkpoint Charlie, as the Friedrichstrasse crossing point quickly came to be known, American and Soviet Bloc tanks faced each other across a hundred-yard strip of road, their guns trained on one another's turrets. Now and then they roared at each other with their engines, supposedly to keep them warm and ready to advance, but in reality they were psyching each other like boxers before the big fight. Somewhere beyond the Wall, networks of British and American and French and West German secret agents had been caught napping. None, to my knowledge, had forecast the event, and now they would have to live with their lack of success. Many of them probably had other allegiances anyway. Others would become what are called stay-behind agents, who would henceforth have to communicate by means of hidden radios and prearranged methods of secret writing, set up just for this eventuality. With the Wall, the espionage industry was going to become more clandestine, more perilous, more questionable, and certainly more overcrowded than ever before. What the Soviet agents thought—those who were now stuck in West Germany—I can only imagine. But of course they were not really stuck, merely condemned to greater inconveniences in the administration of their secret lives.

And the Wall stayed up. It was strengthened and heightened. It was protected by mined strips and earth brushed so fine you could trace a rabbit's paw across it. Occasionally someone climbed over it or crashed through it or dug under it, or made himself a glider and flew through it. There is a whole long history of tales of derring-do and all those men and women who succeeded in escaping were heroes, perhaps because they were so few, certainly because they were so brave. Reading today's news from East Germany, those who remember the Wall can draw a direct line between the heroism of the few and the approaching liberation of the many. Our Western propaganda was in that sense entirely true: the East German régime was indeed hated by those it governed. The escapers were the vanguard of what is now a great popular army, and almost every accusation that was levelled against the corrupt barons of the East German leadership turns out to have been justified. Which perhaps makes my novel the more chilling.

What prompted me to write it? Where did the notion spring from? Oh, at this distance almost any answer is likely to be tendentious. I know that I was deeply unhappy in my professional life, and that I was enduring the extremes of loneliness and personal confusion. Perhaps some of that solitude and bitterness found its way into Alec Leamas. I know that I wanted to be in love, and that my own past, and my own inwardness, made this impossible. So perhaps the barbed wire and the machinations of the plot did duty for other obstacles that stood between myself and freedom. I had been poor too long, I was drinking a lot, I was beginning to doubt, in the deepest of ways, the wisdom of my choice of job. The familiar process of embracing an institution, then fighting my way clear of it, was taking over my relationship to my marriage and to my work. Staring at the Wall was like staring at frustration itself, and it touched an anger in me that found its way into the book. In interviews at the time, I am sure, I said none of this. Perhaps I was still too much of the spy, or perhaps I didn't know myself well enough to understand that, by telling an ingenious tale, I was making some kind of bitter order out of my own chaos.

Certainly I never wrote this way again, and for a while the smart thing to say of me was that I was a one-book man, that *The Spy Who Came In from the Cold* was a grand fluke, and all the rest was aftercare. The book that followed it—*The Looking Glass War*—being much nearer to the reality and pain I had experienced, was dismissed by British critics as boring and unreal. And perhaps it was, for I don't remember a single kindly British voice.

But the acclaim for *The Spy* had been so great that I was in for a hiding anyway, and knew it. My marriage broke up, I went through most of the withdrawal symptoms that fame instils in writers, even if they pretend it doesn't. I found a new wise wife and put myself together. I had survived after all. I had no more excuses for not writing as well as I could, for not going each time to the edge of my talent, and seeing what was or wasn't beyond.

But of course I will never forget the time when a disgusting gesture of history coincided with some desperate mechanism inside myself, and in six weeks gave me the book that altered my life.

JOHN LE CARRÉ, December 1989

1 ❊
CHECKPOINT

The American handed Leamas another cup of coffee and said, "Why don't you go back and sleep? We can ring you if he shows up."

Leamas said nothing, just stared through the window of the checkpoint, along the empty street.

"You can't wait forever, sir. Maybe he'll come some other time. We can have the polizei contact the Agency: you can be back here in twenty minutes."

"No," said Leamas, "it's nearly dark now."

"But you can't wait forever; he's nine hours over schedule."

"If you want to go, go. You've been very good," Leamas added. "I'll tell Kramer you've been damn' good."

"But how long will you wait?"

"Until he comes." Leamas walked to the observation window and stood between the two motionless policemen. Their binoculars were trained on the Eastern checkpoint.

"He's waiting for the dark," Leamas muttered. "I know he is."

"This morning you said he'd come across with the workmen."

Leamas turned on him.

"Agents aren't aeroplanes. They don't have schedules. He's blown, he's on the run, he's frightened. Mundt's after him, now, at this moment. He's only got one chance. Let him choose his time."

The younger man hesitated, wanting to go and not finding the moment.

A bell rang inside the hut. They waited, suddenly alert. A policeman said in German, "Black Opel Rekord, Federal registration."

"He can't see that far in the dusk, he's guessing," the American whispered and then he added: "How did Mundt know?"

"Shut up," said Leamas from the window. One of the policemen left the hut and walked to the sandbag emplacement two feet short of the white demarcation which lay across the road like the base line of a tennis court. The other waited until his companion was crouched behind the telescope in the emplacement, then put down his binoculars, took his black helmet from the peg by the door, and carefully adjusted it on his head. Somewhere high above the checkpoint the arclights sprang to life, casting theatrical beams on to the road in front of them.

The policeman began his commentary. Leamas knew it by heart.

"Car halts at the first control. Only one occupant, a woman. Escorted to the Vopo hut for document check." They waited in silence.

"What's he saying?" said the American. Leamas didn't reply. Picking up a spare pair of binoculars, he gazed fixedly towards the East German controls.

"Document check completed. Admitted to the second control."

"Mr. Leamas, is this your man?" the American persisted. "I ought to ring the Agency."

"Wait."

"Where's the car now? What's it doing?"

"Currency check, Customs," Leamas snapped.

Leamas watched the car. There were two Vopos at the driver's door, one doing the talking, the other standing off, waiting. A third was sauntering round the car. He stopped at the boot, then walked back to the driver. He wanted the key. He opened the boot, looked inside, closed it, returned the key, and walked thirty yards up the road to where, midway between the two opposing checkpoints, a solitary East German sentry was standing, a squat silhouette in boots and baggy trousers. The two stood together talking, self-conscious in the glare of the arclight.

With a perfunctory gesture they waved the car on. It reached the two sentries in the middle of the road and stopped again. They walked round the car, stood off, and talked again; finally, almost unwillingly, they let it continue across the line to the Western sector.

"It is a man you're waiting for, Mr. Leamas?" asked the American.

"Yes, it's a man."

Pushing up the collar of his jacket, Leamas stepped outside into the icy October wind. He remembered the crowd then. It was something you forgot inside the hut, this group of puzzled faces. The people changed but the expressions were the same. It was like the helpless crowd that gathers round in a traffic accident, no one knowing how it happened, whether you should move the body. Smoke or dust rose through the beam of the arclamps, a constant shifting pall between the margins of light.

Leamas walked over to the car, and said to the woman, "Where is he?"

"They came for him and he ran. He took the bicycle. They can't have known about me."

"Where did he go?"

"We had a room near Brandenburg, over a pub. He kept a few things there, money, papers. I think he'll have gone there. Then he'll come over."

"Tonight?"

"He said he would come tonight. The others have all been caught—Paul, Viereck, Ländser, Salomon. He hasn't got long."

Leamas stared at her for a moment in silence.

"Ländser too?"

"Last night."

A policeman was standing at Leamas' side.

"You'll have to move away from here," he said. "It's forbidden to obstruct the crossing point."

Leamas half turned.

"Go to hell," he snapped. The German stiffened, but the woman said:

"Get in. We'll drive down to the corner."

He got in beside her and they moved slowly down the road to a side turning.

"I didn't know you had a car," he said.

"It's my husband's," she replied indifferently. "Karl never told you I was married, did he?" Leamas was silent. "My husband and I work for an optical firm. The let us over to do business. Karl only told you my maiden name. He didn't want me to be mixed up with . . . you."

Leamas took a key from his pocket.

"You'll want somewhere to stay," he said. His voice sounded flat. "There's an apartment in the Albrecht-Dürer-Strasse, next to the Museum. Number 28A. You'll find everything you want. I'll telephone you when he comes."

"I'll stay here with you."

"I'm not staying here. Go to the flat. I'll ring you. There's no point in waiting here now."

"But he's coming to this crossing point."

Leamas looked at her in surprise.

"He told you that?"

"Yes. He knows one of the Vopos there, the son of his landlord. It may help. That's why he chose this route."

"And he told *you* that?"

"He trusts me. He told me everything."

"Christ."

344

He gave her the key and went back to the checkpoint hut, out of the cold. The policemen were muttering to each other as he entered; the larger one ostentatiously turned his back.

"I'm sorry," said Leamas. "I'm sorry I bawled you out." He opened a tattered briefcase and rummaged in it until he found what he was looking for: a half bottle of whisky. With a nod the elder man accepted it, half filled each coffee mug and topped them up with black coffee.

"Where's the American gone?" asked Leamas.

"Who?"

"The CIA boy. The one who was with me."

"Bed time," said the elder man and they all laughed.

Leamas put down his mug and said:

"What are your rules for shooting to protect a man coming over? A man on the run."

"We can only give covering fire if the Vopos shoot into our sector."

"That means you can't shoot until a man's over the boundary?"

The older man said, "We can't give covering fire, Mr. . . . ."

"Thomas," Leamas replied, "Thomas." They shook hands, the two policemen pronouncing their own names as they did so.

"We can't give covering fire. That's the truth. They tell us there'd be war if we did."

"It's nonsense," said the younger policeman, emboldened by the whisky. "If the allies weren't here the Wall would be gone by now."

"So would Berlin," muttered the elder man.

"I've got a man coming over tonight," said Leamas abruptly.

"Here? At this crossing point?"

"It's worth a lot to get him out. Mundt's men are looking for him."

"There are still places where you can climb," said the younger policeman.

"He's not that kind. He'll bluff his way through; he's got papers, if the papers are still good. He's got a bicycle."

There was only one light in the checkpoint, a reading lamp with a green shade, but the glow of the arclights, like artificial moonlight, filled the cabin. Darkness had fallen, and with it silence. They spoke as if they were afraid of being overheard. Leamas went to the window and waited, in front of him the road and to either side the Wall, a dirty, ugly thing of breeze blocks and strands of barbed wire, lit with cheap yellow light, like the backdrop for a concentration camp. East and west of the Wall lay the unrestored part of Berlin, a half-world of ruin, drawn in two dimensions, crags of war.

That damned woman, thought Leamas, and that fool Karl who'd lied about her. Lied by omission, as they all do, agents the world over. You teach them to cheat, to cover their tracks, and they cheat you as well. He'd only produced her once, after that dinner in the Schürzstrasse last year. Karl had just had his big scoop and Control had wanted to meet him. Control always came in on success. They'd had dinner together—Leamas, Control, and Karl. Karl loved that kind of thing. He turned up looking like a Sunday School boy, scrubbed and shining, doffing his hat and all respectful. Control had shaken his hand for five minutes and said: "I want you to know how pleased we are, Karl, damn' pleased." Leamas had watched and thought, "That'll cost us another couple of hundred a year." When they'd finished dinner Control pumped their hands again, nodded significantly and implying that he had to go off and risk his life somewhere else, got back into his chauffeur-driven car. Then Karl had laughed, and Leamas had laughed with him, and they'd finished the champagne, still laughing about Control. Afterwards they'd gone to the "Alter Fass," Karl had insisted on it, and there Elvira was waiting for them, a forty-year-old blonde, tough as nails.

"This is my best kept secret, Alec," Karl had said, and Leamas was furious. Afterwards they'd had a row.

"How much does she know? Who is she? How did you meet her?" Karl sulked and refused to say. After that things went badly. Leamas tried to alter the routine, change the meet-

346

ing places and the catch words, but Karl didn't like it. He knew what lay behind it and he didn't like it.

"If you don't trust her it's too late anyway," he'd said, and Leamas took the hint and shut up. But he went carefully after that, told Karl much less, used more of the hocus-pocus of espionage technique. And there she was, out there in her car, knowing everything, the whole network, the safe house, everything; and Leamas swore, not for the first time, never to trust an agent again.

He went to the telephone and dialled the number of his flat. Frau Martha answered.

"We've got guests at the Dürer-Strasse," said Leamas, "a man and a woman."

"Married?" asked Martha.

"Near enough," said Leamas, and she laughed that frightful laugh. As he put down the recciver one of the policemen turned to him.

"Herr Thomas! Quick!" Leamas stepped to the observation window.

"A man, Herr Thomas," the younger policeman whispered, "with a bicycle." Leamas picked up the binoculars.

It was Karl, the figure was unmistakable even at that distance, shrouded in an old Wehrmacht macintosh, pushing his bicycle. He's made it, thought Leamas, he must have made it, he's through the document check, only currency and Customs to go. Leamas watched Karl lean his bicycle against the railing, walk casually to the Customs hut. Don't overdo it, he thought. At last Karl came out, waved cheerfully to the man on the barrier, and the red and white pole swung slowly upwards. He was through, he was coming towards them, he had made it. Only the Vopo in the middle of the road, the line, and safety.

At that moment, Karl seemed to hear some sound, sense danger; he glanced over his shoulder, began to pedal furiously, bending low over the handlebars. There was still the lonely sentry on the bridge, and he had turned and was watching Karl. Then, totally unexpected, the searchlights went on, white and

347

brilliant, catching Karl and holding him in their beam like a rabbit in the headlights of a car. There came the see-saw wail of a siren, the sound of orders wildly shouted. In front of Leamas the two policemen dropped to their knees, peering through the sandbagged slits, deftly flicking the rapid load on their automatic rifles.

The East German sentry fired, quite carefully, away from them, into his own sector. The first shot seemed to thrust Karl forward, the second to pull him back. Somehow he was still moving, still on the bicycle, passing the sentry, and the sentry was still shooting at him. Then he sagged, rolled to the ground, and they heard quite clearly the clatter of the bike as it fell. Leamas hoped to God he was dead.

2 �֎
THE CIRCUS

He watched the Tempelhof runway sink beneath him. Leamas was not a reflective man and not a particularly philosophical one. He knew he was written off—it was a fact of life which he would henceforth live with, as a man must live with cancer or imprisonment. He knew there was no kind of preparation which could have bridged the gap between then and now. He met failure as one day he would probably meet death, with cynical resentment and the courage of a solitary. He'd lasted longer than most; now he was beaten. It is said a dog lives as long as its teeth; metaphorically, Leamas' teeth had been drawn: and it was Mundt who had drawn them.

Ten years ago he could have taken the other path—there were desk jobs in that anonymous government building in Cambridge Circus which Leamas could have taken and kept till he was God knows how old; but Leamas wasn't made that way. You might as well have asked a jockey to become a totalisator clerk as expect Leamas to abandon operational life for the tendentious theorising and clandestine self-interest of Whitehall.

349

He had stayed on in Berlin, conscious that Personnel had marked his file for review at the end of every year—stubborn, wilful, contemptuous of instruction, telling himself that something would turn up. Intelligence work has one moral law—it is justified by results. Even the sophistry of Whitehall paid court to that law, and Leamas got results. Until Mundt came.

It was odd how soon Leamas had realised that Mundt was the writing on the wall.

Hans-Dieter Mundt, born forty-two years ago in Leipzig. Leamas knew his dossier, knew the photograph on the inside of the cover; the blank, hard face beneath the flaxen hair; knew by heart the story of Mundt's rise to power as second man in the Abteilung and effective head of operations. Mundt was hated even within his own department. Leamas knew that from the evidence of defectors, and from Riemeck, who as a member of the SED Praesidium sat on security committees with Mundt, and dreaded him. Rightly as it turned out, for Mundt had killed him.

Until 1959 Mundt had been a minor functionary of the Abteilung, operating in London under the cove of the East German Steel Mission. He returned to Germany in a hurry after murdering two of his own agents to save his skin and was not heard of for more than a year. Quite suddenly he reappeared at the Abteilung's headquarters in Leipzig as head of the Ways and Means Department, responsible for allocating currency, equipment, and personnel for special tasks. At the end of that year came the big struggle for power within the Abteilung. The number and influence of Soviet liaison officers were drastically reduced, several of the old guard were dismissed on ideological grounds and three men emerged: Fiedler as head of counter intelligence, Jahn took over from Mundt as head of facilities, and Mundt himself got the plum—deputy director of operations—at the age of forty-one. Then the new style began. The first agent Leamas lost was a girl. She was only a small link in the network; she was used for courier jobs. They shot her dead in the street as she left a West Berlin cinema. The police never found the murderer and Leamas was at first inclined to write the incident off as unconnected with her work. A month later a railway porter in Dresden, a discarded agent from Peter Guillam's network, was found dead and mutilated beside a railway track. Leamas knew it wasn't coincidence any longer. Soon after that two members of another network under Leamas' control were arrested and summarily sentenced to death. So it went on: remorseless and unnerving.

And now they had Karl, and Leamas was leaving Berlin as he had come—without a single agent worth a farthing. Mundt had won.

Leamas was a short man with close, iron-grey hair, and the physique of a swimmer. He was very strong. This strength was discernible in his back and shoulders, in his neck, and in the stubby formation of his hands and fingers.

He had a utilitarian approach to clothes, as he did to most other things, and even the spectacles he occasionally wore had steel rims. Most of his suits were of artificial fibre, none of them had waistcoats. He favoured shirts of the American kind with buttons on the points of the collars, and suede shoes with rubber soles.

He had an attractive face, mucular, and a stubborn line to his thin mouth. His eyes were brown and small; Irish, some said. It was hard to place Leamas. If he were to walk into a London club the porter would certainly not mistake him for a member; in a Berlin night club they usually gave him the best table. He looked like a man who could make trouble, a man who looked after his money, a man who was not quite a gentleman.

The air hostess thought he was interesting. She guessed he was North Country, which he might have been, and rich, which he was not. She put his age at fifty, which was about right. She guessed he was single, which was half true. Somewhere long ago there had been a divorce; somewhere there were children, now in their teens, who received their allowance from a rather odd private bank in the City.

"If you want another whisky," said the air hostess, "you'd better hurry. We shall be at London airport in twenty minutes."

"No more." He didn't look at her; he was looking out of the window at the grey-green fields of Kent.

Fawley met him at the airport and drove him to London.

"Control's pretty cross about Karl," he said, looking sideways at Leamas. Leamas nodded.

"How did it happen?" asked Fawley.

"He was shot. Mundt got him."

"Dead?"

"I should think so, by now. He'd better be. He nearly made it. He should never have hurried, they couldn't have been sure. The Abteilung got to the checkpoint just after he'd been let through. They started the siren and a Vopo shot him twenty yards short of the line. He moved on the ground for a moment, then lay still."

"Poor bastard."

"Precisely," said Leamas.

Fawley didn't like Leamas, and if Leamas knew he didn't care. Fawley was a man who belonged to Clubs and wore representative ties, pontificated on the skills of sportsmen, and assumed a service rank in office correspondence. He thought Leamas suspect, and Leamas thought him a fool.

"What section are you in?" asked Leamas.

"Personnel."

"Like it?"

"Fascinating."

"Where do I go now? On ice?"

"Better let Control tell you, old boy."

"Do you know?"

"Of course."

"Then why the hell don't you tell me?"

"Sorry, old man," Fawley replied, and Leamas suddenly very nearly lost his temper. Then he reflected that Fawley was probably lying anyway.

"Well, tell me one thing, do you mind? Have I got to look for a bloody flat in London?"

Fawley scratched at his ear: "I don't think so, old man, no."

"No? Thank God for that."

They parked near Cambridge Circus, at a parking meter, and went together into the hall.

"You haven't got a pass, have you? You'd better fill in a slip, old man."

"Since when have we had passes? McCall knows me as well as his own mother."

"Just a new routine. Circus is growing, you know."

Leamas said nothing, nodded at McCall, and got into the lift without a pass.

Control shook his hand rather carefully, like a doctor feeling the bones.

"You must be awfully tired," he said apologetically, "do sit down." That same dreary voice, the donnish bray.

Leamas sat down in a chair facing an olive green electric fire with a bowl of water balanced on the top of it.

"Do you find it cold?" Control asked. He was stooping over the fire rubbing his hands together. He wore a cardigan under his black jacket, a shabby brown one. Leamas remembered Control's wife, a stupid little woman called Mandy who seemed to think her husband was in the Coal Board. He supposed she had knitted it.

"It's so dry, that's the trouble," Control continued. "Beat the cold and you patch the atmosphere. Just as dangerous." He went to the desk and pressed a button. "We'll try and get some coffee," he said, "Ginnie's on leave, that's the trouble. They've given me some new girl. It really is too bad."

He was shorter than Leamas remembered him: otherwise, just the same. The same affected detachment, the same donnish conceits; the same horror of draughts; courteous according to a formula miles removed from Leamas' experience. The same milk-and-water smile, the same elaborate diffidence, the same

353

apologetic adherence to a code of behaviour which he pretended to find ridiculous. The same banality.

He brought a packet of cigarettes from the desk and gave one to Leamas.

"You're going to find these more expensive," he said, and Leamas nodded dutifully. Slipping the cigarettes into his pocket, Control sat down. There was a pause; finally Leamas said:

"Riemeck's dead."

"Yes, indeed," Control declared, as if Leamas had made a good point. "It is very unfortunate. Most . . . I suppose the girl blew him—Elvira?"

"I suppose so." Leamas wasn't going to ask him how he knew about Elvira.

"And Mundt had him shot," Control added.

"Yes."

Control got up and drifted round the room looking for an ashtray. He found one and put it awkwardly on the floor between their two chairs.

"How did you feel? When Riemeck was shot, I mean? You saw it, didn't you?"

Leamas shrugged. "I was bloody annoyed," he said.

Control put his head on one side and half closed his eyes. "Surely you felt more than that? Surely you were upset? That would be more natural."

"I was upset. Who wouldn't be?"

"Did you like Riemeck—as a man?"

"I suppose so," said Leamas helplessly. "There doesn't seem much point in going into it," he added.

"How did you spend the night, what was left of it, after Riemeck had been shot?"

"Look, what is this?" Leamas asked hotly; "what are you getting at?"

"Riemeck was the last," Control reflected, "the last of a series of deaths. If my memory is right it began with the girl, the one they shot in Wedding, outside the cinema. Then there was the Dresden man, and the arrests at Jena. Like the ten little niggers.

354

Now Paul, Vierek, and Ländser—all dead. And finally Riemeck." He smiled deprecatingly; "that is quite a heavy rate of expenditure. I wondered if you'd had enough."

"What do you mean—enough?"

"I wondered whether you were tired. Burnt out." There was a long silence.

"That's up to you," Leamas said at last.

"We have to live without sympathy, don't we? That's impossible of course. We act it to one another, all this hardness; but we aren't like that really, I mean . . . one can't be out in the cold all the time; one has to come in from the cold . . . d'you see what I mean?"

Leamas saw. He saw the long road outside Rotterdam, the long straight road beside the dunes, and the stream of refugees moving along it; saw the little aeroplane miles away, the procession stop and look towards it; and the plane coming in, nearly over the dunes; saw the chaos, the meaningless hell, as the bombs hit the road.

"I can't talk like this, Control," Leamas said at last. "What do you want me to do?"

"I want you to stay out in the cold a little longer." Leamas said nothing, so Control went on: "The ethic of our work, as I understand it, is based on a single assumption. That is, we are never going to be aggressors. Do you think that's fair?"

Leamas nodded. Anything to avoid talking.

"Thus we do disagreeable things, but we are *defensive*. That, I think, is still fair. We do disagreeable things so that ordinary people here and elsewhere can sleep safely in their beds at night. Is that too romantic? Of course, we occasionally do very wicked things"; he grinned like a schoolboy. "And in weighing up the moralities, we rather go in for dishonest comparisons; after all, you can't compare the ideals of one side with the methods of the other, can you, now?"

Leamas was lost. He'd heard the man talked a lot of drivel before getting the knife in, but he'd never heard anything like this before.

"I mean you've got to compare method with method, and ideal with ideal. I would say that since the war, our methods—ours and those of the opposition—have become much the same. I mean you can't be less ruthless than the opposition simply because your government's *policy* is benevolent, can you now?" He laughed quietly to himself: "That would *never* do," he said.

For God's sake, thought Leamas, it's like working for a bloody clergyman. What *is* he up to?

"That is why," Contol continued, "I think we ought to try and get rid of Mundt . . . Oh really," he said, turning irritably towards the door, "Where is that damned coffee?"

Control crossed to the door, opened it, and talked to some unseen girl in the outer room. As he returned he said: "I really think we *ought* to get rid of him if we can manage it."

"Why? We've got nothing left in East Germany, nothing at all. You just said so—Riemeck was the last. We've nothing left to protect."

Control sat down and looked at his hands for a while.

"That is not altogether true," he said finally; "but I don't think I need to bore you with the details."

Leamas shrugged.

"Tell me," Control continued, "are you tired of spying? Forgive me if I repeat the question. I mean that is a phenomenon we understand here, you know. Like aircraft designers . . . metal fatigue, I think the term is. Do say if you are."

Leamas remembered the flight home that morning and wondered.

"If you were," Control added, "we would have to find some other way of taking care of Mundt. What I have in mind is a little out of the ordinary."

The girl came in with the coffee. She put the tray on the desk and poured out two cups. Control waited till she had left the room.

"Such a *silly* girl," he said, almost to himself. "It seems extraordinary they can't find good ones anymore. I do wish Ginnie wouldn't go on holiday at times like this." He stirred his coffee disconsolately for a while.

"We really must discredit Mundt," he said. "Tell me, do you drink a lot? Whisky and that kind of thing?"

Leamas had thought he was used to Control.

"I drink a bit. More than most I suppose."

Control nodded understandingly. "What do you know about Mundt?"

"He's a killer. He was here a year or two back with the East German Steel Mission. We had an Adviser here then: Maston."

"Quite so."

"Mundt was running an agent, the wife of an FO man. He killed her."

"He tried to kill George Smiley. And of course he shot the woman's husband. He is a very distasteful man. Ex Hitler-Youth and all that kind of thing. Not at all the intellectual kind of Communist. A practitioner of the cold war."

"Like us," Leamas observed drily. Control didn't smile.

"George Smiley knew the case well. He isn't with us anymore, but I think you ought to ferret him out. He's doing things on seventeenth-century Germany. He lives in Chelsea, just behind Sloane Square. Bywater Street, do you know it?"

"Yes."

"And Guillam was on the case as well. He's in Satellites Four, on the first floor. I'm afraid everything's changed since your day."

"Yes."

"Spend a day or two with them. They know what I have in mind. Then I wondered if you'd care to stay with me for the weekend. My wife," he added hastily, "is looking after her mother, I'm afraid. It will be just you and I."

"Thanks. I'd like to."

"We can talk about things in comfort then. It would be very nice. I think you might make a lot of money out of it. You can have whatever you make."

"Thanks."

"That is, of couse, if you're *sure you want* to . . . no metal fatigue or anything?"

"If it's a question of killing Mundt, I'm game."

"Do you really feel that?" Control enquired politely. And then, having looked at Leamas thoughtfully for a moment he observed: "Yes, I really think you do. But you mustn't feel you *have* to say it. I mean in our world we pass so quickly out of the register of hate or love—like certain sounds a dog can't hear. All that's left in the end is a kind of nausea; you never want to cause suffering again. Forgive me, but isn't that rather what you felt when Karl Riemeck was shot? Not hate for Mundt, nor love for Karl, but a sickening jolt like a blow on a numb body . . . They tell me you walked all night—just walked through the streets of Berlin. Is that right?"

"It's right that I went for a walk."

"All night?"

"Yes."

"What happened to Elvira?"

"God knows . . . I'd like to take a swing at Mundt," he said.

"Good . . . good. Incidentally, if you should meet any old friends in the meantime, I don't think there's any point in discussing this with them. In fact," Control added after a moment, "I should be rather short with them. Let them think we've treated you badly. It's as well to begin as one intends to continue, isn't it?"

3 ❋
DECLINE

It surprised no one very much when they put Leamas on the shelf. In the main, they said, Berlin had been a failure for years, and someone had to take the rap. Besides, he was old for operational work, where your reflexes often had to be as quick as those of a professional tennis player. Leamas had done good work in the war, everyone knew that. In Norway and Holland he had somehow remained demonstrably alive, and at the end of it they gave him a medal and let him go. Later, of course, they got him to come back. It was bad luck about his pension, decidedly bad luck. Accounts Section had let it out, in the person of Elsie. Elsie said in the canteen that poor Alec Leamas would only have £400 a year to live on because of his interrupted service. Elsie felt it was a rule they really ought to change; after all, Mr. Leamas had *done* the service, hadn't he? But there they were with Treasury on their backs, not a bit like the old days, and what could they do? Even in the bad days of Maston they'd managed things better.

Leamas, the new men were told, was the old school; blood,

guts and cricket and School Cert. French. In Leamas' case this happened to be unfair, since he was bilingual in German and English and his Dutch was admirable; he also disliked cricket. But it was true that he had no degree.

Leamas' contract had a few months to run, and they put him in Banking to do his time. Banking Section was different from Accounts; it dealt with overseas payments, financing agents and operations. Most of the jobs in Banking could have been done by an office boy were it not for the high degree of secrecy involved, and thus Banking was one of several Sections of the Service which were regarded as laying-out places for officers shortly to be buried.

Leamas went to seed.

The process of going to seed is generally considered to be a protracted one, but in Leamas this was not the case. In the full view of his colleagues he was transformed from a man honourably put aside to a resentful, drunken wreck—and all within a few months. There is a kind of stupidity among drunks, particularly when they are sober, a kind of disconnection which the unobservant interpret as vagueness and which Leamas seemed to acquire with unnatural speed. He developed small dishonesties, borrowed insignificant sums from secretaries and neglected to return them, arrived late or left early under some mumbled pretext. At first his colleagues treated him with indulgence; perhaps his decline scared them in the same way as we are scared by cripples, beggars, and invalids because we fear we could ourselves become them; but in the end his neglect, his brutal, unreasoning malice isolated him.

Rather to people's surprise, Leamas didn't seem to mind being put on the shelf. His well seemed to have collapsed. The débutante secretaries, reluctant to believe that Intelligence Services are peopled by ordinary mortals, were alarmed to notice that Leamas had become definitely seedy. He took less care of his appearance and less notice of his surroundings, he lunched in the canteen which was normally the preserve of junior staff, and it was rumoured that he was drinking. He became a solitary, belonging to that tragic class of active men prematurely deprived of activity; swimmers barred from the water or actors banished from the stage.

Some said he had made a mistake in Berlin, and that was why his network had been rolled up; no one quite knew. All agreed that he had been treated with unusual harshness, even by a personnel department not famed for its philanthropy. They would point to him covertly as he went by, as men will point to an athlete of the past, and say: "That's Leamas. He put up a black in Berlin. Pathetic the way he's let himself go."

And then one day he had vanished. He said good-bye to no one, not even, apparently, Control. In itself that was not surprising. The nature of the Service precluded elaborate farewells and the presentation of gold watches, but even by these standards Leamas' departure seemed abrupt. So far as could be judged, his departure occurred before the statutory termination of his contract. Elsie, of Accounts Section, offered one or two crumbs of information: Leamas had drawn the balance of his pay in cash, which, if Elsie knew anything, meant he was having trouble with his bank. His gratuity was to be paid at the turn of the month, she couldn't say how much but it wasn't four figures, poor lamb. His National Insurance card had been sent on. Personnel had an address for him, Elsie added with a sniff, but of course they weren't revealing it, not Personnel.

Then there was the story about the money. It leaked out— no one, as usual, knew where from—that Leamas' sudden departure was connected with irregularities in the accounts of Banking Section. A largish sum was missing (not three figures but four, according to a lady with blue hair who worked in the telephone room) and they'd got it back, nearly all of it, and they'd stuck a lien on his pension. Others said they didn't believe it—if Alec had wanted to rob the till, they said, he'd know better ways of doing it than fiddling with HQ accounts. Not that he wasn't capable of it—he'd just have done it better. But those less impressed by Leamas' criminal potential pointed at his large consumption of alcohol, at the expense of maintaining a separate household, at the fatal disparity between pay at home and allowances abroad and above all at the temptations put in the way of a man handling large sums of hot money when he knew that his days in the Service were numbered. All agreed that if Alec had dipped his hands in the honey pot he was finished for all time—the Resettlement people wouldn't look at him and Personnel would give him no reference—or one so icy cold that the most enthusiastic employer would shiver at the sight of it. Peculation was the one sin Personnel would never let you forget—and they never forgot it themselves. If it was true that Alec had robbed the Circus, he would take the wrath of Personnel with him to the grave—and Personnel would not so much as pay for the shroud.

For a week or two after his departure, a few people wondered what had become of him. But his former friends had already learnt to keep clear of him. He had become a resentful bore, constantly attacking the Service and its administration, and what he called the "Cavalry boys" who, he said, managed its affairs as if it were a regimental club. He never missed an opportunity of railing against the Americans and their intelligence agencies. He seemed to hate them more than the Abteilung, to which he seldom, if ever, referred. He would hint that it was they who had compromised his network; this seemed to be an obsession with him, and it was poor reward for attempts to console him, it made him bad company, so that those who had known and even tacitly liked him, wrote him off. Leamas' departure caused only a ripple on the water; with other winds and the changing of the seasons it was soon forgotten.

His flat was small and squalid, done in brown paint with photographs of Clovelly. It looked directly on to the grey backs of three stone warehouses, the windows of which were drawn, for aesthetic reasons, in creosote. Above the warehouse there lived an Italian family, quarrelling at night and beating carpets in the morning. Leamas had few possessions with which to brighten his rooms. He bought some shades to cover the light bulbs, and two pairs of sheets to replace the hessian squares provided by the landlord. The rest Leamas tolerated: the flower pattern curtains, not lined or hemmed, the fraying brown carpets, and the clumsy darkwood furniture, like something from a seamen's hostel. From a yellow, crumbling geyser he obtained hot water for a shilling.

He needed a job. He had no money, none at all. So perhaps the stories of embezzlement were true. The offers of resettlement which the Service made had seemed to Leamas lukewarm and peculiarly unsuitable. He tried first to get a job in commerce. A firm of industrial adhesive manufacturers showed interest in his application for the post of assistant manager and personnel officer. Unconcerned by the inadequate reference with which the Service provided him, they demanded no qualifications, and offered him six hundred a year. He stayed for a week, by which time the foul stench of decaying fish oil had permeated his clothes and hair, lingering in his nostrils like the smell of death. No amount of washing would remove it, so that in the end Leamas had his hair cut short to the scalp and threw away two of his best suits. He spent another week trying to sell encyclopaedias to suburban housewives, but he was not a man that housewives liked or understood; they did not want Leamas, let alone his encyclopaedias. Night after night he returned wearily to his flat, his ridiculous sample under his arm. At the end of a week he telephoned the company and told them he had sold nothing. Expressing no surprise, they reminded him of his obligation to return the sample if he discontinued acting on their behalf, and rang off. Leamas stalked out of the telephone booth in a fury, leaving the sample behind him, went to a pub and got very drunk at a cost of twenty-five shillings, which he could not afford. They threw him out for shouting at a woman who tried to pick him up. They told him never to come back, but they'd forgotten all about it a week later. They were beginning to know Leamas there.

They were beginning to know him elsewhere too, the grey, shambling figure from the Mansions. Not a wasted word did he speak, not a friend, neither man, woman, nor beast did he have. They guessed he was in trouble, run away from his wife like as not. He never knew the price of anything, never remembered it when he was told. He patted all his pockets whenever he looked for change, he never remembered to bring a basket, always buying carrier bags. They didn't like him in the Street, but they were almost sorry for him. They thought he was dirty too, the way he didn't shave weekends, and his shirts all grubby.

A Mrs. McCaird from Sudbury Avenue cleaned for him for a week, but having never received a civil word from him withdrew her labour. She was an important source of information in the Street, where tradesmen told one another what they needed to know in case he asked for credit. Mrs. McCaird's advice was against credit. Leamas never had a letter, she said, and they agreed that that was serious. He'd no pictures and only a few books; she thought one of the books was dirty but couldn't be sure because it was in foreign writing. It was her opinion he had a bit to live on, and that that bit was running out. She knew he drew Benefit on Thursdays. Bayswater was warned, and needed no second warning. They heard from Mrs. McCaird that he drank like a fish: this was confirmed by the publican. Publicans and charwomen are not in the way of accommodating their clients with credit; but their information is treasured by those who are.

4 ❋
LIZ

Finally he took the job in the library. The Labour Exchange had put him on to it each Thursday morning as he drew his unemployment benefit, and he'd always turned it down.

"It's not really your cup of tea," Mr. Pitt said, "but the pay's fair and the work's easy for an educated man."

"What sort of library?" Leamas asked.

"It's the Bayswater Library for Psychic Research. It's an endowment. They've got thousands of volumes, all sorts, and they've been left a whole lot more. They want another helper."

He took his dole and the slip of paper. "They're an odd lot," Mr. Pitt added, "but then you're not a stayer anyway, are you? I think it's time you gave them a try, don't you?"

It was odd about Pitt. Leamas was certain he'd seen him before somewhere. At the Circus, during the war.

The library was like a church hall, and very cold. The black oil stoves at either end made it smell of paraffin. In the middle of the room was a cubicle like a witness-box and inside it sat Miss Crail, the librarian.

It had never occurred to Leamas that he might have to work for a woman. No one at the Labour Exchange had said anything about that.

"I'm the new help," he said; "my name's Leamas."

Miss Crail looked up sharply from her card index, as if she had heard a rude word. "Help? What do you mean, help?"

"Assistant. From the Labour Exchange. Mr. Pitt." He pushed across the counter a roneoed form with his particulars entered in a sloping hand. She picked it up and studied it.

"You are Mr. Leamas." This was not a question, but the first stage of a laborious fact-finding investigation.

"And you are from the Labour Exchange."

"No. I was sent by the Exchange. They told me you needed an assistant."

"I see." A wooden smile.

At that moment the telephone rang: she lifted the receiver and began arguing with somebody, fiercely. Leamas guessed they argued all the time; there were no preliminaries. Her voice just rose a key and she began arguing about some tickets for a concert. He listened for a minute or two and then drifted towards the bookshelves. He noticed a girl in one of the alcoves standing on a ladder sorting large volumes.

"I'm the new man," he said, "my name's Leamas."

She came down from the ladder and shook his hand a little formally.

"I'm Liz Gold. How d'you do. Have you met Miss Crail?"

"Yes, but she's on the phone at the moment."

"Arguing with her mother I expect. What are you going to do?"

"I don't know. Work."

"We're marking at the moment; Miss Crail's started a new index."

She was a tall girl, ungainly, with a long waist and long legs. She wore flat, ballet-type shoes to reduce her height. Her face, like her body, had large components which seemed to hesitate between plainness and beauty. Leamas guessed she was twenty-two or three, and Jewish.

"It's just a question of checking that all the books are in the shelves. This is the reference bit, you see. When you've checked you pencil in the new reference and mark it off on the index."

"What happens then?"

"Only Miss Crail's allowed to ink in the reference. It's the rule."

"Whose rule?"

"Miss Crail's. Why don't you start on the archaeology?"

Leamas nodded and together they walked to the next alcove where a shoe-box full of cards lay on the floor.

"Have you done this kind of thing before?" she asked.

"No." He stooped and picked up a handful of cards and shuffled through them. "Mr. Pitt sent me. From the Exchange." He put the cards back.

"Is Miss Crail the only person who can ink the cards, too?" Leamas enquired.

"Yes."

She left him there, and after a moment's hesitation he took out a book and looked at the fly-leaf. It was called *Archaeological Discoveries in Asia Minor,* Volume four. They only seemed to have volume four.

It was one o'clock and Leamas was hungry, so he walked over to where Liz Gold was sorting and said:

"What happens about lunch?"

"Oh, I bring sandwiches." She looked a little embarrassed. "You can have some of mine if that would help. There's no café for miles."

Leamas shook his head.

"I'll go out, thanks. Got some shopping to do." She watched him push his way through the swing doors.

It was half past two when he came back. He smelt of whisky. He had one carrier bag full of vegetables and another containing

367

groceries. He put them down in a corner of the alcove and wearily began again on the archaeology books. He'd been marking for about ten minutes when he became aware that Miss Crail was watching him.

"*Mister* Leamas." He was half-way up the ladder, so he looked down over his shoulder and said:

"Yes?"

"Do you know where these carrier bags come from?"

"They're mine."

"I see. They are yours." Leamas waited. "I regret," she continued at last, "that we do not allow it, bringing shopping into the library."

"Where else can I put it? There's nowhere else I *can* put it."

"Not in the library," she replied. Leamas ignored her, and returned his attention to the archaeology section.

"If you only took the normal lunch break," Miss Crail continued, "you would not have time to go shopping. Neither of *us* does, Miss Gold or myself; *we* do not have time to shop."

"Why don't you take an extra half-hour?" Leamas asked, "you'd have time then. If you're pushed you can work another half-hour in the evening. If you're pressed."

She stayed for some moments, just watching him and obviously thinking of something to say. Finally she announced:

"I shall discuss it with Mr. Ironside," and went away.

At exactly half past five Miss Crail put on her coat and, with a pointed: "Good night, Miss Gold," left. Leamas guessed she had been brooding on the carrier bags all afternoon. He went into the next alcove where Liz Gold was sitting on the bottom rung of her ladder reading what looked like a tract. When she saw Leamas she dropped it guiltily into her handbag and stood up.

"Who's Mr. Ironside?" Leamas asked.

"I don't think he exists," she replied. "He's her big gun when she's stuck for an answer. I asked her once who he was. She went all shifty and mysterious, and said 'Never mind.' I don't think he exists."

"I'm not sure Miss Crail does," said Leamas and Liz Gold smiled.

At six o'clock she locked up and gave the keys to the curator, a very old man with First War shellshock who, said Liz, sat awake all night in case the Germans made a counterattack. It was bitterly cold outside.

"Got far to go?" asked Leamas.

"Twenty minutes' walk. I always walk it. Have you?"

"Not far," said Leamas. "Good night."

He walked slowly back to the flat. He let himself in and turned the light switch. Nothing happened. He tried the light in the tiny kitchen and finally the electric fire that plugged in by his bed. On the door mat was a letter. He picked it up and took it out into the pale, yellow light of the staircase. It was the electricity company, regretting that the area manager had no alternative but to cut off the electricity until the outstanding account of nine pounds four shillings and eightpence had been settled.

He had become an enemy of Miss Crail, and enemies were what Miss Crail liked. Either she scowled at him or she ignored him, and when he came close, she began to tremble, looking to left and right, either for something with which to defend herself, or perhaps for a line of escape. Occasionally she would take immense umbrage, such as when he hung his macintosh on *her* peg, and she stood in front of it shaking, for fully five minutes, until Liz spotted her and called Leamas. Leamas went over to her and said:

"What's troubling you, Miss Crail?"

"Nothing," she replied in a breathy, clipped way, "nothing at all."

"Something wrong with my coat?"

"Nothing at all."

"Fine," he replied, and went back to his alcove. She quivered all that day, and conducted a telephone call in a stage whisper for half the morning.

"She's telling her mother," said Liz. "She always tells her mother. She tells her about me, too."

Miss Crail developed such an intense hatred for Leamas that she found it impossible to communicate with him. On pay days he would come back from lunch and find an envelope on the third rung of his ladder with his name misspelt on the outside. The first time it happened he took the money over to her with the envelope and said; "It's L-E-A, Miss Crail, and only one S," whereupon she was seized with a veritable palsy, rolling her eyes and fumbling erratically with her pencil until Leamas went away. She conspired into the telephone for hours after that.

About three weeks after Leamas began work at the library Liz asked him to supper. She pretended it was an idea that had come to her quite suddenly, at five o'clock that evening; she seemed to realise that if she were to ask him for tomorrow or the next day he would forget or just not come, so she asked him at five o'clock. Leamas seemed reluctant to accept, but in the end he did.

They walked to her flat through the rain and they might have been anywhere—Berlin, London, any town where paving stones turn to lakes of light in the evening rain, and the traffic shuffles despondently through wet streets.

It was the first of many meals which Leamas had at her flat. He came when she asked him, and she asked him often. He never spoke much. When she discovered he would come, she took to laying the table in the morning before leaving for the library. She even prepared the vegetables beforehand and had the candles on the table, for she loved candlelight. She always knew that there was something deeply wrong with Leamas, and that one day, for some reason she could not understand, he might break and she would never see him again. She tried to tell him she knew; she said to him one evening:

"You must go when you want. I'll never follow you, Alec," and his brown eyes rested on her for a moment: "I'll tell you when," he replied.

Her flat was just a bed-sitting-room and a kitchen. In the sitting-room were two armchairs, a divan bed, and a bookcase full of paper-back books, mainly classics which she had never read.

After supper she would talk to him, and he would lie on the divan, smoking. She never knew how much he heard, she didn't care. She could kneel by the bed holding his hand against her cheek, talking.

Then one evening she said to him:

"Alec, what do you believe in? Don't laugh—tell me." She waited and at last he said:

"I believe an eleven bus will take me to Hammersmith. I don't believe it's driven by Father Christmas."

She seemed to consider this and at last she asked again:

"But what do you believe in?"

Leamas shrugged.

"You must believe in something," she persisted: "something like God—I know you do, Alec; you've got that look sometimes, as if you'd got something special to do, like a priest. Alec, don't smile, it's true."

He shook his head.

"Sorry, Liz, you've got it wrong. I don't like Americans and public schools. I don't like military parades and people who play soldiers." Without smiling he added, "And I don't like conversations about Life."

"But, Alec, you might as well say—"

"I should have added," Leamas interrupted, "that I don't like people who tell me what I ought to think." She knew he was getting angry but she couldn't stop herself anymore.

"That's because you don't *want* to think, you don't dare! There's some poison in your mind, some hate. You're a fanatic, Alec. I know you are, but I don't know what about. You're a fanatic who doesn't want to convert people, and that's a dangerous thing. You're like a man who's . . . sworn vengeance or something." The brown eyes rested on her. When he spoke she was frightened by the menace in his voice.

"If I were you," he said roughly, "I'd mind my own business."

And then he smiled, a roguish smile. He hadn't smiled like that before and Liz knew he was putting on the charm.

"What does Liz believe in?" he asked, and she replied:

"I can't be had that easy, Alec."

Later that night they talked about it again. Leamas brought it up—he asked her whether she was religious.

"You've got me wrong," she said, "all wrong. I don't believe in God."

"Then what do you believe in?"

"History."

He looked at her in astonishment for a moment, then laughed.

"Oh, Liz . . . oh *no*. You're not a bloody Communist?" She nodded, blushing like a small girl at his laughter, angry and relieved that he didn't care.

She made him stay that night and they became lovers. He left at five in the morning. She couldn't understand it; she was so proud and he seemed ashamed.

He left her flat and turned down the empty street towards the park. It was foggy. Some way down the road—not far, twenty yards, perhaps a bit more—stood the figure of a man in a raincoat, short and rather plump. He was leaning against the railings of the park, silhouetted in the shifting mist. As Leamas approached, the mist seemed to thicken, closing in around the figure at the railings, and when it parted the man was gone.

5 ❀
CREDIT

Then one day about a week later, he didn't come to the library. Miss Crail was delighted; by half-past eleven she had told her mother, and on returning from lunch she stood in front of the archaeology shelves where he had been working since he came. She stared with theatrical concentration at the rows of books and Liz knew she was pretending to work out whether Leamas had stolen anything.

Liz entirely ignored her for the rest of the day, failed to reply when she addressed her and worked with assiduous application. When the evening came she walked home and cried herself to sleep.

The next morning she arrived early at the library. She somehow felt that the sooner she got there, the sooner Leamas might come; but as the morning dragged on her hopes faded, and she knew he would never come. She had forgotten to make sandwiches for herself that day so she decided to take a bus to the Bayswater Road and go to the ABC. She felt sick and empty, but not hungry. Should she go and find him? She had promised

373

never to follow him, but he had promised to tell her; should she go and find him?

She hailed a taxi and gave his address.

She made her way up the dingy staircase and pressed the bell of his door. The bell seemed to be broken; she heard nothing. There were three bottles of milk on the mat and a letter from the electricity company. She hesitated a moment, then banged on the door, and she heard the faint groan of a man. She rushed downstairs to the flat below, hammered and rang at the door. There was no reply so she ran down another flight and found herself in the back room of a grocer's shop. An old woman sat in a corner, rocking back and forth in her chair.

"The top flat," Liz almost shouted, "somebody's very ill. Who's got a key?"

The old woman looked at her for a moment, then called towards the front room, where the shop was.

"Arthur, come in here, Arthur, there's a girl here!"

A man in a brown overall and grey trilby hat looked round the door and said:

"Girl?"

"There's someone seriously ill in the top flat," said Liz, "he can't get to the front door to open it. Have you got a key?"

"No," replied the grocer, "but I've got a hammer," and they hurried up the stairs together, the grocer, still in his trilby, carrying a heavy screwdriver and a hammer. He knocked on the door sharply, and they waited breathless for an answer. There was none.

"I heard a groan before, I promise I did," Liz whispered.

"Will you pay for this door if I bust it?"

"Yes."

The hammer made a terrible noise. With three blows he had wrenched out a piece of the frame and the lock came with it. Liz went in first and the grocer followed. It was bitterly cold in the room and dark, but on the bed in the corner they could make out the figure of a man.

"Oh God," thought Liz, "if he's dead I don't think I can touch him," but she went to him and he was alive. Drawing the curtains, she knelt beside the bed.

"I'll call you if I need you, thank you," she said without looking back, and the grocer nodded and went downstairs.

"Alec, what is it, what's making you ill? What is it, Alec?"

Leamas moved his head on the pillow. His sunken eyes were closed. The dark beard stood out against the pallor of his face.

"Alec, you must tell me, please, Alec." She was holding one of his hands in hers. The tears were running down her cheeks. Desperately she wondered what to do; then, getting up, she ran to the tiny kitchen and put on a kettle. She wasn't quite clear what she would make, but it comforted her to do something. Leaving the kettle on the gas she picked up her handbag, took Leamas' key from the bedside table and ran downstairs, down the four flights into the street, and crossed the road to Mr. Sleaman, the Chemist. She bought some calves-foot jelly, some essence of beef, and a bottle of aspirin. She got to the door, then went back and bought a packet of rusks. Altogether it cost her sixteen shillings, which left four shillings in her handbag and eleven pounds in her post office book, but she couldn't draw any of that till tomorrow. By the time she returned to his flat the kettle was just boiling.

She made the beef tea like her mother used to, in a glass with a teaspoon in to stop it cracking, and all the time she glanced towards him, as if she were afraid he was dead.

She had to prop him up to make him drink the tea. He only had one pillow and there were no cushions in the room, so taking his overcoat down from the back of the door she made a bundle of it and arranged it behind the pillow. It frightened her to touch him, he was drenched in sweat, so that his short grey hair was damp and slippery. Putting the cup beside the bed she held his head with one hand, and fed him the tea with the other. After he had taken a few spoonfuls, she crushed two aspirin and gave them to him in the spoon. She talked to him as if he were a child, sitting on the edge of the bed looking at him, sometimes letting her fingers run over his head and face, whispering his name over and over again, "Alec, Alec."

Gradually his breathing became more regular, his body more relaxed as he drifted from the taut pain of fever to the calm of sleep; Liz, watching him, sensed that the worst was over. Suddenly she realised it was almost dark.

Then she felt ashamed, because she knew she should have cleaned and tidied. Jumping up, she fetched the carpet sweeper and a duster from the kitchen, and set to work with feverish energy. She found a clean teacloth and spread it neatly on the bedside table and she washed up the odd cups and saucers which lay around the kitchen. When everything was done she looked at her watch and it was half past eight. She put the kettle on and went back to the bed. Leamas was looking at her.

"Alec, don't be cross, please don't," she said. "I'll go. I promise I will, but let me make you a proper meal. You're ill, you can't go on like this, you're . . . oh, Alec," and she broke down and wept, holding both hands over her face, the tears running between her fingers like the tears of a child. He let her cry, watching her with his brown eyes, his hands holding the sheet.

She helped him wash and shave and she found some clean bedclothes. She gave him some calves-foot jelly, and some breast of chicken from the jar she'd bought at Mr. Sleaman's. Sitting on the bed she watched him eat, and she thought she had never been so happy before.

Soon he fell asleep, and she drew the blanket over his shoulders and went to the window. Parting the threadbare curtains, she raised the sash and looked out. Two other windows in the courtyard were lit. In one she could see the flickering blue shadow of a television screen, the figures round it held motionless in its spell; in the other a woman, quite young, was arranging curlers in her hair. Liz wanted to weep at the crabbed delusion of their dreams.

* * *

376

She fell asleep in the armchair and did not wake until it was nearly light, feeling stiff and cold. She went to the bed: Leamas stirred as she looked at him and she touched his lips with the tip of her finger. He did not open his eyes but gently took her arm and drew her down on to the bed and suddenly she wanted him terribly, and nothing mattered, and she kissed him again and again and when she looked at him he seemed to be smiling.

She came every day for six days. He never spoke to her much and once, when she asked him if he loved her, he said he didn't believe in fairy tales. She would lie on the bed, her head against his chest, and sometimes he would put his thick fingers in her hair, holding it quite tight, and Liz laughed and said it hurt. On the Friday evening she found him dressed but not shaved and she wondered why he hadn't shaved. For some imperceptible reason she was alarmed. Little things were missing from the room—his clock and the cheap portable wireless that had been on the table. She wanted to ask and did not dare. She had bought some eggs and ham and she cooked them for their supper while Leamas sat on the bed and smoked one cigarette after another. When it was ready he went to the kitchen and came back with a bottle of red wine.

He hardly spoke at supper, and she watched him, her fear growing until she could bear it no more and she cried out suddenly:

"Alec . . . oh, Alec . . . what is it? Is it good-bye?"

He got up from the table, took her hands, and kissed her in a way he'd never done before and spoke to her softly for a long time, told her things she only dimly understood, only half heard because all the time she knew it was the end and nothing mattered any more.

"Good-bye, Liz," he said. "Good-bye," and then: "Don't follow me. Not again."

Liz nodded and muttered: "Like we said." She was thankful for the biting cold of the street and for the dark which hid her tears.

It was the next morning, the Saturday, that Leamas asked at the grocer's for credit. He did it without much artistry, in a way not calculated to ensure him success. He ordered half a dozen items—they didn't come to more than a pound—and when they had been wrapped and put into the carrier bag he said:

"You'd better send me that account."

The grocer smiled a difficult smile and said:

"I'm afraid I can't do that"; the "Sir" was definitely missing.

"Why the hell not?" asked Leamas, and the queue behind him stirred uneasily.

"Don't know you," replied the grocer.

"Don't be bloody silly," said Leamas, "I've been coming here for four months." The grocer coloured.

"We always ask for a banker's reference before giving credit," he said, and Leamas lost his temper.

"Don't talk bloody cock," he shouted. "Half your customers have never seen the inside of a bank and never bloody well will." This was heresy beyond bearing, since it was true.

"I don't know you," the grocer repeated thickly, "and I don't like you. Now get out of my shop." And he tried to recover the parcel which unfortunately Leamas was already holding. Opinions later differed as to what happened next. Some said the grocer, in trying to recover the bag, pushed Leamas; others say he did not. Whether he did or not, Leamas hit him, most people think twice, without disengaging his right hand, which still held the carrier bag. He seemed to deliver the blow not with the fist but with the side of the left hand, and then, as part of the same phenomenally rapid movement, with the left elbow; and the grocer fell straight over and lay as still as a rock. It was said in court later, and not contested by the defence, that the grocer had two injuries—a fractured cheek bone from the first blow and a dislocated jaw from the second. The coverage in the daily press was adequate, but not over-elaborate.

6 ❀
CONTACT

At night he lay on his bunk listening to the sounds of the prisoners. There was a boy who sobbed and an old lag who sang "On Ilkley Moor bar t'at" beating out the time on his food tin. There was a warder who shouted, "Shut up, George, you miserable sod," after each verse, but no one took any notice. There was an Irishman who sang songs about the IRA, though the others said he was in for rape.

Leamas took as much exercise as he could during the day in the hope that he would sleep at night; but it was no good. At night you knew you were in prison: at night there was nothing, no trick of vision or self-delusion which saved you from the nauseating enclosure of the cell. You could not keep the taste of prison, the smell of prison uniform, the stench of prison sanitation heavily disinfected, the noises of captive men. It was then, at night, that the indignity of captivity became urgently insufferable, it was then that Leamas longed to walk in the friendly sunshine of a London park. It was then that he hated the grotesque steel cage that held him, had to force back the urge to fall upon the bars with his bare fists, to split the skulls of his gaolers and burst into the free, free space of London. Sometimes he thought of Liz. He would direct his mind towards her briefly like the shutter of a camera, recall for a moment the softhard touch of her long body, then put her from his memory. Leamas was not a man accustomed to living on dreams.

He was contemptuous of his cell mates, and they hated him. They hated him because he succeeded in being what each in his heart longed to be: a mystery. He preserved from collectivisation some discernible part of his personality; he could not be drawn at moments of sentiment to talk of his girl, his family or his children. They knew nothing of Leamas; they waited, but he did not come to them. New prisoners are largely of two kinds—there are those who for shame, fear, or shock wait in fascinated horror to be initiated into the lore of prison life, and there are those who trade on their wretched novelty in order to endear themselves to the community. Leamas did neither of these things. He seemed pleased to despise them all, and they hated him because, like the world outside, he did not need them. After about ten days they had had enough. The great had had no homage, the small had had no comfort, so they crowded him in the dinner queue. Crowding is a prison ritual akin to the eighteenth-century practice of jostling. It has the virtue of an apparent accident, in which the prisoner's mess tin is upturned, and its contents spilt on his uniform. Leamas was barged from one side, while from the other an obliging hand descended on his forearm, and the thing was done. Leamas said nothing, looked thoughtfully at the two men on either side of him, and accepted in silence the filthy rebuke of a warder who knew quite well what had happened.

Four days later, while working with a hoe on the prison flower-bed, he seemed to stumble. He was holding the hoe with both hands across his body, the end of the handle protruding about six inches from his right fist. As he strove to recover his balance the prisoner to his right doubled up with a grunt of agony, his arms across his stomach. There was no more crowding after that.

Perhaps the strangest thing of all about prison was the brown paper parcel when he left. In a ridiculous way it reminded him of the marriage service—with this ring I thee wed, with this paper parcel I return thee to society. They handed it to him and made him sign for it, and it contained all he had in the world. There was nothing else. Leamas felt it the most dehumanising moment of the three months, and he determined to throw the parcel away as soon as he got outside.

He seemed a quiet prisoner. There had been no complaints against him. The Governor, who was vaguely interested in his case, secretly put the whole thing down to the Irish blood he swore he could detect in Leamas.

"What are you going to do," he asked, "when you leave here?" Leamas replied, without a ghost of a smile, that he thought he would make a new start, and the Governor said that was an excellent thing to do.

"What about your family?" he asked. "Couldn't you make it up with your wife?"

"I'll try," Leamas had replied indifferently; "but she's re-married."

The probation officer wanted Leamas to become a male nurse at a mental home in Buckinghamshire and Leamas agreed to apply. He even took down the address and noted the train times from Marylebone.

"The rail's electrified as far as Great Missenden, now," the probation officer added, and Leamas said that would be a help. So they gave him the parcel and he left. He took a bus to Marble Arch and walked. He had a bit of money in his pocket and he intended to give himself a decent meal. He thought he would walk through Hyde Park to Piccadilly, then through Green Park and St. James's Park to Parliament Square, then wander down White-hall to the Strand where he could go to the big café near Charing Cross station and get a reasonable steak for six shillings.

London was beautiful that day. Spring was late and the parks were filled with crocuses and daffodils. A cool, cleaning wind was blowing from the south; he could have walked all day. But he still had the parcel and he had to get rid of it. The litter baskets were too small; he'd look absurd trying to push his parcel into one of those. He supposed there were one or two things he ought to take out—his wretched pieces of paper—insurance card, driving licence and his E.93 (whatever that was) in a buff OHMS envelope, but suddenly he couldn't be bothered. He sat down on a bench and put the parcel beside him, not too close, and moved a little away from it. After a couple of minutes he walked back towards the footpath, leaving the parcel where it lay. He had just reached the footpath when he heard a shout; he turned, a little sharply perhaps, and saw a man in an army macintosh beckoning to him, holding the brown paper parcel in the other hand.

Leamas had his hands in his pockets and he left them there, and stood, looking back over his shoulder at the man in the macintosh. The man hesitated, evidently expecting Leamas to come to him or give some sign of interest, but Leamas gave none. Instead, he shrugged and continued along the footpath. He heard another shout and ignored it, and he knew the man was coming after him. He heard the footsteps on the gravel, half running, approaching rapidly, and then a voice, a little breathless, a little aggrieved:

"Here, you—I say!" and then he had drawn level, so that Leamas stopped, turned, and looked at him.

"Yes?"

"This is your parcel, isn't it? You left it on the seat. Why didn't you stop when I called you?"

Tall, with rather curly brown hair, orange tie, and pale green shirt; a little bit petulant, a little bit of a pansy, thought Leamas. Could be a schoolmaster, ex LSE and runs a suburban drama club. Weak-eyed.

"You can put it back," said Leamas. "I don't want it."

The man coloured.

"You can't just leave it there," he said, "it's litter."

"I bloody well can," Leamas replied. "Somebody will find a use for it." He was going to move on, but the stranger was

382

still standing in front of him, holding the parcel in both arms as if it were a baby. "Get out of the light," said Leamas. "Do you mind?"

"Look here," said the stranger, and his voice had risen a key, "I was trying to do you a favour; why do you have to be so damned rude?"

"If you're so anxious to do me a favour," Leamas replied, "why have you been following me for the last half hour?"

He's pretty good, thought Leamas. He hasn't flinched, but he must be shaken rigid.

"I thought you were somebody I once knew in Berlin, if you must know."

"So you followed me for half an hour?"

Leamas' voice was heavy with sarcasm, his brown eyes never left the other's face.

"Nothing like half an hour. I caught sight of you in Marble Arch and I thought you were Alec Leamas, a man I borrowed some money from. I used to be in the BBC in Berlin and there was this man I borrowed some money from. I've had a conscience about it ever since and that's why I followed you. I wanted to be sure."

Leamas went on looking at him, not speaking, and thought he wasn't all that good but he was good enough. His story was scarcely plausible—that didn't matter. The point was that he'd produced a new one and stuck to it after Leamas had wrecked what promised to be a classic approach.

"I'm Leamas," he said at last, "who the hell are you?"

He said his name was Ashe with an 'E' he added quickly, and Leamas knew he was lying. He pretended not to be quite sure that Leamas really was Leamas, so over lunch they opened the parcel and looked at the National Insurance card like, thought Leamas, a couple of cissies looking at a dirty postcard. Ashe ordered lunch with just a fraction too little regard for expense, and they drank some Frankenwein to remind them of the old days. Leamas began by insisting he couldn't remember Ashe,

383

and Ashe said he was surprised. He said it in the sort of tone that suggested he was hurt. They met at a party, he said, which Derek Williams gave in his flat off the Kudamm (he got that right) and all the press boys had been there; surely Alec remembered that? No, Leamas did not. Well, surely he remembered Derek Williams from the *Observer,* that *nice* man who gave such lovely pizza parties? Leamas had a lousy memory for names, after all they were talking about fifty-four; a lot of water had flowed under the bridge since then . . . Ashe remembered (his christian name was William, by the by, most people called him Bill). Ashe remembered *vividly.* They'd been drinking stingers, brandy and créme de menthe, and were all rather tiddly, and Derek had provided some really gorgeous girls, half the cabaret from the Malkasten, *surely* Alec remembered now? Leamas thought it was probably coming back to him, if Bill would go on a bit.

Bill did go on, *ad lib.* no doubt, but he did it well, playing up the sex side a little, how they'd finished up in a night club with three of these girls; Alec, a chap from the political adviser's office, and Bill, and Bill had been so embarrassed because he hadn't any money on him and Alec had paid, and Bill had wanted to take a girl home and Alec had lent him another tenner . . .

"Christ," said Leamas, "I remember now, of course I do."

"I *knew* you would," said Ashe happily, nodding at Leamas over his glass, "look, do let's have the other half, this is *such* fun."

Ashe was typical of that stratum of mankind which conducts its human relationships according to a principle of challenge and response. Where there was softness, he would advance; where he found resistance, retreat. Having himself no particular opinions or tastes he relied upon whatever conformed with those of his companion. He was as ready to drink tea at Fortnum's as beer at the Prospect of Whitby; he would listen to military music in St. James's Park or jazz in a Compton Street cellar; his voice would tremble with sympathy when he spoke of Sharpeville, or with indignation at the growth of Britain's coloured population. To

Leamas this observably passive role was repellent; it brought out the bully in him, so that he would lead the other gently into a position where he was committed, and then himself withdraw, so that Ashe was constantly scampering back from some cul-de-sac into which Leamas had enticed him. There were moments that afternoon when Leamas was so brazenly perverse that Ashe would have been justified in terminating their conversation—not least since he was paying for it; but he did not. The little sad man with spectacles who sat alone at the neighbouring table, deep in a book on the manufacture of ball bearings, might have deduced, had he been listening, that Leamas was indulging a sadistic nature—or perhaps (if he had been a man of particular subtlety) that Leamas was proving to his own satisfaction that only a man with a strong ulterior motive would put up with that kind of treatment.

It was nearly four o'clock before they ordered the bill and Leamas tried to insist on paying his half. Ashe wouldn't hear of it, paid the bill and took out his cheque book in order to settle his debt to Leamas.

"Twenty of the best," he said, and filled in the date on the cheque form.

Then he looked up at Leamas, all wide-eyed and accommodating.

"I say, a cheque is all right by you, isn't it?"

Colouring a little, Leamas replied:

"I haven't got a bank at the moment—only just back from abroad, something I've got to fix up. Better give me a cheque and I'll cash it at your bank."

"My dear chap, I wouldn't *dream* of it! You'd have to go to Rotherhithe to cash this one!" Leamas shrugged and Ashe laughed, and they agreed to meet at the same place on the following day, at one o'clock, when Ashe would have the money in cash.

Ashe took a cab at the corner of Compton Street, and Leamas waved at it until it was out of sight. When it was gone, he looked

385

at his watch. It was four o'clock. He guessed he was still being followed, so he walked down to Fleet Street and had a cup of coffee in the Black and White. He looked at bookshops, read the evening papers displayed in the show windows of newspaper offices, and then quite suddenly, as if the thought had occurred to him at the last minute, he jumped on a bus. The bus went to Ludgate Hill, where it was held up in a traffic jam near a tube station; he dismounted and caught a tube. He bought a sixpenny ticket, stood in the end carriage, and alighted at the next station. He caught another train to Euston, trekked back to Charing Cross. It was nine o'clock when he reached the station and it had turned rather cold. There was a van waiting in the forecourt; the driver was fast asleep. Leamas glanced at the number, went over, and called through the window:

"Are you from Clements?" The driver woke up with a start and asked:

"Mr. Thomas?"

"No," replied Leamas. "Thomas couldn't come. I'm Amies from Hounslow."

"Hop in, Mr. Amies," the driver replied, and opened the door. They drove west, towards the King's Road. The driver knew the way.

Control opened the door.

"George Smiley's out," he said. "I've borrowed his house. Come in." Not until Leamas was inside and the front door closed, did Control put on the hall light.

"I was followed till lunch time," Leamas said. They went into the little drawing-room. There were books everywhere. It was a pretty room; tall, with eighteenth-century mouldings, long windows, and a good fireplace.

"They picked me up this morning. A man called Ashe." He lit a cigarette. "A pansy. We're meeting again tomorrow."

Control listened carefully to Leamas' story, stage by stage, from the day he hit Ford, the grocer, to his encounter that morning with Ashe.

"How did you find prison?" Control enquired. He might

have been asking whether Leamas had enjoyed his holiday. "I am sorry we couldn't improve conditions for you, provide little extra comforts, but that would never have done."

"Of course not."

"One must be consistent. At every turn one must be consistent. Besides, it would be wrong to break the spell. I understand you were ill. I am sorry. What was the trouble?"

"Just fever."

"How long were you in bed?"

"About ten days."

"How very distressing; and nobody to look after you, of course."

There was a very long silence.

"You know she's in the Party, don't you?" Control asked quietly.

"Yes," Leamas replied. Another silence. "I don't want her brought into this."

"Why should she be?" Control asked sharply and for a moment, just for a moment, Leamas thought he had penetrated the veneer of academic detachment. "Who suggested she should be?"

"No one," Leamas replied, "I'm just making the point. I know how these things go—all offensive operations. They have by-products, take sudden turns in unexpected directions. You think you've caught one fish and you find you've caught another. I want her kept clear of it."

"Oh, quite, quite."

"Who's that man in the Labour Exchange—Pitt? Wasn't he in the Circus during the war?"

"I know no one of that name. Pitt, did you say?"

"Yes."

"No, not a name to me. In the Labour Exchange?"

"Oh, for God's sake," Leamas muttered audibly.

"I'm sorry," said Control, getting up, "I'm neglecting my duties as deputy host. Would you care for a drink??"

"No. I want to get away tonight, Control. Go down to the country and get some exercise. Is the House open?"

"I've arranged a car," he said. "What time do you see Ashe tomorrow—one o'clock?"

"Yes."

"I'll ring Haldane and tell him you want some squash. You'd better see a doctor, too. About that fever."

"I don't need a doctor."

"Just as you like."

Control gave himself a whisky and began looking idly at the books in Smiley's shelf.

"Why isn't Smiley here?" Leamas asked.

"He doesn't like the operation," Control replied indifferently. "He finds it distasteful. He sees the necessity but he wants no part in it. His fever," Control added with a whimsical smile, "is recurrent."

"He didn't exactly receive me with open arms."

"Quite. He wants no part in it. But he told you about Mundt; gave you the background?"

"Yes."

"Mundt is a very *hard* man," Control reflected. "We should never forget that. And a good intelligence officer."

"Does Smiley know the reason for the operation? The special interest?"

Control nodded and took a sip of whisky.

"And he still doesn't like it?"

"It isn't a question of moralities. He is like the surgeon who has grown tired of blood. He is content that others should operate."

"Tell me," Leamas continued, "how are you so certain this will get us where we want? How do you know the East Germans are on to it—not the Czechs or the Russians?"

"Rest assured," Control said a little pompously, "that that has been taken care of."

As they got to the door, Control put his hand lightly on Leamas' shoulder.

"This is your last job," he said. "Then you can come in from the cold. About that girl—do you want anything done about her, money or anything?"

"When it's over. I'll take care of it myself then."

"Quite. It would be very insecure to do anything now."

"I just want her left alone," Leamas repeated with emphasis. "I just don't want her to be messed about. I don't want her to have a file or anything. I want her forgotten."

He nodded to Control and slipped out into the night air. Into the cold.

7 ❋

KIEVER

On the following day Leamas arrived twenty minutes late for his lunch with Ashe, and smelt of whisky. Ashe's pleasure on catching sight of Leamas was, however, undiminished. He claimed that he had himself only that moment arrived, he'd been a little late getting to the bank. He handed Leamas an envelope.

"Singles," said Ashe. "I hope that's all right."

"Thanks," Leamas replied, "let's have a drink." He hadn't shaved and his collar was filthy. He called the waiter and ordered drinks, a large whisky for himself and a pink gin for Ashe. When the drinks came Leamas' hand trembled as he poured the soda into the glass, almost slopping it over the side.

They lunched well, with a lot of drink, and Ashe made most of the running. As Leamas had expected he first talked about himself, an old trick but not a bad one.

"To be quite frank, I've got on to rather a good thing recently," said Ashe, "free-lancing English features for the foreign press. After Berlin I made rather a mess of things at first—the

390

Corporation wouldn't renew the contract and I took a job running a dreary toffee-shop weekly about hobbies for the over-sixties. Can you *imagine* anything more frightful? That went under in the first printing strike—I can't tell you how relieved I was. Then I went to live with my mamma in Cheltenham for a time; she runs an antique shop, does very nicely thank you, as a matter of fact. Then I got a letter from an old friend, Sam Kiever his name is actually, who was starting up a new agency for small features on English life specially slanted for foreign papers. You know the sort of thing—six hundred words on Morris dancing. Sam had a new gimmick, though; he sold the stuff already translated and do you know, it makes a hell of a difference. One always imagines anyone can pay a translator to do it themselves, but if you're looking for a half column in-fill for your foreign features you don't *want* to waste time and money on translation. Sam's gambit was to get in touch with the editors direct—he traipsed round Europe like a gypsy, poor thing, but it's paid hands *down*."

Ashe paused, waiting for Leamas to accept the invitation to speak about himself, but Leamas ignored it. He just nodded dully and said: "Bloody good." Ashe had wanted to order wine, but Leamas said he'd stick to whisky and by the time the coffee came he'd had four large ones. He seemed to be in bad shape; he had the drunkard's habit of ducking his mouth towards the rim of his glass just before he drank, as if his hand might fail him and the drink escape.

Ashe fell silent for a moment.

"You don't know Sam, do you?" he asked.

"Sam?"

A note of irritation entered Ashe's voice.

"Sam Kiever, my boss. The chap I was telling you about."

"Was he in Berlin too?"

"No. He knows Germany well, but he's never lived in Berlin. He did a bit of devilling in Bonn, free-lance stuff. You might have met him. He's a dear."

"Don't think so." A pause.

391

"What do you do these days, old chap?" asked Ashe.

Leamas shrugged.

"I'm on the shelf," he replied, and grinned a little stupidly. "Out of the bag and on the shelf."

"I forget what you were doing in Berlin? Weren't you one of the mysterious cold warriors?" My God, thought Leamas, you're stepping things up a bit.

Leamas hesitated, then coloured and said savagely, "Office boy for the bloody Yanks, like the rest of us."

"You know," said Ashe, as if he had been turning the idea over for some time, "you ought to meet Sam. You'd like him," and then, all of a bother, "I say, Alec—I don't even know where to get hold of you!"

"You can't," Leamas replied listlessly.

"I don't get you, old chap. Where are you staying?"

"Around the place. Roughing it a bit. I haven't got a job. Bastards wouldn't give me a proper pension."

Ashe looked horrified.

"But, Alec, that's awful; why didn't you *tell* me? Look, why not come and stay at my place? It's only tiny but there's room for one more if you don't mind a camp bed. You can't just live in the trees, my dear chap!"

"I'm all right for a bit," Leamas replied, tapping at the pocket which contained the envelope. "I'm going to get a job," he nodded with determination; "get one in a week or so. Then I'll be all right."

"What sort of job?"

"Oh, I don't know. Anything."

"But you can't just throw yourself away, Alec! You speak German like a native, I remember you do. There must be all sorts of things you can do!"

"I've done all sorts of things. Selling encyclopaedias for some bloody American firm, sorting books in a psychic library, punching work tickets in a stinking glue factory. What the hell *can* I do?" He wasn't looking at Ashe but at the table before him, his agitated lips moving quickly. Ashe responded to his animation, leaning forward across the table, speaking with emphasis, almost triumph.

"But Alec, you need *contacts,* don't you see? I know what it's like, I've been on the breadline myself. That's when you need to *know* people. I don't know what you were doing in Berlin, I don't want to know, but it wasn't the sort of job where you could meet people who matter, was it? If I hadn't met Sam at Poznan five years ago I'd *still* be on the breadline. Look, Alec, come and stay with me for a week or so. We'll ask Sam round and perhaps one or two of the old press boys from Berlin if any of them are in town."

"But I can't write," said Leamas. "I couldn't write a bloody thing." Ashe had his hand on Leamas' arm: "Now, don't fuss," he said soothingly; "let's just take things one at a time. Where are your bits and pieces?"

"My what?"

"Your things: clothes, baggage and what not?"

"I haven't got any. I've sold what I had—except the parcel."

"What parcel?"

"The brown paper parcel you picked up in the park. The one I was trying to throw away."

Ashe had a flat in Dolphin Square. It was just what Leamas had expected—small and anonymous with a few hastily assembled curios from Germany: beer mugs, a peasant's pipe, and a few pieces of second-rate Nymphenburg.

"I spend the weekends with my mother in Cheltenham," he said. "I just use this place mid-week. It's pretty handy," he added deprecatingly. They fixed the camp bed up in the tiny drawing-room. It was about four-thirty.

"How long have you been here?" asked Leamas.

"Oh—about a year or more."

"Find it easily?"

"They come and go, you know, these flats. You put your name down and one day they ring you up and tell you you've made it."

Ashe made tea and they drank it, Leamas sullen, like a man not used to comfort. Even Ashe seemed a little piano. After tea Ashe said: "I'll go out and do a spot of shopping before the shops close, then we'll decide what to do about everything. I might give Sam a tinkle later this evening—I think the sooner you two get together the better. Why don't you get some sleep—you look all in."

Leamas nodded. "It's bloody good of you—" he made an awkward gesture with his hand, "—all this." Ashe gave him a pat on the shoulder, picked up his army macintosh, and left.

As soon as Leamas reckoned Ashe was safely out of the building, he put the front door of the flat carefully on the latch and made his way downstairs to the centre hall where there were two telephone cabins. He dialled a Maida Vale number and asked for Mr. Thomas' secretary. Immediately a girl's voice said, "Mr. Thomas' secretary speaking."

"I'm ringing on behalf of Mr. Sam Kiever," Leamas said, "he has accepted the invitation and hopes to contact Mr. Thomas personally this evening."

"I'll pass that on to Mr. Thomas. Does he know where to get in touch with you?"

"Dolphin Square," Leamas replied, and gave the address. "Good-bye."

After making some enquiries at the reception desk he returned to Ashe's flat, and sat on the camp bed looking at his clasped hands. After a while he lay down. He decided to accept Ashe's advice and get some rest. As he closed his eyes he remembered Liz lying beside him in the flat in Bayswater, and he wondered vaguely what had become of her.

He was woken up by Ashe, accompanied by a small, rather plump man with long, greying hair swept back and a double-breasted suit. He spoke with a slight central European accent; German perhaps, it was hard to tell. He said his name was Kiever—Sam Kiever.

They had a gin and tonic, Ashe doing most of the talking. It

394

was just like old times, he said, in Berlin: the boys together and the night their oyster. Kiever said he didn't want to be too late; he had to work tomorrow. They agreed to eat at a Chinese restaurant that Ashe knew of—it was opposite Limehouse police station and you brought your own wine. Oddly enough Ashe had some Burgundy in the kitchen, and they took that with them in the taxi.

Dinner was very good and they drank both bottles of wine. Kiever opened up a little on the second: he'd just come back from a tour of West Germany and France. France was in a hell of a mess, de Gaulle was on the way out and God alone knew what would happen then. With a hundred thousand demoralised *colons* returning from Algeria he reckoned Fascism was on the cards.

"What about Germany?" asked Alec, prompting him.

"It's just a question of whether the Yanks can hold them." Kiever looked invitingly at Leamas.

"What do you mean?" asked Leamas.

"What I say. Dulles gave them a foreign policy with one hand, Kennedy takes it away with the other. They're getting waspish."

Leamas nodded abruptly and said, "Bloody typical Yank."

"Alec doesn't seem to like our American cousins," said Ashe, stepping in heavily, and Kiever, with complete disinterest, murmured, "Oh, really?" Kiever played it, Leamas reflected, very long. Like someone used to horses, he let you come to him. He conveyed to perfection a man who suspected that he was about to be asked a favour, and was not easily won.

After dinner Ashe said, "I know a place in Wardour Street— you've been there, Sam. They do you all right there. Why don't we summon a barouche and go along?"

"Just a minute," said Leamas, and there was something in his voice which made Ashe look at him quickly; "just tell me something will you? Who's paying for this jolly?"

"I am," said Ashe quickly, "Sam and I."

"Have you discussed it?"

395

"Well—no."

"Because I haven't got any bloody money; you know that, don't you? None to throw about anyway."

"Of course. Alec. I've looked after you up till now, haven't I?"

"Yes," Leamas replied; "yes, you have."

He seemed to be going to say something else, and then to change his mind. Ashe looked worried, not offended, and Kiever as inscrutable as before.

Leamas refused to speak in the taxi. Ashe attempted some conciliatory remark and he just shrugged irritably. They arrived at Wardour Street and dismounted, neither Leamas nor Kiever making any attempt to pay for the cab. Ashe led them past a shop window full of "girlie" magazines, down a narrow alley, at the far end of which shone a tawdry neon sign: "Pussywillow Club. Members Only." On either side of the door were photographs of girls, and pinned across each was a thin, hand-printed strip of paper which read, "Nature Study. Members only."

Ashe pressed the bell. The door was at once opened by a very large man in a white shirt and black trousers.

"I'm a member," Ashe said. "These two gentlemen are with me."

"See your card?"

Ashe took a buff card from his wallet and handed it over.

"Your guests pay a quid a head temporary membership. Your recommendation, right?" He held out the card and as he did so, Leamas stretched past Ashe and took it. He looked at it for a moment, then handed it back to Ashe.

Taking two pounds from his hip pocket Leamas put them into the waiting hand of the man at the door.

"Two quid," said Leamas, "for the guests," and ignoring the astonished protests of Ashe he guided them through the curtained doorway into the dim hallway of the club. He turned to the doorman.

"Find us a table," said Leamas, "and a bottle of Scotch. And see we're left alone." The doorman hesitated for a moment, decided not to argue, and escorted them downstairs. As they descended they heard the subdued moan of unintelligible music.

They got a table on their own at the back of the room. A two-piece band was playing and girls sat around in twos and threes. Two got up as they came in but the big doorman shook his head.

Ashe glanced at Leamas uneasily while they waited for the whisky. Kiever seemed slightly bored. The waiter brought a bottle and three tumblers and they watched in silence as he poured a little whisky into each glass. Leamas took the bottle from the waiter and added as much again to each. This done, he leant across the table and said to Ashe, "Now perhaps you'll tell me what the bloody hell's going on?"

"What do you mean?" Ashe sounded uncertain. "What *do* you mean, Alec?"

"You followed me from prison the day I was released," he began quietly, "with some bloody silly story of meeting me in Berlin. You gave me money you didn't owe me. You've bought me expensive meals and you're putting me up in your flat."

Ashe coloured and said, "If that's the—"

"Don't attempt," said Leamas fiercely. "Just damn' well wait till I've finished, do you mind? Your membership card for this place is made out for someone called Murphy. Is that your name?"

"No, it is not."

"I suppose a friend called Murphy lent you his membership card?"

"No he didn't as a matter of fact. If you must know I come here occasionally to find a girl. I used a phoney name to join the club."

"Then why," Leamas persisted ruthlessly, "is Murphy registered as the tenant of your flat?"

It was Kiever who finally spoke.

"You run along home," he said to Ashe. "I'll look after this."

* * *

397

A girl performed a striptease, a young, drab girl with a dark bruise on her thigh. She had that pitiful, spindly nakedness which is embarrassing because it is not erotic; because it is artless and undesiring. She turned slowly, jerking sporadically with her arms or legs as if she only heard the music in snatches, and all the time she looked at them with the precocious interest of a child in adult company. The tempo of the music increased abruptly, and the girl responded like a dog to the whistle, scampering back and forth. Removing her brassiere on the last note, she held it above her head, displaying her meagre body with its three tawdry patches of tinsel hanging from it like old Christmas decorations.

They watched in silence, Leamas and Kiever.

"I suppose you're going to tell me that we've seen better in Berlin," Leamas suggested at last, and Kiever saw that he was still very angry.

"I expect *you* have," Kiever replied pleasantly. "I have often been to Berlin, but I am afraid I dislike nightclubs."

Leamas said nothing.

"I'm no prude, mind, just rational. If I want a woman I know cheaper ways of finding one; if I want to dance I know better places to do it." Leamas might not have been listening.

"Perhaps you'll tell me why that cissy picked me up," he suggested. Kiever nodded.

"By all means. I told him to."

"Why?"

"I am interested in you. I want to make you a proposition, a journalistic proposition."

There was a pause.

"Journalistic," Leamas repeated, "I see."

"I run an agency, an international feature service. It pays well—very well—for interesting material."

"Who publishes the material?"

"It pays so well, in fact, that a man with your kind of experience of . . . the international scene, a man with your background, you understand, who provided convincing, factual material, could free himself in a comparatively short time from further financial worry."

"Who publishes the material, Kiever?" There was a threatening edge to Leamas' voice, and for a moment, just for a moment, a look of apprehension seemed to pass across Kiever's smooth face.

"International clients. I have a correspondent in Paris who disposes of a good deal of my stuff. Often I don't even know who *does* publish. I confess," he added with a disarming smile, "that I don't awfully care. They pay and they ask for more. They're the kind of people, you see, Leamas, who don't fuss about awkward details; they pay promptly, and they're happy to pay into foreign banks, for instance, where no one bothers about things like tax."

Leamas said nothing. He was holding his glass with both hands, staring into it.

Christ, they're rushing their fences, Leamas thought; it's indecent. He remembered some silly music-hall joke—"This is an offer no respectable girl could accept—and besides, I don't know what it's worth." Tactically, he reflected, they're right to rush it. I'm on my uppers, prison experience still fresh, social resentment strong. I'm an old horse, I don't need breaking in; I don't have to pretend they've offended my honour as an English gentleman. On the other hand they would expect *practical* objections. They would expect him to be afraid; for his Service pursued traitors as the eye of God followed Cain across the desert.

And finally, they would know it was a gamble. They would know that inconsistency in human decision can make nonsense of the best-planned espionage approach; that cheats, liars, and criminals may resist every blandishment while respectable gentlemen have been moved to appalling treasons by watery cabbage in a Departmental canteen.

"They'd have to pay a hell of a lot," Leamas muttered at last. Kiever gave him some more whisky.

"They are offering a downpayment of fifteen thousand

pounds. The money is already lodged at the Banquet Cantonale in Bern. On production of a suitable identification, with which my clients will provide you, you can draw the money. My clients reserve the right to put questions to you over the period of one year on payment of another five thousand pounds. They will assist you with any . . . resettlement problems that may arise."

"How soon do you want an answer?"

"Now. You are not expected to commit all your reminiscences to paper. You will meet my client and he will arrange to have the material . . . ghost written."

"Where am I supposed to meet him?"

"We felt for everybody's sake it would be simplest to meet outside the United Kingdom. My client suggested Holland."

"I haven't got my passport," Leamas said dully.

"I took the liberty of obtaining one for you," Kiever replied suavely; nothing in his voice or his manner indicated that he had done other than negotiate an adequate business arrangement. "We're flying to The Hague tomorrow morning at nine forty-five. Shall we go back to my flat and discuss any other details?"

Kiever paid and they took a taxi to a rather good address not far from St. James's Park.

Kiever's flat was luxurious and expensive, but its contents somehow gave the impression of having been hastily assembled. It is said that there are shops in London which will sell you bound books by the yard, and interior decorators who will harmonise the colour scheme of the walls with that of a painting. Leamas, who was not particularly receptive to such subtleties, found it hard to remember that he was in a private flat and not an hotel. As Kiever showed him to his room (which looked onto a dingy inner courtyard and not onto the street) Leamas asked him:

"How long have you been here?"

"Oh, not long," Kiever replied lightly, "a few months, not more."

"Must cost a packet. Still, I suppose you're worth it."

"Thanks."

There was a bottle of Scotch in his room and a syphon of soda on a silver-plated tray. A curtained doorway at the further end of the room led to a bathroom and lavatory.

"Quite a little love nest. All paid for by the great Worker State?"

"Shut up," said Kiever savagely, and added, "If you want me, there's an internal telephone to my room. I shall be awake."

"I think I can manage my buttons now," Leamas retorted.

"Then good night," said Kiever shortly, and left the room. He's on edge, too, thought Leamas.

Leamas was woken by the telephone at his bedside. It was Kiever.

"It's six o'clock," he said, "breakfast at half past."

"All right," Leamas replied, and rang off. He had a headache.

Kiever must have telephoned for a taxi because at seven o'clock the door bell rang and Kiever asked, "Got everything?"

"I've no luggage," Leamas replied, "except a toothbrush and a razor."

"That is taken care of. Are you ready otherwise?"

Leamas shrugged. "I suppose so. Have you got any cigarettes?"

"No," Kiever replied, "but you can get some on the plane. You'd better look through this," he added, and handed Leamas a British passport. It was made out in his name with his own photograph mounted in it, embossed by the deep press Foreign Office seal running across the corner. It was neither old nor new; it described Leamas as a clerk, and gave his status as single. Holding it in his hand for the first time, Leamas was a little nervous. It was like getting married: whatever happened, things would never be the same again.

"What about money?" Leamas asked.

"You won't need any. It's on the firm."

8 ✻

LE MIRAGE

It was cold that morning; the light mist was damp and grey, pricking the skin. The airport reminded Leamas of the war: machines, half hidden in the fog, waiting patiently for their masters; the resonant voices and their echoes, the sudden shout and the incongruous clip of a girl's heels on a stone floor; the roar of an engine that might have been at your elbow. Everywhere that air of conspiracy which generates among people who have been up since dawn—of superiority almost, derived from the common experience of having seen the night disappear and the morning come. The staff had that look which is informed by the mystery of dawn and animated by the cold, and they treated the passengers and their baggage with the remoteness of men returned from the front: ordinary mortals had nothing for them that morning.

Kiever had provided Leamas with luggage. It was a nice detail: Leamas admired it. Passengers without luggage attracted attention, and it was not part of Kiever's plan to do that. They checked in at the airline desk and followed the signs to passport control. There was a ludicrous moment when they lost the way and Kiever was rude to a porter. Leamas supposed Kiever was worried about the passport—he needn't be, thought Leamas, there's nothing wrong with it.

The passport officer was a youngish, little man with an Intelligence Corps tie and some mysterious badge in his lapel. He had a ginger moustache, and a North Country accent which was his life's enemy.

"Going to be away for a long time, Sir?" he asked Leamas.

"A couple of weeks," Leamas replied.

"You'll want to watch it, Sir. Your passport's due for renewal on the 31st."

"I know," said Leamas.

They walked side by side into the passengers' waiting room. On the way Leamas said: "You're a suspicious sod, aren't you, Kiever," and the other laughed quietly.

"Can't have you on the loose, can we! Not part of the contract," he replied.

They still had twenty minutes to wait. They sat down at a table and ordered coffee. "And take these things away," Kiever added to the waiter, indicating the used cups, saucers, and ash-trays on the table. "There's a trolley coming round," the waiter replied.

"Take them," Kiever repeated, angry again. "It's disgusting, leaving dirty crockery there like that."

The waiter just turned and walked away. He didn't go near the service counter and he didn't order their coffee. Kiever was white, ill with anger. "For Christ's sake," Leamas muttered, "let it go. Life's too short."

"Cheeky bastard, that's what he is," said Kiever.

"All right, all right, make a scene; you've chosen a good moment. They'll never forget us here."

The formalities at the airport at The Hague provided no problem. Kiever seemed to have recovered from his anxieties. He became jaunty and talkative as they walked the short distance

403

between the plane and the Customs sheds. The young Dutch officer gave a perfunctory glance at their luggage and passports and announced in awkward throaty English: "I hope you have a pleasant stay in the Netherlands."

"Thanks," said Kiever, almost too gratefully, "thanks very much."

They walked from the Customs shed along the corridor to the reception hall on the other side of the airport buildings. Kiever led the way to the main exit, between the little groups of travellers staring vaguely at kiosk displays of scent, cameras, and fruit. As they pushed their way through the revolving glass door, Leamas looked back. Standing at the newspaper kiosk, deep in a copy of the *Continental Daily Mail*, stood a small, froglike figure in glasses, an earnest, worried little man. He looked like a civil servant. Something like that.

A car was waiting for them in the car park, a Volkswagen with a Dutch registration, driven by a woman who ignored them. She drove slowly, always stopping if the lights were amber, and Leamas guessed she had been briefed to drive that way and that they were being followed by another car. He watched the off-side wing mirror, trying to recognise the car, but without success. Once he saw a black Peugeot with a CD number, but when they turned the corner there was only a furniture van behind them. He knew The Hague quite well from the war, and he tried to work out where they were heading. He guessed they were travelling northwest towards Scheveningen. Soon they had left the suburbs behind them and were approaching a colony of villas bordering the dunes along the sea front.

Here they stopped. The woman got out, leaving them in the car, and rang the front door bell of a small cream-coloured bungalow which stood at the near end of the row. A wrought iron sign hung on the porch with the words "Le Mirage" in pale blue Gothic script. There was a notice in the window, which proclaimed that all the rooms were taken.

The door was opened by a kindly, plump woman who looked past the driver towards the car. Her eyes still on the car, she came down the drive towards them, smiling with pleasure. She reminded Leamas of an old aunt he once had who beat him for wasting string.

"How nice that you have come," she declared; "we are so *pleased* that you have come!" They followed her into the bungalow, Kiever leading the way. The driver got back into the car. Leamas glanced down the road which they had just travelled; three hundred yards away a black car, a Fiat perhaps, or a Peugeot, had parked. A man in a raincoat was getting out.

Once in the hall the woman shook Leamas warmly by the hand. "Welcome, welcome to Le Mirage. Did you have a good journey?"

"Fine," Leamas replied.

"Did you fly or come by sea?"

"We flew," Kiever said; "a very smooth flight." He might have owned the airline.

"I'll make your lunch," she declared; "a special lunch. I'll make you something specially good. What shall I bring you?"

"Oh, for God's sake," said Leamas under his breath, and the door bell rang. The woman went quickly into the kitchen; Kiever opened the front door.

He was wearing a macintosh with leather buttons. He was about Leamas' height, but older. Leamas put him at about fifty-five. His face had a hard, grey hue and sharp furrows; he might have been a soldier. He held out his hand.

"My name is Peters," he said. The fingers were slim and polished.

"Did you have a good journey?"

"Yes," said Kiever quickly, "quite uneventful."

"Mr. Leamas and I have a lot to discuss; I do not think we need to keep you, Sam. You could take the Volkswagen back to town."

Kiever smiled. Leamas saw the relief in his smile.

"Good-bye, Leamas," said Kiever, his voice jocular; "good luck, old man."

Leamas nodded, ignoring Kiever's hand.

"Good-bye," Kiever repeated and let himself quietly out of the front door.

Leamas followed Peters into a back room. Heavy lace curtains hung on the window, ornately fringed and draped. The window sill was covered with potted plants; great cacti, a tobacco plant, and some curious tree with wide, rubbery leaves. The furniture was heavy, pseudo-antique. In the centre of the room was a table with two carved chairs. The table was covered with a rust-coloured counterpane more like a carpet; on it before each chair was a pad of paper and a pencil. On a sideboard there was whisky and soda. Peters went over to it and mixed them both a drink.

"Look," said Leamas suddenly, "from now on I can do without the goodwill; do you follow me? We both know what we're about; both professionals. You've got a paid defector—good luck to you. For Christ's sake don't pretend you've fallen in love with me." He sounded on edge, uncertain of himself.

Peters nodded. "Kiever told me you were a proud man," he observed dispassionately. Then he added without smiling, "After all, why else does a man attack tradesmen?"

Leamas guessed he was Russian, but he wasn't sure. His English was nearly perfect, he had the ease and habits of a man long used to civilised comforts.

They sat at the table.

"Kiever told you what I am going to pay you?" Peters enquired.

"Yes. Fifteen thousand pounds to be drawn on a Bern bank."

"Yes."

"He said you might have follow-up questions during the next year," said Leamas, "you would pay another five thousand if I kept myself available."

Peters nodded.

"I don't accept that condition," Leamas continued. "You

know as well as I do it wouldn't work. I want to draw the fifteen thousand and get clear. Your people have a rough way with defected agents; so have mine. I'm not going to sit on my fanny in St. Moritz while you roll up every network I've given you. They're not fools; they'd know who to look for. For all you and I know they're on to us now."

Peters nodded: "You could, of course, come somewhere . . . safer, couldn't you?"

"Behind the Curtain?"

"Yes."

Leamas just shook his head and continued: "I reckon you'll need about three days for a preliminary interrogation. Then you'll want to refer back for a detailed brief."

"Not necessarily," Peters replied.

Leamas looked at him with interest.

"I see," he said, "they've sent the expert. Or isn't Moscow Centre in on this?"

Peters was silent; he was just looking at Leamas, taking him in. At last he picked up the pencil in front of him and said:

"Shall we begin with your war service?"

Leamas shrugged:

"It's up to you."

"That's right. We'll begin with your war service. Just talk."

"I enlisted in the Engineers in 1939. I was finishing my training when a notice came round inviting linguists to apply for specialist service abroad. I had Dutch and German and a good deal of French and I was fed up with soldiering, so I applied. I knew Holland well; my father had a machine tool agency at Leiden; I'd lived there for nine years. I had the usual interviews and went off to a school near Oxford where they taught me the usual monkey tricks."

"Who was running that setup?"

"I didn't know till later. Then I met Steed-Asprey, and an Oxford don called Fielding. They were running it. In forty-one they dropped me into Holland and I stayed there nearly two years. We lost agents quicker than we could find them in those days—it was bloody murder. Holland's a wicked country for that kind of work—it's got no real rough country, nowhere out of the way you can keep a headquarters or a radio set. Always on the move, always running away. It made it a very dirty game. I got out in forty-three and had a couple of months in England, then I had a go at Norway—that was a picnic by comparison. In forty-five they paid me off and I came over here again, to Holland, to try and catch up on my father's old business. That was no good, so I joined up with an old friend who was running a travel agency business in Bristol. That lasted eighteen months then we were sold up. Then out of the blue I got a letter from the Department: would I like to go back? But I'd had enough of all that, I thought, so I said I'd think about it and rented a cottage on Lundy Island. I stayed there a year contemplating my stomach, then I got fed up again so I wrote to them. By late forty-nine I was back on the payroll. Broken service of course—reduction of pension rights and the usual crabbing. Am I going too fast?"

"Not for the moment," Peters replied, pouring him some more whisky; "we'll discuss it again of course, with names and dates."

There was a knock at the door and the woman came in with lunch, an enormous meal of cold meats and bread and soup. Peters pushed his notes aside and they ate in silence. The interrogation had begun.

Lunch was cleared away. "So you went back to the Circus," said Peters.

"Yes. For a while they gave me a desk job, processing reports, making assessments of military strengths in Iron Curtain countries, tracing units and that kind of thing."

"Which section?"

"Satellites Four. I was there from February fifty to May fifty-one."

"Who were your colleagues."

"Peter Guillam, Brian de Grey, and George Smiley. Smiley left us in early fifty-one and went over to Counter Intelligence. In May fifty-one I was posted to Berlin as DCA—Deputy-Controller of Area. That meant all the operational work."

"Who did you have under you?" Peters was writing swiftly. Leamas guessed he had some homemade shorthand.

"Hackett, Sarrow, and de Jong. De Jong was killed in a traffic accident in fifty-nine. We thought he was murdered but we could never prove it. They all ran networks and I was in charge. Do you want details?" he asked drily.

"Of course, but later. Go on."

"It was late fifty-four when we landed our first big fish in Berlin: Fritz Feger, second man in the DDR Defence Ministry. Up till then it had been heavy going—but in November fifty-four we got on to Fritz. He lasted almost exactly two years, then one day we never heard any more. I hear he died in prison. It was another three years before we found anyone to touch him. Then, in 1959, Karl Riemeck turned up. Karl was on the Praesidium of the East German Communist Party. He was the best agent I ever knew."

"He is now dead," Peters observed.

A look of something like shame passed across Leamas' face.

"I was there when he was shot," he muttered. "He had a mistress who came over just before he died. He'd told her everything—she knew the whole damned network. No wonder he was blown."

"We'll return to Berlin later. Tell me this. When Karl died you flew back to London. Did you remain in London for the rest of your service?"

"What there was of it, yes."

"What job did you have in London?"

"Banking section; supervision of agents' salaries, overseas payments for clandestine purposes. A child could have managed it. We got our orders and we signed the drafts. Occasionally there was a security headache."

"Did you deal with agents direct?"

"How could we? The Resident in a particular country would make a requisition. Authority would put a hoofmark on it and pass it to us to make the payment. In most cases we had the money transferred to a convenient foreign bank where the Resident could draw it himself and hand it to the agent."

"How were agents described? By cover names?"

"By figures. The Circus calls them combinations. Every network was given a combination; every agent was described by a suffix attached to the combination. Karl's combination was eight A stroke one."

Leamas was sweating. Peters watched him coolly, appraising him like a professional gambler across the table. What was Leamas worth? What would break him, what attract or frighten him? What did he hate, above all, what did he know? Would he keep his best card to the end and sell it dear? Peters didn't think so; Leamas was too much off balance to monkey about. He was a man at odds with himself, a man who knew one life, one confession, and had betrayed them. Peters had seen it before. He had seen it, even in men who had undergone a complete ideological rehearsal, who in the secret hours of the night had found a new creed, and alone, compelled by the internal power of their convictions, had betrayed their calling, their families, their countries. Even they, filled as they were with new zeal and new hope, had had to struggle against the stigma of treachery; even they wrestled with the almost physical anguish of saying that which they had been trained never, never to reveal. Like apostates who feared to burn the Cross, they hesitated between the instinctive and the material; and Peters, caught in the same polarity, must give them comfort and destroy their pride. It was a situation of which they were both aware; thus Leamas had fiercely rejected a human relationship with Peters, for his pride precluded it. Peters knew that for those reasons, Leamas would lie; lie perhaps only by omission, but lie all the same, for pride, from defiance or through the sheer perversity of his profession; and he, Peters, would have to nail the lies. He knew, too, that the very fact that Leamas was a professional could militate against his interests, for

410

Leamas would select where Peters wanted no selection; Leamas would anticipate the type of intelligence which Peters required—and in doing so might pass by some casual scrap which could be of vital interest to the evaluators. To all that, Peters added the capricious vanity of an alcoholic wreck.

"I think," he said, "we will now take your Berlin service in some detail. That would be from May 1951 to March 1961. Have another drink."

Leamas watched him take a cigarette from the box on the table, and light it. He noticed two things: that Peters was left-handed, and that once again he had put the cigarette in his mouth with the maker's name away from him, so that it burnt first. It was a gesture Leamas liked: it indicated that Peters, like himself, had been on the run.

Peters had an odd face, expressionless and grey. The colour must have left it long ago—perhaps in some prison in the early days of the Revolution—and now his features were formed and Peters would look like that till he died. Only the stiff, grey hair might turn to white, but his face would not change. Leamas wondered vaguely what Peters' real name was, whether he was married. There was something very orthodox about him which Leamas liked. It was the orthodoxy of strength, of confidence. If Peters lied there would be a reason. The lie would be a calculated, necessary lie, far removed from the fumbling dishonesty of Ashe.

Ashe, Kiever, Peters; that was a progression in quality, in authority, which to Leamas was axiomatic of the hierarchy of an intelligence network. It was also, he suspected, a progression in ideology. Ashe, the mercenary, Kiever the fellow traveller, and now Peters, for whom the end and the means were identical.

Leamas began to talk about Berlin. Peters seldom interrupted, seldom asked a question or made a comment, but when he did, he displayed a technical curiosity and expertise which entirely accorded with Leamas' own temperament. Leamas even

411

seemed to respond to the dispassionate professionalism of his interrogator—it was something they had in common.

It had taken a long time to build a decent East Zone network from Berlin, Leamas explained. In the earlier days the city had been thronging with second-rate agents: intelligence was discredited and so much a part of the daily life of Berlin that you could recruit a man at a cocktail party, brief him over dinner, and he would be blown by breakfast. For a professional it was a nightmare: dozens of agencies, half of them penetrated by the opposition, thousands of loose ends; too many leads, too few sources, too little space to operate. They had their break with Feger in 1954, true enough. But by '56 when every Service department was screaming for high-grade intelligence, they were becalmed. Feger had spoilt them for second-rate stuff that was only one jump ahead of the news. They needed the real thing— and they had to wait another three years before they got it.

Then one day de Jong went for a picnic in the woods on the edge of East Berlin. He had a British military number plate on his car, which he parked, locked, in an unmade road beside the canal. After the picnic his children ran on ahead, carrying the basket. When they reached the car they stopped, hesitated, dropped the basket and ran back. Somebody had forced the car door—the handle was broken and the door was slightly open. De Jong swore, remembering that he had left his camera in the glove compartment. He went and examined the car. The handle had been forced; de Jong reckoned it had been done with a piece of steel tubing, the kind of thing you can carry in your sleeve. But the camera was still there, so was his coat, so were some parcels, belonging to his wife. On the driving seat was a tobacco tin, and in the tin was a small nickel cartridge. De Jong knew exactly what it contained: it was the film cartridge of a subminiature camera, probably a Minox.

De Jong drove home and developed the film. It contained the minutes of the last meeting of the Praesidium of the East German Communist Party, the SED. By an odd coincidence there was collateral from another source; the photographs were genuine.

412

Leamas took the case over then. He was badly in need of a success. He'd produced virtually nothing since arriving in Berlin, and he was getting past the usual age limit for full-time operational work. Exactly a week later he took de Jong's car to the same place and went for a walk.

It was a desolate spot that de Jong had chosen for his picnic: a strip of canal with a couple of shell-torn pill-boxes, some parched, sandy fields, and on the Eastern side a sparse pine wood, lying about two hundred yards from the gravel road which bordered the canal. But it had the virtue of solitude—something that was hard to find in Berlin—and surveillance was impossible. Leamas walked in the woods. He made no attempt to watch the car because he did not know from which direction the approach might be made. If he was seen watching the car from the woods, the chances of retaining his informant's confidence were ruined. He need not have worried.

When he returned there was nothing in the car so he drove back to West Berlin, kicking himself for being a damned fool; the Praesidium was not due to meet for another fortnight. Three weeks later he borrowed de Jong's car and took a thousand dollars in twenties in a picnic case. He left the car unlocked for two hours and when he returned there was a tobacco tin in the glove compartment. The picnic case had gone.

The films were packed with first grade documentary stuff. In the next six weeks he did it twice more, and the same thing happened.

Leamas knew he had hit a gold mine. He gave the source the cover name of "Mayfair" and sent a pessimistic letter to London. Leamas knew that if he gave London half an opening they would control the case direct, which he was desperately anxious to avoid. This was probably the only kind of operation which could save him from superannuation and it was just the kind of thing that was big enough for London to want to take over for itself. Even if he kept them at arm's length there was still the danger that the Circus would have theories, make suggestions, urge caution, demand action. They would want him to give only

413

new dollar bills in the hope of tracing them, they would want the film cartridges sent home for examination, they would plan clumsy tailing operations and tell the Departments. Most of all they would want to tell the Departments; and that, said Leamas, would blow the thing sky-high. He worked like a madman for three weeks. He combed the personality files of each member of the Praesidium. He drew up a list of all the clerical staff who might have had access to the minutes. From the distribution list on the pages of the facsimiles he extended the total of possible informants to thirty-one, including clerks and secretarial staff.

Confronted with the almost impossible task of identifying an informant from the incomplete records of thirty-one candidates, Leamas returned to the original material, which, he said, was something he should have done earlier. It puzzled him that in none of the photostat minutes he had so far received were the pages numbered, that none was stamped with a security classification, and that in the second and fourth copy words were crossed out in pencil or crayon. He came finally to an important conclusion: that the photocopies related not to the minutes themselves, but to the *draft* minutes. This placed the source in the Secretariat and the Secretariat was very small. The draft minutes had been well and carefully photographed: that suggested that the photographer had had time and a room to himself.

Leamas returned to the personality index. There was a man called Karl Riemeck in the Secretariat, a former corporal in the Medical Corps, who had served three years as a prisoner of war in England. His sister had been living in Pomerania when the Russians overran it, and he had never heard of her since. He was married and had one daughter named Carla.

Leamas decided to take a chance. He found out from London Riemeck's prisoner of war number, which was 29012, and the date of his release which was November 10th, 1945. He bought an East German children's book of science fiction and wrote in the fly leaf in German in an adolescent hand: "This book belongs to Carla Riemeck, born December 10th, 1945, in Bideford, North Devon. Signed Moonspacewoman 29012," and

414

underneath, he added, "Applicants wishing to make space flights should present themselves for instruction to C. Riemeck in person. An application form is enclosed. Long live the People's Republic of Democratic Space!"

He ruled some lines on a sheet of writing paper, made columns of name, address, and age, and wrote at the bottom of the page:

"Each candidate will be interviewed personally. Write to the usual address stating when and where you wish to be met. Applications will be considered in seven days. C.R."

He put the sheet of paper inside the book. Leamas drove to the usual place, still in de Jong's car, and left the book on the passenger seat with five used one-hundred-dollar bills inside the cover. When Leamas returned the book had gone, and there was a tobacco tin on the seat instead. It contained three rolls of film. Leamas developed them that night: one film contained as usual the minutes of the Praesidium's last meeting; the second showed a draft revision of the East Germans' relationship to COMECON; and the third a breakdown of the East German Intelligence Service, complete with functions of departments and details of personalities.

Peters interrupted: "Just a minute," he said. "Do you mean to say all this intelligence came from Riemeck?"

"Why not? You know how much he saw."

"It's scarcely possible," Peters observed, almost to himself; "he must have had help."

"He did have later on; I'm coming to that."

"I know what you are going to tell me. But did you never have the feeling he got assistance from *above* as well as from the agents he afterwards acquired?"

"No. No, I never did. It never occurred to me."

"Looking back on it now, does it seem likely?"

"Not particularly."

"When you sent all this material back to the Circus, they never suggested that even for a man in Riemeck's position, the intelligence was phenomenally comprehensive."

415

"No."

"Did they ever ask where Riemeck got his camera from, who instructed him in document photography?"

Leamas hesitated.

"No . . . I'm sure they never asked."

"Remarkable," Peters observed drily. "I'm sorry—do go on. I do not mean to anticipate you."

Exactly a week later, Leamas continued, he drove to the canal and this time he felt nervous. As he turned into the unmade road he saw three bicycles lying in the grass and two hundred yards down the canal, three men fishing. He got out of the car as usual and began walking towards the line of trees on the other side of the field. He had gone about twenty yards when he heard a shout. He looked round and caught sight of one of the men beckoning to him. The other two had turned and were looking at him too. Leamas was wearing an old macintosh; he had his hands in the pockets, and it was too late to take them out. He knew that the men on either side were covering the man in the middle and that if he took his hands out of his pockets they would probably shoot him; they would think he was holding a revolver in his pocket. Leamas stopped ten yards from the centre man.

"You want something?" Leamas asked.

"Are you Leamas?" He was a small, plump man, very steady. He spoke English.

"Yes."

"What is your British national identity number?"

"PRT stroke L 58003 stroke one."

"Where did you spend VJ night?"

"At Leiden in Holland in my father's workshop, with some Dutch friends."

"Let's go for a walk, Mr. Leamas. You won't need your macintosh. Take it off and leave it on the ground where you are standing. My friends will look after it."

Leamas hesitated, shrugged, and took off his macintosh. Then they walked together briskly towards the wood.

*   *   *

"You know as well as I do who he was," said Leamas wearily, "third man in the Ministry of the Interior, Secretary to the SED Praesidium, head of the Co-ordinating Committee for the Protection of the People. I suppose that was how he knew about de Jong and me: he'd seen our counter intelligence files in the Abteilung. He had three strings to his bow: the Praesidium, straightforward internal politial and economic reporting, and access to the files of the East German Security Service."

"But only *limited* access. They'd never give an outsider the run of all their files," Peters insisted.

Leamas shrugged.

"They did," he said.

"What did he do with his money?"

"After that afternoon I didn't give him any. The Circus took that over straight away. It was paid into a West German bank. He even gave me back what I'd given him. London banked it for him."

"How much did you tell London?"

"Everything after that. I had to; then the Circus told the Departments. "After that," Leamas added venomously, "it was only a matter of time before it packed up. With the Departments at their backs, London got greedy. They began pressing us for more, wanted to give him more money. Finally we had to suggest to Karl that he recruited other sources and we took them on to form a network. It was bloody stupid, it put a strain on Karl, endangered him, undermined his confidence in us. It was the beginning of the end."

"How much did you get out of him?"

Leamas hesitated.

"How much? Christ, I don't know. It lasted an unnaturally long time. I think he was blown long before he was caught. The standard dropped in the last few months; think they'd begun to suspect him by then and kept him away from the good stuff."

"Altogether, what did he give you?" Peters persisted.

Piece by piece, Leamas recounted the full extent of all Karl

417

Riemeck's work. His memory was, Peters noted approvingly, remarkably precise considering the amount he drank. He could give dates and names, he could remember the reaction from London, the nature of corroboration where it existed. He could remember sums of money demanded and paid, the dates of the conscription of other agents into the network.

"I'm sorry," said Peters at last, "but I do not believe that one man, however well placed, however careful, however industrious, could have acquired such a range of detailed knowledge. For that matter, even if he had he would never have been able to photograph it."

"He *was* able," Leamas persisted, suddenly angry, "he bloody well did and that's all there is to it."

"And the Circus never told you to go into it with him, exactly how and when he saw all this stuff."

"No," snapped Leamas, "Riemeck was touchy about that, and London was content to let it go."

"Well, well," Peters mused.

After a moment Peters said: "You heard about that woman, incidentally?"

"What woman?" Leamas asked sharply.

"Karl Riemeck's mistress, the one who came over to West Berlin the night Riemeck was shot."

"Well?"

"She was found dead a week ago. Murdered. She was shot from a car as she left her flat."

"It used to be my flat," said Leamas mechanically.

"Perhaps," Peters suggested, "she knew more about Riemeck's network than you did."

"What the hell do you mean?" Leamas demanded.

Peters shrugged.

"It's all very strange," he observed. "I wonder who killed her."

When they had exhausted the case of Karl Riemeck, Leamas went on to talk of other less spectacular agents, then of the procedure of his Berlin office, its communications, its staff, its secret ramifications—flats, transport, recording and photographic equipment. They talked long into the night and throughout the next day and when at last Leamas stumbled into bed the following night he knew he had betrayed all that he knew of Allied Intelligence in Berlin, and drunk two bottles of whisky in two days.

One thing puzzled him: Peters' insistence that Karl Riemeck must have had help—must have had a high-level collaborator. Control had asked him the same question—he remembered now—Control had asked about Riemeck's access. How could they both be so sure Karl hadn't managed alone? He'd had helpers, of course; like the guards by the canal the day Leamas met him. But they were small beer—Karl had told him about them. But Peters—and Peters, after all, would know precisely how much Karl had been able to get his hands on—Peters had refused to believe Karl had managed alone. On this point, Peters and Control were evidently agreed.

Perhaps it was true. Perhaps there was somebody else. Perhaps this was the Special Interest whom Control was so anxious to protect from Mundt. That would mean that Karl Riemeck had collaborated with this special interest and provided what both of them had together obtained. Perhaps that was what Control had spoken to Karl about, alone, that evening in Leamas' flat in Berlin.

Anyway, tomorrow would tell. Tomorrow he would play his hand.

He wondered who had killed Elvira. And he wondered *why* they had killed her. Of course—here was a point, here was a possible explanation—Elvira, knowing the identity of Riemeck's special collaborator, had been murdered *by* that collaborator . . . No, that was too far-fetched. It overlooked the difficulty of crossing from East to West: Elvira had after all been murdered in West Berlin.

He wondered why Control had never told him Elvira had been murdered. So that he would react suitably when Peters told him? It was useless speculating. Control had his reasons;

they were usually so bloody tortuous it took you a week to work them out.

As he fell asleep he muttered, "Karl was a damn' fool. That woman did for him, I'm sure she did." Elvira was dead now, and serve her right. He remembered Liz.

9 ❊
THE SECOND DAY

Peters arrived at eight o'clock the next morning, and without ceremony they sat down at the table and began.

"So you came back to London. What did you do there?"

"They put me on the shelf. I knew I was finished when that ass in Personnel met me at the airport. I had to go straight to Control and report about Karl. He was dead—what else was there to say?"

"What did they do with you?"

"They said at first I could hang around in London and wait till I was qualified for a proper pension. They were so bloody decent about it I got angry—I told them that if they were so keen to chuck money at me why didn't they do the obvious thing and count in all my time instead of bleating about broken service. Then they got cross when I told them that. They put me in Banking with a lot of women. I can't remember much about that part—I began hitting the bottle a bit. Had rather a bad patch."

He lit a cigarette. Peters nodded.

"That was why they gave me the push, really. They didn't like me drinking."

"Tell me what you *do* remember about Banking Section," Peters suggested.

"It was a dreary set-up. I never was cut out for desk work, I knew that. That's why I hung on in Berlin. I knew when they recalled me I'd be put on the shelf, but, Christ . . . !"

"What did you do?"

Leamas shrugged.

"Sat on my behind in the same room as a couple of women. Thursby and Larrett. I called them Thursday and Friday." He grinner rather stupidly. Peters looked uncomprehending.

"We just pushed paper. A letter came down from Finance: 'the payment of seven hundred dollars to so and so is authorised with effect from so and so. Kindly get on with it'—that was the gist of it. Thursday and Friday would kick it about a bit, file it, stamp it and I'd sign a cheque or get the bank to make a transfer."

"What bank?"

"Blatt and Rodney, a chichi little bank in the City. There's a sort of theory in the Circus that Etonians are discreet."

"In fact, then, you knew the names of agents all over the world?"

"Not necessarily. That was the cunning thing. I'd sign the cheque, you see, or the order to the bank, but we'd leave a space for the name of the payee. The covering letter or what have you was all signed and then the file would go *back* to Special Despatch."

"Who are they?"

"They're the general holders of agents' particulars. They put in the names and posted the order. Bloody clever, I must say."

Peters looked disappointed.

"You mean you had no way of knowing the names of the payees?"

"Not usually, no."

"But occasionally?"

422

"We got pretty near the knuckle now and again. All the fiddling about between Banking, Finance, and Special Despatch led to cock-ups, of course. Too elaborate. Then occasionally we came in on special stuff which brightened one's life a bit."

Leamas got up. "I've made a list," he said, "of all the payments I can remember. It's in my room. I'll get it."

He walked out of the room, the rather shuffling walk he had affected since arriving in Holland. When he returned he held in his hand a couple of sheets of lined paper torn from a cheap notebook.

"I wrote these down last night," he said; "I thought it would save time."

Peters took the notes and read them slowly and carefully. He seemed impressed.

"Good," he said, "very good."

"Then I remembered best a thing called Rolling Stone. I got a couple of trips out of it. One to Copenhagen and one to Helsinki. Just dumping money at banks."

"How much?"

"Ten thousand dollars in Copenhagen, forty thousand D-Marks in Helsinki."

Peters put down his pencil.

"Who for?" he asked.

"God knows. We worked Rolling Stone on a system of deposit accounts. The service gave me a phoney British passport; I went to the Royal Scandinavian Bank in Copenhagen and the National Bank of Finland in Helsinki, deposited the money, and drew a pass book on a joint account for me in my alias and for someone else—the agent, I suppose, in his alias. I gave the banks a sample of the co-holder's signature. I'd got that from Head Office. Later the agent was given the pass book and a false passport which he showed at the bank when he drew the money. All I knew was the alias." He heard himself talking and it all sounded so ludicrously improbable.

"Was this procedure common?"

"No. It was a special payment. It had a subscription list."

"What's that?"

"It had a code name known to very few people."

"What was the code name?"

"I told you—Rolling Stone. The operation covered irregular payments of ten thousand dollars in different currencies and in different capitals."

"Always in capital towns?"

"Far as I know. I remember reading in the file that there had been other Rolling Stone payments before I came to the section, but in those cases Banking Section got the local Resident to do it."

"These other payments that took place before you came, where were they made?"

"One in Oslo. I can't remember where the other was."

"Was the alias of the agent always the same?"

"No. That was an added security precaution. I heard later we pinched the whole technique from the Russians. It was the most elaborate payment scheme I'd met. In the same way I used a different alias and of course a different passport for each trip." That would please him; help him to fill in the gaps.

"These faked passports the agent was given so that he could draw the money: did you know anything about them, how they were made out and despatched?"

"No. Oh, except that they had to have visas in them for the country where the money was deposited. And entry stamps."

"*Entry stamps?*"

"Yes. I assumed the passports were never used at the border—only presented at the bank for identification purposes. The agent must have travelled on his own passport, quite legally entered the country where the bank was situated, then used the faked passport at the bank. That was my guess."

"Do you know of a reason why earlier payments were made by the Residents, and later payments by someone travelling out from London?"

"I know the reason. I asked the women in Banking Section, Thursday and Friday. Control was anxious that—"

"*Control?* Do you mean to say Control himself was running the case?"

"Yes, he was running it. He was afraid the Resident might be recognised at the bank. So he used a postman: me."

"When did you make your journeys?"

"Copenhagen on the fifteenth of June. I flew back the same night. Helsinki at the end of September. I stayed two nights there, flew back around the twenty-eighth. I had a bit of fun in Helsinki." He grinned but Peters took no notice.

"And the other payments—when were they made?"

"I can't remember. Sorry."

"But one was definitely in Oslo?"

"Yes, in Oslo."

"How much time separated the first two payments, the payments made by the Residents?"

"I don't know. Not long, I think. Maybe a month. A bit more perhaps."

"Was it your impression that the agent had been operating for some time before the first payment was made? Did the file show that?"

"No idea. The file simply covered actual payments. First payments early '59. There was no other data on it. That is the principle that operates where you have a limited subscription. Different files handle different bits of a single case. Only someone with the master file would be able to put it all together."

Peters was writing all the time now. Leamas assumed there was a tape recorder hidden somewhere in the room but the subsequent transcription would take time. What Peters wrote down now would provide the background for this evening's telegram to Moscow, while in the Soviet Embassy in The Hague the girls would sit up all night telegraphing the verbatim transcript on hourly schedules.

"Tell me," said Peters; "these are large sums of money. The arrangements for paying them were elaborate and very expensive. What did you make of it yourself?"

Leamas shrugged.

"What could I make of it? I thought Control must have a bloody good source, but I never saw the material so I don't know. I didn't like the way it was done—it was too high-powered, too complicated, too clever. Why couldn't they just meet him and give him the money in cash? Did they really let him cross borders on his own passport with a forged one in his pocket? I doubt it," said Leamas. It was time he clouded the issue, let him chase a hare.

"What do you mean?"

"I mean, that for all I know the money was never drawn from the bank. Supposing he was a highly placed agent behind the Curtain—the money would be on deposit for him when he could get at it. That was what I reckoned anyway. I didn't think about it all that much. Why should I? It's part of our work only to know pieces of the whole set-up. You know that. If you're curious, God help you."

"If the money wasn't collected, as you suggest, why all the trouble with passports?"

"When I was in Berlin we made an arrangement for Karl Riemeck in case he ever needed to run and couldn't get hold of us. We kept a bogus West German passport for him at an address in Düsseldorf. He could collect it any time by following a pre-arranged procedure. It never expired—Special Travel renewed the passport and the visas as they expired. Control might have followed the same technique with this man. I don't know—it's only a guess."

"How do you know for certain that passports were issued?"

"There were minutes on the file between Banking section and Special Travel. Special Travel is the section which arranges false identity papers and visas."

"I see." Peters thought for a moment and then he asked: "What names did you use in Copenhagen and Helsinki?"

"Robert Lang, electrical engineer from Derby. That was in Copenhagen."

"When exactly were you in Copenhagen?" Peters asked.

"I told you, June the fifteenth. I got there in the morning at about eleven-thirty."

"Which bank did you use?"

"Oh, for Christ's sake, Peters," said Leamas, suddenly angry, "the Royal Scandinavian. You've got it written down."

"I just wanted to be sure," the other replied evenly, and continued writing. "And for Helsinki, what name?"

"Stephen Bennett, marine engineer from Plymouth. I was there," he added sarcastically, "at the end of September."

"You visited the bank on the day you arrived?"

"Yes. It was the 24th or 25th, I can't be sure, as I told you."

"Did you take the money with you from England?"

"Of course not. We just transferred it to the Resident's account in each case. The Resident drew it, met me at the airport with the money in a suitcase, and I took it to the bank."

"Who's the Resident in Copenhagen?"

"Peter Jensen, a bookseller in the University bookshop."

"And what were the names which would be used by the agent?"

"Horst Karlsdorf in Copenhagen. I think that was it, yes it was, I remember. Karlsdorf. I kept on wanting to say Karlshorst."

"Description?"

"Manager, from Klagenfurt in Austria."

"And the other? The Helsinki name?"

"Fechtmann. Adolf Fechtmann from St. Gallen, Switzerland. He had a title—yes, that's right: Doctor Fechtmann, archivist."

"I see; both German-speaking?"

"Yes, I noticed that. But it can't be a German."

"Why not?"

"I was head of the Berlin set-up, wasn't I? I'd have been in on it. A high-level agent in East Germany would have to be run from Berlin. I'd have known." Leamas got up, went to the sideboard, and poured himself some whisky. He didn't bother about Peters.

"You said yourself there were special precautions, special procedures in this case. Perhaps they didn't think you needed to know."

"Don't be bloody silly," Leamas rejoined shortly; "of course I'd have known." This was the point he would stick to through thick and thin; it made them feel they knew better, gave credence to the rest of his information. "They will want to deduce *in spite of you*," Control had said. "We must give them the material and remain sceptical to their conclusions. Rely on their intelligence and conceit, on their suspicion of one another—that's what we must do."

Peters nodded as if he were confirming a melancholy truth. "You are a very proud man, Leamas," he observed once more.

Peters left soon after that. He wished Leamas good day and walked down the road along the seafront. It was lunchtime.

10 ❈
THE THIRD DAY

Peters didn't appear that afternoon, nor the next morning. Leamas stayed in, waiting with growing irritation for some message, but none came. He asked the housekeeper but she just smiled and shrugged her heavy shoulders. At about eleven o'clock the next morning he decided to go out for a walk along the front, bought some cigarettes and stared dully at the sea.

There was a girl standing on the beach throwing bread to the seagulls. Her back was turned to him. The sea wind played with her long black hair and pulled at her coat, making an arc of her body, like a bow strung towards the sea. He knew what it was then that Liz had given him; the thing that he would have to go back and find if ever he got home to England: it was the caring about little things—the faith in ordinary life; the simplicity that made you break up a bit of bread into a paper bag, walk down to the beach, and throw it to the gulls. It was this respect for triviality which he had never been allowed to possess; whether it was bread for the seagulls or love, whatever it was he would go back and find it; he would make Liz find it for him.

429

A week, two weeks perhaps, and he would be home. Control had said he could keep whatever they paid—and that would be enough. With fifteen thousand pounds, a gratuity, and a pension from the Circus, a man—as Control would say—can afford to come in from the cold.

He made a detour and returned to the bungalow at a quarter to twelve. The woman let him in without a word, but when he had gone into the back room he heard her lift the receiver and dial a telephone number. She only spoke for a few seconds. At half past twelve she brought him lunch, and, to his pleasure, some English newspapers, which he read contentedly until three o'clock. Leamas who normally read nothing, read newspapers slowly and with concentration. He remembered details, like the names and addresses of people who were the subject of small news items. He did it almost unconsciously as a kind of private pelmanism, and it absorbed him entirely.

At three o'clock Peters arrived, and as soon as Leamas saw him he knew that something was up. They did not sit at the table; Peters did not take off his macintosh.

"I've got bad news for you," he said, "they're looking for you in England. I heard this morning. They're watching the ports."

Leamas replied impassively: "On what charge?"

"Nominally for failing to report to a police station within the statutory period after release from prison."

"And in fact?"

"The word is going around that you're wanted for an offence under the Official Secrets Act. Your photograph's in all the London evening papers. The captions are very vague."

Leamas was standing very still.

Control had done it. Control had started the hue and cry. There was no other explanation. If Ashe or Kiever had been pulled in, if they had talked—even then, the responsibility for the hue and cry was still Control's. "A couple of weeks," he'd said; "I expect they'll take you off somewhere for the interrogation—it may even be abroad. A couple of weeks should see

430

you through, though. After that, the thing should run itself. You'll have to lie low over here while the chemistry works itself out; but you won't mind that I'm sure. I've agreed to keep you on operational subsistence until Mundt is eliminated: that seemed the fairest way."

And now this.

This wasn't part of the bargain; this was different. What the hell was he supposed to do? By pulling out now, by refusing to go along with Peters, he was wrecking the operation. It was just possible that Peters was lying, that this was the test—all the more reason that he should agree to go. But if he went, if he agreed to go east, to Poland, Czechoslovakia, or God knows where, there was no good reason why they should ever let him out—there was no good reason (since he was notionally a wanted man in the West) why he should *want* to be let out.

Control had done it—he was sure. The terms had been too generous, he'd known that all along. They didn't throw money about like that for nothing—not unless they thought they might lose you. Money like that was a *douceur* for discomfort and dangers Control would not openly admit to. Money like that was a warning; Leamas had not heeded the warning.

"Now how the devil," he asked quietly, "could they get on to that?" A thought seemed to cross his mind and he said, "Your friend Ashe could have told them, of course, or Kiever . . ."

"It's possible," Peters replied. "You know as well as I do that such things are always possible. There is no certainty in our job. The fact is," he added with something like impatience, "that by now every country in Western Europe will be looking for you."

Leamas might not have heard what Peters was saying. "You've got me on the hook now, haven't you, Peters?" he said. "Your people must be laughing themselves sick. Or did they give the tip-off themselves?"

"You overrate your own importance," Peters said sourly.

"Then why do you have me followed, tell me that? I went for a walk this morning. Two little men in brown suits, one twenty

431

yards behind the other, trailed me along the seafront. When I came back the housekeeper rang you up."

"Let us stick to what we know," Peters suggested. "How your own authorities have got on to you does not at the moment acutely concern us. The fact is, they have."

"Have you brought the London evening papers with you?"

"Of course not. They are not available here. We received a telegram from London."

"That's a lie. You know perfectly well your apparatus is only allowed to communicate with Centre."

"In this case a direct link between two outstations was permitted," Peters retorted angrily.

"Well, well," said Leamas with a wry smile, "you must be quite a big wheel. Or"—a thought seemed to strike him—"isn't Centre in on this?"

Peters ignored the question.

"You know the alternative. You let us take care of you, let us arrange your safe passage, or you fend for yourself—with the certainty of eventual capture. You've no false papers, no money, nothing. Your British passport will have expired in ten days."

"There's a third possibility. Give me a Swiss passport and some money and let me run. I can look after myself."

"I am afraid that is not considered desirable."

"You mean you haven't finished the interrogation. Until you have I am not expendable?"

"That is roughly the position."

"When you have completed the interrogation, what will you do with me?"

Peters shrugged. "What do you suggest?"

"A new identity. Scandinavian passport perhaps. Money."

"It's very academic," Peters replied, "but I will suggest it to my superiors. Are you coming with me?" Leamas hesitated then he smiled a little uncertainly and asked:

"If I didn't, what would you do? After all I've quite a story to tell, haven't I?"

"Stories of that kind are hard to substantiate. I shall be gone

432

tonight. Ashe and Kiever . . ." he shrugged, "what do they add up to?"

Leamas went to the window. A storm was gathering over the grey North Sea. He watched the gulls wheeling against the dark clouds. The girl had gone.

"All right," he said at last, "fix it up."

"There's no plane East until tomorrow. There's a flight to Berlin in an hour. We shall take that. It's going to be very close."

Leamas' passive role that evening enabled him once again to admire the unadorned efficiency of Peters' arrangements. The passport had been put together long ago—Centre must have thought of that. It was made out in the name of Alexander Thwaite, travel agent, and filled with visas and frontier stamps— the old, well-fingered passport of the professional traveller. The Dutch frontier guard at the airport just nodded and stamped it for form's sake—Peters was three or four behind him in the queue and took no interest in the formalities.

As they entered the "passengers only" enclosure Leamas caught sight of a bookstall. A selection of international newspapers was on show: *Figaro, Monde, Neue Zürcher Zeitung, Die Welt,* and half a dozen British dailies and weeklies. As he watched, the girl came round to the front of the kiosk and pushed an *Evening Standard* into the rack. Leamas hurried across to the bookstall and took the paper from the rack.

"How much?" he asked. Thrusting his hand into his trouser pocket he suddenly realised that he had no Dutch currency.

"Thirty cents," the girl replied. She was rather pretty; dark and jolly.

"I've only got two English sillings. That's a guilder. Will you take them?"

"Yes, please," she replied, and Leamas gave her the florin. He looked back; Peters was still at the passport desk, his back turned to Leamas. Without hesitation he made straight for the men's lavatory. There he glanced rapidly but thoroughly at each page, then shoved the paper in the litter basket and re-emerged.

433

It was true: there was his photograph with the vague little passage underneath. He wondered if Liz had seen it. He made his way thoughtfully to the passengers' lounge. Ten minutes later they boarded the plane for Hamburg and Berlin. For the first time since it all began, Leamas was frightened.

11 ❈
FRIENDS OF ALEC

The men called on Liz the same evening.

Liz Gold's room was at the northern end of Bayswater. It had two single beds in it, and a gas fire, rather a pretty one in charcoal grey, which made a modern hiss instead of an old fashioned bubble. She used to gaze into it sometimes when Leamas was there, when the gas fire shed the only light in the room. He would lie on the bed, hers, the one furthest from the door, and she would sit beside him and kiss him, or watch the gas fire with her face pressed against his. She was afraid to think of him too much now because then she forgot what he looked like, so she let her mind think of him for brief moments like running her eyes across a faint horizon, and then she would remember some small thing he had said or done, some way he had looked at her, or, more often, ignored her. That was the terrible thing, when her mind dwelled on it: she had nothing to remember him by—no photograph, no souvenir, nothing. Not even a mutual friend—only Miss Crail in the library, whose hatred of him had been vindicated by his spectacular departure. Liz had been round to his room once and seen

435

the landlord. She didn't know why she did it quite, but she plucked up courage and went. The landlord was very kind about Alec; Mr. Leamas had paid his rent like a gentleman, right till the end, then there'd been a week or two owing and a chum of Mr. Leamas had dropped in and paid up handsome, no queries or nothing. He'd always said it of Mr. Leamas, always would, he was a gent. Not public school, mind, nothing arsy-tansy but a real gent. He liked to scowl a bit occasionally, and of course he drank a drop more than was good for him, though he never acted tight when he came home. But this little bloke who come round, funny little shy chap with specs, *he* said Mr. Leamas had particularly requested, quite particularly, that the rent owing should be settled up. And if that wasn't gentlemanly the landlord was damned if he knew what was. Where he got the money from Heaven knows, but that Mr. Leamas was a deep one and no mistake. He only did to Ford the grocer what a good many had been wanting to do ever since the war. The room? Yes, the room had been taken—a gentleman from Korea, two days after they took Mr. Leamas away.

That was probably why she went on working at the library— because there, at least, he still existed; the ladders, shelves, the books, the card index, were things he had known and touched, and one day he might come back to them. He had said he would never come back, but she didn't believe it. It was like saying you would never get better, to believe a thing like that. Miss Crail thought he would come back: she had discovered she owed him some money—wages underpaid—and it infuriated her that her monster had been so unmonstrous as not to collect it. After Leamas had gone, Liz had never given up asking herself the same question; why had he hit Mr. Ford? She knew he had a terrible temper, but that was different. He had intended to do it right from the start as soon as he had got rid of his fever. Why else had he said good-bye to her the night before? He knew that he would hit Mr. Ford on the following day. She refused to accept the only other possible interpretation: that he had grown tired

436

of her and said good-bye, and the next day, still under the emotional strain of their parting, had lost his temper with Mr. Ford and struck him. She knew, she had always known, that there was something Alec had got to do. He'd even told her that himself. What it was she could only guess.

First, she thought he had a quarrel with Mr. Ford, some deep-rooted hatred going back for years. Something to do with a girl, or Alec's family perhaps. But you only had to look at Mr. Ford and it seemed ridiculous. He was the archetypal *petit-bourgeois*, cautious, complacent, mean. And anyway, if Alec had a vendetta on with Mr. Ford, why did he go for him in the shop on a Saturday, in the middle of the weekend shopping rush, when everyone could see?

They'd talked about it in the meeting of her party branch. George Hanby, the branch treasurer, had actually been passing Ford the grocer's as it happened, he hadn't seen much because of the crowd, but he'd talked to a bloke who'd seen the whole thing. Hanby had been so impressed that he'd rung the *Worker*, and they'd sent a man to the trial—that was why the *Worker* had given it a middle page spread as a matter of fact. It was just a straight case of protest—of sudden social awareness and hatred against the boss class, as the *Worker* said. This bloke that Hanby spoke to (he was just a little ordinary chap with specs, white collar type) said it had been so sudden—spontaneous was what he meant—and it just proved to Hanby once again how incendiary was the fabric of the capitalist system. Liz had kept very quiet while Hanby talked: none of them knew, of course, about her and Leamas. She realised then that she hated George Hanby; he was a pompous, dirty-minded little man, always leering at her and trying to touch her.

Then the men called.

She thought they were a little too smart for policemen: they came in a small black car with an aerial on it. One was short and rather plump. He had glasses and wore odd, expensive clothes; he was a kindly, worried little man and Liz trusted him somehow without knowing why. The other was smoother, but not glossy—rather a boyish figure, although she guessed he wasn't less than forty. They said they came from Special Branch, and they had printed cards with photographs in cellophane cases. The plump one did most of the talking.

"I believe you were friendly with Alec Leamas," he began. She was prepared to be angry, but the plump man was so earnest that it seemed silly.

"Yes," Liz answered. "How did you know?"

"We found out quite by chance the other day. When you go to . . . prison, you have to give next of kin. Leamas said he hadn't any. That was a lie as a matter of fact. They asked him whom they should inform if anything happened to him in prison. He said you."

"I see."

"Does anyone else know you were friendly with him?"

"No."

"Did you go to the trial?"

"No."

"No press men called, creditors, no one at all?"

"No, I've told you. No one else knew. Not even my parents, no one. We worked together in the library, of course—the Psychical Research Laboratory—but only Miss Crail, the librarian, would know that. I don't think it occurred to her that there was anything between us. She's queer," Liz added simply.

The little man peered very seriously at her for a moment, then asked:

"Did it surprise you when Leamas beat up Mr. Ford?"

"Yes, of course."

"Why did you think he did it?"

"I don't know. Because Ford wouldn't give him credit, I suppose. But I think he always meant to." She wondered if she was saying too much, but she longed to talk to somebody about it, she was so alone and there didn't seem any harm.

"But that night, the night before it happened, we talked together. We had supper, a sort of special one; Alec said we should and I knew that it was our last night. He'd got a bottle of red wine from somewhere; I didn't like it much. Alec drank most of it. And then I asked him, 'Is this good-bye'—whether it was all over."

"What did he say?"

"He said there was a job he'd got to do. I didn't really understand it all, not really."

There was a very long silence and the little man looked more worried than ever. Finally he asked her:

"Do you believe that?"

"I don't know." She was suddenly terrified for Alec, and she didn't know why. The man asked:

"Leamas has got two children by his marriage, did he tell you?" Liz said nothing. "In spite of that he gave your name as next of kin. Why do you think he did that?" The little man seemed embarrassed by his own question. He was looking at his hands, which were pudgy and clasped together on his lap. Liz blushed.

"I was in love with him," she replied.

"Was he in love with you?"

"Perhaps. I don't know."

"Are you still in love with him?"

"Yes."

"Did he ever say he would come back?" asked the younger man.

"No."

"But he did say good-bye to you?" the other asked quickly.

"Did he say good-bye to you?" The little man repeated his question slowly, kindly. "Nothing more can happen to him, I promise you. But we want to help him, and if you have any idea of why he hit Ford, if you have the slightest notion from something he said, perhaps casually, or something he did, then tell us for Alec's sake."

Liz shook her head.

"Please go," she said, "please don't ask any more questions. Please go now."

439

As he got to the door, the elder man hesitated, then took a card from his wallet and put it on the table, gingerly, as if it might make a noise. Liz thought he was a very shy little man.

"If you ever want any help—if anything happens about Leamans or . . . ring me up," he said. "Do you understand?"

"Who are you?"

"I'm a friend of Alec Leamas." He hesitated. "Another thing," he added, "one last question. Did Alec know you were . . . did Alec know about the Party?"

"Yes," she replied, hopelessly, "I told him."

"Does the Party know about you and Alec?"

"I've told you. No one knew." Then, white-faced, she cried out suddenly, "Where is he; tell me where he is. Why won't you tell me where he is? I can help him, don't you see; I'll look after him . . . even if he's gone mad, I don't care, I swear I don't . . . I wrote to him in prison; I shouldn't have done, I know. I just said he could come back any time. I'd wait for him always . . ." She couldn't speak any more, just sobbed and sobbed, standing there in the middle of the room, her broken face buried in her hands; the little man watching her.

"He's gone abroad," he said gently. "We don't quite know where he is. He isn't mad, but he shouldn't have said all that to you. It was a pity."

The younger man said:

"We'll see you're looked after. For money and that kind of thing."

"Who are you?" Liz asked again.

"Friends of Alec," the young man repeated; "good friends."

She heard them go quietly down the stairs and into the street. From her window she watched them get into the small black car and drive away in the direction of the park.

Then she remembered the card. Going to the table she picked it up and held it to the light. It was expensively done, more than a polceman could afford, she thought. Engraved. No rank in front of the name, no police station or anything.

Just the name with "Mister"—and whoever heard of a police-man living in Chelsea?

"Mr. George Smiley. 9 Bywater Street, Chelsea." Then the telephone number underneath.

It was very strange.

12 ✼
EAST

Leamas unfastened his seat belt.

It is said that men condemned to death are subject to sudden moments of elation; as if, like moths in the fire, their destruction were coincidental with attainment. Following directly upon his decision, Leamas was aware of a comparable sensation; relief, short-lived but consoling, sustained him for a time. It was followed by fear and hunger.

He was slowing down. Control was right.

He'd noticed it first during the Riemeck case, early last year. Karl had sent a message: he'd got something special for him and was making one of his rare visits to Western Germany; some legal conference at Karlsruhe. Leamas had managed to get an air passage to Cologne, and picked up a car at the airport. It was still quite early in the morning and he'd hoped to miss most of the autobahn traffic to Karlsruhe but the heavy lorries were already on the move. He drove seventy kilometres in half an hour, weaving between the traffic, taking risks to beat the clock, when a small car, a Fiat probably, nosed its way out into the fast lane

442

forty yards ahead of him. Leamas stamped on the brake, turning his headlights full on and sounding his horn, and by the grace of God he missed it; missed it by a fraction of a second. As he passed the car he saw out of the corner of his eye four children in the back, waving and laughing, and the stupid, frightened face of their father at the wheel. He drove on, cursing, and suddenly it happened; suddenly his hands were shaking feverishly, his face was burning, his heart palpitating wildly. He managed to pull off the road into a lay-by, scrambled out of the car, and stood breathing heavily, staring at the hurtling stream of giant lorries. He had a vision of the little car caught among them, pounded and smashed, until there was nothing left, nothing but the frenetic whine of klaxons and the blue lights flashing; and the bodies of the children, torn, like the murdered refugees on the road across the dunes.

He drove very slowly the rest of the way and missed his meeting with Karl.

He never drove again without some corner of his memory recalling the tousled children waving to him from the back of that car, and their father grasping the wheel like a farmer at the shafts of a hand plough.

Control would call it fever.

He sat dully in his seat over the wing. There was an American woman next to him wearing high-heeled shoes in polythene wrappers. He had a momentary notion of passing her some note for the people in Berlin, but he discarded it at once. She'd think he was making a pass at her, Peters would see it. Besides, what was the point? Control knew what had happened; Control had made it happen. There was nothing to say.

He wondered what would become of him. Control hadn't talked about that—only about the technique:

"Don't give it to them all at once, make them work for it. Confuse them with detail, leave things out, go back on your tracks. Be testy, be cussed, be difficult. Drink like a fish; don't give way on the ideology, they won't trust that. They want to deal with a man they've bought; they want the clash of opposites,

Alec, not some half-cock convert. Above all, they want to *deduce.* The ground's prepared; we did it long ago, little things, difficult clues. You're the last stage in the treasure hunt."

He'd had to agree to do it; you can't back out of the big fight when all the preliminary ones have been fought for you.

"One thing I can promise you: it's worth it. It's worth it for our special interest, Alec. Keep alive and we've won a great victory."

He didn't think he could stand torture. He remembered a book by Koestler where the old revolutionary had conditioned himself for torture by holding lighted matches to his fingers. He hadn't read much but he'd read that and he remembered it.

It was nearly dark as they landed at Tempelhof. Leamas watched the lights of Berlin rise to meet them, felt the thud as the plane touched down, saw the Customs and immigration officials move forward out of the half light.

For a moment Leamas was anxious lest some former acquaintance should chance to recognise him at the airport. As they walked side by side, Peters and he, along the interminable corridors, through the cursory Customs and immigration check, and still no familiar face turned to greet him, he realised that his anxiety had in reality been hope; hope that somehow his tacit decision to go on would be revoked by circumstance.

It interested him that Peters no longer bothered to disown him; it was as if Peters regarded West Berlin as safe ground, where vigilance and security could be relaxed; a mere technical staging post to the East.

They were walking through the big reception hall to the main entrance when Peters suddenly seemed to alter his mind, abruptly changed direction and led Leamas to a smaller side entrance which gave on to a car park and taxi rank. There Peters hesitated a second, standing beneath the light over the door, then put his suitcase on the ground beside him, deliberately removed his newspaper from beneath his arm, folded it, pushed it into the left pocket of his raincoat and picked up his suitcase again. Immediately, from the direction of the car

444

park, a pair of headlights sprang to life, were dipped and then extinguished.

"Come on," said Peters and started to walk briskly across the tarmac, Leamas following more slowly. As they reached the first row of cars the rear door of a black Mercedes was opened from the inside, and the courtesy light went on. Peters, ten yards ahead of Leamas, went quickly to the car, spoke softly to the driver, then called to Leamas.

"Here's the car. Be quick."

It was an old Mercedes 180 and he got in without a word. Peters sat beside him in the back. As they pulled out they overtook a small DKW with two men sitting in the front. Twenty yards down the road there was a telephone kiosk. A man was talking into the telephone, and he watched them go by, talking all the time. Leamas looked out of the back window and saw the DKW following them. Quite a reception, he thought.

They drove quite slowly. Leamas sat with his hands on his knees, looking straight in front of him. He didn't want to see Berlin that night. This was his last chance, he knew that. The way he was sitting now he could drive the side of his right hand into Peters' throat, smashing the promontory of the thorax. He could get out and run, weaving to avoid the bullets from the car behind. He would be free—there were people in Berlin who would take care of him—he could get away.

He did nothing.

It was so easy crossing the sector border. Leamas had never expected it to be quite that easy. For about ten minutes they dawdled, and Leamas guessed that they had to cross at a pre-arranged time. As they approached the West German checkpoint, the DKW pulled out and overtook them with the ostentatious roar of a laboured engine, and stopped at the police hut. The Mercedes waited thirty yards behind. Two minutes later the red and white pole lifted to let through the DKW and as it did so both cars drove over together, the Mercedes engine screaming in second gear, the driver pressing himself back against his seat, holding the wheel at arms' length.

As they crossed the fifty yards which separated the two checkpoints, Leamas was dimly aware of the new fortifications on the Eastern side of the wall—dragons' teeth, observation towers, and double aprons of barbed wire. Things had brightened up.

The Mercedes didn't stop at the second checkpoint; the booms were already lifted and they drove straight through, the Vopos just watching them through binoculars. The DKW had disappeared, and when Leamas sighted it ten minutes later it was behind them again. They were driving fast now—Leamas had thought they would stop in East Berlin, change cars perhaps, and congratulate one another on a successful operation, but they drove on eastwards through the city.

"Where are we going?" he asked Peters.

"We are there. The German Democratic Republic. They have arranged accommodation for you."

"I thought we'd be going further east."

"We are. We are spending a day or two here first. We thought the Germans ought to have a talk with you."

"I see."

"After all, most of your work has been on the German side. I sent them details from your statement."

"And they asked to see me?"

"They've never had anything quite like you, nothing quite so . . . near the source. My people agreed that they should have the chance to meet you."

"And from there? Where do we go from Germany?"

"East again."

"Who will I see on the German side?"

"Does it matter?"

"Not particularly. I know most of the Abteilung people by name, that's all. I just wondered."

"Who would you expect to meet?"

"Fiedler," Leamas replied promptly, "deputy head of security. Mundt's man. He does all the big interrogations. He's a bastard."

446

"Why?"

"A savage little bastard. I've heard about him. He caught an agent of Peter Guillam's and bloody nearly killed him."

"Espionage is not a cricket game," Peters observed sourly and after that they sat in silence. So it is Fiedler, Leamas thought.

Leamas knew Fiedler all right. He knew him from the photographs on the file and the accounts of his former subordinates. A slim, neat man, quite young, smooth-faced. Dark hair, bright brown eyes; intelligent and savage, as Leamas had said. A lithe, quick body containing a patient, retentive mind; a man seemingly without ambition for himself but remorseless in the destruction of others. Fiedler was a rarity in the Abteilung—he took no part in its intrigues, seemed content to live in Mundt's shadow without prospect of promotion. He could not be labelled as a member of this or that clique; even those who had worked close to him in the Abteilung could not say where he stood in its power complex. Fiedler was a solitary; feared, disliked, and mistrusted. Whatever motives he had were concealed beneath a cloak of destructive sarcasm.

"Fiedler is our best bet," Control had explained. They'd been sitting together over dinner—Leamas, Control, and Peter Guillam—in the dreary little seven-dwarfs house in Surrey where Control lived with his beady wife, surrounded by carved Indian tables with brass tops. "Fiedler is the acolyte who one day will stab the high priest in the back. He's the only man who's a match for Mundt"—here Guillam had nodded—" and he hates his guts. Fiedler's a Jew of course, and Mundt is quite the other thing. Not at all a good mixture. It has been our job," he declared, indicating Guillam and himself, "to give Fiedler the weapon with which to destroy Mundt. It will be yours, my dear Leamas, to encourage him to use it. Indirectly, of course, because you'll never meet him. At least I certainly hope you won't."

They'd all laughed then, Guillam too. It had seemed a good joke at the time; good by Control's standards anyway.

∗   ∗   ∗

It must have been after midnight.

For some time they had been travelling an unmade road, partly through a wood and partly across open country. Now they stopped and a moment later the DKW drew up beside them. As he and Peters got out Leamas noticed that there were now three people in the second car. Two were already getting out. The third was sitting in the back seat looking at some papers by the light from the car roof, a slight figure half in shadow.

They had parked by some disused stables; the building lay thirty yards back. In the headlights of the car Leamas had glimpsed a low farmhouse with walls of timber and whitewashed brick. They got out. The moon was up, and shone so brightly that the wooded hills behind were sharply defined against the pale night sky. They walked to the house, Peters and Leamas leading and the two men behind. The other man in the second car had still made no attempt to move; he remained there, reading.

As they reached the door Peters stopped, waiting for the other two to catch them up. One of them carried a bunch of keys in his left hand, and while he fiddled with them the other stood off, his hands in his pockets, covering him.

"They're taking no chances," Leamas observed to Peters, "what do they think I am?"

"They are not paid to think," Peters replied, and turning to one of them he asked in German:

"Is he coming?"

The German shrugged and looked back towards the car.

"He'll come," he said; "he likes to come alone."

They went into the house, the man leading the way. It was got up like a hunting lodge, part old, part new. It was badly lit with pale overhead lights. The place had a neglected, musty air as if it had been opened for the occasion. There were little touches of officialdom here and there—a notice of what to do in case of fire, institutional green paint on the door, and heavy spring-cartridge locks; and in the drawing-room, which was quite comfortably done, dark, heavy furniture, badly scratched, and the inevitable photographs of Soviet leaders. To Leamas

448

these lapses from anonymity signified the involuntary identification of the Abteilung with bureaucracy. That was something he was familiar with in the Circus.

Peters sat down, and Leamas did the same. For ten minutes, perhaps longer, they waited, then Peters spoke to one of the two men standing awkwardly at the other end of the room.

"Go and tell him we're waiting. And find us some food, we're hungry." As the man moved towards the door Peters called, "And whisky—tell them to bring whisky and some glasses." The man gave an uncooperative shrug of his heavy shoulders and went out, leaving the door open behind him.

"Have you been here before?" asked Leamas.

"Yes," Peters replied, "several times."

"What for?"

"This kind of thing. Not the same, but our kind of work."

"With Fiedler?"

"Yes."

"Is he good?"

Peters shrugged. "For a Jew, he's not bad," he replied, and Leamas, hearing a sound from the other end of the room, turned and saw Fiedler standing in the doorway. In one hand he held a bottle of whisky, and in the other, glasses and some mineral water. He couldn't have been more than five foot six. He wore a dark blue single-breasted suit; the jacket was cut too long. He was sleek and slightly animal; his eyes were brown and bright. He was not looking at them but at the guard beside the door.

"Go away," he said. He had a slight Saxonian twang: "Go away and tell the other one to bring us food."

"I've told him," Peters called; "they know already. But they've brought nothing."

"They are great snobs," Fiedler observed drily in English. "They think we should have servants for the food."

Fiedler had spent the war in Canada. Leamas remembered that, now that he detected the accent. His parents had been German Jewish refugees, Marxists, and it was not until 1946 that the family returned home, anxious to take part, whatever the personal cost, in the construction of Stalin's Germany.

"Hello," he added to Leamas, almost by the way, "glad to see you."

"Hello, Fiedler."

"You've reached the end of the road."

"What the hell d'you mean?" asked Leamas quickly.

"I mean that contrary to anything Peters told you, you are not going further east. Sorry." He sounded amused.

Leamas turned to Peters.

"Is this true?" His voice was shaking with rage. "Is it true? Tell me!"

Peters nodded: "Yes. I am the go-between. We had to do it that way. I'm sorry," he added.

"Why?"

"*Force majeure*," Fiedler put in. "Your initial interrogation took place in the West, where only an embassy could provide the kind of link we needed. The German Democratic Republic has no embassies in the West. Not yet. Our liaison section therefore arranged for us to enjoy facilities and communications and immunities which are at present denied to us."

"You bastard," hissed Leamas, "you lousy bastard! You knew I wouldn't trust myself to your rotten Service; that was the reason, wasn't it? That was why you used a Russian."

"We used the Soviet Embassy at The Hague. What else could we do? Up till then it was our operation. That's perfectly reasonable. Neither we nor anyone else could have known that your own people in England would get on to you so quickly."

"No? Not even when you put them on to me yourselves? Isn't that what happened, Fiedler? Well, isn't it?" Always remember to dislike them, Control had said. Then they will treasure what they get out of you.

"That is an absurd suggestion," Fiedler replied shortly. Glancing towards Peters he added something in Russian. Peters nodded and stood up.

"Good-bye," he said to Leamas. "Good luck."

450

He smiled wearily, nodded to Fiedler, then walked to the door. He put his hand on the door handle, then turned and called to Leamas again:

"Good luck." He seemed to want Leamas to say something, but Leamas might not have heard. He had turned very pale, he held his hands loosely across his body, the thumbs upwards as if he were going to fight. Peters remained standing at the door.

"I should have known," said Leamas, and his voice had the odd, faulty note of a very angry man, "I should have guessed you'd never have the guts to do your own dirty work, Fiedler. It's typical of your rotten little half-country and your squalid little Service that you get big uncle to do your pimping for you. You're not a country at all, you're not a government, you're a fifth-rate dictatorship of political neurotics." Jabbing his finger in Fiedler's direction, he shouted:

"I know you, you sadistic bastard; it's typical of you. You were in Canada in the war, weren't you; a bloody good place to be then, wasn't it? I'll bet you stuck your fat head into Mummy's apron any time an aeroplane flew over. What are you now? A creeping little acolyte to Mundt and twenty-two Russian divisions sitting on your mother's doorstep. Well, I pity you, Fiedler, the day you wake up and find them gone. There'll be a killing then, and not Mummy or big uncle will save you from getting what you deserve."

Fiedler shrugged.

"Regard it as a visit to the dentist, Leamas. The sooner it's all done, the sooner you can go home. Have some food and go to bed."

"You know perfectly well I can't go home," Leamas retorted. "You've seen to that. You blew me sky high in England, you had to, both of you. You knew damn' well I'd never come here unless I had to."

Fiedler looked at his thin, strong fingers.

"This is hardly the time to philosophise," he said, "but you can't really complain, you know. All our work—yours and mine—is rooted in the theory that the whole is more important

451

than the individual. That is why a Communist sees his secret service as the natural extension of his arm, and that is why in your own country intelligence is shrouded in a kind of *pudeur anglaise.* The exploitation of individuals can only be justified by the collective need, can't it? I find it slightly ridiculous that you should be so indignant. We are not here to observe the ethical laws of English country life. After all," he added silkily, "your own behaviour has not, from the purist's point of view, been irreproachable."

Leamas was watching Fiedler with an expression of disgust.

"I know your set-up. You're Mundt's poodle, aren't you? They say you want his job. I suppose you'll get it now. It's time the Mundt dynasty ended; perhaps this is it."

"I don't understand," Fiedler replied.

"I'm your big success, aren't I?" Leamas sneered. Fiedler seemed to reflect for a moment, then he shrugged and said, "The operation was successful. Whether you were worth it is questionable. We shall see. But it was a good operation. It satisfied the only requirement of our profession: it worked."

"I suppose you take the credit?" Leamas persisted, with a glance in the direction of Peters.

"There is no question of credit," Fiedler replied crisply, "none at all." He sat down on the arm of a sofa, looked at Leamas thoughtfully for a moment and then said:

"Nevertheless you are right to be indignant about one thing. Who told your people we had picked you up? We didn't. You may not believe me, but it happens to be true. We didn't tell them. We didn't even want them to know. We had ideas then of getting you to work for us later—ideas which I now realise to be ridiculous. So who told them? You were lost, drifting around, you had no address, no ties, no friends. Then how the devil did they know you'd gone? Someone told them—scarcely Ashe or Kiever, since they are both now under arrest."

"Under arrest?"

"So it appears. Not specifically for their work on your case, but there were other things . . ."

"Well, well."

"It is true, what I said just now. We would have been content with Peters' report from Holland. You could have had your money and gone. But you hadn't told us everything; and I want to know everything. After all, your presence here provides us with problems too, you know."

"Well, you've boobed. I know damn' well—and you're welcome to it."

There was a silence, during which Peters, with an abrupt and by no means friendly nod in Fiedler's direction, quietly let himself out of the room.

Fiedler picked up the bottle of whisky and poured a little into each glass.

"We have no soda, I'm afraid," he said. "Do you like water? I ordered soda, but they brought some wretched lemonade."

"Oh, go to hell," said Leamas. He suddenly felt very tired.

Fiedler shook his head.

"You are a very proud man," he observed, "but never mind. Eat your supper and go to bed."

"One of the guards came in with a tray of food—black bread, sausage, and cold green salad.

"It is a little crude," said Fiedler, "but quite satisfying. No potato, I'm afraid. There is a temporary shortage of potato."

They began eating in silence, Fiedler very carefully, like a man who counted his calories.

The guards showed Leamas to his bedroom. They let him carry his own luggage—the same luggage that Kiever had given him before he left England—and he walked between them along the wide central corridor which led through the house from the front door. They came to a large double door, painted dark green, and one of the guards unlocked it; they beckoned to Leamas to go first. He pushed open the door and found himself in a small barrack bedroom with two bunk beds, a chair and a rudimentary desk. It was like something in prison camp. There were pictures of girls on the walls and the windows were shuttered.

At the far end of the room was another door. They signalled him forward again. Putting down his baggage he went and opened the door. The second room was identical to the first, but there was one bed and the walls were bare.

"You bring those cases," he said; "I'm tired." He lay on the bed, fully dressed, and within a few minutes he was fast asleep.

A sentry woke him with breakfast: black bread and *ersatz* coffee. He got out of bed and went to the window.

The house stood on a high hill. The ground fell steeply away from beneath his window, the crowns of pine trees visible above the crest. Beyond them, spectacular in their symmetry, unending hills, heavy with trees, stretched into the distance. Here and there a timber gully or fire-break formed a thin brown divide between the pines, seeming like Aaron's rod miraculously to hold apart massive seas of encroaching forest. There was no sign of man; not a house or church, not even the ruin of some previous habitation—only the road, the yellow unmade road, a crayon line across the basin of the valley. There was no sound. It seemed incredible that anything so vast could be so still. The day was cold but clear. It must have rained in the night; the ground was moist, and the whole landscape so sharply defined against the white sky that Leamas could distinguish even single trees on the furthest hills.

He dressed slowly, drinking the sour coffee meanwhile. He had nearly finished dressing and was about to start eating the bread when Fiedler came into the room.

"Good morning," he said cheerfully. "Don't let me keep you from your breakfast." He sat down on the bed. Leamas had to hand it to Fiedler; he had guts. Not that there was anything brave about coming to see him—the sentries, Leamas supposed, were still in the adjoining room. But there was an endurance, a defined purpose in his manner which Leamas could sense and admire.

"You have presented us with an intriguing problem," he observed.

454

"I've told you all I know."

"Oh no." He smiled. "Oh no, you haven't. You have told us all you are *conscious* of knowing."

"Bloody clever," Leamas muttered pushing his food aside and lighting a cigarette—his last.

"Let me ask *you* a question," Fiedler suggested with the exaggerated bonhomie of a man proposing a party game. "As an experienced intelligence officer, what would *you* do with the information you have given us?"

"What information?"

"My dear Leamas, you have only given us one piece of intelligence. You have told us about Riemeck: we knew about Riemeck. You have told us about the dispositions of your Berlin organisation, about its personalities and its agents. That, if I may say so, is old hat. Accurate—yes. Good background, fascinating reading, here and there good collateral, here and there a little fish which we shall take out of the pool. But not—if I may be crude—not fifteen thousand pounds' worth of intelligence. Not," he smiled again, "at current rates."

"Listen," said Leamas, "I didn't propose this deal—you did. You, Kiever, and Peters. I didn't come crawling to your cissy friends, peddling old intelligence. You people made the running, Fiedler; you named the price and took the risk. Apart from that, I haven't had a bloody penny. So don't blame me if the operation's a flop." Make them come to you, Leamas thought.

"It isn't a flop," Fiedler replied, "it isn't finished. It can't be. You haven't told us what you *know*. I said you had given us one piece of intelligence. I'm talking about Rolling Stone. Let me ask you again—what would *you* do if I, if Peters or someone like us, had told *you* a similar story?"

Leamas shrugged:

"I'd feel uneasy," he said; "it's happened before. You get an indication, several perhaps, that there's a spy in some department or at a certain level. So what? You can't arrest the whole government service. You can't lay traps for a whole department. You just sit tight and hope for more. You bear it in

455

mind. In Rolling Stone you can't even tell what country he's working in."

"You are an operator, Leamas," Fiedler observed with a laugh, "not an evaluator. That is clear. Let me ask you some elementary questions."

Leamas said nothing.

"The file—the actual file on operation Rolling Stone. What colour was it?"

"Grey with a red cross on it—that means limited subscription."

"Was anything attached to the outside?"

"Yes, the Caveat. That's the subscription label. With a legend saying that any unauthorised person not named on this label finding the file in his possession must at once return it unopened to Banking Section."

"Who was on the subscription list?"

"For Rolling Stone?"

"Yes."

"PA to Control, Control, Control's secretary; Banking Section, Miss Bream of Special Registry and Satellites Four. That's all, I think. And Special Despatch, I suppose—I'm not sure about them."

"Satellites Four? What do they do?"

"Iron Curtain countries excluding the Soviet Union and China. The Zone."

"You mean the GDR?"

"I mean the Zone."

"Isn't it unusual for a whole section to be on a subscription list?"

"Yes, it probably is. I wouldn't know—I've never handled limited subscription stuff before. Except in Berlin, of course; it was all different there."

"Who was in Satellites Four at that time?"

"Oh, God. Guillam, Haverlake, de Jong, I think. De Jong was just back from Berlin."

"Were they *all* allowed to see this file?"

"I don't know, Fiedler," Leamas retorted irritably; "and if I were you—"

"Then isn't it odd that a whole section was on the subscription list while all the rest of the subscribers are individuals."

"I tell you I don't know—how could I know? I was just a clerk in all this."

"Who carried the file from one subscriber to another?"

"Secretaries, I suppose—I can't remember. It's bloody months since—"

"Then why weren't the secretaries on the list? Control's Secretary was." There was a moment's silence.

"No, you're right; I remember now," Leamas said, a note of surprise in his voice; "we passed it by hand."

"Who else in Banking dealt with that file?"

"No one. It was my pigeon when I joined the section. One of the women had done it before, but when I came I took it over and they were taken off the list."

"Then you alone passed the file by hand to the next reader?"

"Yes . . . yes, I suppose I did."

"To whom did you pass it?"

"I . . . I can't remember."

"Think!" Fiedler had not raised his voice, but it contained a sudden urgency which took Leamas by surprise.

"To Control's PA, I think, to show what action we had taken or recommended."

"Who brought the file?"

"What do you mean?" Leamas sounded off balance.

"Who brought you the file to read? Somebody on the list must have brought it to you."

Leamas' fingers touched his cheek for a moment in an involuntary nervous gesture.

"Yes, they must. It's difficult, you see, Fiedler; I was putting back a lot of drink in those days"; his tone was oddly conciliatory. "You don't realise how hard it is to—"

"I ask you again. Think. Who brought you the file?"

Leamas sat down at the table and shook his head.

457

"I can't remember. It may come back to me. At the moment I just can't remember, really I can't. It's no good chasing it."

"It can't have been Control's girl, can it? You always handed the file *back* to Control's PA. You said so. So those on the list must all have seen it *before* Control."

"Yes, that's it, I suppose."

"Then there is Special Registry, Miss Bream."

"She was just the woman who ran the strong room for subscription list files. That's where the file was kept when it wasn't in action."

"Then," said Fiedler silkily, "it must have been Satellites Four who brought it, mustn't it?"

"Yes, I suppose it must," said Leamas helplessly, as if he were not quite up to Fiedler's brilliance.

"Which floor did Satellites Four work on?"

"The second."

"And Banking?"

"The fourth. Next to Special Registry."

"Do you remember *who* brought it up? Or do you remember, for instance, going downstairs ever to collect the file from them?"

In despair, Leamas shook his head; then suddenly he turned to Fiedler and cried:

"Yes, yes I do! Of course I do! I got it from Peter!" Leamas seemed to have woken up, his face was flushed, excited. "That's it: I once collected the file from Peter in his room. We chatted together about Norway. We'd served there together, you see."

"Peter Guillam?"

"Yes, Peter—I'd forgotten about him. He'd come back from Ankara a few months before. He was on the list! Peter was—of course! That's it. It was Satellite Four and PG in brackets, Peter's initials. Someone else had done it before and Special Registry had glued a bit of white paper over the old name and put Peter's initials."

"What territory did Guillam cover?"

"The Zone. East Germany. Economic stuff; ran a small

458

section, sort of backwater. He was the chap. He brought the file up to me once too, I remember that now. He didn't run agents though: I don't quite know how he came into it—Peter and a couple of others were doing some research job on food shortages. Evaluation really."

"Did you not discuss it with him?"

"No, that's taboo. It isn't done with subscription files. I got a homily from the woman in Special Registry about it—Bream—no discussion, no questions."

"But taking into account the elaborate security precautions surrounding Rolling Stone, it is possible, is it not, that Guillam's so-called research job might have involved the partial running of this agent, Rolling Stone?"

"I've told Peters," Leamas almost shouted, banging his fist on the desk, "it's just bloody silly to imagine that any operation could have been run against East Germany without my knowledge—without the knowledge of the Berlin organisation. I would have known, d'you see? How many times do I have to say that? I would have known!"

"Quite so," said Fiedler softly, "of course you would." He stood up and went to the window.

"You should see it in the Autumn," he said, looking out; "it's magnificent when the beeches are on the turn."

13 ❉
PINS OR PAPER CLIPS

Fiedler loved to ask questions. Sometimes, because he was a lawyer, he asked them for his own pleasure alone, to demonstrate the discrepancy between evidence and perfective truth. He possessed, however, that persistent inquisitiveness which for journalists and lawyers is an end in itself.

They went for a walk that afternoon, following the gravel road down into the valley, then branching into the forest along a broad, pitted track lined with felled timber. All the time, Fiedler probed, giving nothing. About the building in Cambridge Circus, and the people who worked there. What social class did they come from, what parts of London did they inhabit, did husbands and wives work in the same Department? He asked about the pay, the leave, the morale, the canteen; he asked about their love-life, their gossip, their philosophy. Most of all he asked about their philosophy.

To Leamas that was the most difficult question of all.

"What do you mean, a philosophy?" he replied; "we're not Marxists, we're nothing. Just people."

"Are you Christians, then?"

"Not many, I shouldn't think. I don't know many."

"What makes them do it, then?" Fiedler persisted; "they must have a philosophy."

"Why must they? Perhaps they don't know; don't even care. Not everyone has a philosophy," Leamas answered, a little helplessly.

"Then tell me what is your philosophy?"

"Oh for Christ's sake," Leamas snapped, and they walked on in silence for a while. But Fiedler was not to be put off.

"If they do not know what they want, how can they be so certain they are right?"

"Who the hell said they were?" Leamas replied irritably.

"But what is the justification then? What is it? For us it is easy, as I said to you last night. The Abteilung and organisations like it are the natural extension of the Party's arm. They are in the vanguard of the fight for Peace and Progress. They are to the Party what the Party is to socialism: they *are* the vanguard. Stalin said so"—he smiled drily, "it is not fashionable to quote Stalin—but he said once 'half a million liquidated is a statistic, and one man killed in a traffic accident is a national tragedy.' He was laughing, you see, at the bourgeois sensitivities of the mass. He was a great cynic. But what he meant is still true: a movement which protects itself against counter-revolution can hardly stop at the exploitation—or the elimination, Leamas—of a few individuals. It is all one, we have never pretended to be wholly just in the process of rationalistic society. Some Roman said it, didn't he, in the Christian Bible—it is expedient that one man should die for the benefit of many."

"I expect so," Leamas replied wearily.

"Then what do you think? What is your philosophy?"

"I just think the whole lot of you are bastards," said Leamas savagely.

Fiedler nodded, "That is a viewpoint I understand. It is primitive, negative, and very stupid—but it is a viewpoint, it exists. But what about the rest of the Circus?"

461

"I don't know. How should I know?"

"Have you never discussed philosophy with them?"

"No. We're not Germans." He hesitated, then added vaguely: "I suppose they don't like Communism."

"And that justifies, for instance, the taking of human life? That justifies the bomb in the crowded restaurant; that justifies your write-off rate of agents—all that?"

Leamas shrugged. "I suppose so."

"You see, for us it does," Fiedler continued, "I myself would have put a bomb in a restaurant if it brought us further along the road. Afterwards I would draw the balance—so many women, so many children; and so far along the road. But Christians—and yours is a Christian society—Christians may not draw the balance."

"Why not. They've got to defend themselves, haven't they?"

"But they believe in the sanctity of human life. They believe every man has a soul which can be saved. They believe in sacrifice."

"I don't know. I don't much care," Leamas added. "Stalin didn't either, did he?"

Fiedler smiled; "I like the English," he said, almost to himself; "my father did too. He was very fond of the English."

"That gives me a nice, warm feeling," Leamas retorted, and relapsed into silence.

They stopped while Fiedler gave Leamas a cigarette and lit it for him.

They were climbing steeply now. Leamas liked the exercise, walking ahead with long strides, his shoulders thrust forward. Fiedler followed, slight and agile, like a terrier behind his master. They must have been walking for an hour, perhaps more, when suddenly the trees broke above them and the sky appeared. They had reached the top of a small hill, and could look down on the solid mass of pine broken only here and there by grey clusters of beech. Across the valley Leamas could glimpse the hunting lodge, perched below the crest of the opposite hill, low and dark against the trees. In the middle of the clearing was

462

a rough bench beside a pile of logs and the damp remnants of a charcoal fire.

"We'll sit down for a moment," said Fiedler, "then we must go back." He paused. "Tell me: this money, these large sums in foreign banks—what did you think they were for?"

"What do you mean? I've told you, they were payments to an agent."

"An agent from behind the Iron Curtain?"

"Yes, I thought so," Leamas replied wearily.

"Why did you think so?"

"First, it was a hell of a lot of money. Then the complications of paying him; the special security. And of course, Control being mixed up in it."

"What did you think the agent did with the money?"

"Look, I've told you—I don't know. I don't even know if he collected it. I didn't know anything—I was just the bloody office boy."

"What did you do with the pass books for the accounts?"

"I handed them in as soon as I got back to London—together with my phoney passport."

"Did the Copenhagen or Helsinki banks ever write to you in London—to your alias, I mean?"

"I don't know. I suppose any letters would have been passed straight to Control anyway."

"The false signatures you used to open the accounts—Control had a sample of them?"

"Yes. I practised them a lot and they had samples."

"More than one?"

"Yes. Whole pages."

"I see. Then letters could have gone to the banks after you had opened the accounts. You need not have known. The signatures could have been forged and the letters sent without your knowledge."

"Yes. That's right. I suppose that's what happened. I signed a lot of blank sheets too. I always assumed someone else took care of the correspondence."

"But you never did actually *know* of such correspondence?"

Leamas shook his head: "You've got it all wrong," he said; "you've got it all out of proportion. There was a lot of paper going around—this was just part of the day's work. It wasn't something I gave much thought to. Why should I? It was hush-hush, but I've been in on things all my life where you only know a little and someone else knows the rest. Besides, paper bores me stiff. I didn't lose any sleep on it. I liked the trips of course—I drew operational subsistence which helped. But I didn't sit at my desk all day, wondering about Rolling Stone. Besides," he added a little shamefacedly, "I was hitting the bottle a bit."

"So you said," Fiedler commented, "and of course, I believe you."

"I don't give a damn whether you believe me or not," Leamas rejoined hotly.

Fiedler smiled.

"I am glad. That is your virtue," he said, "that is your great virtue. It is the virtue of indifference. A little resentment here, a little pride there, but that is nothing: the distortions of a tape recorder. You are objective. It occurred to me," Fiedler continued after a slight pause, "that you could still help us to establish whether any of that money was ever drawn. There is nothing to stop you writing to each bank and asking for a current statement. We could say you were staying in Switzerland; use an accommodation address. Do you see any objection to that?"

"It might work. It depends on whether Control has been corresponding with the bank independently, over my forged signature. It might not fit in."

"I do not see that we have much to lose."

"What have you got to win?"

"If the money has been drawn, which I agree is doubtful, we shall know where the agent was on a certain day. That seems to be a useful thing to know."

"You're dreaming. You'll never find him, Fiedler, not on that kind of information. Once he's in the West he can go to any Consulate, even in a small town, and get a visa for another country.

464

How are you any the wiser? You don't even know whether the man is East German. What are you after?"

Fiedler did not answer at once. He was gazing distractedly across the valley.

"You said you are accustomed to knowing only a little, and I cannot answer your question without telling you what you should not know." He hesitated; "but Rolling Stone was an operation against us, I can assure you."

"Us?"

"The GDR." He smiled, "the Zone if you prefer. I am not really so sensitive."

He was watching Fiedler now, his brown eyes resting on him reflectively.

"But what about me?" Leamas asked. "Suppose I don't write letters?" His voice was rising. "Isn't it time to talk about me, Fiedler!"

Fiedler nodded.

"Why not?" he replied, agreeably. There was a moment's silence, then Leamas said:

"I've done my bit, Fiedler. You and Peters between you have got all I know. I never agreed to write letters to banks—it could be bloody dangerous, a thing like that. That doesn't worry you, I know. As far as you're concerned I'm expendable."

"Now let me be frank," Fiedler replied. "There are, as you know, two stages in the interrogation of a defector. The first stage in your case is nearly complete: you have told us all we can reasonably record. You have not told us whether your Service favours pins or paper clips because we haven't asked you, and because you did not consider the answer worth volunteering. There is a process on both sides of unconscious selection. Now it is always possible—and this is the worrying thing, Leamas—it is always entirely possible that in a month or two we shall unexpectedly and quite desperately need to know about the pins and paper clips. That is normally accounted for in the second stage—that part of the bargain which you refused to accept in Holland."

"You mean you're going to keep me on ice?"

465

"The profession of defector," Fiedler observed with a smile, "demands great patience. Very few are suitably qualified."

"How long?" Leamas insisted.

Fiedler was silent.

"Well?"

Fiedler spoke with sudden urgency. "I give you my word that as soon as I possibly can, I will tell you the answer to your question. Look—I could lie to you, couldn't I? I could say one month or less, just to keep you sweet. But I am telling you I don't know because that is the truth. You have given us some indications: until we have run them to earth I cannot listen to talk of letting you go. But afterwards if things are as I think they are, you will need a friend and that friend will be me. I give you my word as a German."

Leamas was so taken aback that for a moment he was silent.

"All right," he said finally, "I'll play, Fiedler, but if you are stringing me along, somehow I'll break your neck."

"That may not be necessary," Fiedler replied evenly.

A man who lives apart, not to others but alone, is exposed to obvious psychological dangers. In itself, the practice of deception is not particularly exacting; it is a matter of experience, of professional expertise, it is a facility most of us can acquire. But while a confidence trickster, a play-actor, or a gambler can return from his performance to the ranks of his admirers, the secret agent enjoys no such relief. For him, deception is first a matter of self-defence. He must protect himself not only from without but from within, and against the most natural of impulses; though he earn a fortune, his role may forbid him the purchase of a razor, though he be erudite, it can befall him to mumble nothing but banalities; though he be an affectionate husband and father, he must under all circumstances withhold himself from those in whom he should naturally confide.

Aware of the overwhelming temptations which assail a man permanently isolated in his deceit, Leamas resorted to the course which armed him best; even when he was alone, he compelled himself to live with the personality he had assumed. It is said that

Balzac on his deathbed enquired anxiously after the health and prosperity of characters he had created. Similarly Leamas, without relinquishing the power of invention, identified himself with what he had invented. The qualities he exhibited to Fiedler, the restless uncertainty, the protective arrogance concealing shame, were not approximations but extensions of qualities he actually possessed; hence also the slight dragging of the feet, the aspect of personal neglect, the indifference to food, and an increasing reliance on alcohol and tobacco. When alone, he remained faithful to these habits. He would even exaggerate them a little, mumbling to himself about the iniquities of his Service.

Only very rarely, as now, going to bed that evening, did he allow himself the dangerous luxury of admitting the great lie he lived.

Control had been phenomenally right. Fiedler was walking like a man led in his sleep, into the net which Control had spread for him. It was uncanny to observe the growing identity of interest between Fiedler and Control: it was as if they had agreed on the same plan, and Leamas had been despatched to fulfill it.

Perhaps that was the answer. Perhaps Fiedler was the special interest Control was fighting so desperately to preserve. In matters of that kind he was wholly uninquisitive: he knew that no conceivable good could come of his deductions. Nevertheless, he hoped to God it was true. It was possible, just possible in that case, that he would get home.

14 ❊
LETTER TO A CLIENT

Leamas was still in bed the next morning when Fiedler brought him the letters to sign. One was on the thin, blue writing paper of the Seiler Hotel Alpenblick, Lake Spiez, Switzerland, the other from the Palace Hotel, Gstaad.

Leamas read the first letter:

To the Manager,
The Royal Scandinavian Bank Ltd.,
Copenhagen.

Dear Sir,

I have been travelling for some weeks and have not received any mail from England. Accordingly I have not had your reply to my letter of March 3rd requesting a current statement of the deposit account of which I am a joint signatory with Herr Karlsdorf. To avoid further delay, would you be good enough to forward a duplicate

468

statement to me at the following address, where I shall be staying for two weeks beginning April 21st:

c/o Madame Y. de Sanglot,
13 Avenue des Colombes,
Paris XII,
France.
I apologise for this confusion,

Yours faithfully,
(Robert Lang)

"What's all this about a letter of March 3rd? he asked. "I didn't write them any letter."

"No, you didn't. As far as we know, no one did. That will worry the bank. If there is any inconsistency between the letter we are sending them now and letters they have had from Control, they will assume the solution is to be found in the *missing* letter of March 3rd. Their reaction will be to send you the statement as you ask, with a covering note regretting that they have not received your letter of the third."

The second letter was the same as the first; only the names were different. The address in Paris was the same. Leamas took a blank piece of paper and his fountain pen and wrote half a dozen times in a fluent hand "Robert Lang"; then signed the first letter. Sloping his pen backwards he practised the second signature until he was satisfied with it, then wrote "Stephen Bennett" under the second letter.

"Admirable," Fiedler observed, "quite admirable."

"What do we do now?"

"They will be posted in Switzerland tomorrow, in Interlaken and Gstaad. Our people in Paris will telegraph the replies to me as soon as they arrive. We shall have the answer in a week."

"And until then?"

"We shall be constantly in one another's company. I know that is distasteful to you, and I apologise. I thought we could go for walks, drive round in the hills a bit, kill time. I want you to relax and talk; talk about London, about Cambridge Circus and working in the Department; tell me the gossip, talk about the pay, the leave, the rooms, the paper, and the people. The pins and the paper clips. I want to know all the little things that don't matter. Incidentally . . ." A change of tone.

"Yes?"

"We have facilities here for people, who . . . for people who are spending some time with us. Facilities for diversion and so on."

"Are you offering me a woman?" he asked.

"Yes."

"No, thank you. Unlike you, I haven't reached the stage where I need a pimp."

Fiedler seemed indifferent to his reply. He went on quickly.

"But you had a woman in England, didn't you—the girl in the library."

Leamas turned on him, his hands open at his sides.

"One thing!" he shouted. "Just that one thing—don't ever mention that again, not as a joke, not as a threat, not even to turn the screws, Fiedler, because it won't work, not ever; I'd dry up, d'you see, you'd never get another bloody word from me as long as I lived. Tell that to them, Fiedler, to Mundt and Stammberger or whichever little alley-cat told you to say it— tell them what I said."

"I'll tell them," Fiedler replied; "I'll tell them. It may be too late."

In the afternoon they went walking again. The sky was dark and heavy, and the air warm.

"I've only been to England once," Fiedler observed casually, "that was on my way to Canada, with my parents before the war. I was a child then of course. We were there for two days."

Leamas nodded.

"I can tell you this now," Fiedler continued. "I nearly went

470

there a few years back. I was going to replace Mundt on the Steel Mission—did you know he was once in London?"

"I knew," Leamas replied cryptically.

"I always wondered what it would have been like, that job."

"Usual game of mixing with the other Bloc Missions I suppose. Certain amount of contact with British business—not much of that." Leamas sounded bored.

"But Mundt got about all right: he found it quite easy."

"So I hear," said Leamas; "he even managed to kill a couple of people."

"So you heard about that too?"

"From Peter Guillam. He was in on it with George Smiley. Mundt bloody nearly killed George as well."

"The Fennan case," Fiedler mused. "It was amazing that Mundt managed to escape at all, wasn't it?"

"I suppose it was."

"You wouldn't think that a man whose photograph and personal particulars were filed at the Foreign Office as a member of a Foreign Mission would have a chance against the whole of British Security."

"From what I hear," Leamas said, "they weren't too keen to catch him anyway."

Fiedler stopped abruptly.

"What did you say?"

"Peter Guillam told me he didn't reckon they wanted to catch Mundt, that's all I said. We had a different set-up then— an Adviser instead of an Operational Control—a man called Maston. Maston had made a bloody awful mess of the Fennan case from the start, that's what Guillam said. Peter reckoned that if they'd caught Mundt it would have made a hell of a stink—they'd have tried him and probably hanged him. The dirt that came out in the process would have finished Maston's career. Peter never knew quite what happened, but he was bloody sure there was no full-scale search for Mundt."

"You are sure of that, you are sure Guillam told you that in as many words? No full-scale search?"

471

"Of course I am sure."

"Guillam never suggested any other reason why they might have let Mundt go?"

"What do you mean?"

Fiedler shook his head and they walked on along the path.

"The Steel Mission was closed down after the Fennan case," Fiedler observed a moment later, "that's why I didn't go."

"Mundt must have been mad. You may be able to get away with assassination in the Balkans—or here—but not London."

"He did get away with it though, didn't he?" Fiedler put in quickly. "And he did good work."

"Like recruiting Kiever and Ashe? God help him."

"They ran the Fennan woman for long enough."

Leamas shrugged.

"Tell me something else about Karl Riemeck," Fiedler began again. "He met Control once, didn't he?"

"Yes, in Berlin about a year ago, maybe a bit more."

"Where did they meet?"

"We all met together in my flat."

"Why?"

"Control loved to come in on success. We'd got a hell of a lot of good stuff from Karl—I suppose it had gone down well with London. He came out on a short trip to Berlin and asked me to fix up for them to meet."

"Did you mind?"

"Why should I?"

"He was your agent. You might not have liked him to meet other operators."

"Control isn't an operator, he's head of Department. Karl knew that and it tickled his vanity."

"Were you all three together, all the time?"

"Yes. Well, not quite. I left them alone for a quarter of an hour or so—not more. Control wanted that—he wanted a few minutes alone with Karl, God knows why, so I left the flat on some excuse, I forget what. Oh—I know, I pretended we'd run

472

out of Scotch. I actually went and collected a bottle from de Jong in fact."

"Do you know what passed between them while you were out?"

"How could I? I wasn't that interested, anyway."

"Didn't Karl tell you afterwards?"

"I didn't ask him. Karl was a cheeky sod in some ways, always pretending he had something over me. I didn't like the way he sniggered about Control. Mind you, he had every right to snigger—it was a pretty ridiculous performance. We laughed about it together a bit, as a matter of fact. There wouldn't have been any point in pricking Karl's vanity; the whole meeting was supposed to give him a shot in the arm."

"Was Karl depressed then?"

"No, far from it. He was spoilt already. He was paid too much, loved too much, trusted too much. It was partly my fault, partly London's. If we hadn't spoilt him he wouldn't have told that bloody woman of his about his network."

"Elvira?"

"Yes." They walked on in silence for a while, until Fiedler interrupted his own reverie to observe:

"I'm beginning to like you. But there's one thing that puzzles me. It's odd—it didn't worry me before I met you."

"What's that?"

"Why you ever came. Why you defected." Leamas was going to say something when Fiedler laughed. "I'm afraid that wasn't very tactful, was it?" he said.

They spent that week walking in the hills. In the evenings they would return to the lodge, eat a bad meal washed down with a bottle of rank white wine, sit endlessly over their Steinhäger in front of the fire. The fire seemed to be Fiedler's idea—they didn't have it to begin with, then one day Leamas overheard him telling a guard to bring logs. Leamas didn't mind the evening then; after the fresh air all day, the fire and the rough spirit, he would talk unprompted, rambling on about his service. Leamas supposed it was recorded. He didn't care.

As each day passed in this way Leamas was aware of an increasing tension in his companion. Once they went out in the DKW—it was late in the evening—and stopped at a call-box. Fiedler left him in the car with the keys and made a long phone call. When he came back Leamas said:

"Why didn't you ring from the house?" But Fiedler just shook his head.

"We must take care," he replied; "you too, you must take care."

"Why? What's going on?"

"The money you paid into the Copenhagen bank—we wrote, you remember?"

"Of course I remember."

Fiedler wouldn't say any more, but drove on in silence into the hills. There they stopped. Beneath them, half screened by the ghostly patchwork of tall pine trees, lay the meeting point of two great valleys. The steep wooded hills on either side gradually yielded their colours to the gathering dusk until they stood grey and lifeless in the twilight.

"Whatever happens," Fiedler said, "don't worry. It will be all right, do you understand?" His voice was heavy with emphasis, his slim hand rested on Leamas' arm. "You may have to look after yourself a little, but it won't last long, do you understand?" he asked again.

"No. And since you won't tell me I shall have to wait and see. Don't worry too much for my skin, Fiedler." He moved his arm, but Fiedler's hand still held him. Leamas hated being touched.

"Do you know Mundt?" asked Fiedler, "do you know about him?"

"We've talked about Mundt."

"Yes," Fiedler repeated, "we've talked about him. He shoots first and asks questions afterwards. The deterrent principle. It's an odd system in a profession where the questions are always supposed to be more important than the shooting."

Leamas knew what Fiedler wanted to tell him. "It's an odd system unless you're frightened of the answers," Fiedler continued under his breath.

Leamas waited. After a moment Fiedler said:

"He's never taken on an interrogation before. He's left it to me before, always. He used to say to me—'You interrogate them, Jens, no one can do it like you. I'll catch them and you make them sing.' He used to say that people who do counter-espionage are like painters—they need a man with a hammer standing behind them to strike when they have finished their work, otherwise they forget what they're trying to achieve. 'I'll be your hammer,' he used to say to me. It was a joke between us, at first, then it began to matter; when he began to kill, kill them before they sang, just as you said: one here, another there, shot or murdered. I asked him, I begged him, 'Why not arrest them? Why not let me have them for a month or two? What good to you are they when they are dead?' He just shook his head at me and said there was a law that thistles must be cut down before they flower. I had the feeling that he'd prepared the answer before I ever asked the question. He's a good operator, very good. He's done wonders with the Abteilung—you know that. He's got theories about it; I've talked to him late at night. Coffee he drinks—nothing else—just coffee all the time. He says Germans are too introspective to make good agents, and it all comes out in counter-intelligence. He says counter-intelligence people are like wolves chewing dry bones—you have to take away the bones and make them find new quarry—I see all that, I know what he means. But he's gone too far. Why did he kill Viereck? Why did he take him away from me? Viereck was fresh quarry, we hadn't even taken the meat from the bone, you see. So why did he take him? Why, Leamas, why?" The hand on Leamas' arm was clasping it tightly; in the total darkness of the car Leamas was aware of the frightening intensity of Fiedler's emotion.

"I've thought about it night and day. Ever since Viereck was shot, I've asked for a reason. At first it seemed fantastic. I told myself I was jealous, that the work was going to my head, that I was seeing treachery behind every tree; we get like that, people in our world. But I couldn't help myself, Leamas, I had to work it out. There'd been other things before. He was afraid—he was afraid that we would catch one who would talk too much!"

"What are you saying? You're out of your mind," said Leamas, and his voice held a trace of fear.

"It all held together, you see. Mundt escaped so easily from England; you told me yourself he did. And what did Guillam say to you? He said they didn't *want* to catch him! Why not? I'll tell you why—he was their man; they turned him, they caught him, don't you see and that was the price of his freedom—that and the money he was paid."

"I tell you you're out of your mind!" Leamas hissed. "He'll kill you if he ever thinks you make up this kind of stuff. It's sugar candy, Fiedler. Shut up and drive us home." At last the hot grip on Leamas' arm relaxed.

"That's where you're wrong. You provided the answer, you yourself, Leamas. That's why we need one another."

"It's not true!" Leamas shouted. "I've told you again and again, they couldn't have done it. The Circus couldn't have run him against the Zone without my knowing! It just wasn't an administrative possibility. You're trying to tell me Control was personally directing the deputy head of the Abteilung without the knowledge of the Berlin station. You're mad, Fiedler, you're just bloody well off your head!" Suddenly he began to laugh quietly. "You may want his job, you poor bastard; that's not unheard of, you know. But this kind of thing went out with bustles." For a moment neither spoke.

"That money," Fiedler said, "in Copenhagen. The bank replied to your letter. The manager is very worried lest there has been a mistake. The money was drawn by your co-signatory exactly one week after you paid it in. The date it was drawn coincides with a two-day visit which Mundt paid to

476

Denmark in February. He went there under an alias to meet an American agent we have who was attending a world scientists' conference." Fiedler hesitated, then added, "I suppose you ought to write to the bank and tell them everything is quite in order?"

15 ❋
COME TO THE BALL

Liz looked at the letter from Party Centre and wondered what it was about. She found it a little puzzling. She had to admit she was pleased, but why hadn't they consulted her first? Had the District Committee put up her name, or was it Centre's own choice? But no one in Centre knew her, so far as she was aware. She'd met odd speakers of course, and at District Congress she'd shaken hands with the Party Organiser. Perhaps that man from Cultural Relations had remembered her—that fair, rather effeminate man who was so ingratiating. Ashe, that was his name. He'd taken a bit of interest in her and she supposed he might have handed her name on, or remembered her when the Scholarship came up. An odd man, he was; took her to the Black and White for coffee after the meeting and asked her about her boyfriends. He hadn't been amorous or anything—she'd thought he was a bit queer to be honest—but he asked her masses of questions about herself. How long had she been in the Party, did she get homesick living away from her parents? Had she lots of boyfriends or was there a

478

special one she carried a torch for? She hadn't cared for him much but his talk had gone down quite well—the worker-state in the German Democratic Republic, the concept of the worker-poet and all that stuff. He certainly knew all about Eastern Europe, he must have travelled a lot. She'd guessed he was a schoolmaster, he had that rather didactic, fluent way with him. They'd had a collection for the Fighting Fund afterwards, and Ashe had put a pound in; she'd been absolutely amazed. That was it, she was sure now: it was Ashe who'd remembered her. He'd told someone at London District, and District had told Centre or something like that. It still seemed a funny way to go about things, but then the Party always was secretive—it was part of being a revolutionary party, she supposed. It didn't appeal to Liz much, the secrecy, it seemed dishonest. But she supposed it was necessary, and Heaven knows, there were plenty who got a kick out of it.

She read the letter again. It was on Centre's writing paper; with the thick red print at the top and it began, "Dear Comrade," it sounded so military to Liz, and she hated that; she'd never quite got used to "Comrade."

Dear Comrade,
We have recently had discussions with our Comrades in the Socialist Unity Party of the German Democratic Republic on the possibility of effecting exchanges between party members over here and our comrades in democratic Germany. The idea is to create a basis of exchange at the rank and file level between our two parties. The SUP is aware that the existing discriminatory measures by the British Home Office make it unlikely that their own delegates will be able to come to the United Kingdom in the immediate future, but they feel that an exchange of experiences is all the more important for this reason. They have generously invited us to select five Branch Secretaries with good experience and a good record of stimulating mass action at street level.

Each selected comrade will spend three weeks attending Branch discussions, studying progress in industry and social welfare and seeing at first hand the evidence of fascist provocation by the West. This is a grand opportunity for our comrades to profit from the experience of a young socialist system.

We therefore asked District to put forward the names of young Cadre workers from your areas who might get the biggest advantage from the trip, and your name has been put forward. We want you to go if you possibly can, and carry out the second part of the scheme—which is to establish contact with a Party Branch in the GDR whose members are from similar industrial backgrounds and have the same kind of problems as your own. The Bayswater South Branch has been paired with Neuenhagen, a suburb of Leipzig. Freda Lüman, Secretary of the Neuenhagen branch, is preparing a big welcome. We are sure you are just the Comrade for the job, and that it will be a terrific success. All expenses will be paid by the GDR Cultural Office.

We are sure you realise what a big honour this is, and are confident you will not allow personal considerations to prevent you from accepting. The visits are due to take place at the end of next month, about the 23rd, but the selected Comrades will travel separately as their invitations are not all concurrent. Will you please let us know as soon as possible whether you can accept, and we will let you know further details.

The more she read it, the odder it seemed. Such short notice for a start—how could they know she could get away from the Library? Then to her surprise she recalled that Ashe had asked her what she did for her holidays, whether she had taken her leave this year, and whether she had to give a lot of notice if she wanted to claim free time. Why hadn't they told her who the other nominees were? There was no particular reason why they should, perhaps, but it somehow looked odd when they didn't. It was such a *long* letter, too. They were so hard up for secretarial help at Centre they usually kept their letters short, or asked Comrades to ring up. This was so efficient, so well typed it might not have been done at Centre at all. But it *was* signed by the Cultural Organiser; it was his signature all right, no doubt of that. She'd seen it at the bottom of roneoed notices masses of times. And the letter had that awkward, semi-bureaucratic, semi-Messianic style she had grown accustomed to without ever liking. It was stupid to say she had a good record of stimulating mass action at street level. She hadn't. As a matter of fact she hated that side of party work—the loudspeakers at the factory gates, selling the *Daily Worker* at the street corner, going from door to door at the local elections. Peace Work she didn't mind so much, it meant something to her, it made sense. You could look at the kids in the street as you went by, at the mothers pushing their prams and the old people standing in doorways, and you could say, "I'm doing it for them." That really *was* fighting for peace.

But she never quite saw the fighting for votes and the fighting for sales in the same way. Perhaps that was because it cut them down to size, she thought. It was easy when there were a dozen or so together at a Branch meeting to rebuild the world, march at the vanguard of socialism, and talk of the inevitability of history. But afterwards she'd go out into the streets with an armful of *Daily Workers,* often waiting an hour, two hours, to sell a copy. Sometimes she'd cheat, as the others cheated, and pay for a dozen herself just to get out of it and go home. At the next meeting they'd boast about it—forgetting they'd bought them themselves—"Comrade Gold sold eighteen copies on Saturday night—eighteen!" It would go in the Minutes then, and the Branch bulletin as well. District would rub their hands, and perhaps she'd get a mention in that little panel on the front page about the Fighting Fund. It was such a little world, and she wished they could be more honest. But she lied to herself about it all, too. Perhaps they all did. Or perhaps the others understood

481

more *why* you had to lie so much. It seemed so odd they'd made her Branch Secretary. It was Mulligan who'd proposed it—"Our young, vigorous, *and* attractive comrade—" He'd thought she'd sleep with him if he got her made secretary. The others had voted for her because they liked her, and because she could type. Because she'd do the work and not try and make them go canvassing at weekends. Not too often anyway. They'd voted for her because they wanted a decent little club, nice and revolutionary and no fuss. It was all such a fraud. Alec had seemed to understand that; he just hadn't taken it seriously. "Some people keep canaries, some people join the Party," he'd said once, and it was true. In Bayswater South it was true anyway, and District knew that perfectly well. That's why it was so peculiar that she had been nominated; that was why she was extremely reluctant to believe that District had even had a hand in it. The explanation, she was sure, was Ashe. Perhaps he had a crush on her, perhaps he wasn't queer but just looked it.

Liz made a rather exaggerated shrug, the kind of overstressed gesture people do make when they are excited and alone. It was abroad anyway, it was free and it sounded interesting. She had never been abroad, and she certainly couldn't afford the fare herself. It would be rather fun. She had reservations about Germans, that was true. She knew, she had been told, that West Germany was militarist and revanchist, and that East Germany was democratic and peace-loving. But she doubted whether all the good Germans were on one side and all the bad ones on the other. And it was the bad ones who had killed her father. Perhaps that was why the Party had chosen her—as a generous act of reconciliation. Perhaps that was what Ashe had had in mind when he asked her all those questions. Of course—that was the explanation. She was suddenly filled with a feeling of warmth and gratitude towards the Party. They really were decent people and she was proud and thankful to belong. She went to the desk and opened the drawer where, in an old school satchel, she kept the Branch stationery and the dues stamps. Putting a sheet of paper into her old Underwood typewriter—they'd sent it down from District

482

when they heard she could type: it jumped a bit but otherwise was fine—she typed a neat, grateful letter of acceptance. Centre was such a wonderful thing—stern, benevolent, impersonal, perpetual. They were good, good people. People who fought for peace. As she closed the drawer she caught sight of Smiley's card.

She remembered the little man with the earnest, puckered face, standing at the doorway of her room and saying: "Did the Party know about you and Alec?" How silly she was. Well, this would take her mind off it.

16 ❧
ARREST

Fiedler and Leamas drove back the rest of the way in silence. In the dusk the hills were black and cavernous, the pinpoint lights struggling against the gathering darkness like the lights of distant ships at sea.

Fiedler parked the car in a shed at the side of the house and they walked together to the front door. They were about to enter the lodge when they heard a shout from the direction of the trees, followed by someone calling Fiedler's name. They turned, and Leamas distinguished in the twilight twenty yards away three men standing, apparently waiting for Fiedler to come.

"What do you want?" Fiedler called.

"We want to talk to you. We're from Berlin."

Fiedler hesitated. "Where's that damn' guard?" he asked Leamas; "there should be a guard on the front door."

Leamas shrugged.

"Why aren't the lights on in the hall?" he asked again: then, still unconvinced, he began walking slowly towards the men.

Leamas waited a moment, then, hearing nothing, made his

way through the unlit house to the annexe behind it. This was a shoddy barrack but attached to the back of the building and hidden from all sides by close plantations of young pine trees. The hut was divided into three adjoining bedrooms; there was no corridor. The centre room had been given to Leamas, and the room nearest to the main building was occupied by two guards. Leamas never knew who occupied the third. He had once tried to open the connecting door between it and his own room, but it was locked. He had only discovered it was a bedroom by peering through a narrow gap in the lace curtains early one morning as he went for a walk. The two guards, who followed him everywhere at fifty yards' distance, had not rounded the corner of the hut, and he looked in at the window. The room contained a single bed, made, and a small writing-desk with papers on it. He supposed that someone, with what passes for German thoroughness, watched him from that bedroom. But Leamas was too old a dog to allow himself to be bothered by surveillance. In Berlin it had been a fact of life—if you couldn't spot it so much the worse: it only meant they were taking greater care, or you were losing your grip. Usually, because he was good at that kind of thing, because he was observant and had an accurate memory—because, in short, he was good at his job—he spotted them anyway. He knew the formations favoured by a shadowing team, he knew the tricks, the weaknesses, the momentary lapses that could give them away. It meant nothing to Leamas that he was watched, but as he walked through the improvised doorway from the lodge to the hut, and stood in the guards' bedroom, he had the distinct feeling that something was wrong.

The lights in the annexe were controlled from some central point. They were put on and off by an unseen hand. In the mornings he was often woken by the sudden blaze of the single overhead light in his room. At night he would be hastened to bed by perfunctory darkness. It was only nine o'clock as he entered the annexe, and the lights were already out. Usually they stayed on till eleven, but now they were out and the shutters had

485

been lowered. He had left the connecting door from the house open, so that the pale twilight from the hallway reached, but scarcely penetrated, the guards' bedroom, and by it he could just see the two empty beds. As he stood there peering into the room, surprised to find it empty, the door behind him closed. Perhaps by itself, but Leamas made no attempt to open it. It was pitch dark. No sound accompanied the closing of the door, no click nor footstep. To Leamas, his instinct suddenly alert, it was as if the sound-track had stopped. Then he smelt the cigar smoke. It must have been hanging in the air but he had not noticed it till now. Like a blind man, his senses of touch and smell were sharpened by the darkness.

There were matches in his pocket but he did not use them. He took one pace sideways, pressed his back against the wall and remained motionless. To Leamas there could only be one explanation—they were waiting for him to pass from the guards' room to his own and therefore he determined to remain where he was. Then from the direction of the main building whence he had come he heard clearly the sound of a footstep. The door which had just closed was tested, the lock turned and made fast. Still Leamas did not move. Not yet. There was no pretence: he was a prisoner in the hut. Very slowly, Leamas now lowered himself into a crouch putting his hand in the side pocket of his jacket as he did so. He was quite calm, almost relieved at the prospect of action, but memories were racing through his mind. "You've nearly always got a weapon: an ash-tray, a couple of coins, a fountain-pen—anything that will gouge or cut." It was the favourite dictum of the mild little Welsh sergeant at that house near Oxford in the war; "Never use both hands at once, not with a knife, a stick or a pistol; keep your left arm free, and hold it across the belly. If you can't find anything to hit with, keep the hands open and the thumbs stiff." Taking the box of matches in his right hand he clasped it longways, and deliberately crushed it, so that the small, jagged edges of boxwood protruded from between his fingers. This done, he edged his way along the wall until he came to a chair which he knew was in the corner of the room. Indifferent now to the noise he made, he shoved the chair into the centre of the floor. Counting his footsteps as he moved back from the chair, he positioned himself in the angle of the two walls. As he did so, he heard the door of his own bedroom flung open. Vainly he tried to discern the figure who must be standing in the doorway, but there was no light from his own room either. The darkness was impenetrable. He dared not move forward to attack, for the chair was now in the middle of the room; it was his tactical advantage, for he knew where it was, and they did not. They must come for him, they must; he could not let them wait until their helper outside had reached the master switch and put on the lights.

"Come on, you windy bastards," he hissed in German; "I'm here, in the corner. Come and get me, can't you?" Not a move, not a sound.

"I'm here, can't you see me? What's the matter then? What's the matter, children, come on, can't you?" And then he heard one stepping forward, and another following; and then the oath of a man as he stumbled on the chair, and that was the sign that Leamas was waiting for. Tossing away the box of matches he slowly, cautiously crept forward, pace by pace, his left arm extended in the attitude of a man warding off twigs in a wood until, quite gently, he had touched an arm and felt the warm prickly cloth of a military uniform. Still with his left hand Leamas deliberately tapped the arm twice—two distinct taps—and heard a frightened voice whisper close to his ear in German:

"Hans, is it you?"

"Shut up, you fool," Leamas whispered in reply, and in that same moment reached out and grasped the man's hair, pulling his head forward and down, then in a terrible cutting blow drove the side of his right hand on to the nape of the neck, pulled him up again by the arm, hit him in the throat with an upward thrust of his open fist, then released him to fall where the force of gravity took him. As the man's body hit the ground, the lights went on.

In the doorway stood a young captain of the People's Police

487

smoking a cigar, and behind him two men. One was in civilian clothes, quite young. He held a pistol in his hand. Leamas thought it was the Czech kind with a loading lever on the spine of the butt. They were all looking at the man on the floor. Somebody unlocked the outer door and Leamus turned to see who it was. As he turned, there was a shout—Leamas thought it was the captain—telling him to stand still. Slowly he turned back and faced the three men.

His hands were still at his side as the blow came. It seemed to crush his skull. As he fell, drifting warmly into unconsciousness, he wondered whether he had been hit with a revolver, the old kind with a swivel on the butt where you fastened the lanyard.

He was woken by the lag singing and the warder yelling at him to shut up. He opened his eyes and like a brilliant light the pain burst upon his brain. He lay quite still, refusing to close them, watching the sharp, coloured fragments racing across his vision. He tried to take stock of himself: his feet were icy cold and he was aware of the sour stench of prison denims. The singing had stopped and suddenly Leamas longed for it to start again, although he knew it never would. He tried to raise his hand and touch the blood that was caked on his cheek, but his hands were behind him, locked together. His feet too must be bound: the blood had left them, that was why they were cold. Painfully he looked about him, trying to lift his head an inch or two from the floor. To his surprise he saw his own knees in front of him. Instinctively he tried to stretch his legs and as he did so his whole body was seized with a pain so sudden and terrible that he screamed out a sobbing agonised cry of self-pity, like the last cry of a man upon the rack. He lay there panting, attempting to master the pain, then through the sheer perversity of his nature, he tried again, quite slowly, to straighten his legs. At once the agony returned, but Leamas had found the cause: his hands and feet were chained together behind his back. As soon as he attempted to stretch his legs the chain tightened, forcing his shoulders down and his damaged head on to

488

the stone floor. They must have beaten him up while he was un-conscious, his whole body was stiff and bruised and his groin ached. He wondered if he'd killed the guard. He hoped so.

Above him shone the light, large, clinical, and fierce. No furniture, just whitewashed walls, quite close all round, and the grey steel door, a smart charcoal grey, the colour you see on clever London houses. There was nothing else. Nothing at all. Nothing to think about, just the savage pain.

He must have lain there hours before they came. It grew hot from the light, he was thirsty but he refused to call out. At last the door opened and Mundt stood there. He knew it was Mundt from the eyes. Smiley had told him about them.

17 ❀
MUNDT

They untied him and let him try to stand. For a moment he almost succeeded, then, as the circulation returned to his hands and feet, and as the joints of his body were released from the contraction to which they had been subject, he fell. They let him lie there, watching him with the detachment of children looking at an insect. One of the guards pushed past Mundt and yelled at Leamas to get up. Leamas crawled to the wall and put the palms of his throbbing hands against the white brick. He was half-way up when the guard kicked him and he fell again. He tried once more and this time the guard let him stand with his back against the wall. He saw the guard move his weight on to his left leg and he knew he would kick him again. With all his remaining strength Leamas thrust himself forward, driving his lowered head into the guard's face. They fell together, Leamas on top. The guard got up and Leamas lay there waiting for the pay-off. But Mundt said something to the guard and Leamas felt himself being picked up by the shoulders and

490

feet and heard the door of his cell close as they carried him down the corridor. He was terribly thirsty.

They took him to a small comfortable room, decently furnished with a desk and armchairs. Swedish blinds half covered the barred windows. Mundt sat at the desk and Leamas in an armchair, his eyes half closed. The guards stood at the door.

"Give me a drink," said Leamas.

"Whisky?"

"Water."

Mundt filled a carafe from a basin in the corner, and put it on the table beside him with a glass.

"Bring him something to eat," he ordered, and one of the guards left the room, returning with a mug of soup and some sliced sausage. He drank and ate, and they watched him in silence.

"Where's Fiedler?" Leamas asked finally.

"Under arrest," Mundt replied curtly.

"What for?"

"Conspiring to sabotage the security of the people."

Leamas nodded slowly. "So you won," he said. "When did you arrest him?"

"Last night."

Leamas waited a moment, trying to focus again on Mundt.

"What about me?" he asked.

"You're a material witness. You will of course stand trial yourself later."

"So I'm part of a put-up job by London to frame Mundt, am I?"

Mundt nodded, lit a cigarette and gave it to one of the sentries to pass to Leamas. "That's right," he said. The sentry came over, and with a gesture of grudging solicitude, put the cigarette between Leamas' lips.

"A pretty elaborate operation," Leamas observed, and added stupidly, "clever chaps these Chinese."

Mundt said nothing. Leamas became used to his silences as the interview progressed. Mundt had rather a pleasant voice, that was something Leamas hadn't expected, but he seldom spoke. It was part of Mundt's extraordinary self-confidence perhaps, that he did not speak unless he specifically wished to, that he was prepared to allow long silences to intervene rather than exchange pointless words. In this he differed from professional interrogators who set store by initiative, by the evocation of atmosphere and the exploitation of that psychological dependency of a prisoner upon his inquisitor. Mundt despised technique: he was a man of fact and action. Leamas preferred that.

Mundt's appearance was fully consistent with his temperament. He looked an athlete. His fair hair was cut short. It lay matt and neat. His young face had a hard, clean line, and a frightening directness; it was barren of humour or fantasy. He looked young but not youthful; older men would take him seriously. He was well built. His clothes fitted him because he was an easy man to fit. Leamas found no difficulty in recalling that Mundt was a killer. There was a coldness about him, a rigorous self-sufficiency which perfectly equipped him for the business of murder. Mundt was a very hard man.

"The other charge on which you will stand trial, if necessary," Mundt added quietly, "is murder."

"So the sentry died, did he?" Leamas replied.

A wave of intense pain passed through his head.

Mundt nodded: "That being so," he said, "your trial for espionage is somewhat academic. I propose that the case against Fiedler should be publicly heard. That is also the wish of the Praesidium."

"And you want my confession?"

"Yes."

"In other words you haven't any proof."

"We shall have proof. We shall have your confession." There was no menace in Mundt's voice. There was no style, no theatrical twist.

"On the other hand, there could be mitigation in your case. You were blackmailed by British Intelligence; they accused you

492

of stealing money and then coerced you into preparing a revanchist trap against myself. The court would have sympathy for such a plea."

Leamas seemed to be taken off his guard.

"How did you know they accused me of stealing money?" But Mundt made no reply.

"Fiedler has been very stupid," Mundt observed. "As soon as I read the report of our friend Peters I knew why you had been sent, and I knew that Fiedler would fall into the trap. Fiedler hates me so much." Mundt nodded, as if to emphasise the truth of his observation. "Your people knew that of course. It was a very clever operation. Who prepared it, tell me. Was it Smiley? Did he do it?" Leamas said nothing.

"I wanted to see Fiedler's report of his own interrogation of you, you see. I told him to send it to me. He procrastinated and I knew I was right. Then yesterday he circulated it among the Praesidium, and did not send me a copy. Someone in London has been very clever."

Leamas said nothing.

"When did you last see Smiley?" Mundt asked casually. Leamas hesitated, uncertain of himself. His head was aching terribly.

"When did you last see him?" Mundt repeated.

"I don't remember," Leamas said at last, "he wasn't really in the outfit any more. He'd drop in from time to time."

"He is a great friend of Peter Guillam, is he not?"

"I think so, yes."

"Guillam, you thought, studied the economic situation in the GDR. Some odd little section in your Service, you weren't quite sure what it did."

"Yes." Sound and sight were becoming confused in the mad throbbing in his brain. His eyes were hot and painful. He felt sick.

"Well, when did you last see Smiley?"

"I don't remember . . . I don't remember."

Mundt shook his head.

"You have a very good memory—for anything that incriminates me. We can all remember when we *last* saw somebody. Did you for instance see him after you returned from Berlin?"

"Yes, I think so. I bumped into him . . . in the Circus once, in London." Leamas had closed his eyes and he was sweating. "I can't go on, Mundt . . . not much longer, Mundt; I'm sick," he said.

"After Ashe had picked you up, after he had walked into the trap that had been set for him, you had lunch together, didn't you?"

"Yes. Lunch together."

"Lunch ended at about four o'clock. Where did you go then?"

"I went down to the City, I think. I don't remember for sure . . . for Christ's sake, Mundt," he said holding his head with his hand, "I can't go on. My bloody head's . . ."

"And after that where did you go? Why did you shake off your followers, why were you so keen to shake them off?"

Leamas said nothing: he was breathing in sharp gasps, his head buried in his hands.

"Answer this one question, then you can go. You shall have a bed. You can sleep if you want. Otherwise you must go back to your cell, do you understand? You will be tied up again and fed on the floor like an animal, do you understand? Tell me where you went."

The wild pulsation of his brain suddenly increased, the room was dancing; he heard voices around him and the sound of footsteps; spectral shapes passed and re-passed, detached from sound and gravity; someone was shouting, but not at him; the door was open, he was sure someone had opened the door. The room was full of people, all shouting now, and then they were going, some of them had gone, he heard them marching away, the stamping of their feet was like the throbbing of his head; the echo died and there was silence. Then like the touch of mercy itself, a cool cloth was laid across his forehead, and kindly hands carried him away.

He woke on a hospital bed, and standing at the foot of it was Fiedler, smoking a cigarette.

18 ❊
FIEDLER

Leamas took stock. A bed with sheets. A single ward with no bars in the windows, just curtains and frosted glass. Pale green walls, dark green linoleum; and Fiedler watching him, smoking.

A nurse brought him food: an egg, some thin soup and fruit. He felt like death, but he supposed he'd better eat it. So he did and Fiedler watched.

"How do you feel?" he asked.

"Bloody awful," Leamas replied.

"But better?"

"I suppose so." He hesitated, "Those sods beat me up."

"You killed a sentry, you know that?"

"I guessed I had . . . What do they expect if they mount such a damn' stupid operation. Why didn't they pull us both in at once? Why put all the lights out? If anything was over-organised, that was."

"I am afraid that as a nation we tend to over-organise. Abroad that passes for efficiency."

496

Again there was a pause.

"What happened to you?" Leamas asked.

"Oh, I too was softened for interrogation."

"By Mundt's men?"

"By Mundt's men *and* Mundt. It was a very peculiar sensation!"

"That's one way of putting it."

"No, no; not physically. Physically it was a nightmare, but you see Mundt had a special interest in beating me up. Apart from the confession."

"Because you dreamed up that story about—"

"Because I am a Jew."

"Oh Christ," said Leamas softly.

"That is why I got special treatment. All the time he whispered to me. It was very strange."

"What did he say?"

Fiedler didn't reply. At last he muttered:

"That's all over."

"Why? What's happened?"

"The day we were arrested I had applied to the Praesidium for a civil warrant to arrest Mundt as an enemy of the people."

"But you're mad—I told you, you're raving mad, Fiedler! He'll never—"

"There was other evidence against him apart from yours. Evidence I have been accumulating over the last three years, piece by piece. Yours provided the proof we need; that's all. As soon as that was clear I prepared a report and sent it to every member of the Praesidium except Mundt. They received it on the same day that I made my application for a warrant."

"The day we were pulled in."

"Yes. I knew Mundt would fight. I knew he had friends on the Praesidium, or yes-men at least, people who were sufficiently frightened to go running to him as soon as they got my report. And in the end, I knew he would lose. The Praesidium had the weapon it needed to destroy him; they had the report, and for those few days while you and I were being questioned they read

497

it and re-read it until they knew it was true and each knew the others knew. In the end they acted. Herded together by their common fear, their common weakness, and their common knowledge they turned against him and ordered a Tribunal."

"Tribunal?"

"A secret one, of course. It meets tomorrow. Mundt is under arrest."

"What is this other evidence? The evidence you've collected."

"Wait and see," Fiedler replied with a smile. "Tomorrow you will see."

Fiedler was silent for a time, watching Leamas eat.

"This Tribunal," Leamas asked, "how is it conducted?"

"That is up to the President. It is not a People's Court—it is important to remember that. It is more in the nature of an enquiry—a committee of enquiry, that's it, appointed by the Praesidium to investigate and report upon a certain . . . subject. Its report contains a recommendation. In a case like this the recommendation is tantamount to a verdict, but remains secret, as part of the proceedings of the Praesidium."

"How does it work? Are there counsel and judges?"

"There are three judges," Fiedler said; "and in effect, there are counsel. Tomorrow I myself shall put the case against Mundt. Karden will defend him."

"Who's Karden?"

Fiedler hesitated.

"A very tough man," he said. "Looks like a country doctor, small and benevolent. He was at Buchenwald."

"Why can't Mundt defend himself?"

"It was Mundt's wish. It is said that Karden will call a witness."

Leamas shrugged.

"That's your affair," he said. Again there was silence. At last Fiedler said reflectively:

"I wouldn't have minded—I don't think I would have minded, not so much anyway—if he had hurt me for myself,

498

for hate or jealousy. Do you understand that? That long, long pain and all the time you say to yourself, 'Either I shall faint or I shall grow to bear the pain, nature will see to that' and the pain just increases like a violinist going up the E string. You think it can't get any higher and it does—the pain's like that, it rises and rises, and all that nature does is bring you on from note to note like a deaf child being taught to hear. And all the time he was whispering Jew . . . Jew. I could understand, I'm sure I could, if he had done it for the idea, for the Party, if you like, or if he had hated *me*. But it wasn't that; he hated—"

"All right," said Leamas shortly, "you should know. He's a bastard."

"Yes," said Fiedler, "he is a bastard." He seemed excited; he wants to boast to somebody, thought Leamas.

"I thought a lot about you," Fiedler added. "I thought about that talk we had—you remember—about the motor."

"What motor?"

Fiedler smiled. "I'm sorry, that is a direct translation. I mean '*Motor*,' the engine, spirit, urge; whatever Christians call it."

"I'm not a Christian."

Fiedler shrugged. "You know what I mean." He smiled again, "the thing that embarrasses you . . . I'll put it another way. Suppose Mundt is right. He asked me to confess, you know; I was to confess that I was in league with British spies who were plotting to murder him. You see the argument—that the whole operation was mounted by British Intelligence in or-der to entice us—me, if you like—into liquidating the best man in the Abteilung. To turn our own weapon against us."

"He tried that on me," said Leamas indifferently. And he added, "As if I'd cooked up the whole bloody story."

"But what I mean is this: suppose you had done that, sup-pose it were true—I am taking an example, you understand, a hypothesis, would you kill a man, an innocent man—"

"Mundt's a killer himself."

"Suppose he wasn't. Suppose it were me they wanted to kill: would London do it?"

"It depends . . . it depends on the need . . ."

"Ah," said Fiedler contentedly, "it depends on the need. Like Stalin, in fact. The traffic accident and the statistics. That is a great relief."

"Why?"

"You must get some sleep," said Fiedler. "Order what food you want. They will bring you whatever you want. Tomorrow you can talk." As he reached the door he looked back and said, "We're all the same, you know, that's the joke."

Soon Leamas was asleep, content in the knowledge that Fiedler was his ally and that they would shortly send Mundt to his death. That was something which he had looked forward to for a very long time.

19 ❁
BRANCH MEETING

Liz was happy in Leipzig. Austerity pleased her—
it gave her the comfort of sacrifice. The little house she stayed
in was dark and meagre, the food was poor and most of it had
to go to the children. They talked politics at every meal, she and
Frau Ebert, Branch Secretary for the Ward Branch of Leipzig-
Hohengrün, a small, grey woman whose husband managed a
gravel quarry on the outskirts of the city. It was like living in a
religious community, Liz thought; a convent or a kibbutz or
something. You felt the world was better for your empty stomach. Liz had some German which she had learnt from her aunt,
and she was surprised how quickly she was able to use it. She
tried it on the children first and they grinned and helped her.
The children treated her oddly to begin with, as if she were a
person of great quality or rarity value, and on the third day one
of them plucked up courage and asked her if she had brought
any chocolate from *"drüben"*—from "over there." She'd never
thought of that and she felt ashamed. After that they seemed to
forget about her.

501

In the evenings there was Party Work. They distributed literature, visited Branch members who had defaulted on their dues or lagged behind in their attendance at meetings, called in at District for a discussion on "Problems connected with the centralised distribution of agricultural produce" at which all local Branch Secretaries were present, and attended a meeting of the Workers' Consultative Council of a machine tool factory on the outskirts of the town.

At last, on the fourth day, the Thursday, came their own Branch Meeting. This was to be, for Liz at least, the most exhilarating experience of all; it would be an example of all that her own Branch in Bayswater could one day be. They had chosen a wonderful title for the evening's discussions—"Coexistence after two wars"—and they expected a record attendance. The whole ward had been circularised, they had taken care to see that there was no rival meeting in the neighbourhood that evening; it was not a late shopping day.

Seven people came.

Seven people and Liz and the Branch Secretary and the man from District. Liz put a brave face on it but she was terribly upset. She could scarcely concentrate on the speaker, and when she tried he used long German compounds that she couldn't work out anyway. It was like the meetings in Bayswater, it was like mid-week evensong when she used to go to church—the same dutiful, little group of lost faces, and same fussy self-consciousness, the same feeling of a great idea in the hands of little people. She always felt the same thing—it was awful, really, but she did—she wished no one would turn up, because that was absolute and it suggested persecution, humiliation—it was something you could react to.

But seven people were nothing: they were worse than nothing, because they were evidence of the inertia of the uncapturable mass. They broke your heart.

The room was better than the schoolroom in Bayswater, but even that was no comfort. In Bayswater it had been fun trying to *find* a room. In the early days they had pretended they were

502

something else, not the Party at all. They'd taken back rooms in pubs, a committee room at the Ardena Café, or met secretly in one another's houses. Then Bill Hazel had joined from the Secondary School and they'd used his classroom. Even that was a risk—the headmaster thought Bill ran a drama group, so theoretically at least they might still be chucked out. Somehow that fitted better than this Peace Hall in pre-cast concrete with the cracks in the corners and the picture of Lenin. Why did they have that silly frame thing all round the picture? Bundles of organ pipes sprouting from the corners and the bunting all dusty. It looked like something from a fascist funeral. Sometimes she thought Alec was right—you believed in things because you needed to; what you believed in had no value of its own, no function. What did he say: "A dog scratches where it itches. Different dogs itch in different places." No, it was wrong, Alec was wrong—it was a wicked thing to say. Peace and freedom and equality—they were facts, of course they were. And what about history—all those laws of the Party proved. No, Alec was wrong: truth existed outside people, it was demonstrated in history, individuals must bow to it, be crushed by it if necessary. The Party was the vanguard of history, the spearpoint in the fight for Peace . . . she went over the rubric a little uncertainly. She wished more people had come. Seven was so few. They looked so cross; cross and hungry.

The meeting over, Liz waited for Frau Ebert to collect the unsold literature from the heavy table by the door, fill in her attendance book, and put on her coat, for it was cold that evening. The speaker had left—rather rudely, Liz thought—before the general discussion. Frau Ebert was standing at the door with her hand on the light switch when a man appeared out of the darkness, framed in the doorway. Just for a moment Liz thought it was Ashe. He was tall and fair and wore one of those raincoats with leather buttons.

"Comrade Ebert?" he enquired.

"Yes?"

"I am looking for an English Comrade, Gold. She is staying with you?"

"I'm Elizabeth Gold," Liz put in, and the man came into the hall, closing the door behind him, so that the light shone full upon his face.

"I am Holten from District." He showed some paper to Frau Ebert who was still standing at the door, and she nodded and glanced a little anxiously towards Liz.

"I have been asked to give a message to Comrade Gold from the Praesidium," he said. "It concerns an alteration in your programme; an invitation to attend a special meeting."

"Oh," said Liz rather stupidly. It seemed fantastic that the Praesidium should even have heard of her.

"It is a gesture," Holten said. "A gesture of goodwill."

"But I—but Frau Ebert . . ." Liz began helplessly.

"Comrade Ebert, I am sure, will forgive you under the circumstances."

"Of course," said Frau Ebert quickly.

"Where is the meeting to be held?"

"It will necessitate your leaving tonight," Holten replied. "We have a long way to go. Nearly to Görlitz."

"To Görlitz . . . Where's that?"

"East," said Frau Ebert quickly. "On the Polish border."

"We can drive you home now. You can collect your things and we will continue the journey at once."

"Tonight? Now?"

"Yes." Holten didn't seem to consider Liz had much choice.

A large black car was waiting for them. There was a driver in the front and a flagpost on the bonnet. It looked rather a military car.

20 ❀
TRIBUNAL

The court was no larger than a schoolroom. At one end, on the mere five or six benches which were provided, sat guards and warders and here and there among them spectators—members of the Praesidium and selected officials. At the other end of the room sat the three members of the Tribunal on tall-backed chairs at an unpolished oak table. Above them, suspended from the ceiling by three loops of wire, was a large red star made of plywood. The walls of the courtroom were white like the walls of Leamas' cell.

On either side, their chairs a little forward of the table, and turned inwards to face one another, sat two men; one was middle-aged, sixty perhaps, in a black suit and a grey tie, the kind of suit they wear in church in German country districts. The other was Fiedler.

Leamas sat at the back, a guard on either side of him. Between the heads of the spectators he could see Mundt, himself surrounded by police, his fair hair cut very short, his broad shoulders covered in the familiar grey of prison uniform. It seemed to Leamas a curious commentary on the mood of the court—or the influence of Fiedler—that he himself should be wearing his own clothes, while Mundt was in prison uniform.

Leamas had not long been in his place when the president of the Tribunal, sitting at the centre of the table, rang the bell. The sound directed his attention towards it, and a shiver passed over him as he realised that the president was a woman. He could scarcely be blamed for not noting it before. She was fifty-ish, small-eyed and dark. Her hair was cut short like a man's, and she wore the kind of functional dark tunic favoured by Soviet wives. She looked sharply round the room, nodded to a sentry to close the door, and began at once without ceremony to address the court.

"You all know why we are here. The proceedings are secret, remember that. This is a Tribunal convened expressly by the Praesidium. It is to the Praesidium alone that we are responsible. We shall hear evidence as we think fit." She pointed perfunctorily towards Fiedler. "Comrade Fiedler, you had better begin."

Fiedler stood up. Nodding briefly towards the table he drew from the brief-case beside him a sheaf of papers held together in one corner by a piece of black cord.

He talked quietly and easily, with a diffidence which Leamas had never seen in him before. Leamas considered it a good performance, well adjusted to the role of a man regretfully hanging his superior.

"You should know first, if you do not know already," Fiedler began, "that on the day that the Praesidium received my report on the activities of Comrade Mundt I was arrested, together with the defector Leamas. Both of us were imprisoned and both of us . . . invited, under extreme duress, to confess that this whole terrible charge was a fascist plot against a loyal comrade.

"You can see from the report I have already given you how it was that Leamas came to our notice: we ourselves sought him out, induced him to defect, and finally brought him to Democratic Germany. Nothing could more clearly demonstrate the

506

impartiality of Leamas than this: that he still refuses, for reasons I will explain, to believe that Mundt was a British agent. It is therefore grotesque to suggest that Leamas is a plant: the initiative was ours, and the fragmentary but vital evidence of Leamas provides only the final proof in a long chain of indications reaching back over the last three years.

"You have before you the written record of this case. I need do no more than interpret for you facts of which you are already aware.

"The charge against Comrade Mundt is that he is the agent of an imperialist power. I could have made other charges—that he passed information to the British Secret Service, that he turned his Department into the unconscious lackey of a bourgeois state, that he deliberately shielded revanchist anti-Party groups and accepted sums of foreign currency in reward. These other charges would derive from the first; that Hans-Dieter Mundt is the agent of an imperialist power. The penalty for this crime is death. There is no crime more serious in our penal code, none which exposes our state to greater danger, nor demands more vigilance of our Party organs." Here he puts the papers down.

"Comrade Mundt is forty-two years old. He is deputy head of the Department for the Protection of the People. He is unmarried. He has always been regarded as a man of exceptional capabilities, tireless in serving the Party's interests, ruthless in protecting them.

"Let me tell you some details of his career. He was recruited into the Department at the age of twenty-eight and underwent the customary instruction. Having completed his probationary period he undertook special tasks in Scandinavian countries—notably Norway, Sweden, and Finland—where he succeeded in establishing an intelligence network which carried the battle against fascist agitators into the enemy's camp. He performed this task well, and there is no reason to suppose that at that time he was other than a diligent member of his Department. But, Comrades, you should not forget this early connection with

Scandinavia. The networks established by Comrade Mundt soon after the war provided the excuse, many years later, for him to travel to Finland and Norway, where his commitments became a cover enabling him to draw thousands of dollars from foreign banks in return for his treacherous conduct. Make no mistake: Comrade Mundt has not fallen victim to those who try to disprove the arguments of history. First cowardice, then weakness, then greed were his motives; the acquirement of great wealth his dream. Ironically, it was the elaborate system by which his lust for money was satisfied that brought the forces of justice on his trail."

Fiedler paused, and looked round the room, his eyes suddenly alight with fervour. Leamas watched, fascinated.

"Let that be a lesson," Fiedler shouted, "to those other enemies of the state, whose crime is so foul that they must plot in the secret hours of the night!" A dutiful murmur rose from the tiny group of spectators at the back of the room.

"They will not escape the vigilance of the people whose blood they seek to sell!" Fiedler might have been addressing a large crowd rather than a handful of officials and guards assembled in the tiny, white-walled room.

Leamas realised at that moment that Fiedler was taking no chances: the deportment of the Tribunal, prosecutors, and witnesses must be politically impeccable. Fiedler, knowing no doubt that the danger of a subsequent counter-charge was inherent in such cases, was protecting his own back: the polemic would go down in the record and it would be a brave man who set himself to refute it.

Fiedler now opened the file that lay on the desk before him.

"At the end of 1956 Mundt was posted to London as a member of the East German Steel Mission. He had the additional special task of undertaking counter-subversionary measures against *emigré* groups. In the course of his work he exposed himself to great dangers—of that there is no doubt—and he obtained valuable results."

Leamas' attention was again drawn to the three figures at the centre table. To the President's left a youngish man, dark. His eyes seemed to be half closed. He had lank, unruly hair and the grey, meagre complexion of an ascetic. His hands were slim, restlessly toying with the corner of a bundle of papers which lay before him. Leamas guessed he was Mundt's man; he found it hard to say why. On the other side of the table sat a slightly older man, balding, with an open agreeable face. Leamas thought he looked rather an ass. He guessed that if Mundt's fate hung in the balance the young man would defend him and the woman condemn. He thought the second man would be embarrassed by the difference of opinion and side with the President.

Fiedler was speaking again.

"It was at the end of his service in London that recruitment took place. I have said that he exposed himself to great dangers; in doing so he fell foul of the British secret police, and they issued a warrant for his arrest. Mundt, who had no diplomatic immunity (NATO Britain does not recognise our sovereignty), went into hiding. Ports were watched, his photograph and description were distributed throughout the British Isles. Yet, after two days in hiding, Comrade Mundt took a taxi to London Airport and flew to Berlin. 'Brilliant,' you will say, and so it was. With the whole of Britain's police force alerted, her roads, railways, shipping, and air routes under constant surveillance, Comrade Mundt takes a plane from London Airport. Brilliant indeed. Or perhaps you may feel, Comrades, with the advantage of hindsight, that Mundt's escape from England was a little *too* brilliant, a little *too* easy, that without the connivance of the British authorities it would never have been possible at all!" Another murmur, more spontaneous than the first, rose from the back of the room.

"The truth is this: Mundt *was* taken prisoner by the British; in a short historic interview they offered him the classic alternative. Was it to be years in an imperialist prison, the end of a brilliant career, or was Mundt to make a dramatic return to his home country, against all expectation, and fulfil the promise he had shown? The British, of course, made it a condition of his return

509

that he should provide them with information, and they would pay him large sums of money. With the carrot in front and the stick behind, Mundt was recruited.

"It was now in the British interest to promote Mundt's career. We cannot yet prove that Mundt's success in liquidating minor Western intelligence agents was the work of his imperialist masters betraying their own collaborators—those who were expendable—in order that Mundt's prestige should be enhanced. We cannot prove it, but it is an assumption which the evidence permits.

"Ever since 1960—the year Comrade Mundt became Head of the Counter Espionage section of the Abteilung—indications have reached us from all over the world that there was a highly placed spy in our ranks. You all know Karl Riemeck was a spy; we thought when he was eliminated that the evil had been stamped out. But the rumours persisted.

"In late 1960 a former collaborator of ours approached an Englishman in the Lebanon known to be in contact with their Intelligence Service. He offered him—we found out soon afterwards—a complete breakdown of the two sections of the Abteilung for which he had formerly worked. His offer, after it had been transmitted to London, was rejected. That was a very curious thing. It could only mean that the British already possessed the intelligence they were being offered, *and that it was up to date.*

"From mid-1960 onwards we were losing collaborators abroad at an alarming rate. Often they were arrested within a few weeks of their despatch. Sometimes the enemy attempted to turn our own agents back on us, but not often. It was as if they could scarcely be bothered.

"And then—it was early 1961 if my memory is correct—we had a stroke of luck. We obtained by means I will not describe, a summary of the information which British Intelligence held about the Abteilung. It was complete, it was accurate, and it was astonishingly up to date. I showed it to Mundt, of course—he was my superior. He told me it came as no surprise to him: he

510

had certain enquiries in hand and I should take no action for fear of prejudicing them. And I confess that at that moment the thought crossed my mind, remote and fantastic as it was, that Mundt himself could have provided the information. There were other indications too . . .

"I need hardly tell you that the last, the very last person to be suspected of espionage is the head of the Counter Espionage section. The notion is so appalling, so melodramatic that few would entertain it, let alone give expression to it! I confess that I myself have been guilty of excessive reluctance in reaching such a seemingly fantastic deduction. That was erroneous.

"But, Comrades, the final evidence has been delivered into our hands. I propose to call that evidence now." He turned, glancing towards the back of the room. "Bring Leamas forward."

The guards on either side of him stood up and Leamas edged his way along the row to the rough gangway which ran, not more than two feet wide, down the middle of the room. A guard indicated to him that he should stand facing the table. Fiedler stood a bare six feet away from him. First the President addressed him.

"Witness, what is your name?" she asked.

"Alec Leamas."

"What is your age?"

"Fifty."

"Are you married?"

"No."

"But you were."

"I'm not married now."

"What is your profession?"

"Assistant librarian."

Fiedler angrily intervened. "You were formerly employed by British Intelligence, were you not?" he snapped.

"That's right. Till a year ago."

"The Tribunal has read the reports of your interrogation," Fiedler continued. "I want you to tell them again about the conversation you had with Peter Guillam some time in May last year."

"You mean when we talked about Mundt?"

"Yes."

"I've told you. It was at the Circus, the office in London, our headquarters in Cambridge Circus. I bumped into Peter in the corridor. I knew he was mixed up with the Fennan case and I asked him what had become of George Smiley. Then we got talking about Dieter Frey, who died, and Mundt, who was mixed up in the thing. Peter said he thought that Maston—Maston was effectively in charge of the case then—had not wanted Mundt to be caught."

"How did you interpret that?" asked Fiedler.

"I knew Maston had made a mess of the Fennan case. I supposed he didn't want any mud raked up by Mundt appearing at the Old Bailey."

"If Mundt had been caught, would he have been legally charged?" the President put in.

"It depends who caught him. If the police got him they'd report it to the Home Office. After that no power on earth could stop him being charged."

"And what if your Service had caught him?" Fiedler enquired.

"Oh, that's a different matter. I suppose they would either have interrogated him and then tried to exchange him for one of our own people in prison over here; or else they'd have given him a ticket."

"What does that mean?"

"Get rid of him."

"Liquidate him?" Fiedler was asking all the questions now, and the members of the Tribunal were writing diligently in the files before them.

"I don't know what they do. I've never been mixed up in that game."

"Might they not have tried to recruit him as their agent?"

"Yes, but they didn't succeed."

512

"How do you know that?"

"Oh, for God's sake, I've told you over and over again. I'm not a bloody performing seal . . . I was head of the Berlin Command for four years. If Mundt had been one of our people, I would have known. I couldn't help knowing."

"Quite."

Fiedler seemed content with that answer, confident perhaps that the remainder of the Tribunal was not. He now turned his attention to Operation "Rolling Stone"; took Leamas once again through the special security complexities governing the circulation of the file, the letters to the Copenhagen and Helsinki banks and the one reply which Leamas had received. Addressing himself to the Tribunal, Fiedler commented:

"We had no reply from Helsinki. I do not know why. But let me recapitulate for you. Leamas deposited money at Copenhagen on June 15th. Among the papers before you there is the facsimile of a letter from the Royal Scandinavian Bank addressed to Robert Lang. Robert Lang was the name Leamas used to open the Copenhagen deposit account. From that letter (it is the twelfth serial in your files) you will see that the entire sum—ten thousand dollars—was drawn by the co-signatory to the account one week later. I imagine," Fiedler continued, indicating with his head the motionless figure of Mundt in the front row, "that it is not disputed by the Defendant that he was in Copenhagen on June 21st, nominally engaged in secret work on behalf of the Abteilung." He paused and then continued:

"Leamas' visit to Helsinki—the second visit he made to deposit money—took place on about September 24th." Raising his voice he turned and looked directly at Mundt. "On the third of October Comrade Mundt made a clandestine journey to Finland—once more allegedly in the interests of the Abteilung." There was silence. Fiedler turned slowly and addressed himself once more to the Tribunal. In a voice at once subdued and threatening he asked:

"Are you complaining that the evidence is circumstantial? Let me remind you of something more." He turned to Leamas.

513

"Witness, during your activities in Berlin you became associated with Karl Riemeck, formerly Secretary to the Praesidium of the Socialist Unity Party. What was the nature of that association?"

"He was my agent, until he was shot by Mundt's men."

"Quite so. He was shot by Mundt's men. One of several spies who were summarily liquidated by Comrade Mundt before they could be questioned. But before he was shot by Mundt's men he was an agent of the British Secret Service?"

Leamas nodded.

"Will you describe Riemeck's meeting with the man you call Control."

"Control came over to Berlin from London to see Karl. Karl was one of the most productive agents we had, I think, and Control wanted to meet him."

Fiedler put in: "He was also one of the most trusted?"

"Yes, oh yes. London loved Karl; he could do no wrong. When Control came out I fixed up for Karl to come to my flat and the three of us dined together. I didn't like Karl coming there really, but I couldn't tell Control that. It's hard to explain but they get ideas in London, they're so cut off from it and I was frightened stiff they'd find some excuse for taking over Karl themselves—they're quite capable of it."

"So you arranged for the three of you to meet," Fiedler put in curtly, "what happened?"

"Control asked me beforehand to see that he had a quarter of an hour alone with Karl, so during the evening I pretended to have run out of Scotch. I left the flat and went over to de Jong's place. I had a couple of drinks there, borrowed a bottle and came back."

"How did you find them?"

"What do you mean?"

"Were Control and Riemeck talking still? If so, what were they talking about?"

"They weren't talking at all when I came back."

"Thank you. You may sit down."

514

Leamas returned to his seat at the back of the room. Fiedler turned to the three members of the Tribunal and began:

"I want to talk first about the spy Riemeck, who was shot: Karl Riemeck. You have before you a list of all the information which Riemeck passed to Alec Leamas in Berlin, so far as Leamas can recall it. It is a formidable record of treachery. Let me summarise it for you. Riemeck gave to his masters a detailed breakdown of the work and personalities of the whole Abteilung. He was able, if Leamas is to be believed, to describe the workings of our most secret sessions. As secretary of the Praesidium he gave minutes of its most secret proceedings.

"That was easy for him; he himself compiled the record of every meeting. But Riemeck's *access* to the secret affairs of the Abteilung is a different matter. Who at the end of 1959 co-opted Riemeck onto the Committee for the Protection of the People, that vital subcommittee of the Praesidium which coordinates and discusses the affairs of our security organs? Who proposed that Riemeck should have the privilege of access to the files of the Abteilung? Who at every stage in Riemeck's career *since* 1959 (the year Mundt returned from England, you remember) singled him out for posts of exceptional responsibility? I will tell you," Fiedler proclaimed. "The same man who was uniquely placed to shield him in his espionage activities: Hans-Dieter Mundt. Let us recall how Riemeck contacted the Western Intelligence Agencies in Berlin—how he sought out de Jong's car on a picnic and put the film inside it. Are you not amazed at Riemeck's foreknowledge? How could he have known where to find that car, and on that very day? Riemeck had no car himself, he could not have followed de Jong from his house in West Berlin. There was only one way he could have known—through the agency of our own Security police, who reported de Jong's presence as a matter of routine as soon as the car passed the Inter Sector checkpoint. That knowledge was available to Mundt, and Mundt made it available to Riemeck. *That* is the case against Hans-Dieter Mundt—I tell you, Riemeck was his creature, the link between Mundt and his imperialist masters!"

515

Fiedler paused, then added quietly:

"Mundt—Riemeck—Leamas: that was the chain of command, and it is axiomatic of intelligence technique the whole world over that each link of the chain be kept, as far as possible, in ignorance of the others. Thus it is *right* that Leamas should maintain he knows nothing to the detriment of Mundt: that is no more than the proof of good security by his masters in London.

"You have also been told how the whole case known as 'Rolling Stone' was conducted under conditions of special secrecy, how Leamas knew in vague terms of the intelligence section under Peter Guillam which was supposedly concerned with economic conditions in our Republic—a section which surprisingly was on the distribution list of 'Rolling Stone.' Let me remind you that that same Peter Guillam was one of several British security officers who were involved in the investigation of Mundt's activities while he was in England."

The youngish man at the table lifted his pencil, and looking at Fiedler with his hard, cold eyes wide open he asked:

"Then why did Mundt liquidate Riemeck, if Riemeck was his agent?"

"He had no alternative. Riemeck was under suspicion. His mistress had betrayed him by boastful indiscretion. Mundt gave the order that he be shot on sight, got word to Riemeck to run, and the danger of betrayal was eliminated. Later, Mundt assassinated the woman.

"I want to speculate for a moment on Mundt's technique. After his return to Germany in 1959 British Intelligence played a waiting game. Mundt's willingness to cooperate with them had yet to be demonstrated, so they gave him instructions and waited, content to pay their money and hope for the best. At that time Mundt was not a senior functionary of our Service—nor of our Party—but he saw a good deal, and what he saw he began to report. He was, of course, communicating with his masters unaided. We must suppose that he was met in West Berlin, that on his short journeys abroad to Scandinavia and elsewhere he was contacted and interrogated. The British must have been wary to

516

begin with—who would not be?—they weighed what he gave them with painful care against what they already knew, they feared that he would play a double game. But gradually they realised they had hit a gold mine. Mundt took to his treacherous work with the systematic efficiency for which he is renowned. At first—this is my guess, but it is based, Comrades, on long experience of this work and on the evidence of Leamas—for the first few months they did not dare to establish any kind of network which included Mundt. They let him be a lone wolf, they serviced him, paid and instructed him independently of their Berlin organisation. They established in London, under Guillam (for it was he who recruited Mundt in England), a tiny undercover section whose function was not known even within the Service save to a select circle. They paid Mundt by a special system which they called Rolling Stone, and no doubt they treated the information he gave them with prodigious caution. Thus, you see, it is consistent with Leamas' protestations that the existence of Mundt was unknown to him although—as you will see—he not only paid him, but in the end *actually received from Riemeck and passed to London the intelligence which Mundt obtained.*

"Towards the end of 1959 Mundt informed his London masters that he had found within the Praesidium a man who would act as intermediary between them and Mundt. That man was Karl Riemeck.

"How did Mundt find Riemeck? How did he dare to establish Riemeck's willingness to cooperate? You must remember Riemeck's exceptional position: he had access to all the security files, could tap telephones, open letters, employ watchers; he could interrogate anyone with undisputed right, and had before him the most detailed picture of their private life. Above all he could silence suspicion in a moment by turning against the people the very weapon"—Fiedler's voice was trembling with fury—"which was designed for their protection." Returning effortlessly to his former rational style, he continued:

"You can see now what London did. Still keeping Mundt's identity a close secret, they connived at Riemeck's enlistment

517

and enabled indirect contact to be established between Mundt and the Berlin command. That is the significance of Riemeck's contact with de Jong and Leamas. *That* is how you should interpret Leamas' evidence, *that* is how you should measure Mundt's treachery." He turned and, looking Mundt full in the face, he shouted:

"There is your saboteur, terrorist! There is the man who has sold the people's right!

"I have nearly finished. Only one more thing needs to be said. Mundt gained a reputation as a loyal and astute protector of the people, and he silenced for ever those tongues that could betray his secret. Thus he killed in the name of the people to protect his fascist treachery and advanced his own career within our Service. It is not possible to imagine a crime more terrible than this. That is why—in the end—having done what he could to protect Karl Riemeck from the suspicion which was gradually surrounding him he gave the order that Riemeck be shot on sight. That is why he arranged for the assassination of Riemeck's mistress. When you come to give your judgement to the Praesidium, do not shrink from recognising the full bestiality of this man's crime. For Hans-Dieter Mundt, death is a judgement of mercy."

21 ✻
THE WITNESS

The President turned to the little man in the black suit sitting directly opposite Fiedler.

"Comrade Karden, you are speaking for Comrade Mundt. Do you wish to examine the witness Leamas?"

"Yes, yes, I should like to in one moment" he replied, getting laboriously to his feet and pulling the end of his gold-rimmed spectacles over his ears. He was a benign figure, a little rustic, and his hair was white.

"The contention of Comrade Mundt," he began—his mild voice was rather pleasantly modulated—"is that Leamas is lying; that Comrade Fiedler either by design or ill chance has been drawn into a plot to disrupt the Abteilung, and thus bring into disrepute the organs for the defence of our socialist state. We do not dispute that Karl Riemeck was a British spy—there is evidence for that. But we dispute that Mundt was in league with him, or accepted money for betraying our Party. We say there is no objective evidence for this charge, that Comrade Fiedler is intoxicated by dreams of power and blinded to rational thought.

519

We maintain that from the moment Leamas returned from Berlin to London he lived a part; that he simulated a swift decline into degeneracy, drunkenness, and debt, that he assaulted a tradesman in full public view and affected anti-American sentiment—all solely in order to attract the attention of the Abteilung. We believe that British Intelligence has deliberately spun around Comrade Mundt a mesh of circumstantial evidence—the payment of money to foreign banks, its withdrawal to coincide with Mundt's presence in this or that country, the casual hearsay evidence from Peter Guillam, the secret meeting between Control and Riemeck at which matters were discussed that Leamas could not hear: these all provided a spurious chain of evidence and Comrade Fiedler, on whose ambitions the British so accurately counted, accepted it; and thus he became party to a monstrous plot to destroy—to murder in fact, for Mundt now stands to lose his life—one of the most vigilant defenders of our Republic.

"Is it not consistent with their record of sabotage, subversion, and human trafficking that the British should devise this desperate plot? What other course lies open to them now that the rampart has been built across Berlin and the flow of Western spies has been checked? We have fallen victim to their plot; at best Comrade Fiedler is guilty of a most serious error; at worst of conniving with imperialist spies to undermine the security of the worker state, and shed innocent blood.

"We also have a witness." He nodded benignly at the court. "Yes. We too have a witness. For do you really suppose that all this time Comrade Mundt has been in ignorance of Fiedler's fevered plotting? Do you really suppose that? For months he has been aware of the sickness in Fiedler's mind. It was Comrade Mundt himself who authorised the approach that was made to Leamas in England: do you think he would have taken such an insane risk if he were himself to be implicated?

"And when the reports of Leamas' first interrogation in The Hague reached the Praesidium, do you suppose Comrade Mundt threw his away unread? And when, after Leamas had

520

arrived in our country and Fiedler embarked on his own interrogation, no further reports were forthcoming, do you suppose Comrade Mundt was then so obtuse that he did not know what Fiedler was hatching? When the first reports came in from Peters in The Hague, Mundt had only to look at the dates of Leamas' visits to Copenhagen and Helsinki to realise that the whole thing was a plant—a plant to discredit Mundt himself. Those dates did indeed coincide with Mundt's visits to Denmark and Finland: they were chosen by London for that very reason. Mundt had known of those 'earlier indications' as well as Fiedler—remember that. Mundt too was looking for a spy within the ranks of the Abteilung . . .

"And so by the time Leamas arrived in Democratic Germany, Mundt was watching with fascination how Leamas nourished Fiedler's suspicions with hints and oblique indications—never overdone, you understand, never emphasised, but dropped here and there with perfidious subtlety. And by then the ground had been prepared . . . the man in the Lebanon, the miraculous scoop to which Fiedler referred, both seeming to confirm the presence of a highly placed spy within the Abteilung . . .

"It was wonderfully well done. It could have turned—it could still turn—the defeat which the British suffered through the loss of Karl Riemeck into a remarkable victory.

"Comrade Mundt took one precaution while the British, with Fiedler's aid, planned his murder.

"He caused scrupulous enquiries to be made in London. He examined every tiny detail of that double life which Leamas led in Bayswater. He was looking, you see, for some human error in a scheme of almost superhuman subtlety. Somewhere, he thought, in Leamas' long sojourn in the wilderness, he would have to break faith with his oath of poverty, drunkenness, degeneracy, above all of solitude. He would need a companion, a mistress perhaps; he would long for the warmth of human contact, long to reveal a part of the other soul within his breast. Comrade Mundt was right you see. Leamas, that skilled, experienced operator, made a mistake so elementary, so human that . . ." He smiled. "You shall hear the witness, but not yet. The witness is here; procured by Comrade Mundt. It was an admirable precaution. Later I shall call—that witness." He looked a trifle arch, as if to say he must be allowed his little joke. "Meanwhile I should like, if I may, to put one or two questions to this reluctant incriminator, Mr. Alec Leamas."

"Tell me," he began, "are you a man of means?"

"Don't be bloody silly," said Leamas shortly; "you know how I was picked up."

"Yes, indeed," Karden declared, "it was masterly. I may take it, then, that you have no money at all?"

"You may."

"Have you friends who would lend you money, give it to you perhaps? Pay your debts?"

"If I had I wouldn't be here now."

"You have none? You cannot imagine that some kindly benefactor, someone perhaps you have almost forgotten about, would ever concern himself with putting you on your feet . . . settling with creditors and that kind of thing?"

"No."

"Thank you. Another question: do you know George Smiley?"

"Of course I do. He was in the Circus."

"He has now left British Intelligence?"

"He packed it up after the Fennan case."

"Ah—the case in which Mundt was involved. Have you ever seen him since?"

"Once or twice."

"Have you seen him since you left the Circus?"

Leamas hesitated.

"No," he said.

"He didn't visit you in prison?"

"No. No one did."

"And before you went to prison?"

"No."

"After you left prison—the day of your release in fact—you were picked up, weren't you, by a man called Ashe?"

"Yes."

"You had lunch with him in Soho. After the two of you had parted, where did you go?"

"I don't remember. Probably I went to a pub. No idea."

"Let me help you. You went to Fleet Street eventually and caught a bus. From there you seem to have zigzagged by bus, tube, and private car, rather inexpertly for a man of your experience, to Chelsea. Do you remember that? I can show you the report if you like, I have it here."

"You're probably right. So what?"

"George Smiley lives in Bywater Street, just off the King's Road, that is my point. Your car turned into Bywater Street and our agent reported that you were dropped at number nine. That happens to be Smiley's house."

"That's drivel," Leamas declared. "I should think I went to the Eight Bells; it's a favourite pub of mine."

"By private car?"

"That's nonsense too. I went by taxi, I expect. If I have money I spend it."

"But why all the running about beforehand?"

"That's just cock. They were probably following the wrong man. That would be bloody typical."

"Going back to my original question, you cannot imagine that Smiley would have taken any interest in you after you left the Circus?"

"God, no."

"Nor in your welfare after you went to prison, nor spent money on your dependents, nor wanted to see you after you had met Ashe?"

"No. I haven't the least idea what you're trying to say, Karden, but the answer's no. If you'd ever met Smiley you wouldn't ask. We're about as different as we could be."

Karden seemed rather pleased with this, smiling and nodding

to himself as he adjusted his spectacles and referred elaborately to his file.

"Oh yes," he said, as if he had forgotten something; "when you asked the grocer for credit, how much money had you?"

"Nothing," said Leamas carelessly. "I'd been broke for a week. Longer, I should think."

"What had you lived on?"

"Bits and pieces. I'd been ill; some fever. I'd hardly eaten anything for a week. I suppose that made me nervous too— tipped the scales."

"You were, of course, still owed money at the library, weren't you?"

"How did you know that?" asked Leamas sharply. "Have you been—"

"Why didn't you go and collect it? Then you wouldn't have had to ask for credit, would you, Leamas?"

He shrugged.

"I forget. Probably because the library was closed on Saturday mornings."

"I see. Are you sure it was closed on Saturday mornings?"

"No, it's just a guess."

"Quite. Thank you, that is all I have to ask." Leamas was sitting down as the door opened, and a woman came in. She was large and ugly, wearing a grey overall with chevrons on one sleeve. Behind her stood Liz.

22 ❀
THE PRESIDENT

She entered the court slowly, looking around her, wide-eyed, like a half-woken child entering a brightly lit room. Leamas had forgotten how young she was. When she saw him sitting between two guards she stopped.

"Alec."

The guard beside her put his hand on her arm and guided her forward to the spot where Leamas had stood. It was very quiet in the courtroom.

"What is your name, child?" the President asked abruptly. Liz's long hands hung at her sides, the fingers straight.

"What is your name?" she repeated, loudly this time.

"Elizabeth Gold."

"You are a member of the British Communist Party?"

"Yes."

"And you have been staying in Leipzig?"

"Yes."

"When did you join the Party?"

525

"1955. No—fifty-four, I think it was—"

She was interrupted by the sound of movement; the screech of furniture forced aside, and Leamas' voice, hoarse, high-pitched, ugly, filling the room.

"You bastards! Leave her alone!"

Liz turned in terror and saw him standing, his white face bleeding and his clothes awry, saw a guard hit him with his fist, so that he half fell; then they were both upon him, had lifted him up, thrusting his arms high behind his back. His head fell forward on his chest, then jerked sideways in pain.

"If he moves again, take him out," the President ordered, and she nodded to Leamas in warning, adding: "You can speak again later if you want. Wait." Turning to Liz she said sharply, "Surely you know when you joined the Party?"

Liz said nothing, and after waiting a moment the President shrugged. Then leaning forward and staring at Liz intently she asked:

"Elizabeth, have you ever been told in your Party about the need for secrecy?"

Liz nodded.

"And you have been told never, never to ask questions of another Comrade on the organisation and dispositions of the Party?"

Liz nodded again. "Yes," she said, "of course."

"Today you will be severely tested in that rule. It is better for you, far better, that you should know nothing. Nothing," she added with sudden emphasis. "Let this be enough: we three at this table hold very high rank in the Party. We are acting with the knowledge of our Praesidium, in the interests of Party security. We have to ask you some questions, and your answers are of the greatest importance. By replying truthfully, and bravely, you will help the cause of Socialism."

"But *who*," she whispered, "*who* is on trial? What's Alec done?"

The President looked past her at Mundt and said, "Perhaps no one is on trial. That is the point. Perhaps only the accusers.

526

It can make no difference *who* is accused," she added, "it is a guarantee of your impartiality that you cannot know."

Silence descended for a moment on the little room; and then, in a voice so quiet that the President instinctively turned her head to catch her words, she asked:

"Is it Alec? Is it Leamas?"

"I tell you," the President insisted, "it is better for you—far better—you should not know. You must tell the truth and go. That is the wisest thing you can do."

Liz must have made some sign or whispered some words the others could not catch, for the President again leant forward and said, with great intensity:

"Listen, child, do you want to go home? Do as I tell you and you shall. But if you . . ." She broke off, indicated Karden with her hand and added cryptically, "this Comrade wants to ask you some questions, not many. Then you shall go. Tell the truth."

Karden stood again, and smiled his kindly, churchwarden smile.

"Elizabeth," he enquired, "Alec Leamas was your lover, wasn't he?"

She nodded.

"You met at the library in Bayswater, where you work."

"Yes."

"You had not met him before?"

She shook her head: "We met at the library," she said.

"Have you had many lovers, Elizabeth?"

Whatever she said was lost as Leamas shouted again: "Karden, you swine," but as she heard him she turned and said, quite loud:

"Alec, don't. They'll take you away."

"Yes," observed the President drily; "they will."

"Tell me," Karden resumed smoothly, "was Alec a Communist?"

"No."

"Did he know you were a Communist?"

"Yes. I told him."

"What did he say when you told him then, Elizabeth?"

She didn't know whether to lie, that was the terrible thing. The questions came so quickly she had no chance to think. All the time they were listening, watching, waiting for a word, a gesture, perhaps, that could do terrible harm to Alec. She couldn't lie unless she knew what was at stake; she would fumble on and Alec would die—for there was no doubt in her mind that Leamas was in danger.

"What did he say then?" Karden repeated.

"He laughed. He was above all that kind of thing."

"Do you believe he was above it?"

"Of course."

The young man at the Judges' table spoke for the second time. His eyes were half closed:

"Do you regard that as a valid judgement of a human being? That he is *above* the course of history and the compulsion of dialectic?"

"I don't know. It's what I believed, that's all."

"Never mind," said Karden; "tell me, was he a *happy* person, always laughing and that kind of thing?"

"No. He didn't often laugh."

"But he laughed when you told him you were in the Party. Do you know why?"

"I think he despised the Party."

"Do you think he *hated* it?" Karden asked casually.

"I don't know," Liz replied pathetically.

"Was he a man of strong likes and dislikes?"

"No . . . no; he wasn't."

"But he assaulted a grocer. Now why did he do that?"

Liz suddenly didn't trust Karden any more. She didn't trust the caressing voice and the good-fairy face.

"I don't know."

"But you thought about it?"

"Yes."

"Well, what conclusion did you come to?"

"None," said Liz flatly.

528

Karden looked at her thoughtfully, a little disappointed perhaps, as if she had forgotten her catechism.

"Did you," he asked—it might have been the most obvious of questions—"did you *know* that Leamas was going to hit the grocer?"

"No," Liz replied, perhaps too quickly, so that in the pause that followed Karden's smile gave way to a look of amused curiosity.

"Until now, until today," he asked finally, "when had you last seen Leamas?"

"I didn't see him again after he went to prison," Liz replied.

"When did you see him last, then?"—the voice was kind but persistent. Liz hated having her back to the court; she wished she could turn and see Leamas, see his face perhaps; read in it some guidance, some sign telling how to answer. She was becoming frightened for herself; these questions which proceeded from charges and suspicions of which she knew nothing. They must know she wanted to help Alec, that she was afraid, but no one helped her—why would no one help her?

"Elizabeth, when was your last meeting with Leamas until today?" Oh that voice, how she hated it, that silken voice.

"The night before it happened," she replied, "the night before he had the fight with Mr. Ford."

"The fight? It wasn't a fight, Elizabeth. The grocer never hit back, did he—he never had a chance. Very unsporting!" Karden laughed, and it was all the more terrible because no one laughed with him.

"Tell me, where did you meet Leamas that last night?"

"At his flat. He'd been ill, not working. He'd been in bed and I'd been coming in and cooking for him."

"And buying the food? Shopping for him?"

"Yes."

"How kind. It must have cost you a lot of money," Karden observed sympathetically: "could you afford to keep him?"

"I didn't keep him. I got it from Alec. He . . ."

"Oh," said Karden sharply, "so he *did* have some money?"

529

Oh God, thought Liz, oh God, oh dear God, what have I said?

"Not much," she said quickly, "not much, I know. A pound, two pounds, not more. He didn't have more than that. He couldn't pay his bills—his electric light and his rent—they were all paid afterwards, you see, after he'd gone, by a friend. A friend had to pay, not Alec."

"Of course," said Karden quietly, "a friend paid. Came specially and paid all his bills. Some old friend of Leamas, someone he knew before he came to Bayswater perhaps. Did you ever meet this friend, Elizabeth?"

She shook her head.

"I see. What other bills did this good friend pay, do you know?"

"No . . . no."

"Why do you hesitate?"

"I said I don't know," Liz retorted fiercely.

"But you hesitated," Karden explained, "I wondered if you had second thoughts."

"No."

"Did Leamas ever speak of this friend? A friend with money who knew where Leamas lived?"

"He never mentioned a friend at all. I didn't think he had any friends."

"Ah."

There was a terrible silence in the courtroom, more terrible to Liz because like a blind child among the seeing she was cut off from all those around her, they could measure her answers against some secret standard, and she could not know from the dreadful silence what they had found.

"How much money do you earn, Elizabeth?"

"Six pounds a week."

"Have you any savings?"

"A little. A few pounds."

"How much is the rent of your flat?"

"Fifty shillings a week."

"That's quite a lot, isn't it, Elizabeth? Have you paid your rent recently?"

She shook her head helplessly.

"Why not," Karden continued. "Have you no money?"

In a whisper she replied: "I've got a lease. Someone bought the lease and sent it to me."

"Who?"

"I don't know." Tears were running down her face, "I don't know . . . Please don't ask any more questions. I don't know who it was . . . six weeks ago they sent it, a bank in the City . . . some Charity had done it . . . a thousand pounds. I swear I don't know who . . . a gift from a Charity they said. You know everything— you tell me who . . ."

Burying her face in her hands she wept, her back still turned to the court, her shoulders moving as the sobs shook her body. No one moved, and at length she lowered her hands but did not look up.

"Why didn't you enquire?" Karden asked simply, "or are you used to receiving anonymous gifts of a thousand pounds?"

She said nothing and Karden continued: "You didn't enquire because you guessed. Isn't that right?"

Raising her hand to her face again, she nodded.

"You guessed it came from Leamas, or from Leamas' friend, didn't you?"

"Yes," she managed to say. "I heard in the street that the grocer had got some money, a lot of money from somewhere after the trial. There was a lot of talk about it, and I knew it must be Alec's friend . . ."

"How very strange," said Karden almost to himself. "How odd." And then: "Tell me, Elizabeth, did anyone get in touch with you after Leamas went to prison?"

"No," she lied. She knew now, she was sure they wanted to prove something against Alec, something about the money or his friends; something about the grocer.

"Are you sure?" Karden asked, his eyebrows raised above the gold rims of his spectacles.

"Yes."

"But your neighbour, Elizabeth," Karden objected patiently, "says that men called—two men—quite soon after Leamas had been sentenced; or were they just lovers, Elizabeth? Casual lovers, like Leamas, who gave you money?"

"Alec *wasn't* a casual lover," she cried, "how can you . . ."

"But he gave you money. Did the men give you money, too?"

"Oh God," she sobbed, "don't ask . . ."

"Who were they?" She did not reply, then Karden shouted, quite suddenly; it was the first time he had raised his voice.

"*Who?*"

"I don't know. They came in a car. Friends of Alec."

"*More* friends? What did they want?"

"I don't know. They kept asking me what he had told me . . . they told me to get in touch with them if . . ."

"*How? How* get in touch with them?"

At last she replied:

"He lived in Chelsea . . . his name was Smiley . . . George Smiley . . . I was to ring him."

"And did you?"

"No!"

Karden had put down his file. A deathly silence had descended on the court. Pointing towards Leamas Karden said, in a voice more impressive because it was perfectly under control:

"Smiley wanted to know whether Leamas had told her too much. Leamas had done the one thing British Intelligence had never expected him to do: he had taken a girl and wept on her shoulder." Then Karden laughed quietly, as if it were all such a neat joke:

"Just as Karl Riemeck did. He's made the same mistake."

"Did Leamas ever talk about himself?" Karden continued.

"No."

"You know nothing about his past?"

"No. I knew he'd done something in Berlin. Something for the government."

"Then he did talk about his past, didn't he? Did he tell you he had been married?"

There was a long silence. Liz nodded.

"Why didn't you see him after he went to prison? You could have visited him."

"I didn't think he'd want me to."

"I see. Did you write to him?"

"No. Yes, once . . . just to tell him I'd wait. I didn't think he'd mind."

"You didn't think he would want that either?"

"No."

"And when he had served his time in prison, you didn't try and get in touch with him?"

"No."

"Did he have anywhere to go, did he have a job waiting for him—friends who would take him in?"

"I don't know . . . I don't know."

"In fact you were finished with him, were you?" Karden asked with a sneer. "Had you found another lover?"

"No! I waited for him . . . I'll always wait for him." She checked herself. "I wanted him to come back."

"Then why had you not written? Why didn't you try and find out where he was?"

"He didn't want me to, don't you see? He made me promise . . . never to follow him . . . never to . . ."

"*So he expected to go to prison, did he?*" Karden demanded triumphantly.

"No . . . I don't know. How can I tell what I don't know . . ."

"And on that last evening," Karden persisted, his voice harsh and bullying, "on the evening before he hit the grocer, did he make you renew your promise? . . . Well, did he?"

With infinite weariness, she nodded in a pathetic gesture of capitulation. "Yes."

"And you said good-bye?"

"We said good-bye."

"After supper, of course. It was quite late. Or did you spend the night with him?"

"After supper. I went home . . . not straight home . . . I went for a walk first, I don't know where. Just walking."

"What reason did he give for breaking off your relationship?"

"He didn't break it off," she said. "Never. He just said there was something he had to do; someone he had to get even with, whatever it cost, and afterwards, one day perhaps, when it was all over . . . he would . . . come back, if I was still there and . . ."

"And you said," Karden suggested with irony, "that you would always wait for him, no doubt? That you would always love him?"

"Yes," Liz replied simply.

"Did he say he would send you money?"

"He said . . . he said things weren't as bad as they seemed . . . that I would be . . . looked after."

"And that was why you didn't enquire, wasn't it, afterwards, when some charity in the City casually gave you a thousand pounds?"

"Yes! Yes, that's right. Now you know everything—you knew it all already . . . Why did you send for me if you knew?"

Imperturbably Karden waited for her sobbing to stop.

"That," he observed finally to the Tribunal before him, "is the evidence of the defence. I am sorry that a girl whose perception is clouded by sentiment, and whose alertness is blunted by money, should be considered by our British comrades a suitable person for Party office."

Looking first at Leamas and then at Fiedler he added brutally:

"She is a fool. It is fortunate, nevertheless, that Leamas met her. This is not the first time that a revanchist plot has been uncovered through the decadence of its architects."

With a little precise bow towards the Tribunal, Karden sat down.

As he did so, Leamas rose to his feet, and this time the guards left him alone.

London must have gone raving mad. He'd told them—that was the joke—he'd told them to leave her alone. And now it was clear that from the moment, the very moment he left England—before that, even, as soon as he went to prison—some bloody fool had gone round tidying up—paying the bills, settling the grocer, the landlord; above all, Liz. It was insane, fantastic. What were they trying to do—kill Fiedler, kill their agent? Sabotage their own operation? Was it just Smiley—had his wretched little conscience driven him to this? There was only one thing to do—get Liz and Fiedler out of it and carry the can. He was probably written off anyway. If he could save Fiedler's skin—if he could do that—perhaps there was a chance that Liz would get away.

How the hell did they know so much? He was sure, he was absolutely sure, he hadn't been followed to Smiley's house that afternoon. And the money—how did they pick up the story about him stealing money from the Circus? That was designed for internal consumption only . . . then how? For God's sake, how?

Bewildered, angry and bitterly ashamed he walked slowly up the gangway, stiffly, like a man going to the scaffold.

23 ❧

CONFESSION

"All right, Karden," his face was white and hard as stone, his head tilted back, a little to one side; in the attitude of a man listening to some distant sound. There was a frightful stillness about him, not of resignation but of self-control, so that his whole body seemed to be in the iron grip of his will.

"All right, Karden, let her go."

Liz was staring at him, her face crumpled and ugly, her dark eyes filled with tears.

"No, Alec . . . no," she said. There was no one else in the room—just Leamas tall and straight like a soldier.

"Don't tell them," she said, her voice rising, "whatever it is, don't tell them just because of me . . . I don't mind anymore, Alec; I promise I don't."

"Shut up, Liz," said Leamas awkwardly. "It's too late now." His eyes turned to the President.

"She knows nothing. Nothing at all. Get her out of here and send her home. I'll tell you the rest."

The President glanced briefly at the men on either side of her. She deliberated, then said:

"She can leave the court; but she cannot go home until the hearing is finished. Then we shall see."

"She knows nothing, I tell you," Leamas shouted. "Karden's right, don't you see? It was an operation, a planned operation. How could she know that! She's just a frustrated little girl from a crackpot library—she's no good to you!"

"She is a witness," replied the President shortly. "Fiedler may want to question her." It wasn't Comrade Fiedler any more.

At the mention of his name, Fiedler seemed to wake from the reverie into which he had sunk, and Liz looked at him consciously for the first time. His deep brown eyes rested on her for a moment, and he smiled very slightly, as if in recognition of her race. He was a small, forlorn figure, oddly relaxed she thought.

"She knows nothing," Fiedler said. "Leamas is right, let her go." His voice was tired.

"You realise what you are saying?" the President asked. "You realise what this means? Have *you* no questions to put to her?"

"She has said what she had to say." Fiedler's hands were folded on his knees and he was studying them as if they interested him more than the proceedings of the court. "It was all most cleverly done." He nodded. "Let her go. She cannot tell us what she does not know." With a certain mock formality he added, "I have no questions for the witness."

A guard unlocked the door and called into the passage outside. In the total silence of the court they heard a woman's answering voice, and her ponderous footsteps slowly approaching. Fiedler abruptly stood up, and taking Liz by the arm, he guided her to the door. As she reached the door she turned and looked back towards Leamas, but he was staring away from her like a man who cannot bear the sight of blood.

"Go back to England," Fiedler said to her. "You go back

to England." Suddenly Liz began to sob uncontrollably. The wardress put an arm round her shoulder, more for support than comfort, and led her from the room. The guard closed the door. The sound of her crying faded gradually to nothing.

"There isn't much to say," Leamas began. "Karden's right. It was a put-up job. When we lost Karl Riemeck we lost our only decent agent in the Zone. All the rest had gone already. We couldn't understand it—Mundt seemed to pick them up almost before we'd recruited them. I came back to London and saw Control. Peter Guillam was there and George Smiley. George was in retirement really, doing something clever. Philology or something.

"Anyway, they'd dreamed up this idea. Set a man to trap himself, that's what Control said. Go through the motions and see if they bite. Then we worked it out—backwards so to speak. 'Inductive' Smiley called it. If Mundt *were* our agent how would we have paid him, how would the files look, and so on. Peter remembered that some Arab had tried to sell us a breakdown of the Abteilung a year or two back and we'd sent him packing. Afterwards we found out we'd made a mistake. Peter had the idea of fitting that in—as if we'd turned it down because we already knew. That was clever.

"You can imagine the rest. The pretence of going to pieces; drink, money troubles, the rumours that Leamas had robbed the till. It all hung together. We got Elsie in Accounts to help with the gossip, and one or two others. They did it bloody well," he added with a touch of pride. "Then I chose a morning—a Saturday morning, lots of people about—and broke out. It made the local press—it even made the *Worker* I think—and by that time you people had picked it up. From then on," he added with contempt, "you dug your own graves."

"Your grave," said Mundt quietly. He was looking thoughtfully at Leamas with his pale, pale eyes. "And perhaps Comrade Fiedler's."

"You can hardly blame Fiedler," said Leamas indifferently,

"he happened to be the man on the spot; he's not the only man in the Abteilung who'd willingly hang you, Mundt."

"We shall hang you, anyway," said Mundt reassuringly. "You murdered a guard. You tried to murder me."

Leamas smiled drily.

"All cats are alike in the dark, Mundt . . . Smiley always said it could go wrong. He said it might start a reaction we couldn't stop. His nerve's gone—you know that. He's never been the same since the Fennan case—since the Mundt affair in London. They say something happened to him then—that's why he left the Circus. That's what I can't make out, why they paid off the bills, the girl and all that. It must have been Smiley wrecking the operation on purpose, it must have been. He must have had a crisis of conscience, thought it was wrong to kill or something. It was mad after all that preparation, all that work, to mess up an operation that way.

"But Smiley hated you, Mundt. We all did, I think, although we didn't say it. We planned the thing as if it was all a bit of a game . . . it's hard to explain now. We knew we had our backs to the wall: we'd failed against Mundt and now we were going to try and kill him. But it was still a game." Turning to the Tribunal he said: "You're wrong about Fiedler, he's not ours. Why would London take this kind of risk with a man in Fiedler's position? They counted on him, I admit. They knew he hated Mundt—why shouldn't he? Fiedler's a Jew, isn't he? You know, you must know, all of you, what Mundt's reputation is, what he thinks about Jews.

"I'll tell you something, no one else will, so I'll tell you: Mundt had Fiedler beaten up, and all the time, while it was going on, Mundt baited him and jeered at him for being a Jew. You all know what kind of man Mundt is, and you put up with him because he's good at his job. But . . ." he faltered for a second, then continued: "But for God's sake . . . enough people have got mixed up in all this without Fiedler's head going into the basket. Fiedler's all right, I tell you . . . ideologically sound, that's the expression, isn't it?"

He looked at the Tribunal. They watched him impassively, curiously almost, their eyes steady and cold. Fiedler, who had returned to his chair and was listening with rather studied detachment, looked at Leamas blandly for a moment:

"And you messed it all up, Leamas, is that it?" he asked. "An old dog like Leamas, engaged in the crowning operation of his career, falls for a . . . what did you call her? . . . a frustrated little girl in a crackpot library? London must have known; Smiley couldn't have done it alone." Fiedler turned to Mundt: "Here's an odd thing, Mundt; they must have known you'd check up on every part of his story. That was why Leamas lived the life. Yet afterwards they sent money to the grocer, paid up the rent; and they bought the lease for the girl. Of all the extraordinary things for them to do . . . people of their experience . . . to pay a thousand pounds, to a girl—*to a member of the Party*—who was supposed to believe he was broke. Don't tell me Smiley's conscience goes that far. London must have done it. What a risk!"

Leamas shrugged.

"Smiley was right. We couldn't stop the reaction. We never expected you to bring me here—Holland yes—but not here." He fell silent for a moment, then continued. "And I never thought you'd bring the girl. I've been a bloody fool."

"But Mundt hasn't," Fiedler put in quickly. "Mundt knew what to look for—he even knew the girl would provide the proof—very clever of Mundt I must say. He even knew about that lease—amazing really. I mean, how *could* he have found out; she didn't tell anyone. I know that girl; I understand her . . . she wouldn't tell anyone at all." He glanced towards Mundt. "Perhaps Mundt can tell us how he knew?"

Mundt hesitated, a second too long, Leamas thought.

"It was her subscription," he said; "a month ago she increased her Party contribution by ten shillings a month. I heard about it. And so I tried to establish how she could afford it. I succeeded."

"A masterly explanation," Fiedler replied coolly.

There was silence.

540

"I think," said the President, glancing at her two colleagues, "that the Tribunal is now in a position to make its report to the Praesidium. That is," she added, turning her small, cruel eyes on Fiedler, "unless you have anything more to say."

Fiedler shook his head. Something still seemed to amuse him.

"In that case," the President continued, "my colleagues are agreed that Comrade Fiedler should be relieved of his duties until the disciplinary committee of the Praesidium has considered his position.

"Leamas is already under arrest. I would remind you all that the Tribunal has no executive powers. The people's prosecutor, in collaboration with Comrade Mundt, will no doubt consider what action is to be taken against a British *agent provocateur* and murderer."

She glanced past Leamas at Mundt. But Mundt was looking at Fiedler with the dispassionate regard of a hangman measuring his subject for the rope.

And suddenly, with the terrible clarity of a man too long deceived, Leamas understood the whole ghastly trick.

24 ❀
THE COMMISSAR

Liz stood at the window, her back to the wardress, and stared blankly into the tiny yard outside. She supposed the prisoners took their exercise there. She was in somebody's office; there was food on the desk beside the telephone but she couldn't touch it. She felt sick and terribly tired; physically tired. Her legs ached, her face felt stiff and raw from weeping. She felt dirty and longed for a bath.

"Why don't you eat?" the woman asked again. "It's all over now." She said this without compassion, as if the girl were a fool not to eat when the food was there.

"I'm not hungry."

The wardress shrugged: "You may have a long journey," she observed, "and not much the other end."

"What do you mean?"

"The workers are starving in England," she declared complacently. "The capitalists let them starve."

Liz thought of saying something but there seemed no point.

542

Besides, she wanted to know; she had to know, and this woman could tell her.

"What is this place?"

"Don't you know?" the wardress laughed. "You should ask them over there," she nodded towards the window. "They can tell you what it is."

"Who are they?"

"Prisoners."

"What kind of prisoners?"

"Enemies of the state," she replied promptly. "Spies, agitators."

"How do you know they are spies?"

"The Party knows. The Party knows more about people than they know themselves. Haven't you been told that?" The wardress looked at her, shook her head and observed, "The English! The rich have eaten your future and your poor have given them the food—that's what's happened to the English."

"Who told you that?"

The woman smiled and said nothing. She seemed pleased with herself.

"And this is a prison for spies?" Liz persisted.

"It is a prison for those who fail to recognise Socialist reality; for those who think they have the right to err; for those who slow down the march. Traitors," she concluded briefly.

"But what have they done?"

"We cannot build Communism without doing away with individualism. You cannot plan a great building if some swine builds his sty on your site."

Liz looked at her in astonishment.

"Who told you all this?"

"I am Commissar here," she said proudly, "I work in the prison."

"You are very clever," Liz observed, approaching her.

"I am a worker," the woman replied acidly. "The concept of brain workers as a higher category must be destroyed. There are no categories, only workers; no antithesis between physical and mental labour. Haven't you read Lenin?"

"Then the people in this prison are intellectuals?"

The woman smiled. "Yes," she said, "they are reactionaries who call themselves progressive: they defend the individual against the state. Do you know what Khrushchev said about the counter-revolution in Hungary?"

Liz shook her head. She must show interest, she must make the woman talk.

"He said it would never have happened if a couple of writers had been shot in time."

"Who will they shoot now?" Liz asked quickly. "After the trial?"

"Leamas," she replied indifferently, "and the Jew, Fiedler." Liz thought for a moment she was going to fall but her hand found the back of a chair and she managed to sit down.

"What has Leamas done?" she whispered. The woman looked at her with her small, cunning eyes. She was very large; her hair was scant, stretched over her head to a bun at the nape of her thick neck. Her face was heavy, her complexion flaccid and watery.

"He killed a guard," she said.

"Why?"

The woman shrugged.

"As for the Jew," she continued, "he made an accusation against a loyal comrade."

"Will they shoot Fiedler for that?" asked Liz incredulously.

"Jews are all the same," the woman commented. "Comrade Mundt knows what to do with Jews. We don't need their kind here. If they join the Party they think it belongs to them. If they stay out, they think it is conspiring against them. It is said that Leamas and Fiedler plotted against Mundt. Are you going to eat that?" she enquired, indicating the food on the desk. Liz shook her head. "Then I must," she declared, with a grotesque attempt at reluctance. "They have given you potato. You must have a lover in the kitchen." The humour of this observation sustained her until she had finished the last of Liz's meal.

Liz went back to the window.

In the confusion of Liz's mind, in the turmoil of shame and grief and fear there predominated the appalling memory of Leamas, as she had last seen him in the courtroom, sitting stiffly in his chair, his eyes averted from her own. She had failed him and he dared not look at her before he died; would not let her see the contempt, the fear perhaps, that was written on his face.

But how could she have done otherwise? If Leamas had only told her what he had to do—even now it wasn't clear to her—she would have lied and cheated for him, anything, if he had only told her! Surely he understood that; surely he knew her well enough to realise that in the end she would do whatever he said, that she would take on his form and being, his will, life, his image, his pain, if she could; that she prayed for nothing more than the chance to do so? But how could she have known, if she was not told, how to answer those veiled, insidious questions? There seemed no end to the destruction she had caused. She remembered, in the fevered condition of her mind, how, as a child, she had been horrified to learn that with every step she made, thousands of minute creatures were destroyed beneath her foot; and now, whether she had lied or told the truth—or even, she was sure, had kept silent—she had been forced to destroy a human being; perhaps two, for was there not also the Jew, Fiedler, who had been gentle with her, taken her arm and told her to go back to England? They would shoot Fiedler, that's what the woman said. Why did it have to be Fiedler—why not the old man who asked the questions, or the fair one in the front row between the soldiers, the one who smiled all the time; whenever she turned round she had caught sight of his smooth, blond head and his smooth, cruel face smiling as if it were all a great joke. It comforted her that Leamas and Fiedler were on the same side. She turned to the woman again and asked:

545

"Why are we waiting here?"

The wardress pushed the plate aside and stood up.

"For instructions," she replied. "They are deciding whether you must stay."

"Stay?" repeated Liz blankly.

"It is a question of evidence. Fiedler may be tried, I told you: they suspect conspiracy between Fiedler and Leamas."

"But who against? How could he conspire in England? How did he come here? He's not in the Party."

The woman shook her head.

"It is secret," she replied. "It concerns only the Praesidium. Perhaps the Jew brought him here."

"But *you* know," Liz insisted, a note of blandishment in her voice, "you are Commissar at the prison. Surely they told *you*?"

"Perhaps," the woman replied, complacently. "It is very secret," she repeated.

The telephone rang. The woman lifted the receiver and listened. After a moment she glanced at Liz.

"Yes, Comrade. At once," she said, and put down the receiver.

"You are to stay," she said shortly. "The Praesidium will consider the case of Fiedler. In the meantime you will stay here. That is the wish of Comrade Mundt."

"Who is Mundt?"

The woman looked cunning.

"It is the wish of the Praesidium," she said.

"I don't want to stay," Liz cried. "I want . . ."

"The Party knows more about us than we know ourselves," the woman replied. "You must stay here. It is the Party's wish."

"Who is Mundt?" Liz asked again, but still she did not reply.

Slowly Liz followed her along endless corridors, through grilles manned by sentries, past iron doors from which no sound came, down endless stairs, across whole courtyards far beneath the ground, until she thought she had descended to the

bowels of hell itself, and no one would even tell her when Leamas was dead.

She had no idea what time it was when she heard the footsteps
in the corridor outside her cell. It could have been five in the
evening—it could have been midnight. She had been awake,
staring blankly into the pitch darkness, longing for a sound.
She had never imagined that silence could be so terrible. Once
she had cried out, and there had been no echo, nothing. Just the
memory of her own voice. She had visualised the sound breaking against the solid darkness like a fist against a rock. She had
moved her hands about her as she sat on the bed, and it seemed
to her that the darkness made them heavy, as if she were groping in the water. She knew the cell was small; that it contained
the bed on which she sat, a handbasin without taps, and a crude
table: she had seen them when she first entered. Then the light
had gone out, and she had run wildly to where she knew the
bed had stood, and struck it with her shins, and had remained
there, shivering with fright. Until she heard the footsteps, and
the door of her cell was opened abruptly.

She recognised him at once, although she could only discern his silhouette against the pale blue light in the corridor.
The trim, agile figure, the clear line of the cheek and the short
fair hair just touched by the light behind him.

"It's Mundt," he said. "Come with me, at once." His voice
was contemptuous yet subdued, as if he were not anxious to be
overheard.

Liz was suddenly terrified. She remembered the wardress:
"Mundt knows what to do with Jews." She stood by the bed,
staring at him, not knowing what to do.

"Hurry, you fool." Mundt had stepped forward and seized
her wrist. "Hurry." She let herself be drawn into the corridor.
Bewildered, she watched Mundt quietly relock the door of
her cell. Roughly he took her arm and forced her quickly along
the first corridor, half running, half walking. She could hear the

distant whirr of air conditioners; and now and then the sound of other footsteps from passages branching from their own. She noticed that Mundt hesitated, drew back even, when they came upon other corridors, would go ahead and confirm that no one was coming, then signal her forward. He seemed to assume that she would follow, that she knew the reason. It was almost as if he was treating her as an accomplice.

And suddenly he had stopped, was thrusting a key into the keyhole of a dingy metal door. She waited, panic-stricken. He pushed the door savagely outwards and the sweet, cold air of a winter's evening blew against her face. He beckoned to her again, still with the same urgency, and she followed him down two steps on to a gravel path which led through a rough kitchen garden.

They followed the path to an elaborate Gothic gateway which gave on to the road beyond. Parked in the gateway was a car. Standing beside it was Alec Leamas.

"Keep your distance," Mundt warned her as she started to move forward:

"Wait here."

Mundt went forward alone and for what seemed an age she watched the two men standing together, talking quietly between themselves. Her heart was beating madly, her whole body shivering with cold and fear. Finally Mundt returned.

"Come with me," he said, and led her to where Leamas stood. The two men looked at one another for a moment.

"Good-bye," said Mundt indifferently. "You're a fool, Leamas," he added. "She's trash, like Fiedler." And he turned without another word and walked quickly away into the twilight.

She put her hand out and touched him, and he half turned from her, brushing her hand away as he opened the car door. He nodded to her to get in, but she hesitated.

"Alec," she whispered, "Alec, what are you doing? Why is he letting you go?"

"Shut up!" Leamas hissed. "Don't even think about it, d'you hear? Get in."

"What is it he said about Fiedler? Alec, why is he letting us go?"

"He's letting us go because we've done our job. Get into the car, quick!" Under the compulsion of his extraordinary will she got into the car and closed the door. Leamas got in beside her.

"What bargain have you struck with him?" she persisted, suspicion and fear rising in her voice. "They said you had tried to conspire against him, you and Fiedler. Then why is he letting you go?"

Leamas had started the car and was soon driving fast along the narrow road. On either side, bare fields; in the distance, dark monotonous hills were mingling with the gathering darkness. Leamas looked at his watch.

"We're five hours from Berlin," he said. "We've got to make Köpenick by quarter to one. We should do it easily."

For a time Liz said nothing; she stared through the windscreen down the empty road, confused and lost in a labyrinth of half formed thoughts. A full moon had risen and the frost hovered in long shrouds across the fields. They turned on to an autobahn.

"Was I on your conscience, Alec?" she said at last. "Is that why you made Mundt let me go?"

Leamas said nothing.

"You and Mundt are enemies, aren't you?"

Still he said nothing. He was driving fast now, the needle showed a hundred and twenty kilometres; the autobahn was pitted and bumpy. He had his headlights on full, she noticed, and didn't bother to dip for oncoming traffic on the other lane. He drove roughly, leaning forward, his elbows almost on the wheel.

"What will happen to Fiedler?" Liz asked suddenly and this time Leamas answered.

"He'll be shot."

"Then why didn't they shoot you?" Liz continued quickly.

"You conspired with Fiedler against Mundt, that's what they said. You killed a guard. Why has Mundt let you go?"

"All right!" Leamas shouted suddenly. "I'll tell you. I'll tell you what you were never, never to know, neither you nor I. Listen: Mundt is London's man, their agent; they bought him when he was in England. We are witnessing the lousy end to a filthy, lousy operation to save Mundt's skin. To save him from a clever little Jew in his own department who had begun to suspect the truth. They made us kill him, d'you see, kill the Jew. Now you know, and God help us both."

25 ✿

THE WALL

"If that is so, Alec," she said at last, "what was my part in all this?" Her voice was quite calm almost matter-of-fact.

"I can only guess, Liz, from what I know and what Mundt told me before we left. Fiedler suspected Mundt; had suspected him ever since Mundt came back from England; he thought Mundt was playing a double game. He hated him, of course—why shouldn't he—but he was right too: Mundt was London's man. Fiedler was too powerful for Mundt to eliminate alone, so London decided to do it for him. I can see them working it out, they're so damned academic; I can see them sitting round a fire in one of their smart bloody clubs. They knew it was no good just eliminating Fiedler—he might have told friends, published accusations: they had to eliminate *suspicion*. Public rehabilitation, that's what they organised for Mundt."

He swung into the left-hand lane to overtake a lorry and trailer. As he did so the lorry unexpectedly pulled out in front of him, so that he had to brake violently one the pitted road to avoid being forced into the crash-fence on his left.

"They told me to frame Mundt," he said simply; "they said he had to be killed, and I was game. It was going to be my last job. So I went to seed, and punched the grocer . . . you know all that."

"And made love?" she asked quietly. Leamas shook his head. "But this is the point, you see," he continued, "Mundt knew it all; he knew the plan; he had me picked up, he and Fiedler. Then he let Fiedler take over, because he knew in the end Fiedler would hang himself. My job was to let them think what in fact was the truth: that Mundt was a British spy." He hesitated. "Your job was to discredit me. Fiedler was shot and Mundt was saved, mercifully delivered from a fascist plot. It's the old principle of love on the rebound."

"But how could they know about me; how could they know we would come together?" Liz cried. "Heavens above, Alec, can they even tell when people will fall in love?"

"It didn't matter—it didn't depend on that. They chose you because you were young and pretty and in the Party, because they knew you would come to Germany if they rigged an invitation. That man in the Labour Exchange, Pitt, he sent me up there; they knew I'd work at the Library. Pitt was in the Service during the war and they squared him, I suppose. They only had to put you and me in contact, even for a day, it didn't matter; then afterwards they could call on you, send you the money, make it look like an affair even if it wasn't, don't you see? Make it look like an infatuation, perhaps. The only material point was that after bringing us together they should send you money as if it came at my request. As it was, we made it very easy for them . . ."

"Yes, we did." And then she added, "I feel dirty, Alec, as if I'd been put out to stud."

Leamas said nothing.

"Did it ease your Department's conscience at all? Exploiting . . . somebody in the Party, rather than just anybody?" Liz continued.

552

Leamas said, "Perhaps. They don't really think in those terms. It was an operational convenience."

"I might have stayed in that prison, mightn't I? That's what Mundt wanted, wasn't it? He saw no point in taking the risk—I might have heard too much, guessed too much. After all, Fiedler was innocent, wasn't he? But then he's a Jew," she added excitedly. "So that doesn't matter so much, does it?"

"Oh, for God's sake," Leamas exclaimed.

"It seems odd that Mundt let me go, all the same—even as part of the bargain with you," she mused. "I'm a risk now, aren't I? When we get back to England, I mean: a Party member knowing all this . . . It doesn't seem logical that he should let me go."

"I expect," Leamas replied, "he is going to use our escape to demonstrate to the Praesidium that there are other Fiedlers in his department who must be hunted down."

"And other Jews?"

"It gives him a chance to secure his position," Leamas replied curtly.

"By killing more innocent people? It doesn't seem to worry you much."

"Of course it worries me. It makes me sick with shame and anger and . . . but I've been brought up differently, Liz; I can't see it in black and white. People who play this game take risks. Fiedler lost and Mundt won. London won—that's the point. It was a foul, foul operation. But it's paid off, and that's the only rule." As he spoke his voice rose, until finally he was nearly shouting.

"You're trying to convince yourself," Liz cried. "They've done a wicked thing. How can you kill Fiedler—he was good, Alec; I know he was. And Mundt—"

"What the hell are you complaining about," Leamas demanded roughly. "Your Party's always at war, isn't it? Sacrificing the individual to the mass. That's what it says. Socialist reality: fighting night and day—that relentless battle—that's what they say, isn't it? At least you've survived. I never heard that Communists preached the sanctity of human life—perhaps I've got it wrong," he added sarcastically. "I agree, yes, I agree, you might have been destroyed. That was on the cards. Mundt's a vicious swine; he saw no point in letting you survive. His promise—I suppose he gave a promise to do his best by you—isn't worth a great deal. So you might have died—today, next year, or twenty years on—in a prison in the worker's paradise. And so might I. But I seem to remember the Party is aiming at the destruction of a whole class. Or have I got it wrong?" Extracting a packet of cigarettes from his jacket he handed her two, together with a box of matches. Her fingers trembled as she lit them and passed one back to Leamas.

"You've thought it all out, haven't you?" she asked.

"We happened to fit the mould," Leamas persisted, "and I'm sorry. I'm sorry for the others too—the others who fit the mould. But don't complain about the terms, Liz; they're Party terms. A small price for a big return. One sacrificed for many. It's not pretty, I know, choosing who it'll be—turning the plan into people."

She listened in the darkness, for a moment scarcely conscious of anything except the vanishing road before them, and the numb horror in her mind.

"But they let me love you," she said at last. "And you let me believe in you and love you."

"They used us," Leamas replied pitilessly. "They cheated us both because it was necessary. It was the only way. Fiedler was bloody nearly home already, don't you see? Mundt would have been caught, can't you understand that?"

"How can you turn the world upside down?" Liz shouted suddenly. "Fiedler was kind and decent; he was only doing his job, and now you've killed him. Mundt is a spy and a traitor and you protect him. Mundt is a Nazi, do you know that? He hates Jews . . . what side are you on? How can you . . . ?"

"There's only one law in this game," Leamas retorted. "Mundt is their man; he gives them what they need. That's easy enough to understand, isn't it? Leninism—the expediency of temporary alliances. What do you think spies are: priests, saints, and martyrs? They're a squalid procession of vain fools, traitors too, yes; pansies, sadists, and drunkards, people who play cowboys and Indians to brighten their rotten lives. Do you think they sit like monks in London balancing the rights and wrongs? I'd have killed Mundt if I could, I hate his guts; but not now. It so happens that they need him. They need him so that the great moronic mass that you admire can sleep soundly in their beds at night. They need him for the safety of ordinary, crummy people like you and me."

"But what about Fiedler—don't you feel anything for him?"

"This is a war," Leamas replied. "It's graphic and unpleasant because it's fought on a tiny scale, at close range; fought with a wastage of innocent life sometimes, I admit. But it's nothing, nothing at all besides other wars—the last or the next."

"Oh God," said Liz softly. "You don't understand. You don't want to. You're trying to persuade yourself. It's far more terrible, what they are doing; to find the humanity in people, in me and whoever else they use, to turn it like a weapon in their hands, and use it to hurt and kill . . ."

"Christ Almighty!" Leamas cried. "What else have men done since the world began? I don't believe in anything, don't you see—not even destruction or anarchy. I'm sick, sick of killing but I don't see what else they can do. They don't proselytise; they don't stand in pulpits or on party platforms and tell us to fight for Peace or for God or whatever it is. They're the poor sods who try to keep the preachers from blowing each other sky high."

"You're wrong," Liz declared hopelessly; "they're more wicked than all of us."

"Because I made love to you when you thought I was a tramp?" Leamas asked savagely.

"Because of their contempt," Liz replied; "contempt for what is real and good; contempt for love, contempt for—"

"Yes," Leamas agreed, suddenly weary. "That is the price

they pay; to despise God and Karl Marx in the same sentence. If that is what you mean."

"It makes you the same," Liz continued; "the same as Mundt and all the rest . . . I should know, I was the one who was kicked about, wasn't I? By them, by you because you don't care. Only Fiedler didn't . . . But the rest of you . . . you all treated me as if I was . . . nothing . . . just currency to pay with . . . You're all the same, Alec."

"Oh, Liz," he said desperately, "for God's sake believe me: I hate it, I hate it all; I'm tired. But it's the world, it's mankind that's gone mad. We're a tiny price to pay . . . but everywhere's the same, people cheated and misled, whole lives thrown away, people shot and in prison, whole groups and classes of men written off for nothing. And you, your party—God knows it was built on the bodies of ordinary people. You've never seen men die as I have, Liz . . ."

As he spoke Liz remembered the drab prison courtyard, and the wardress saying: "It is a prison for those who slow down the march . . . for those who think they have the right to err."

Leamas was suddenly tense, peering forward through the windscreen. In the headlights of the car Liz discerned a figure standing in the road. In his hand was a tiny light which he turned on and off as the car approached. "That's him," Leamas muttered; switched off the headlights and engine, and coasted silently forward. As they drew up, Leamas leant back and opened the rear door.

Liz did not turn round to look at him as he got in. She was staring stiffly forward, down the street at the falling rain.

"Drive at thirty kilometres," the man said. His voice was taut, frightened. "I'll tell you the way. When we reach the place you must get out and run to the wall. The searchlight will be shining at the point where you must climb. Stand in the beam of the searchlight. When the beam moves away begin to climb. You will have ninety seconds to get over. You go first," he said to Leamas; "and the girl follows. There are iron rungs in the lower part—after that you must pull yourself up as best you can. You'll have to sit on top and pull the girl up. Do you understand?"

"We understand," said Leamas. "How long have we got?"

"If you drive at thirty kilometres we shall be there in about nine minutes. The searchlight will be on the wall at five past one exactly. They can give you ninety seconds. Not more."

"What happens after ninety seconds?" Leamas asked.

"They can only give you ninety seconds," the man repeated; "otherwise it is too dangerous. Only one detachment has been briefed. They think you are being infiltrated into West Berlin. They've been told not to make it too easy. Ninety seconds are enough."

"I bloody well hope so," said Leamas drily. "What time do you make it?"

"I checked my watch with the sergeant in charge of the detachment," the man replied. A light went on and off briefly in the back of the car. "It is twelve forty-eight. We must leave at five to one. Seven minutes to wait."

They sat in total silence save for the rain pattering on the roof. The cobble road reached out straight before them, staged by dingy street lights every hundred metres. There was no one about. Above them the sky was lit with the unnatural glow of arclights. Occasionally the beam of a searchlight flickered overhead, and disappeared. Far to the left Leamas caught sight of a fluctuating light just above the sky-line, constantly altering in strength, like the reflection of a fire.

"What's that?" he asked, pointing towards it.

"Information Service," the man replied. "A scaffolding of lights. It flashes news headlines into East Berlin."

"Of course," Leamas muttered. They were very near the end of the road.

"There is no turning back," the man continued; "he told you that? There is no second chance."

"I know," Leamas replied.

"If something goes wrong—if you fall or get hurt—don't

557

turn back. They shoot on sight within the area of the wall. You *must* get over."

"We know," Leamas repeated; "he told me."

"From the moment you get out of the car you are in the area."

"We know. Now shut up," Leamas retorted. And then he added: "Are you taking the car back?"

"As soon as you get out of the car I shall drive it away. It is a danger for me, too," the man replied.

"Too bad," said Leamas drily.

Again there was silence; then Leamas asked: "Have you got a gun?"

"Yes," said the man; "but I can't give it to you; he said I shouldn't give it to you . . . that you were sure to ask for it."

Leamas laughed quietly. "He would," he said.

Leamas pulled the starter. With a noise that seemed to fill the street the car moved slowly forward.

They had gone about three hundred yards when the man whispered excitedly, "Go right here, then left." They swung into a narrow side street. There were empty market stalls on either side so that the car barely passed between them.

"Left here, now!"

They turned again, fast, this time between two tall buildings into what looked like a cul-de-sac. There was washing across the street, and Liz wondered whether they would pass under it. As they approached what seemed to be the dead end the man said: "Left again—follow the path." Leamas mounted the curb, crossed the pavement, and they followed a broad footpath bordered by a broken fence to their left, and a tall, windowless building to their right. They heard a shout from somewhere above them, a woman's voice, and Leamas muttered: "Oh, shut up," as he steered clumsily round a right-angle bend in the path and came almost immediately upon a major road.

"Which way?" he demanded.

"Straight across—past the chemist—between the chemist and the post office—there!" The man was leaning so far forward that his face was almost level with theirs. He pointed now, reaching past Leamas, the tips of his fingers pressed against the windscreen.

"Get back," Leamas hissed. "Get your hand away. How the hell can I see if you wave your hand around like that?" Slamming the car into first gear he drove fast across the wide road. Glancing to his left he was astonished to glimpse the plump silhouette of the Brandenburg Gate three hundred yards away, and the sinister grouping of military vehicles at the foot of it.

"Where are we going?" asked Leamas suddenly.

"We're nearly there. Go slowly now . . . left, left, go left!" he cried, and Leamas jerked the wheel in the nick of time; they passed under a narrow archway into a courtyard. Half the windows were missing or boarded up; the empty doorways gaped sightlessly at them. At the other end of the yard was an open gateway. "Through there," came the whispered command, urgent in the darkness; "then hard right. You'll see a street lamp on your right. The one beyond it is broken. When you reach the second lamp switch off the engine and coast until you see a fire hydrant. "That's the place."

"Why the hell didn't you drive yourself?"

"He said you should drive; he said it was safer."

They passed through the gate and turned sharply to the right. They were in a narrow street, pitch dark.

"Lights out!"

Leamas switched off the car lights, drove slowly forwards towards the first street lamp. Ahead, they could just see the second. It was unlit. Switching off the engine they coasted silently past it, until twenty yards ahead of them they discerned the dim outline of the fire hydrant. Leamas braked; the car rolled to a standstill.

"Where are we?" Leamas whispered. "We crossed the Lenin-Allee, didn't we?"

"Griefswalder Strasse. Then we turned north. We're north of Bernauerstrasse."

"Pankow?"

"Just about. Look," the man pointed down a side street to the left. At the far end they saw a brief stretch of wall, grey-brown in the weary arclight. Along the top ran a triple strand of barbed wire.

"How will the girl get over the wire?"

"It is already cut where you climb. There is a small gap. You have one minute to reach the wall. Good-bye."

They got out of the car, all three of them. Leamas took Liz by the arm, and she started from him as if he had hurt her.

"Good-bye," said the German.

Leamas just whispered: "Don't start the car till we're over."

Liz looked at the German for a moment in the pale light. She had a brief impression of a young, anxious face; the face of a boy trying to be brave.

"Good-bye," said Liz. She disengaged her arm and followed Leamas across the road and into the narrow street that led towards the wall.

As they entered the street they heard the car start up behind them, turn, and move quickly away in the direction they had come.

"Pull up the ladder, you bastard," Leamas muttered, glancing back at the retreating car.

Liz hardly heard him.

26 ✺
IN FROM THE COLD

They walked quickly, Leamas glancing over his shoulder from time to time to make sure she was following. As he reached the end of the alley, he stopped, drew into the shadow of a doorway and looked at his watch.

"Two minutes," he whispered.

She said nothing. She was staring straight ahead towards the wall, and the black ruins rising behind it.

"Two minutes," Leamas repeated.

Before them was a strip of thirty yards. It followed the wall in both directions. Perhaps seventy yards to their right was a watch tower; the beam of its searchlight played along the strip. The thin rain hung in the air, so that the light from the arclamps was sallow and chalky, screening the world beyond. There was no one to be seen; not a sound. An empty stage.

The watch tower's searchlight began feeling its way along the wall towards them, hesitant; each time it rested they could see the separate bricks and the careless lines of mortar hastily

561

put on. As they watched the beam stopped immediately in front of them. Leamas looked at his watch.

"Ready?" he asked.

She nodded.

Taking her arm he began walking deliberately across the strip. Liz wanted to run, but he held her so tightly that she could not. They were half-way towards the wall now, the brilliant semi-circle of light drawing them forward, the beam directly above them. Leamas was determined to keep Liz very close to him, as if he were afraid that Mundt would not keep his word and somehow snatch her away at the last moment.

They were almost at the wall when the beam darted to the north leaving them momentarily in total darkness. Still holding Liz's arm, Leamas guided her forward blindly, his left hand reaching ahead of him until suddenly he felt the coarse, sharp contact of the cinder brick. Now he could discern the wall and, looking upwards, the triple-strand of wire and the cruel hooks which held it. Metal wedges, like climbers' pitons, had been driven into the brick. Seizing the highest one, Leamas pulled himself quickly upwards until he had reached the top of the wall. He tugged sharply at the lower strand of wire and it came towards him, already cut.

"Come on," he whispered urgently, "start climbing."

Laying himself flat he reached down, grasped her upstretched hand and began drawing her slowly upwards as her foot found the first metal rung.

Suddenly the whole world seemed to break into flame; from everywhere, from above and beside them, massive lights converged, bursting upon them with savage accuracy.

Leamas was blinded, he turned his head away, wrenching wildly at Liz's arm. Now she was swinging free; he thought she had slipped and he called frantically, still drawing her upwards. He could see nothing—only a mad confusion of colour dancing in his eyes.

Then came the hysterical wail of sirens, orders frantically shouted. Half kneeling astride the wall he grasped both her arms in his, and began dragging her to him inch by inch, himself on the verge of falling.

Then they fired—single rounds, three or four, and he felt her shudder. Her thin arms slipped from his hands. He heard a voice in English from the Western side of the wall:

"Jump, Alec! Jump, man!"

Now everyone was shouting, English, French, and German mixed; he heard Smiley's voice from quite close:

"The girl, where's the girl?"

Shielding his eyes he looked down at the foot of the wall and at last he managed to see her, lying still. For a moment he hesitated, then quite slowly he climbed back down the same rungs, until he was standing beside her. She was dead; her face was turned away, her black hair drawn across her cheek as if to protect her from the rain.

They seemed to hesitate before firing again; someone shouted an order, and still no one fired. Finally they shot him, two or three shots. He stood glaring round him like a blinded bull in the arena. As he fell, Leamas saw a small car smashed between great lorries, and the children waving cheerfully through the window.